Nationwide Acclaim for

Great Stories of the American West:

Edited by Martin Greenberg

GREAT STORIES OF THE AMERICAN WEST
GREAT STORIES OF THE AMERICAN WEST II

Great Stories

of the

American West II

Stories by
Louis L'Amour, John Jakes, Loren D. Estleman, Marcia Muller, and many others

Edited by Martin H. Greenberg

B

BERKLEY BOOKS, NEW YORK

This is a work of fiction. Names, characters, places, and incidents are either the product of the author's imaginations or are used fictitiously, and any resemblance to actual persons, living or dead, events, or locales is entirely coincidental.

GREAT STORIES OF THE AMERICAN WEST II

A Berkley Book / published by arrangement with
Donald I. Fine Books, an imprint of Penguin Books USA Inc.

PRINTING HISTORY
Donald I. Fine edition published 1996
Berkley edition / April 1997

All rights reserved.
Copyright © 1996 by Martin H. Greenberg.
A continuation of copyright credits appears on pages 475-76.
This book may not be reproduced in whole or in part,
by mimeograph or any other means, without permission.
For information address: Donald I. Fine Books, Penguin Books USA Inc.,
375 Hudson Street, New York, New York 10014.

The Penguin Putnam Inc. World Wide Web site address is
http://www.penguinputnam.com

ISBN: 0-425-15936-1

BERKLEY®
Berkley Books are published by The Berkley Publishing Group,
a division of Penguin Putnam Inc.
375 Hudson Street, New York, New York 10014.
BERKLEY and the "B" design
are trademarks belonging to Penguin Putnam Inc.

PRINTED IN THE UNITED STATES OF AMERICA

10 9 8 7 6 5 4 3

AUTHOR NOTES

BRET HARTE   Literary historians love to recount the
two-month job that Francis Bret Harte held as the shotgun rider on a Wells Fargo stage in the early 1860s.
Harte was a dandy of sorts, and not at all equipped to
handle the rougher activities of his adopted West. It is
difficult to imagine that he presented a formidable presence atop the stage. Fortunately for Harte, he was able
to find work as a journalist, and ultimately as a fiction
writer, his tales bringing a tart and ironic slant to the
chronicling of the West. Though he hired Mark Twain
to work for his newspaper, Harte and Twain ended up
despising each other, with Twain becoming somewhat
obsessive on the subject of his former mentor. ''The Idyl
of Red Gulch'' is Harte at his best.

O. HENRY   O. Henry has been so long despised by the
American critical establishment that it's impressive he's

in print at all. ''A respectable rival to the pulps'' was
how W.H. Auden once described the establishment's
view of Poe; and much the same might be said of O.
Henry. No, he was not a profound writer. No, he did not
deal especially well with the serious topical themes of
his time. And no, his prose rarely sang with poetry. But
he was a first-rate teller of tales and his glimpses of last
century's New York and Texas and Alaska are as fetch-
ing today as they were when originally published. An
especially well-turned O. Henry piece is ''The Lonesome
Road.''

CHAD OLIVER   As a writer, Chad Oliver never quite got
his due. Though he excelled at both science fiction and
the Western, and though critics took proper note of his
literary virtues, he never found the large audience he
deserved. By any estimation, his body of work is an
impressive one, and deserves to be read by succeeding
generations. By calling, he was an anthropologist, and
this shows in all of his work. He had a knack for defining
cultures and the people of those cultures. The West he
created was a true one. He died too young but at least
we have the books and stories of his four decades of
professional writing. To know him even slightly was a
true honor.

OWEN WISTER   Several generations of Western writers
stood and saluted when one spoke the name Owen
Wister. His novel *The Westerner* was the seminal
Western of its era, turning the American cowboy into a
literary (and filmic) icon. The product of exclusive
Eastern prep schools, where he made plans to become
a composer, he took the advice of his friend Teddy

Roosevelt and traveled west. Wister was ailing and Roosevelt insisted that the West would revive him. As it did. While some carp that *The Westerner* romanticized the West, one should note that Wister was not afraid to capture its violence and anger. The Eastern prep-school boy had written the most influential Western of all time.

JACK LONDON Though not usually associated with stories of the West, Jack London wrote innumerable "Northerns" about the Yukon and Alaska and the days of the gold rush, and occasionally turned his hand to more conventional Western fiction, as well. London was the preeminent storyteller of his time. He wrote in every genre, and wrote well, too. Many of his stories remain staples in textbooks even today. He was brilliant, brash, sad, scared, capable of both great poetry and great hackery, and one of the most fascinating men of this American century. One of his problems was that he couldn't tell the difference between a foolish idea and a good one. But that was also one of his blessings. He was the original boy-man, and that was the source of his poetry. If he prefigured any movement, it was the Beats of the fifties, the men and the women who found beauty in the experiences of the everyday, and mystical powers in the Whitmanesque symbols of the hobo, the sailor and the gold miner.

LOREN D. ESTLEMAN Loren D. Estleman is generally considered the best Western writer of his generation. Such novels as *Aces & Eights*, *The Stranglers* and *Bloody Season* rank with the very best Western novels ever written. As will be seen here, Estleman brings high style to his writing, the sentences things of beauty in and of themselves. Few writers of prose can claim that. Estleman's most recent novel, *City of Widows* (Tor), demonstrates why so many critics have singled Estleman out for the highest honors. ''Mago's Bride'' also demonstrates his way with words, and his ability to tell finely crafted stories.

LENORE CARROLL The Western field has a long tradition of honoring its female writers. Dorothy Johnson, Peggy Simpson Curry, Leigh Brackett—all received great acknowledgment during their lifetimes. Unfortunately, the bestselling Western writers were always men, so women looked to other genres to work in. Over the past fifteen years, that has changed significantly. Not only have many more women entered the Western field, but the majority of them have provided fresh new ideas and insights. Lenore Carroll is a good example. ''Cowboy Blues'' is a story that honors certain Western traditions but that turns them to unexpected purposes and themes. We can reasonably expect even better work from Lenore in the future.

MARK TWAIN Hemingway once said that nobody ever changed American literature as much as Mark Twain. While this overlooks such writers as Stephen Crane and Walt Whitman, still, in the broadest sense, Hemingway was probably correct. Twain banished forever the stilted and florid prose of early America, and replaced it with the cadences and ''rude wit'' (to borrow from Raymond Chandler) of the vernacular. Twain was anything but the wise and knowing grandpa stereotype that certain stage entertainers like to present. He was, in every sense, a literary roughneck, and when he came after you, it was to street fight. May God have mercy on the soul of James Fenimore Cooper.

GERTRUDE ATHERTON   Gertrude Atherton wrote a number of books, fiction and nonfiction alike, during her long career as a professional writer. Her subject was usually California, and how it had evolved over a century and a half. She was able to fill her stories with journalistic detail without ever sacrificing her ability to excite and entertain. She was frequently compared to O. Henry. Here is a very slick, very knowing story about her favorite period, that of Old California.

STEPHEN CRANE   Stephen Crane was the greatest psychological writer of his time. From ''The Open Boat'' to *Maggie: A Girl of the Streets*, Crane helped fix and define the American soul in a way that influenced such later writers as Hemingway, John Dos Passos, John Steinbeck and William Styron. Though he is taught in the school system, one senses that he has never been properly appreciated or understood, that his spiritual coarseness (much like Robert Stone's today) is celebrated without being quite acceptable to people of more epicene tastes. The formalists, for instance, have never known what to do with him, so they praise him, and then quickly dismiss him. Every literary virtue he could claim is amply displayed in ''The Blue Hotel.''

JOHN JAKES   John Jakes started out as a writer of genre science fiction, fantasy, suspense and Western novels. In the seventies, he became one of America's all-time bestselling writers with his historical novels about the origins of America. Since then, Jakes's books have continued to sell in the millions. And many of his older books have been brought back for new generations. "The Naked Gun" is an early story that demonstrates just how good Jakes can be.

LOUIS L'AMOUR   Louis L'Amour was the bestselling Western writer of all time. For a number of reasons, it's unlikely that his sales records will ever be equaled by anybody. He wrote a lot of material—far more than most people realize—and from the very start he seemed to understand the mass market better than any other writer of his generation. For all his reliance on careful research, he wrote of the mythic West, of good and evil, in an exciting way that appealed to millions and millions of readers. "War Party" is one of his very best stories.

EVAN HUNTER   You may know Evan Hunter as the *New York Times* bestselling author of *The Blackboard Jungle* and *Strangers When We Meet*. Or you may know him as Ed McBain, the author of the 87th Precinct novels that have sold in the millions around the world. Though he published only a handful of Westerns, each was a carefully crafted story as filled with emotions as it was surprises. A notably good Hunter story from his formative years as a writer is "The Killing at Triple Tree."

BILL PRONZINI   Bill Pronzini has worked in virtually every genre of popular fiction. Though he's best known as the creator of the Nameless mystery novels, he has written several first-rate Westerns, as well as a half-dozen remarkable novels of dark suspense. In addition to his novels, Pronzini is an especially gifted short story writer, several of his pieces winning prestigious awards, including the Shamus. His *Blue Lonesome* is one of the most important crime novels to be published in this decade.

MARCIA MULLER Marcia Muller is one of the best crime novelists anywhere in the world. Her character Sharon McCone changed the course of crime fiction forever. McCone was the first really modern woman in the genre of private-eye fiction, and she remains in the forefront of that genre today. The same high style, grace and hard-wrought wisdom of her crime fiction is also evident in her Western stories. As in "Sweet Cactus Wine."

HAMLIN GARLAND As a reviewer noted, "Hamlin Garland (1860–1940) wrote about the Midwestern states with the ear of a journalist and the heart of a preacher. He was always listening for the false statement in human discourse, apparently believing that by the false he could also identify the truth." Though he was probably a minor artist, Garland wrote beautiful and powerful stories about the heartland, showing us the people and the customs of early America. "The Return of a Private" is an especially well-realized story that reads, in places, much like Chekhov.

ERLE STANLEY GARDNER As the creator of Perry Mason, one of the world's all-time sales champions, Erle Stanley Gardner had the success that only a handful of writers per century ever enjoy. Unfortunately, because he was so prolific, he was dismissed even within the mystery field as a skilled but empty hack. This wasn't true. The Masons, right up to the final years of the sixties, offered a complicated view of American business that Theodore Dreiser would have agreed with. Gardner knew his businessmen, and drew some of them in his darkest hues. But Mason wasn't his best series. That honor belongs to the Donald Lam/Bertha Cool novels he wrote as Nero Wolfe knockoffs. Heretical as it may sound, some people actually prefer the Lam novels to the Wolfes. The ones from the thirties and forties are especially enjoyable, screwball comedy combined with noir. "Singing Sand" is from Gardner's salad days in the pulps. The desert fascinated Gardner, so much so that he built an entire series of novelettes around it. This is one of the best ones, which made its initial appearance in *Argosy* for November 7, 1931. Dashiell Hammett always insisted that the private eye really came out of the Western story. In "Singing Sand" we see a perfect fusion of the two forms.

ED GORMAN   Quoting from the dust jacket of the original edition of *What the Dead Men Say*: "Gorman writes 'Westerns for grownups,'" said *Publishers Weekly*. *Booklist* said: "Filled with obsession and revenge, this powerful tale is a gripping coming-of-age story." The *Rocky Mountain News* noted: "Gorman's novels are violent, parablelike stories with brilliant characterizations. His *What the Dead Men Say*, set in turn-of-the-century Iowa, typifies the author's always fresh approach to the Western." Here is the short but remarkably complex novel *What the Dead Men Say*.

CONTENTS

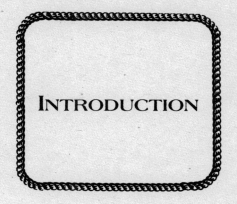

INTRODUCTION

SOMEBODY ONCE SAID that there are only three art forms original to the United States: jazz, the private detective and the Western.

Given the recent success of Clint Eastwood's excellent film *Unforgiven*, the Western story has come back into fashion once again.

Studios have scheduled several Western productions; and word has it that two or three publishers are considering relaunching their former Western lines.

As forgettable as most Western movies, and many Western novels, can be, the great ones remain great.

The Ox-Bow Incident, *The Gunfighter*, *The High Country*, *The Wild Bunch*—these are films that can be appreciated on the level of Fellini and Bergman.

The same can be said for the books of Jack Schaefer, Dorothy M. Johnson, Loren D. Estleman and Elmore Leonard.

The Western story is the one true American folk literature, and it is especially gratifying to display it here in so many of its different forms.

—ED GORMAN

Great
Stories
of the
American
West II

THE IDYL
OF RED GULCH

Bret Harte

SANDY WAS VERY drunk. He was lying under an azalea-bush, in pretty much the same attitude in which he had fallen some hours before. How long he had been lying there he could not tell, and didn't care; how long he should lie there was a matter equally indefinite and un-considered. A tranquil philosophy, born of his physical condition, suffused and saturated his moral being.

The spectacle of a drunken man, and of this drunken man in particular, was not, I grieve to say, of sufficient novelty in Red Gulch to attract attention. Earlier in the day some local satirist had erected a temporary tomb-stone at Sandy's head, bearing the inscription, "Effects of McCorkle's whiskey,—kills at forty rods," with a hand pointing to McCorkle's saloon. But this, I imagine, was, like most local satire, personal; and was a reflection upon the unfairness of the process rather than a com-mentary upon the impropriety of the result. With this

1

facetious exception, Sandy had been undisturbed. A wandering mule, released from his pack, had cropped the scant herbage beside him, and sniffed curiously at the prostrate man; a vagabond dog, with that deep sympathy which the species have for drunken men, had licked his dusty boots, and curled himself up at his feet, and lay there, blinking one eye in the sunlight, with a simulation of dissipation that was ingenious and dog-like in its implied flattery of the unconscious man beside him.

Meanwhile the shadows of the pine-trees had slowly swung around until they crossed the road, and their trunks barred the open meadow with gigantic parallels of black and yellow. Little puffs of red dust, lifted by the plunging hoofs of passing teams, dispersed in a grimy shower upon the recumbent man. The sun sank lower and lower; and still Sandy stirred not. And then the repose of this philosopher was disturbed, as other philosophers have been, by the intrusion of an unphilosophical sex.

"Miss Mary," as she was known to the little flock that she had just dismissed from the log school-house beyond the pines, was taking her afternoon walk. Observing an unusually fine cluster of blossoms on the azalea-bush opposite, she crossed the road to pluck it,— picking her way through the red dust, not without certain fierce little shivers of disgust, and some feline circumlocution. And then she came suddenly upon Sandy!

Of course she uttered the little *staccato* cry of her sex. But when she had paid that tribute to her physical weakness she became overbold, and halted for a moment,— at least six feet from this prostrate monster,—with her white skirts gathered in her hand, ready for flight. But neither sound nor motion came from the bush. With one little foot she then overturned the satirical head-board, and muttered "Beasts!"—an epithet which probably, at that moment, conveniently classified in her mind the entire male population of Red Gulch. For Miss Mary, being possessed of certain rigid notions of her own, had not, perhaps, properly appreciated the demonstrative gallantry for which the Californian has been so justly celebrated by his brother Californians, and had, as a new-comer, perhaps, fairly earned the reputation of being "stuck up."

As she stood there she noticed, also, that the slant sunbeams were heating Sandy's head to what she judged to be an unhealthy temperature, and that his hat was lying uselessly at his side. To pick it up and to place it over his face was a work requiring some courage, particularly as his eyes were open. Yet she did it and made good her retreat. But she was somewhat concerned, on looking back, to see that the hat was removed, and that Sandy was sitting up and saying something.

The truth was, that in the calm depths of Sandy's mind he was satisfied that the rays of the sun were beneficial and healthful; that from childhood he had objected to lying down in a hat; that no people but condemned fools, past redemption, ever wore hats; and that his right to dispense with them when he pleased was inalienable. This was the statement of his inner consciousness. Unfortunately, its outward expression was vague, being limited to a repetition of the following formula,—"Su'shine all ri'! Wasser maär, eh? Wass up, su'shine?"

Miss Mary stopped, and, taking fresh courage from

her vantage of distance, asked him if there was anything that he wanted.

"Wass up? Wasser maär?" continued Sandy, in a very high key.

"Get up, you horrid man!" said Miss Mary, now thoroughly incensed, "get up, and go home."

Sandy staggered to his feet. He was six feet high, and Miss Mary trembled. He started forward a few paces and then stopped.

"Wass I go home for?" he suddenly asked, with great gravity.

"Go and take a bath," replied Miss Mary, eyeing his grimy person with great disfavor.

To her infinite dismay, Sandy suddenly pulled off his coat and vest, threw them on the ground, kicked off his boots, and plunging wildly forward, darted headlong over the hill, in the direction of the river.

"Goodness Heavens!—the man will be drowned!" said Miss Mary; and then, with feminine inconsistency, she ran back to the school-house, and locked herself in.

That night, when seated at supper with her hostess, the blacksmith's wife, it came to Miss Mary to ask, demurely, if her husband ever got drunk. "Abner," responded Mrs. Stidger reflectively, "let's see: Abner hasn't been tight since last 'lection." Miss Mary would have liked to ask if he preferred lying in the sun on these occasions, and if a cold bath would have hurt him; but this would have involved an explanation which she did not then care to give. So she contented herself with opening her gray eyes widely at the red-cheeked Mrs. Stidger,—a fine specimen of Southwestern efflorescence,—and then, dismissed the subject altogether. The next day she wrote to her dearest friend, in Boston: "I think I find the intoxicated portion of this community the least objectionable. I refer, my dear, to the men, of course. I do not know anything that could make the women tolerable.''

In less than a week Miss Mary had forgotten this episode, except that her afternoon walks took thereafter, almost unconsciously, another direction. She noticed, however, that every morning a fresh cluster of azalea-blossoms appeared among the flowers on her desk. This was not strange, as her little flock were aware of her fondness for flowers, and invariably kept her desk bright with anemones, syringas, and lupines; but, on questioning them, they, one and all, professed ignorance of the azaleas. A few days later, Master Johnny Stidger, whose desk was nearest to the window, was suddenly taken with spasms of apparently gratuitous laughter, that threatened the discipline of the school. All that Miss Mary could get from him was, that some one had been ''looking in the winder.'' Irate and indignant, she sallied from her hive to do battle with the intruder. As she turned the corner of the school-house she came plump upon the quondam drunkard,—now perfectly sober, and inexpressibly sheepish and guilty-looking.

These facts Miss Mary was not slow to take a feminine advantage of, in her present humor. But it was somewhat confusing to observe, also, that the beast, despite some faint signs of past dissipation, was amiable-looking,—in fact, a kind of blond Samson, whose corn-colored, silken beard apparently had never yet known the touch of barber's razor or Delilah's shears. So that the cutting speech which quivered on her ready tongue died upon her lips, and she contented herself with receiving his stammering apology with supercilious eyelids and the gathered skirts of uncontamination. When she re-entered the school-room, her eyes fell upon the azaleas with a new sense of revelation. And then she laughed, and the little people all laughed, and they were all unconsciously very happy.

It was on a hot day—and not long after this—that two short-legged boys came to grief on the threshold of the school with a pail of water, which they had laboriously brought from the spring, and that Miss Mary compassionately seized the pail and started for the spring herself. At the foot of the hill a shadow crossed her path, and a blue-shirted arm dexterously, but gently relieved her of her burden. Miss Mary was both embarrassed and angry. "If you carried more of that for yourself," she said, spitefully, to the blue arm, without deigning to raise her lashes to its owner, "you'd do better." In the submissive silence that followed she regretted the speech, and thanked him so sweetly at the door that he stumbled. Which caused the children to laugh again,—a laugh in which Miss Mary joined, until the color came faintly into her pale cheeks. The next day a barrel was mysteriously placed beside the door, and as mysteriously filled with fresh spring-water every morning.

Nor was this superior young person without other quiet attentions. "Profane Bill," driver of the Slumgullion Stage, widely known in the newspapers for his "gallantry" in invariably offering the box-seat to the fair sex, had excepted Miss Mary from this attention, on the ground that he had a habit of "cussin' on up grades," and gave her half the coach to herself. Jack Hamlin, a gambler, having once silently ridden with her in the same coach, afterward threw a decanter at the head of a confederate for mentioning her name in a bar-room.

The over-dressed mother of a pupil whose paternity was doubtful had often lingered near this astute Vestal's temple, never daring to enter its sacred precincts, but content to worship the priestess from afar.

With such unconscious intervals the monotonous procession of blue skies, glittering sunshine, brief twilights, and starlit nights passed over Red Gulch. Miss Mary grew fond of walking in the sedate and proper woods. Perhaps she believed, with Mrs. Stidger, that the balsamic odors of the firs "did her chest good," for certainly her slight cough was less frequent and her step was firmer; perhaps she had learned the unending lesson which the patient pines are never weary of repeating to heedful or listless ears. And so, one day, she planned a picnic on Buckeye Hill, and took the children with her. Away from the dusty road, the straggling shanties, the yellow ditches, the clamor of restless engines, the cheap finery of shop-windows, the deeper glitter of paint and colored glass, and the thin veneering which barbarism takes upon itself in such localities,—what infinite relief was theirs! The last heap of ragged rock and clay passed, the last unsightly chasm crossed,—how the waiting woods opened their long files to receive them! How the children—perhaps because they had not yet grown quite away from the breast of the bounteous Mother—threw themselves face downward on her brown bosom with uncouth caresses, filling the air with their laughter; and how Miss Mary herself—felinely fastidious and intrenched as she was in the purity of spotless skirts, collar, and cuffs—forgot all, and ran like a crested quail at the head of her brood, until, romping, laughing, and panting, with a loosened braid of brown hair, a hat hanging by a knotted ribbon from her throat, she came suddenly and violently, in the heart of the forest, upon—the luckless Sandy!

The explanations, apologies, and not overwise conversation that ensued, need not be indicated here. It would seem, however, that Miss Mary had already established some acquaintance with this ex-drunkard. Enough that he was soon accepted as one of the party; that the children, with that quick intelligence which Providence gives the helpless, recognized a friend, and played with his blond beard, and long silken mustache, and took other liberties,—as the helpless are apt to do. And when he had built a fire against a tree, and had shown them other mysteries of wood-craft, their admiration knew no bounds. At the close of two such foolish, idle, happy hours he found himself lying at the feet of the schoolmistress, gazing dreamily in her face, as she sat upon the sloping hillside, weaving wreaths of laurel and syringa, in very much the same attitude as he had lain when first they met. Nor was the similitude greatly forced. The weakness of an easy, sensuous nature, that had found a dreamy exaltation in liquor, it is to be feared was now finding an equal intoxication in love.

I think that Sandy was dimly conscious of this himself. I know that he longed to be doing something,— slaying a grizzly, scalping a savage, or sacrificing himself in some way for the sake of this sallow-faced, gray-eyed schoolmistress. As I should like to present him in a heroic attitude, I stay my hand with great difficulty at this moment, being only withheld from introducing such an episode by a strong conviction that it does not usually occur at such times. And I trust that my fairest reader, who remembers that, in a real crisis, it is always some uninteresting stranger or unromantic policeman, and not

Adolphus, who rescues, will forgive the omission.

So they sat there undisturbed,—the woodpeckers chattering overhead, and the voices of the children coming pleasantly from the hollow below. What they said matters little. What they thought—which might have been interesting—did not transpire. The woodpeckers only learned how Miss Mary was an orphan; how she left her uncle's house, to come to California, for the sake of health and independence; how Sandy was an orphan, too; how he came to California for excitement; how he had lived a wild life, and how he was trying to reform; and other details, which, from a woodpecker's viewpoint, undoubtedly must have seemed stupid, and a waste of time. But even in such trifles was the afternoon spent; and when the children were again gathered, and Sandy, with a delicacy which the school-mistress well understood, took leave of them quietly at the outskirts of the settlement, it had seemed the shortest day of her weary life.

As the long, dry summer withered to its roots, the school term of Red Gulch—to use a local euphuism— "dried up" also. In another day Miss Mary would be free; and for a season, at least, Red Gulch would know her no more. She was seated alone in the school-house, her cheek resting on her hand, her eyes half closed in one of those day-dreams in which Miss Mary—I fear, to the danger of school discipline—was lately in the habit of indulging. Her lap was full of mosses, ferns, and other woodland memories. She was so preoccupied with these and her own thoughts that a gentle tapping at the door passed unheard, or translated itself into the remembrance of far-off woodpeckers. When at last it asserted itself more distinctly, she started up with a flushed cheek and opened the door. On the threshold stood a woman, the self-assertion and audacity of whose dress were in singular contrast to her timid irresolute bearing.

Miss Mary recognized at a glance the dubious mother of her anonymous pupil. Perhaps she was disappointed, perhaps she was only fastidious; but as she coldly invited her to enter, she half consciously settled her white cuffs and collar, and gathered closer her own chaste skirts. It was, perhaps, for this reason that the embarrassed stranger, after a moment's hesitation, left her gorgeous parasol open and sticking in the dust beside the door, and then sat down at the farther end of a long bench. Her voice was husky as she began:—

"I heerd tell that you were goin' down to the Bay tomorrow, and I couldn't let you go until I came to thank you for your kindness to my Tommy."

Tommy, Miss Mary said, was a good boy, and deserved more than the poor attention she could give him.

"Thank you, miss; thank ye!" cried the stranger, brightening even through the color which Red Gulch knew facetiously as her "war paint," and striving, in her embarrassment, to drag the long bench nearer the school-mistress. "I thank you, miss, for that! and if I am his mother, there ain't a sweeter, dearer, better boy lives than him. And if I ain't much as says it, thar ain't a sweeter, dearer, angeler teacher lives than he's got."

Miss Mary, sitting primly behind her desk, with a ruler over her shoulder, opened her gray eyes widely at this, but said nothing.

"It ain't for you to be complimented by the like of me, I know," she went on, hurriedly. "It ain't for me to be comin' here, in broad day, to do it either; but I come to ask a favor,—not for me, miss,—not for me, but for the darling boy.''

Encouraged by a look in the young schoolmistress's eye, and putting her lilac-gloved hands together, the fingers downward, between her knees, she went on, in a low voice:—

''You see, miss, there's no one the boy has any claim on but me, and I ain't the proper person to bring him up. I thought some, last year, of sending him away to 'Frisco to school, but when they talked of bringing a school-ma'am here, I waited till I saw you, and then I knew it was all right, and I could keep my boy a little longer. And O, miss, he loves you so much; and if you could hear him talk about you, in his pretty way, and if he could ask you what I ask you now, you couldn't refuse him.

''It is natural,'' she went on, rapidly, in a voice that trembled strangely between pride and humility,—''it's natural that he should take to you, miss, for his father, when I first knew him, was a gentleman,—and the boy must forget me, sooner or later,—and so I ain't agoin' to cry about that. For I come to ask you to take my Tommy,—God bless him for the bestest, sweetest boy that lives,—to—to—take him with you.''

She had risen and caught the young girl's hand in her own and had fallen on her knees beside her.

''I've money plenty, and it's all yours and his. Put him in some good school, where you can go and see him, and help him to—to—to forget his mother. Do with him what you like. The worst you can do will be kindness to what he will learn with me. Only take him out of this wicked life, this cruel place, this home of shame and sorrow. You will; I know you will,—won't you?

You will,—you must not, you cannot say no! You will make him as pure, as gentle as yourself; and when he has grown up, you will tell him his father's name,—the name that hasn't passed my lips for years,—the name of Alexander Morton, whom they call here Sandy! Miss Mary!—do not take your hand away! Miss Mary speak to me! You will take my boy? Do not put your face from me. I know it ought not to look on such as me. Miss Mary!—my God, be merciful!—she is leaving me!''

Miss Mary had risen, and, in the gathering twilight, had felt her way to the open window. She stood there, leaning against the casement, her eyes fixed on the last rosy tints that were fading from the western sky. There was still some of its light on her pure young forehead, on her white collar, on her clasped white hands, but all fading slowly away. The suppliant had dragged herself, still on her knees, beside her.

''I know it takes time to consider. I will wait here all night; but I cannot go until you speak. Do not deny me now. You will!—I see it in your sweet face,—such a face as I have seen in my dreams. I see it in your eyes, Miss Mary!—you will take my boy!''

The last red beam crept higher, suffused Miss Mary's eyes with something of its glory, flickered, and faded, and went out. The sun had set on Red Gulch. In the twilight and silence Miss Mary's voice sounded pleasantly.

''I will take the boy. Send him to me to-night.''

The happy mother raised the hem of Miss Mary's skirts to her lips. She would have buried her hot face in its virgin folds, but she dared not. She rose to her feet.

"Does—this man—know of your intention?" asked Miss Mary, suddenly.

"No, nor cares. He has never even seen the child to know it."

"Go to him at once,—to-night,—now! Tell him what you have done. Tell him I have taken his child, and tell him—he must never see—see—the child again. Wherever it may be, he must not come; wherever I may take it, he must not follow! There, go now, please,— I'm weary, and—have much yet to do!"

They walked together to the door. On the threshold the woman turned.

"Good night."

She would have fallen at Miss Mary's feet. But at the same moment the young girl reached out her arms, caught the sinful woman to her own pure breast for one brief moment and then closed and locked the door.

It was with a sudden sense of great responsibility that Profane Bill took the reins of the Slumgullion Stage the next morning for the schoolmistress was one of his passengers. As he entered the high-road, in obedience to a pleasant voice from the "inside," he suddenly reined up his horses and respectfully waited, as "Tommy" hopped out at the command of Miss Mary.

"Not that bush, Tommy,—the next."

Tommy whipped out his new pocket-knife, and, cutting a branch from a tall azalea-bush, returned with it to Miss Mary.

"All right now?"

"All right."

And the stage-door closed on the Idyl of Red Gulch.

THE LONESOME ROAD

O. Henry

BROWN AS A coffee-berry, rugged, pistoled, spurred, wary, indefeasible, I saw my old friend, Deputy-Marshal Buck Caperton, stumble, with jingling rowels, into a chair in the marshal's outer office.

And because the courthouse was almost deserted at that hour, and because Buck would sometimes relate to me things that were out of print, I followed him in and tricked him into talk through knowledge of a weakness he had. For, cigarettes rolled with sweet corn husk were as honey to Buck's palate; and though he could finger the trigger of a forty-five with skill and suddenness, he never could learn to roll a cigarette.

It was through no fault of mine (for I rolled the cigarettes tight and smooth), but the upshot of some whim of his own, that instead of to an Odyssey of the chaparral, I listened to—a dissertation upon matrimony! This from Buck Caperton! But I maintain that the cigarettes were impeccable, and crave absolution for myself.

"We just brought in Jim and Bud Granberry," said Buck. "Train robbing, you know. Held up the Aransas Pass last month. We caught 'em in the Twenty-Mile pear flat, south of the Nueces."

"Have much trouble coralling them?" I asked, for here was the meat that my hunger for epics craved.

"Some," said Buck; and then, during a little pause, his thoughts stampeded off the trail. "It's kind of queer about women," he went on, "and the place they're supposed to occupy in botany. If I was asked to classify them I'd say they was a human loco weed. Ever see a bronc that had been chewing loco? Ride him up to a puddle of water two feet wide, and he'll give a snort and fall back on you. It looks as big as the Mississippi River to him. Next trip he'd walk into a cañon a thousand feet deep thinking it was a prairie-dog hole. Same way with a married man.

"I was thinking of Perry Rountree, that used to be my sidekicker before he committed matrimony. In them days me and Perry hated indisturbances of any kind. We roamed around considerable, stirring up the echoes and making 'em attend to business. Why, when me and Perry wanted to have some fun in a town it was a picnic for the census takers. They just counted the marshal's posse that it took to subdue us, and there was your population. But then there came along this Mariana Good-night girl and looked at Perry sideways, and he was all bridle-wise and saddle-broke before you could skin a yearling.

"I wasn't even asked to the wedding. I reckon the bride had my pedigree and the front elevation of my habits all mapped out, and she decided that Perry would trot better in double harness without any unconverted mustang like Buck Caperton whickering around on the matrimonial range. So it was six months before I saw Perry again.

"One day I was passing on the edge of town, and I see something like a man in a little yard by a little house with a sprinkling-pot squirting water on a rosebush. Seemed to me, I'd seen something like it before, and I stopped at the gate, trying to figure out its brands. 'Twas not Perry Rountree, but 'twas the kind of a curdled jellyfish matrimony had made out of him.

"Homicide was what that Mariana had perpetrated. He was looking well enough, but he had on a white collar and shoes, and you could tell in a minute that he'd speak polite and pay taxes and stick his little finger out while drinking, just like a sheep man or a citizen. Great skyrockets! but I hated to see Perry all corrupted and Willie-ized like that.

"He came out to the gate and shook hands; and I says, with scorn, and speaking like a paroquet with the pip: 'Beg pardon—Mr. Rountree, I believe. Seems to me I sagatiated in your associations once, if I am not mistaken.'

" 'Oh, go to the devil, Buck,' says Perry, polite, as I was afraid he'd be.

" 'Well, then,' says I, 'you poor, contaminated adjunct of a sprinkling-pot and degraded household pet, what did you go and do it for? Look at you, all decent and unriotous, and only fit to sit on juries and mend the wood-house door. You was a man once. I have hostility for all such acts. Why don't you go in the house and count the tidies or set the clock, and not stand out here in the atmosphere? A jackrabbit might come along and bite you.'

" 'Now, Buck,' says Perry, speaking mild, and some sorrowful, 'you don't understand. A married man has got to be different. He feels different from a tough old cloudburst like you. It's sinful to waste time pulling up towns just to look at their roots, and playing faro and looking upon red liquor, and such restless policies as them.'

" 'There was a time,' I says, and I expect I sighed when I mentioned it, 'when a certain domesticated little Mary's lamb I could name was some instructed himself in the line of pernicious sprightliness. I never expected, Perry, to see you reduced down from a full-grown pestilence to such a frivolous fraction of a man. Why,' says I, 'you've got a necktie on; and you speak a senseless kind of indoor drivel, that reminds me of a storekeeper or a lady. You look to me like you might tote an umbrella and wear suspenders, and go home of nights.'

" 'The little woman,' says Perry, 'has made some improvements, I believe. You can't understand, Buck. I haven't been away from the house at night since we was married.'

"We talked on a while, me and Perry, and, as sure as I live, that man interrupted me in the middle of my talk to tell me about six tomato plants he had growing in his garden. Shoved his agricultural degradation right up under my nose while I was telling him about the fun we had tarring and feathering that faro dealer at California Pete's layout! But by and by Perry shows a flicker of sense.

" 'Buck,' says he, 'I'll have to admit that it is a little dull at times. Not that I'm not perfectly happy with the little woman, but a man seems to require some excitement now and then. Now, I'll tell you: Mariana's gone visiting this afternoon, and she won't be home till seven o'clock. That's the limit for both of us—seven o'clock. Neither of us ever stays out a minute after that time unless we are together. Now, I'm glad you came along, Buck,' says Perry, 'for I'm feeling just like having one more rip-roaring razoo with you for the sake of old times. What you say to us putting in the afternoon having fun?—I'd like it fine,' says Perry.

"I slapped that old captive range-rider half across his little garden.

" 'Get your hat, you old dried-up alligator,' I shouts, 'you ain't dead yet. You're part human, anyhow, if you did get all bogged up in matrimony. We'll take this town to pieces and see what makes it tick. We'll make all kinds of profligate demands upon the science of cork pulling. You'll grow horns yet, old muley cow,' says I, punching Perry in the ribs, 'if you trot around on the trail of vice with your Uncle Buck.'

" 'I'll have to be home by seven, you know,' says Perry again.

" 'Oh, yes,' says I, winking to myself, for I knew the kind of seven o'clocks Perry Rountree got back by after he once got to passing repartee with the bartenders.

"We goes down to the Gray Mule saloon—that old 'dobe building by the depot.

" 'Give it a name,' says I, as soon as we got one hoof on the footrest.

" 'Sarsaparilla,' says Perry.

"You could have knocked me down with a lemon peeling.

" 'Insult me as much as you want to,' I says to Perry, 'but don't startle the bartender. He may have heart-disease. Come on, now; your tongue got twisted. The tall glasses,' I orders, 'and the bottle in the left-hand corner of the ice-chest.'

" 'Sarsaparilla,' repeats Perry, and then his eyes get animated, and I see he's got some great scheme in his mind he wants to emit.

" 'Buck,' he says, all interested, 'I'll tell you what! I want to make this a red-letter day. I've been keeping close at home, and I want to turn myself a-loose. We'll have the highest old time you ever saw. We'll go in the back room here and play checkers till half-past six.'

"I leaned against the bar, and I says to Gotch-eared Mike, who was on watch:

" 'For God's sake don't mention this. You know what Perry used to be. He's had the fever, and the doctor says we must humor him.'

" 'Give us the checker-board and the men, Mike,' says Perry. 'Come on, Buck, I'm just wild to have some excitement.'

"I went in the back room with Perry. Before we closed the door, I says to Mike:

" 'Don't ever let it straggle out from under your hat that you seen Buck Caperton fraternal with sarsaparilla or *persona grata* with a checkerboard, or I'll make a swallow-fork in your other ear.'

"I locked the door and me and Perry played checkers. To see that poor old humiliated piece of household bric-à-brac sitting there and sniggering out loud whenever he jumped a man, and all obnoxious with animation when he got into my king row, would have made a sheep-dog sick with mortification. Him that was once satisfied only when he was pegging six boards at keno or giving the faro dealers nervous prostration—to see him pushing them checkers about like Sally Louisa at a schoolchildren's party—why, I was all smothered up with mortification.

"And I sits there playing the black men, all sweating for fear somebody I knew would find it out. And I thinks to myself some about this marrying business, and how it seems to be the same kind of a game as that Mrs. Delilah played. She give her old man a hair cut, and everybody knows what a man's head looks like after a woman cuts his hair. And then when the Pharisees came around to guy him he was so 'shamed he went to work and kicked the whole house down on top of the whole outfit. 'Them married men,' thinks I, 'lose all their spirit and instinct for riot and foolishness. They won't drink, they won't buck the tiger, they won't even fight. What do they want to go and stay married for?' I asks myself.

"But Perry seems to be having hilarity in considerable quantities.

" 'Buck old hoss,' says he, 'isn't this just the hell-roaringest time we ever had in our lives? I don't know when I've been stirred up so. You see, I've been sticking pretty close to home since I married, and I haven't been on a spree in a long time.'

" 'Spree!' Yes, that's what he called it. Playing checkers in the back room of the Gray Mule! I suppose it did seem to him a little immoral and nearer to a prolonged debauch than standing over six tomato plants with a sprinkling pot.

"Every little bit Perry looks at his watch and says:

" 'I got to be home, you know, Buck, at seven.'

" 'All right,' I'd say. 'Romp along and move. This here excitement's killing me. If I don't reform some, and loosen up the strain of this checkered dissipation I won't have a nerve left.'

"It might have been half-past six when commotions began to go on outside in the street. We heard a yelling and a six-shootering, and a lot of galloping and maneuvers.

" 'What's that?' I wonders.

" 'Oh, some nonsense outside,' says Perry. 'It's your move. We just got time to play this game.'

" 'I'll just take a peep through the window,' says I, 'and see. You can't expect a mere mortal to stand the excitement of having a king jumped and listen to an unidentified conflict going on at the same time.'

"The Gray Mule saloon was one of them old Spanish 'dobe buildings, and the back room only had two little windows a foot wide, with iron bars in 'em. I looked out one, and I see the cause of the rucus.

"There was the Trimble gang—ten of 'em—the worst outfit of desperadoes and horse-thieves in Texas, coming up the street shooting right and left. They was coming right straight for the Gray Mule. Then they got past the range of my sight, but we heard 'em ride up to the front door, and then they socked the place full of lead. We heard the big looking-glass behind the bar knocked all to pieces and the bottles crashing. We could see Gotch-eared Mike in his apron running across the plaza like a coyote, with the bullets puffing up the dust all around him. Then the gang went to work in the saloon, drinking what they wanted and smashing what they didn't.

"Me and Perry both knew that gang, and they knew us. The year before Perry married, him and me was in the same ranger company—and we fought that outfit down on the San Miguel, and brought back Ben Trimble and two others for murder.

" 'We can't get out,' says I. 'We'll have to stay in here till they leave.'

"Perry looked at his watch.

" 'Twenty-five to seven,' says he. 'We can finish that game. I got two men on you. It's your move, Buck. I got to be home at seven, you know.'

"We sat down and went on playing. The Trimble gang had a roughhouse for sure. They were getting good and drunk. They'd drink a while and holler a while, and then they'd shoot up a few bottles and glasses. Two or three times they came and tried to open our door. Then there was some more shooting outside, and I looked out the window again. Ham Gossett, the town marshal, had a posse in the houses and stores across the street, and was trying to bag a Trimble or two through the windows.

"I lost that game of checkers. I'm free in saying that I lost three kings that I might have saved if I had been corralled in a more peaceful pasture. But that drivelling married man sat there and cackled when he won a man like an unintelligent hen picking up a grain of corn.

"When the game was over Perry gets up and looks at his watch.

" 'I've had a glorious time, Buck,' says he, 'but I'll have to be going now. It's a quarter to seven, and I got to be home by seven, you know.'

"I thought he was joking.

" 'They'll clear out or be dead drunk in half an hour or an hour,' says I. 'You ain't that tired of being married that you want to commit any more sudden suicide, are you?' says I, giving him the laugh.

" 'One time,' says Perry, 'I was half an hour late getting home. I met Mariana on the street looking for me. If you could have seen her, Buck—but you don't understand. She knows what a wild kind of a snoozer I've been, and she's afraid something will happen. I'll never be late getting home again. I'll say good-bye to you now, Buck.'

"I got between him and the door.

"'Married man,' says I, 'I know you was christened a fool the minute the preacher tangled you up, but don't you never sometimes think one little think on a human basis? There's ten of that gang in there, and they're pizen with whisky and desire for murder. They'll drink you up like a bottle of booze before you get halfway to the door. Be intelligent, now, and use at least wild-hog sense. Sit down and wait till we have some chance to get out without being carried in baskets.'

"'I got to be home by seven, Buck,' repeats this henpecked thing of little wisdom, like an unthinking poll parrot. 'Mariana,' says he, "ll be looking out for me.' And he reaches down and pulls a leg out of the checker table. 'I'll go through this Trimble outfit,' says he, 'like a cottontail through a brush corral. I'm not pestered any more with a desire to engage in rucuses, but I got to be home by seven. You lock the door after me, Buck. And don't you forget—I won three out of them five games. I'd play longer, but Mariana—'

"'Hush up, you old locoed road runner,' I interrupts. 'Did you ever notice your Uncle Buck locking doors against trouble? I'm not married,' says I, 'but I'm as big a d—n fool as any Mormon. One from four leaves three,' says I, and I gathers out another leg of the table. 'We'll get home by seven,' says I, 'whether it's the heavenly one or the other. May I see you home?' says I, 'you sarsaparilla-drinking, checker-playing glutton for death and destruction.'

"We opened the door easy, and then stampeded for the front. Part of the gang was lined up at the bar; part of 'em was passing over the drinks, and two or three was peeping out the door and window taking shots at the marshal's crowd. The room was so full of smoke we got halfway to the front door before they noticed us. Then I heard Berry Trimble's voice somewhere yell out:

" 'How'd that Buck Caperton get in here?' and he skinned the side of my neck with a bullet. I reckon he felt bad over that miss, for Berry's the best shot south of the Southern Pacific Railroad. But the smoke in the saloon was some too thick for good shooting.

"Me and Perry smashed over two of the gang with our table legs, which didn't miss like the guns did, and as we run out the door I grabbed a Winchester from a fellow who was watching the outside, and I turned and regulated the account of Mr. Berry.

"Me and Perry got out and around the corner all right. I never much expected to get out, but I wasn't going to be intimidated by that married man. According to Perry's idea, checkers was the event of the day, but if I am any judge of gentle recreations that little table-leg parade through the Gray Mule saloon deserved the head-lines in the bill of particulars.

" 'Walk fast,' says Perry, 'it's two minutes to seven, and I got to be home by—'

" 'Oh, shut up,' says I. 'I had an appointment as chief performer at an inquest at seven, and I'm not kicking about not keeping it.'

"I had to pass by Perry's little house. His Mariana was standing at the gate. We got there at five minutes past seven. She had on a blue wrapper, and her hair was pulled back smooth like little girls do when they want to look grown-folksy. She didn't see us till we got close, for she was gazing up the other way. Then she backed around, and saw Perry, and a kind of look scooted around over her face—danged if I can describe it. I heard her breathe long, just like a cow when you turn her calf in the lot, and she says: 'You're late, Perry.'

" 'Five minutes,' says Perry, cheerful. 'Me and old Buck was having a game of checkers.'

"Perry introduces me to Mariana, and they ask me to come in. No, siree. I'd had enough truck with married folks for that day. I says I'll be going along, and that I've spent a very pleasant afternoon with my old partner—'especially,' says I, just to jostle Perry, 'during that game when the table legs came all loose.' But I'd promised him not to let her know anything.

"I've been worrying over that business ever since it happened," continued Buck. "There's one thing about it that's got me all twisted up, and I can't figure it out."

"What was that?" I asked, as I rolled and handed Buck the last cigarette.

"Why, I'll tell you: When I saw the look that little woman give Perry when she turned round and saw him coming back to the ranch safe—why was it I got the idea all in a minute that that look of hers was worth more than the whole caboodle of us—sarsaparilla, checkers, and all, and that the d—n fool in the game wasn't named Perry Rountree at all?"

ONE NIGHT AT MEDICINE TAIL

Chad Oliver

THE GRAYING HAIR on Ed Avery's scalp did not actually
stand on end when he saw the blaze-faced sorrel, but he
felt a definite prickling sensation. The white-stockinged
horse was grazing alone in the folded brown hills to the
left of the ranger station. It did not seem to be tethered,
and it was little more than a quarter of a mile away. The
sorrel was a dead ringer for Vic.

"Jesus," Ed Avery said.

He stopped the rental Chevy at the barrier, and Julie
handed their receipt to the ranger in the tall box. It cost
three bucks to get into Custer Battlefield National Monument the first time, but the pass was then good for
weeks. Ed didn't recognize the ranger—a new one,
probably—but he leaned across Julie and asked his question, anyway.

"Park Service stick that sorrel out there?"

The ranger, who did not have the most fascinating job

27

in the world, welcomed some conversation. There were no cars backed up this time of the year.

"Doesn't belong to us, far as I know," he said. "He's just there sometimes. Four or five more horses on the other side of this road. Walk down here after you park and you can see them from that little ridge. They're Crow horses, most likely. This whole place is pretty well surrounded by the Crow Reservation, you know."

Ed Avery knew all about the Crows. It was the sorrel that interested him. It stretched coincidence about as far as it could go. Obviously the young ticket-taking ranger didn't know much more about the horse than he did.

"Thanks very much," he said, straightening up behind the wheel. He moved the car on up to the parking lot below the museum.

"Weird," he said, opening his door against the hammer of the wind. He walked around the tomato-red Chevy to get Julie's door, but Julie had beaten him to it. It wasn't eagerness on her part. Julie's generation made a statement by opening doors and piling into chairs without assistance.

Ed did not insult his younger wife by explaining that the lone sorrel looked like Vic, and that Vic had been the horse that Custer rode that terrible Sunday more than a century ago. Julie had been married to him long enough to know the basics. He did yield to the temptation to dazzle her with trivia, although he was well aware that Julie didn't dazzle much these days.

He gestured toward the cemetery that nestled up against the parking lot. It was a neat little graveyard, he thought, just large enough so that it took you a while to locate particular headstones. The watered grass was a startling green against the barren brown of the battlefield, and the wind was slowed slightly by the dark planted pines.

"Bet you don't know who's buried in there," he said.

"Elvis Presley," Julie offered. She had reached the stage where she really didn't give much of a damn.

Ed smiled to show that he was not offended, and then he pressed on with the lost cause. Maybe he *had* gone a bit ape over this Custer business. Certainly it had hurt him professionally. He was supposed to be interested in other things.

"Remember Captain Fetterman at Fort Phil Kearny?" he asked.

Julie responded almost in spite of herself. There had been a time when she had considered Ed Avery the most interesting man she had ever met, and some of what she had learned had stuck. "That name," she said. "Captain Fetterman. It always reminded me of a Groucho Marx routine. It was a classic line, wasn't it? *'Give me eighty men and I'll ride through the whole Sioux nation!'* "

"That's our boy. Fetterman's in that cemetery, what's left of him. There are also soldiers from two World Wars, Korea, and Vietnam. But there's only one man from Custer's mess at the Little Big Horn—one with a positive ID, anyhow."

"You're lecturing again."

"I know it," he said, and waited.

"Well, who is it?" she said finally.

"Crittenden." There was a touch of triumph in his voice. "John Jordan Crittenden. He was a second lieutenant attached to L Company. With Custer's battalion, right? Did you know that Crittenden only had one eye?"

"That fact had escaped me," Julie admitted.

"Come on," he said. "I'll show you the marker."

Ed Avery knew that he was driving Julie away from him, but he could not help himself. He had reached an age—fifty plus a few birthdays that were a royal pain in the tailbone—where he could no longer pretend an interest in fashionable things. It was the Custer Fight that was the bee in his bonnet. He had to share it or go nuts.

There were more than a few others like him. He wasn't the first historian to get trapped by the Seventh Cavalry.

There was nothing to impede his movement in the well-manicured little cemetery. There were just the white headstones and the wind and the pale Montana sky.

He went straight to the Crittenden marker and could not find it. He knew exactly where it was, but it wasn't there. He shook his head and checked his bearings by walking to the Fetterman stone in the row nearest the parking lot. It was right where it should have been.

Of course.

But John J. Crittenden wasn't home.

"Odd," Ed Avery said. "Damned odd."

"The reburials continue," Julie said. She could not conceal her pleasure in her husband's mistake. "Can't we get out of this damned wind?"

He nodded and they walked up to the Visitor Center. Battle Ridge, which was also known as Last Stand Hill, was in plain view a short distance beyond the Center. It wasn't much of a hill, Ed thought as he had thought before. Just a treeless slope in the middle of nowhere. No sane man would have tried to defend it by choice . . .

The Center was about one quarter bookstore and souvenir shop, and the rest museum. He knew it by heart, and by now so did Julie. He only checked it out as part of the ritual.

Julie hit the rest room to try to undo some of the effects of the hurricane outside. Ed took in the familiar things without really looking at them. All the paintings, including an imaginative portrait of Crazy Horse. It had to be imaginative, since there was no authentic photograph of the Oglala leader. At least ten different versions of Custer's death. They ranged from the ignorant—Custer with long hair and a saber, for God's sake—to the informed. About all they had in common was that there were lots of Indians and that Custer certainly did not survive the fight. Books on the Cheyenne and the Sioux and the archaeology of the battlefield. The Boy General's own book, *My Life on the Plains*. Not as good as Elizabeth Custer's assorted memoirs in Ed's opinion, but probably not a book that deserved the title Benteen gave it: *My Lie on the Plains*. Ah, if only Custer had lived long enough to add one more chapter to that book!

"Ed," Julie said when she came out of the rest room, "I think you'd better take me back to the motel. I'm not feeling so hot." There was no hostility in her voice. She sounded tired.

She did look a little pale around the gills, he thought. It had happened to her before, going all the way back to when she had still been Julie Castlemeyer. She leaned against the thick glass casing of a diorama that was just inside the museum part of the Center.

Ed had never noticed the diorama before. It was credited to a Cheyenne artist from Lame Deer. There was a red thing in it that looked more like an ambulance wagon than anything else. Funny. Ed did not recall hearing about such a wagon on Last Stand Hill. And yet that had to be the site of the diorama. There was Custer's swallow-tailed personal flag with the crossed swords . . .

''Sure, babe,'' he said, turning away from the diorama with an effort. They always kept a medical kit with antibiotics in the car, but she would rest easier in Hardin. He could drive there and back in an hour. ''Just need to get off your feet.''

She let him take her arm as they walked back to the Japanese-made Chevy. The Thrifty rental sticker almost pulsated on the windshield. It wasn't only the hard, dry, rocking wind. There was something like heat lightning flickering on the horizon. There were scarecrow tumbleweeds lurching through straw-colored grass. Ed could almost swear that he saw orange sparks sputtering up out of the tough brown earth.

In late September?

Across from a graveyard that held Fetterman but not Crittenden?

In a world where Custer's horse or a clone grazed placidly across from the ticket-taking ranger station?

Ed shook his head and gunned the Chevy for Hardin.

The afternoon sun was beginning to push shadows from the blue rattlesnake warning signs on the battlefield. It had taken Ed Avery longer than he had expected to get Julie settled and comfortable at the American Inn. The giant cheeseburger and fries and coffee at the Purple Cow had also cost him some time.

He was not overly concerned about the hour. There was plenty of daylight left. The Park Service lowered the barrier across the road early in the evening, but it was no great trick to drive around it. Nobody much cared if a car came *out* of the National Monument area after hours. They wouldn't hunt you down.

It wouldn't be the first time that Ed had spent the better part of a night in this place. There were some things a man could see more clearly in the darkness and the silence.

He did not stop at the Visitor Center. He drove on up the narrow paved trail that looped around the crest of Battle Ridge and eased the Chevy more or less south toward Reno Hill. That was upstream along the Little Big Horn, and it was more than four miles to the plateau where Reno and Benteen had dug in their heels.

It was not his intention to go much beyond Weir Point. He could park the car at the marker and climb the hill on either side of the deserted little road. That way he could see pretty much the same terrain that Captain Weir had seen when Weir had left Reno Hill and tried to go to Custer's aid. Ed Avery had followed Weir's path many times. He was damned sure that Weir could have seen Custer's last position from Weir Point. It was a tough couple of miles, but Ed could see it, and his eyes were not as sharp as they once had been.

He reached Weir Point and noticed that the marker had been changed. Something about the red ambulance wagon spotted there by the Indians. How could that be? He didn't worry about it. He was far past the stage where he could learn anything about that fight from markers or books. It was in his guts.

What Ed Avery was really doing was simple: He was soaking up the feel of this haunted place. He knew that his colleagues viewed this work of his with amused contempt. They were all glued to computers. They didn't believe in anything they couldn't count.

Well, to hell with all of them. This was his leave and

his money. He was old enough to be stubborn. Even with Julie . . .

He did not know what made him turn the Chevy around—not so easy on that narrow trail—and go back to Medicine Tail. It may have been a whisper he caught in the wind. It might have been a distant throbbing or the quicksilver notes of a sweat-stained bugle he could almost hear.

Or it could have been that evening was coming on and Medicine Tail was a place he liked to be.

The wide draw of Medicine Tail was between Weir Point and Last Stand Hill. Ed parked the car and climbed out. He felt it as he always did.

This was the place. Something vitally important had happened here. Somehow Medicine Tail was the key to everything.

See? There is the winding river, a trout stream, flat and shallow at the Medicine Tail ford. No high bluffs here, and no deep, swift water. Across the Little Big Horn—ah, there were irrigated Crow farms there now. But *then* it had been a sight to stir the blood. A forest of tipis. Band upon band of the Sioux, and the Cheyenne camp circle downstream across from Battle Ridge. Crazy Horse and Sitting Bull and Gall and Two Moons. Hear them? The dogs yipping, the children yelling, the horses blowing and snorting. How many horses for a village of dreams? How many horses for three thousand warriors?

Don't bother to punch it up on the old computer. Don't try to look it up somewhere. Nobody counted them.

The ford was so *accessible*. The slope was so gentle, the opening so wide. In this raw and brutal land, Medicine Tail had everything but a welcoming Burger King.

After he sent Benteen on his wild-goose chase and ordered poor Reno to attack that immense Indian camp with three below-strength troops of cavalry, Custer had to have tried crossing the Little Big Horn at Medicine Tail. He *had* to. It was only common sense, and Custer was not so irrational that he didn't recognize a ford when he saw one.

Something had stopped him. Something had driven him that bloody mile to Last Stand Hill. Something had put those rifle bullets in his body, one in the chest and one in the head . . .

Ed Avery was not aware of any transition. He did not remember the sunset. It was just suddenly dark. He was not in a trance. He was not hallucinating.

He knew exactly where he was and what he was doing. Here. In the night. At Medicine Tail.

There was a hushed and pulsing glow in the sky, the kind of light that sometimes comes between sunset and starshine. There was enough light to see.

A single rider splashed across the ford at Medicine Tail. Ed saw him and heard him. There was nothing dreamlike about the rider.

The rider was a Crow. He was young, barely out of his teens. He was dressed in a checked cowboy shirt, boots, and jeans. His horse was a spotted gelding. He was pushing a small herd of cattle through the ford and up the draw. He had a big wet dog with him. The dog eyed Ed's throat and slavered.

Well, no big deal. This was cattle country, Crow land, and herds had to be moved to fresh grazing occasionally. Better to do it when there were no crowds of tourists. The young man could control that dog, certainly.

"Howdy, friend," Ed said. His voice positively oozed hearty friendliness. "Am I in your way?"

The Crow did not reply. He rode his horse straight at Ed, letting the cattle pick their own way. The Crow did not seem to be hostile. Ed almost smiled at that archaic word. There was something about the Indian that stopped the smile before it started.

The Crow reined in right next to where Ed stood. Ed could smell the river-wet horse. He could see the waterline on the Indian's scuffed boots.

The Crow unfastened his left shirt pocket and took out a folded piece of white paper. He handed the paper to Ed. He drilled Ed with his black eyes. He kicked his horse—he wore no spurs—and whistled to his dog.

The Crow trotted after the cattle, topped an indistinct ridge, and was gone.

Feeling very much that he should have stayed with Julie back in Hardin, Ed Avery unfolded the sheet of paper and stared at it.

He could see it plain enough. He had, in fact, seen it before.

It was a handwritten message. It read: "Benteen. Come on. Big village. Be quick. Bring packs. P.S. Bring packs."

The message was signed just above the postscript with the name of W. W. Cooke. Cooke, of course, had been Custer's adjutant. The last message had been dictated by Custer and written by Cooke.

Had been?

Ed Avery was in a state close to shock. His mind tumbled with thoughts he could not sort out. What was a Crow cowboy doing with that piece of paper? Yes, there had been some Crow scouts with Custer, but the message had been carried by a trooper named Martini. God! What was he thinking?

That spelling error in the final line. That rang true. Cooke had been in a hurry. The mistake was in the original.

The last time Ed had seen that message—in the museum at West Point—the paper had been old and the creases stained with age. That wasn't the half of it. After he had gotten the message, Benteen had scrawled a translation of Cooke's hasty handwriting at the top of the page. Benteen had showed the note to Captain Weir and then pocketed it.

Benteen's version of the message was not on this piece of paper. The paper was fresh, not aged. It damned sure was not in Benteen's pocket.

In other words, Ed figured, Benteen hadn't gotten the message yet.

Ed Avery took a very deep breath.

It was right about then that the world turned over.

Quite suddenly it was early afternoon, and a blood-red sun burned down on dust and death. Ed could hear the deep grunting of the Springfields, the lighter cracking of Henrys and Winchesters, the sharp slapping of Colts. He could hear shouted curses and wild screams and the strange, high moans of mortally wounded horses.

There was no need to draw him any pictures. He knew where he was: right there at Medicine Tail, the Thrifty rental Chevy still in place. He knew when he was: Sunday, the twenty-fifth day of June, 1876.

Ed Avery neither cried out at the impossibility of it all, nor cowered in terror. He flashed the widest smile he had managed in years. He didn't give a rattler's left eye why or how this thing had happened.

He was where he had always wanted to be.

He had Custer's last message to Benteen in his hand. *And he knew where everyone was. He knew more than the participants in the fight. He had a lifetime of knowledge in his head. He knew exactly what to do. He was the only man in Montana Territory who knew what would work and what wouldn't.*

One of the reasons why Custer had attacked when he did, and how he did, was that he was convinced that a victory here would get him the nomination for president of the United States. What sweet revenge on Grant that would be!

Ed Avery, when you dig all the way down to the bottom line, was not overly concerned about who won this battle. It would not affect the final fate of the Indians much one way or the other. He also was not a blind worshiper of Iron Butt Custer. He certainly did not care whether or not Custer made it to the highest office in the land. He probably wouldn't have been much worse than some other presidents he could think of.

No. All that was the kind of garbage you use to impress your biographer, if you have one. The truth of the matter was a whole lot simpler. Ed Avery did not kid himself. He saw Old Doc Avery clear as crystal.

Ed Avery was a man who had specialized knowledge that he had never been able to use. He was a maverick academic. The world had not kicked him in the teeth. The world had ignored him.

Nobody had cared what he knew or what he did. Even Julie . . .

That big smile came again.

Why, by God, here he was at the Little Big Horn!

Question: Would the Chevy still run?

Question: If it would run, where should it go?

Question: If the paved road disappeared, would there be a trail he could follow?

There was nothing wrong with Ed Avery's mind. He knew precisely what the situation was. And he knew that time was running out.

It was the Chevy or nothing.

He scrambled up the draw, nicking his ankle on some grabbing brush. Nobody tried to stop him. The brown dust was like a layer of mustard gas in the heat. He could see knots of Indians riding both upstream and downstream along the ridges. The Indians were not wearing blue jeans. They weren't decked out in anything fancy, really. They were half naked, glistening with sweat, and their feathers drooped. They looked like what they were: men caught by surprise.

If they found it incredible that a few hundred soldiers had attacked a village that size, God only knew what they thought of a tomato-soup-colored Chevrolet from Thrifty car rentals in Billings, Montana.

They had more important things to worry about.

Ed piled into the car. He shut the door gently. He hit the starter. The engine caught without even a preliminary cough. Ed squinted through the sun-streaked dust. Where was the wind when you wanted it? It seemed to him that there was pavement directly under the car and nowhere else.

Earth, then. Dirt and grass. The ground was packed hard. He could move. Not just anywhere, and the ride was a genuine tooth shaker, but he could *move*.

He stayed with what he knew. Forget that the displaced Crow had seemingly come from the other side of the river, the village side. Never mind how that young Indian had wound up with Custer's message to Benteen.

All that had been in another world, or between worlds.

Custer had never made it across the Little Big Horn. He was on this side, probably wounded by now. Benteen was on this side. He couldn't have joined Reno yet, because he had not received the message, but Reno already must have been driven back from the village and holed up on the hill.

As for the damned pack-train mules . . .

Jolting along on the roughest ride of his life, Ed took care to think the situation through. This was emphatically not the time to make a big fat mistake.

Benteen and his three troops of cavalry, dispatched on a long, looping scouting expedition by the Boy General, was not with the pack train. That was one of the items that had fouled things up originally. Benteen did not know that Reno's three companies had separated from Custer's five. It was one of Custer's cute little tricks never to tell his officers what they needed to know. Captain McDougall, escorting the pack mules, not only had B Company but also small detachments from each of the other companies. Maybe one hundred soldiers tied up with McDougall . . .

No matter what you think you know, don't play master strategist. Your job is to get the message to Benteen at the right place. The message tells Benteen what to do. It always had. Benteen had more plain old horse sense than any officer on the field. What he didn't have was accurate information. So all you have to do is to tell him what he needs to know and get the hell out of the way.

Ed Avery bucketed his Chevy through screaming ghost riders and smoke-laced dust. More than once the hard rubber tires thumped over mounds that were more yielding than the earth. His knuckles were bone-white, gripping the wheel as he bounced over terrain that was never designed for an automobile that lacked high clearance and four-wheel drive. He didn't know how he got through. He suspected that medicine had something to do with it. Not just the power the Indians must have attributed to this horseless wagon from nowhere, but some real-for-sure medicine that protected the rash and the insane.

"From Medicine Tail!" he hollered. He was astonished at the pitch of his own voice.

He bucked down the long, open slope from the plateau where Reno's shattered command was digging in. God, he wanted to look at it, drink it in, but there wasn't time. Getting fouled up with Reno simply would be repeating one of the larger errors of history.

He kept going until he spotted the snakelike blue column coming at a trot out of the badlands. He didn't have to make out the fluttering guidon of H Company to know who was leading that dust-drenched battalion.

Frederick William Benteen, the senior captain of the Seventh Cavalry.

Well, it wasn't just any old day in June when Benteen got his orders from a rental Chevrolet.

Ed gave a yell he hadn't known was in him and gunned his engine.

Handing Custer's message to Benteen was more than a little eerie. Ed had seen plenty of photographs of the captain, of course, but in the flesh the resemblance of Benteen to Ed Avery was uncanny.

Benteen was a couple of years on the wrong side of forty, and so he was a few years younger than Ed. He was harder, too, as though carved out of oak. Otherwise the two men could almost have been twins. Cold-eyed, round-faced, gray-haired, inclined to be chunky and disheveled—

If Fred Benteen was startled by the Chevy, he didn't show it. That wasn't totally weird, Ed thought. At this very moment, in Philadelphia, the Centennial Exposition was going full-blast, and everyone knew they had miracles there.

The near mirror-image civilian brother didn't bother him, either. Benteen did not rattle easily. The man had orders to Benteen from Custer. The handwriting was Adjutant Cooke's. The message was clear: Custer had found the village, it was a big one, and he wanted Benteen to move up fast with the packs.

That was good enough for Benteen.

"What is Custer's condition?" he snapped. Ed Avery blinked. He had never heard Benteen's voice before. It was deeper than he had imagined.

"It is desperate, Captain," he said. "He is on this side of the river, he has separated from Reno, and he is outgunned and outnumbered."

Benteen wiped sweat out of his eyes with a dust-streaked hand. Two other officers had joined him. One was Captain Weir of D Company, Ed knew. The other was First Lieutenant Edward Settle Godfrey, commanding K Company. Godfrey looked quite young. He had gone on to become a general, and most of his photographs had been taken later in his life.

"Reno's situation?" Benteen asked.

"He has what is left of three troops. He has been hit hard, but he is in a solid defensive position. He is on a hilltop between you and Custer."

"Asshole," Benteen said surprisingly. He was anything but fond of Custer, but he respected him as a fighter. For Reno he had only contempt.

"Position of pack train?" Benteen asked crisply.

Ed told him. McDougall and the mules were nearly in eyeball range.

"Custer's position?"

Ed drew him a map in the dirt. He pointed. He gave him the exact distance.

And Ed Avery grinned. He had done everything that he needed to do. The rest was up to Benteen. Ed had no doubts concerning what Benteen would do. In a sense he had already done it. The first time, when he had joined Reno under the impression that Reno and Custer were together, he had found himself hopelessly outnumbered. Benteen had charged. He had sailed into shocked warriors with bugles blowing and Colt revolvers blasting.

Benteen would do it again. His men were no wearier than they had been the first time.

"Can you lead me to him in that contraption?"

"I can, but the machine is not as fast as a horse in this terrain. You can go straight, more or less. I'll have to feel my way."

Benteen nodded. "You are dismissed," he said. "Well done, courier!"

Feeling not at all like a fool, Ed Avery saluted and climbed back into the Chevy. He had left the motor running. He was not about to miss the finish of this one.

Benteen had to get the word to McDougall. He had to detach ammo mules for Reno and for his own escort. He had to get McDougall's force on the right trail.

Ed Avery's problem was simpler.

He just had to drive a red Chevrolet to Last Stand Hill.

Ed Avery got through to Custer after Benteen's noisy, bluffing charge had lifted the siege, but before Captain Thomas McDougall came swearing in with the mules. He actually got to see the augmented B Troop ride through Gall's confused Sioux warriors with only light casualties.

That was something, but Ed could see more. Calhoun was still alive. There was Myles Keogh, but the horse Comanche was already wounded. Tom Custer, next to his brother Boston. Young Autie Reed. And, by God, Mark Kellogg taking notes—

There was still more. From the ridge he could see across the Little Big Horn into that immense village swarming with Sioux and Cheyenne. Two Moons had to be there. Sitting Bull had never left. Crazy Horse, whose vision was clearer than most, had pulled back into the camp. Ed couldn't pick him out through the haze and dust and distance, but he saw Crazy Horse clearly in his imagination. Not a big man but lithe. Bare-chested with painted hail spots. Lightning streaking from his forehead to his chin. Hair unbound, a brown pebble behind his ear, a red-backed hawk fastened to his head . . .

To be so close to such a man and have to turn away!

But Ed Avery was locked on a course he dared not alter. He wasn't sure how much time he had, but it couldn't be much.

He knew that the Indians would protect the village now. They had the long wisdom of experience. One regiment of cavalry could not dislodge them. They would pull out in their own good time, before Terry and Gibbon arrived.

And Custer? He would do exactly what General Crook had done on the Rosebud a little more than a week ago. Crook had encountered the same Indians. He had fought an inconclusive draw and had declared a mighty victory. Custer could claim the same, with one important difference.

Custer had fewer men than Crook had commanded.

That would make the victory sweeter. It would, in fact, make it presidential—

There was one slight catch, of course.

Custer had to live.

Ed Avery abandoned his Chevy wagon on the slope of Battle Ridge. It had two blown tires and a twisted axle. Steam was hissing from its radiator. That car would never start again. No matter. It had done its job.

Ed snatched up the square tin medical kit that was a part of any automobile driven by him or Julie. He ran for it.

There were a lot of bodies and clouds of flies, but there was very little firing now. The heavy fighting was over. The wounded Custer had fallen back from Medicine Tail, and Benteen had come roaring in at the last possible moment. Hell! Wasn't this the Seventh Cavalry?

Nobody bothered Ed Avery. He was neither fish nor fowl. Benteen waved at him, and that was the only recognition he got.

Ed knew precisely where Custer was. The scene had

been described a thousand times. Ed went straight to him.

George Armstrong Custer was in a sitting position, his back propped up against a dead corporal. He had lost his hat, and someone had stuck a broad-brimmed straw hat on his head to shield his fair skin from the Montana sun. Ed remembered that quite a few of those straw hats had been bought on the *Far West*. Custer was still dressed, which seemed odd. Everybody knew that he had been stripped naked after the battle, and the appearance of the body had been discussed endlessly. He wore his fringed buckskin outfit, and there was a bloody stain seeping through from the front of his blouse. He had a Remington sporting rifle gripped in his hands.

The Boy General looked like hell. He was, in fact, thirty-six years old; he was tired and unshaven; he was dirty; and he had a rifle bullet in his chest. His hair was short, and what Ed could see of it was a neutral color; it just looked like sweaty hair. Custer's eyes were more lively than the rest of him. They were blue and bloodshot and they flashed with anger.

The firing grew somewhat heavier. Ed ignored it, and so did Custer.

Custer turned his head toward Adjutant Cooke. Cooke was on one knee, methodically shooting and reloading a Springfield carbine. It didn't jam on *him*. Cooke, who had positively luxuriant chin whiskers, was known as the best shot in the regiment.

"Cookey," he said. His voice was a shade high and had a braying quality to it. "Who is this man? If it is Captain Benteen again, repeat my orders to attack."

"Not Benteen, General. Rest easy now. Never saw him before."

Ed took a deep breath. "I'm a doctor," he said.

Custer coughed. There were blood bubbles around his mouth. "If you're a doctor," he said, "you'd better be a good one."

"I am," Ed Avery said, and went to work.

He didn't try to get the bullet out. His job was to keep this man alive until the real surgeons took over. He knew enough to get the bleeding stopped and the correct antibiotics applied. His medical kit was over a century advanced beyond anything else on this battlefield.

He did not forget that Custer had sustained two wounds.

Ed Avery knew exactly when to lift his head.

He had a split second of knowledge when the rifle bullet pierced his temple. It was a clean shot. Quick. Not a bad way to go.

Ed Avery could not manage a smile. He didn't have enough control for that.

But he did sense a certain flash of contentment. He had not failed, after all, and he was where he had wanted to be.

It had become more of a ritual than anything else.

Every September, within a day or two of the date of that last trip she had taken with Ed, Julie Castlemeyer flew to Billings and rented a car at Thrifty. She tried to get a red one, like the Chevy.

She drove the lonely miles to Hardin and got the same room at the American Inn. They usually had the courtesy coffee waiting for her. She didn't have to go into the lounge with the washing machines to get it. That gave her a headache.

She wondered sometimes if it would have made any

difference if she had gone ahead and married Ed. Certainly he had been the most unusual man she had ever known.

But as attentive as Ed had been, he was inclined to be forgetful. If ever a man had been wrapped up with his own private set of dreams, that man was Ed Avery. He lived in a different world.

Still, it was not like him to go off and leave her as he had done. Just drive away and never come back!

She had not been feeling well that afternoon, and that made it worse. It hurt her. It still hurt, across the years.

Something had happened to her Ed. He wouldn't have deserted her for no reason . . .

She got into her red car, checking to make sure that her medical kit was in place, and drove on out to the Custer Presidential Library. She didn't spend much time in the Library itself, although she did look again at the diorama that showed President Custer's greatest victory. That peculiar ambulance wagon there on Turnaround Hill often seemed to be trying to speak to her across the chasm of time.

She felt like walking, wind or no wind. She climbed the ridge where Benteen had saved Custer's hide. It was Benteen who had pulled the fat out of the fire; that was what Ed used to say. Of course, Ed had looked enough like Benteen to be his brother, and President Custer had told a somewhat different story in *My Life on the Plains*.

She supposed that it really didn't matter now. Julie was getting a little old to walk these hills. Her breath came hard sometimes.

She walked along the paved pathway until she came to Medicine Tail. It was getting on toward evening, and she left the pavement and picked her way down the draw until she could hear the whispering glide of the Little Big Horn beneath the wind.

There were times when a human being needed to get away from paved roads. You needed the earth under your feet and the sweet smell of old grass.

Ed Avery had taught her that.

Julie closed her eyes just for a moment, and knew a kind of happiness.

She always felt so close to him here.

TIMBERLINE

Owen Wister

JUST AS THE blaze of the sun seems to cast wild birds, when, by yielding themselves they invite it, into a sort of trance, so that they sit upon the ground tilted sidewise, their heads in the air, their beaks open, their wings hanging slack, their feathers ruffled and their eyes vacantly fixed, so must the spot of yellow at which I had sat staring steadily and idly have done something like this to me—given me a spell of torpor in which all thoughts and things receded far away from me. It was a yellow poster, still wet from rain.

A terrifying thunderstorm had left all space dumb and bruised, as it were, with the heavy blows of its noise. The damp seemed to make the yellow paper yellower, the black letters blacker. A dollar sign, figures and zeros, exclamation points and the two blackest words of all, *reward* and *murder*, were what stood out of the yellow.

Two feet from it, on the same shed, was another

poster, white, concerning some stallion, his place of residence, and his pedigree. This also I had read, with equal inattention and idleness, but my eyes had been drawn to the yellow spot and held by it.

Not by its news; the news was now old, since at every cabin and station dotted along our lonely road the same poster had appeared. They had discussed it, and whether he would be caught, and how much money he had got from his victim.

The body hadn't been found on Owl Creek for a good many weeks. Funny his friend hadn't turned up. If they'd killed him, why wasn't his body on Owl Creek, too? If he'd got away, why didn't he turn up? Such comments, with many more, were they making at Lost Soldier, Bull Spring, Crook's Gap and Sweetwater Bridge.

I sat in the wagon waiting for Scipio Le Moyne to come out of the house; there in my nostrils was the smell of the wet sagebrush and of the wet straw and manure, and there, against the gray sky, was an afterimage of the yellow poster, square, huge and blue. It moved with my eyes as I turned them to get rid of the annoying vision, and it only slowly dissolved away over the head of the figure sitting on the corral with its back to me, the stock-tender of this stage section. He sang: "*If that I was where I would be, Then should I be where I am not; Here am I where I must be, And where I would be I cannot.*"

I could not see the figure's face, or that he moved. One boot was twisted between the bars of the corral to hold him steady, its trodden heel was worn to a slant; from one seat pocket a soiled rag protruded and through a hole below this a piece of his red shirt or drawers stuck

out. A coat much too large for him hung from his neck
rather than from his shoulders, and the damp, limp hat
that he wore, with its spotted, unraveled hat band,
somehow completed the suggestion that he was not alive
at all, but had been tied together and stuffed and set out
in joke. Certainly there were no birds, or crops to
frighten birds from; the only thing man had sown the
desert with at Rongis was empty bottles. These lay
everywhere.

As he sat and repeated his song there came from his
back and his hat and his voice an impression of loneliness, poignant and helpless. A windmill turned and
turned and creaked near the corral, adding its note of
forlornness to the song.

A man put his head out of the house. "Stop it," he
said, and shut the door again.

The figure obediently climbed down and went over to
the windmill, where he took hold of the rope hanging
from its rudder and turned the contrivance slowly out of
the wind, until the wheel ceased revolving.

The man put his head out of the house, this second
time speaking louder: "I didn't say stop that. I said stop
it; stop your damned singing." He withdrew his head
immediately.

The boy—the mild, new yellow hair on his face was
the unshaven growth of adolescence—stood a long
while looking at the door in silence, with eyes and
mouth expressing futile injury. Finally he thrust his
hands into bunchy pockets, and said:

"I ain't no two-bit man."

He watched the door, as if daring it to deny this, then,
as nothing happened, he slowly drew his hands from the
bunchy pockets, climbed the corral at the spot nearest

him, twisted the boot between the bars and sat as before only without singing.

Thus we sat waiting, I for Scipio to come out of the house with the information he had gone in for, while the boy waited for nothing. *Waiting for nothing* was stamped plain upon him from head to foot. This boy's eyebrows were insufficient, and his front was as ragged as his back. He just sat and waited.

Presently the same man put his head out of the door. "You after sheep?"

I nodded.

"I could a-showed you sheep. Rams. Horns as big as your thigh—bigger'n *your* thigh. That was before tenderfeet came in and spoiled this country. Counted seven thousand on that there butte one morning before breakfast. Seven thousand and twenty-three, if you want exact figgers. Quit your staring!" This was addressed to the boy on the corral. "Why, you're not a-going without another?" This convivial question was to Scipio, who now came out of the house and across to me with the news that he had failed on what he had went in for.

"I could a-showed you sheep—" resumed the man, but I was now attending to Scipio.

"He don't know anything," said Scipio, "nor any of 'em in there. But we haven't got this country rounded up yet. He's just come out of a week of snake fits, and, by the way it looks, he'll enter on another about tomorrow morning. But drink can't stop *him* lying."

"Bad weather," said the man, watching us make ready to continue our long drive. "Lot o' lightning loose in the air right now. Kind o' weather you're liable to see fire on the horns of the stock some night."

This sounded like such a good one that I encouraged

him. "We have nothing like that in the East."

"Hm. Guess you've not. Guess you never seen six-teen thousand steers with a light at the end of every horn in the herd."

"Are they going to catch that man?" inquired Scipio, pointing to the yellow poster.

"Catch him? Them? No! But I could tell 'em where he's went. He's went to Idaho."

"Thought the '76 outfit had sold Auctioneer," Scipio continued conversationally.

"That stallion? No! But I could tell 'em they'd ought to." This was his good-bye to us; he removed himself and his alcoholic omniscience into the house.

"Wait," I said to Scipio as he got in and took the reins from me. "I'm going to deal some magic to you. Look at that poster. No, not the stallion, the yellow one. Keep looking at it hard." While he obeyed me I made solemn passes with my hands over his head. "Now look anywhere you please."

Scipio looked across the corral at the gray sky. A slight stiffening of figure ensued, and he knit his brows. Then he rubbed a hand over his eyes and looked again.

"You after sheep?" It was the boy sitting on the cor-ral. We paid him no attention.

"It's about gone," said Scipio, rubbing his eyes again. "Did you do that to me? Of course you didn't! What did?"

I adopted the manner of the professor who lectured on light to me when I was nineteen. "The eye being normal in structure and focus, the color of an afterimage of the negative variety is complementary to that of the object causing it. If, for instance, a yellow disk (or loz-enge in this case) be attentively observed, the yellow-

perceiving elements of the retina become fatigued.
Hence, when the mixed rays which constitute white light
fall upon that portion of the retina which has thus been
fatigued, the rays which produce the sensation of yellow
will cause less effect than the other rays for which the
eye has not been fatigued. Therefore, white light to an
eye fatigued for yellow will appear blue—blue being
yellow's complementary color. Now, shall I go on?'' I
asked.

"Don't y'u!" Scipio begged. "I'd sooner believe y'u
done it to me."

"I can show you sheep." It was the boy again. We
had not noticed him come from the corral to our wagon,
by which he now stood. His eyes were eagerly fixed
upon me; as they looked into mine they seemed almost
burning with some sort of appeal.

"Hello, Timberline!" said Scipio, not at all unkindly.
"Still holding your job here? Well, you better stick to
it. You're inclined to drift some."

He touched the horses and we left the boy standing
and looking after us, lonely and baffled.

"Why Timberline?" I asked after several miles.

"Well, he came into this country the long, lanky innocent kid you saw him, and he'd always get too tall in
the legs for his latest pair of pants. They'd be half up
to his knees. So we called him that. Guess he's most
forgot his real name."

"What is his real name?"

"I've quite forgot."

This much talk did for us for two or three miles more.

"Do you suppose the man really did go to Idaho?" I
asked then.

"They do go there—and they go everywhere else

that's convenient—Canada, San Francisco, some Indian reservation. He'll never get found. I expect like as not he killed the confederate along with the victims—it's claimed there was a cook along, too. He's never showed up. It's a bad proposition to get tangled up with a murderer.''

I sat thinking of this and that and the other.

''That was a superior lie about the lights on the steers' horns,'' I remarked next.

Scipio shoved one hand under his hat and scratched his head. ''They say that's so,'' he said. ''I've heard it. Never seen it. But—tell y'u—he ain't got brains enough to invent a thing like that. And he's too conceited to tell another man's lie.''

''There's St. Elmo's fire,'' I pondered. ''That's genuine.''

Scipio desired to know about this, and I told him of the lights that are seen at the ends of the yards and spars of ships at sea in atmospheric conditions of a certain kind. He let me also tell him of the old Breton sailor belief that these lights are the souls of dead sailor men come back to pray for the living in peril; but stopped me soon when I attempted to speak of charged thunder clouds, and the positive, and the negative, and conductors and Leyden jars.

''That's a heap worse than the other stuff about yellow and blue,'' he objected. ''Here's Broke Axle. We'll camp here.''

Scipio's sleep was superior to mine, coming sooner, burying him deeper from the world of wakefulness. Thus, he did not become aware of a figure sitting by our little fire of embers, whose presence penetrated my thinner sleep until my eyes opened and saw it. I lay still drawing my gun stealthily into a good position and thinking what were best to do; but he must have heard me.

"Lemme show you sheep."

"What's that?" It was Scipio starting to life and action.

"Don't shoot Timberline," I said. "He's come to show us sheep."

Scipio sat staring stupefied at the figure by the embers, and then he slowly turned his head around to me, and I thought he was going to pour out one of those long corrosive streams of comment that usually burst from him when he was enough surprised. But he was too much surprised.

"His name is Henry Hall," he said to me very mildly. "I've just remembered it."

The patient figure by the embers rose. "There's sheep in the Washakie Needles. Lots and lots and lots. I seen 'em myself in the spring. I can take you right to 'em. Don't make me go back and be stocktender." He recited all this in a sort of rising rhythm until the last sentence, in which the entreaty shook his voice.

"Washakie Needles is the nearest likely place," muttered Scipio.

"If you don't get any you needn't to pay me any," urged the boy; and he stretched out an arm to mark his words and his prayer.

We sat in our beds and he stood waiting by the embers to hear his fate, while nothing made a sound but Broke Axle.

"Why not?" I said. "We were talking a ways back of taking on a third man."

"A man," said Scipio. "Yes."

"I can cook, I can pack. I can cook good bread, and I can show you sheep, and if I don't you won't have to pay me a cent," stated the boy.

"He sure means what he says," Scipio commented. "It's your trip."

Thus it was I came to hire Timberline.

Dawn showed him in the same miserable rags he wore on my first sight of him at the corral, and these provided his sole visible property of any kind; he didn't possess a change of anything, he hadn't brought away from Rongis so much as a handkerchief tied up with things inside it. Most wonderful of all, he owned not even a horse—and in that country in those days five dollars' worth of horse was within the means of almost anybody.

But he was unclean, as I had feared. He washed his one set of rags, and his skin-and-bones body, by the light of that first sunrise on Broke Axle, and this proved a habit with him, which made all the more strange his neglect to throw the rags away and wear the new clothes I bought as we passed through Lander, and gave him.

"Timberline," said Scipio the next day, "If Anthony Comstock came up in this country he'd jail you."

"Who's he?" Timberline screamed sharply.

"He lives in New York and he's agin the nood. That costume of yours is getting close on to what they claim Venus and other Greek statuary used to wear."

After this Timberline put on the Lander clothes, but we found that he kept the rags next his skin. This clinging to such worthless things seemed probably the result of destitution, of having had nothing, day after day and month after month.

His help in camp was real, not merely well meant; the curious haze or blur in which his mind had seemed to be at the corral cleared away, and he was worth his wages. What he had said he could do he did, and more. And yet, when I looked at him he was somehow forever pitiful.

"Do you think anything is the matter with him?" I asked Scipio.

"Only just one thing. He'd oughtn't never have been born."

We continued along the trail, engrossed in our several thoughts, and I could hear Timberline, behind us with the pack horses, singing: "*If that I was where I would be. Then should I be where I am not.*"

Our mode of travel had changed at Fort Washakie: we had left the wagon and put ourselves and our baggage upon horses because we should presently be in a country where wagons could not go.

Once the vigorous words of some bypasser on a horse caused Scipio and me to discuss dropping the Washakie Needles for the country at the head of Green River. None of us had ever been in the Green River country, while Timberline evidently knew the Washakie Needles well, and this decided us. But Timberline had been thrown into the strangest agitation by our uncertainty. He had said nothing, but he walked about, coming near, going away, sitting down, getting up, instead of placidly watching his fire and cooking; until at last I told him not to worry, that I should keep him and pay him in any case. Then he spoke:

"I didn't hire to go to Green River."

"What have you got against Green River?"

"I hired to go to the Washakie Needles."

His agitation left him immediately upon our turning

our faces in that direction. What had so disturbed him
we could not guess; but, later that day, Scipio rode up
to me, bursting with a solution. He had visited a
freighter's camp, and the freighter, upon learning our
destination, had said he supposed we were "after the
reward."

It did not get through my head at once, but when
Scipio reminded me of the yellow poster and the murder,
it got through fast enough; the body had been found on
Owl Creek, and the middle fork of Owl Creek headed
among the Washakie Needles. There might be another
body—the other Eastern man who had never been seen
since—and there was a possible third, the confederate,
the cook; many held it was the murderer's best policy
to destroy him as well.

So now we had Timberline accounted for satisfacto-
rily to ourselves: he was "after the reward." We never
said this to him, but we worked out his steps from the
start. As stocktender at Rongis he had seen that yellow
poster pasted up, and had read it, day after day, with its
promise of what to him was a fortune. My sheep hunt
had dropped like a Providence into his hand.

We got across the hot country where rattlesnakes were
thick, where neither man lived nor water ran, and came
to the first lone habitation in this new part of the world—
a new set of mountains, a new set of creeks. A man
stood at the door, watching us come.

"Do you know him?" I asked Scipio.

"Well, I've heard of him," said Scipio. "He went
and married a squaw."

We were now opposite the man's door. "You folks
after the reward?" said he.

"After mountain sheep," I replied, somewhat angry.

We camped some ten miles beyond him, and the next day crossed a not high range, stopping near another cabin for noon. Two men were living here, cutting hay in a wild park. They gave us a quantity of berries they had picked, and we gave them some potatoes.

"After the reward?" said one of them as we rode away, and I contradicted him with temper.

"Lie to 'em," said Scipio. "Say yes."

Something had begun to weigh upon our cheerfulness in this new country. The reward dogged us, and we met strange actions of people, twice. We came upon some hot sulphur springs and camped near them, with a wide creek between us and another camp. Those people—two men and two women—emerged from their tent, surveyed us, nodded to us, and settled down again.

Next morning they had vanished; we could see empty bottles where they had been. And once, coming out of a little valley, we sighted close to us through cottonwoods a horseman leading a pack horse coming out of the next little valley. He did not nod to us, but pursued his parallel course some three hundred yards off, until a rise in the ground hid him for a while; when this was passed he was no longer where he should have been, abreast of us, but far to the front, galloping away. That was our last sight of him.

We spoke of these actions a little. Did these people suspect us, or were they afraid we suspected them? All we ever knew was that suspicion now closed down upon all things like a change of climate.

I drove up the narrowing canyon of Owl Creek, a constant prey to such ill-ease, such distaste for continuing my sheep-hunt here, that shame alone prevented my giving it up and getting into another country out of sight and far away from these Washakie Needles, these twin spires of naked rock that rose in front of us now, high above the clustered mountaintops, closing the canyon in, shutting the setting sun away.

"He *can* talk when he wants to." This was Scipio, riding behind me.

"What has Timberline been telling you?"

"Nothing. But he's telling himself a heap of something." In the rear of our single-file party Timberline rode, and I could hear him. It was a relief to have a practical trouble threatening us; if the boy was going off his head we should have something real to deal with. But when I had chosen a camp and we were unsaddling and throwing the packs on the ground, Timberline was in his customary silence.

Next morning, the three of us left camp. It was warm summer in the valley by the streaming channel of our creek, and the quiet days smelled of the pines. By three o'clock we stood upon a lofty, wet, slippery ledge that fell away on three sides, sheer or broken, to the summer and the warmth thousands of feet below. Here it began to be very cold, and to the west the sky now clotted into advancing lumps of thick thunder cloud, black, weaving and merging heavily and swiftly in a fierce rising wind.

We got away from this promontory to follow a sheep trail, and as we went along the backbone of the mountain, two or three valleys off to the right, long black streamers let down from the cloud. They hung and wavered mistily close over the pines that did not grow within a thousand feet of our high level. I gazed hard at the streamers and discerned water, or something pouring down in them. Above our heads the day was still serene, and we had a chance to make camp without a wetting.

"No! No!" said Timberline hoarsely. "See there! We can get them. We're above them. They don't see us."

I saw no sheep where he pointed but he insisted they had merely moved behind a point, and so we went on to a junction of the knife-ridges upon which a second storm was hastening from the southwest over deep valleys that we turned our backs on to creep near the Great Washakie Needle.

Below us there was a new valley like the bottom of a caldron; on the far side of the caldron the air, like a stroke of magic became thick white, and through it leaped the first lightning, a blinding violet. A sheet of the storm crossed over to us, the caldron sank from sight in its white sea, and the hail cut my face, so I bowed it down. On the ground I saw what looked like a tangle of old footprints in the hard-crusted mud.

These the pellets of the swarming hail soon filled. This tempest of flying ice struck my body, my horse, raced over the ground like spray on the crest of breaking waves, and drove me to dismount and sit under the horse, huddled together even as he was huddled against the fury and the biting pain of the hail.

From under the horse's belly I looked out upon a chaos of shooting, hissing white, through which, in every direction, lightning flashed and leaped, while the fearful crashes behind the curtain of the hail sounded as if I should see a destroyed world when the curtain lifted. The place was so flooded with electricity that I gave up the shelter of my horse, and left my rifle on the ground, and moved away from the vicinity of these points of attraction.

At length the hailstones fell more gently, the near

view opened, revealing white winter on all save the steep, gray needles; the thick white curtain of hail departed slowly, the hail where I was fell more scantily still.

Something somewhere near my head set up a delicate sound. It seemed in my hat. I rose and began to wander, bewildered by this. The hail was now falling very fine and gentle, when suddenly I was aware of its stinging me behind my ear more sharply than it had done before. I turned my face in its direction and found its blows harmless, while the stinging in my ear grew sharper. The hissing continued close to my head wherever I walked. It resembled the little watery escape of gas from a charged bottle whose cork is being slowly drawn.

I was now more really disturbed than I had been during the storm's worst, and meeting Scipio, who was also wandering, I asked if he felt anything. He nodded uneasily, when, suddenly—I know not why—I snatched my hat off. The hissing was in the brim, and it died out as I looked at the leather binding and the stitches.

I expected to see some insect there, or some visible reason for the noise. I saw nothing, but the pricking behind my ear had also stopped. Then I knew my wet hat had been charged like a Leyden jar with electricity. Scipio, who had watched me, jerked his hat off also.

"Lights on steer horns are nothing to this," I began, when he cut me short with an exclamation.

Timberline, on his knees, with a frightful countenance, was tearing off his clothes. He had felt the prickling, but it caused him thought different from mine.

"Leave me go!" he screamed. "I didn't push you over! He made me push you. I never knowed his game. I was only the cook. I wish't I'd followed you. There!

There! Take it back! There's your money! I never spent a cent of it!''

And from those rags he had cherished he tore the bills that had been sewed in them. But this confession seemed not to stop the stinging. He rose, stared wildly, and, screaming wildly, "You've got it all" plunged into the caldron from our sight. The fluttered money—some of the victim's, hush-money hapless Timberline had accepted from the murderer—was only five ten dollar bills; but it had been enough load of guilt to draw him to the spot of the crime.

We found the two bodies, the old and the new, and buried them both. But the true murderer was not caught, and no one ever claimed the reward.

ALL GOLD CANYON

Jack London

IT WAS THE green heart of the canyon, where the walls swerved back from the rigid plan and relieved their harshness of line by making a little sheltered nook and filling it to the brim with sweetness and roundness and softness. Here all things rested. Even the narrow stream ceased its turbulent down-rush long enough to form a quiet pool. Knee-deep in the water, with drooping head and half-shut eyes, drowsed a red-coated, many-antlered buck.

On one side, beginning at the very lip of the pool, was a tiny meadow, a cool, resilient surface of green that extended to the base of the frowning wall. Beyond the pool a gentle slope of earth ran up and up to meet the opposing wall. Fine grass covered the slope—grass that was spangled with flowers, with here-and-there patches of color, orange and purple and golden. Below, the canyon was shut in. There was no view. The walls leaned together abruptly, and the canyon ended in a chaos of rocks, moss-covered and hidden by a green screen of vines and creepers and boughs of trees. Up the canyon rose far hills and peaks, the big foothills, pine-covered and remote. And far beyond, like clouds upon the border of the sky, towered minarets of white, where the Sierra's eternal snows flashed austerely the blazes of the sun.

There was no dust in the canyon. The leaves and flowers were clean and virginal. The grass was young velvet. Over the pool three cottonwoods sent their snowy fluffs fluttering down the quiet air. On the slope the blossoms of the wine-wooded manzanita filled the air with spring-time odors, while the leaves, wise with experience, were already beginning their vertical twist against the coming aridity of summer. In the open spaces on the slope, beyond the farthest shadow-reach of the manzanita, poised the mariposa lilies, like so many flights of jewelled moths suddenly arrested and on the verge of trembling into flight again. Here and there that woods harlequin, the madrone, permitting itself to be caught in the act of changing its pea green trunk to madder red, breathed its fragrance into the air from great clusters of waxen bells. Creamy white were these bells, shaped like lilies of the valley, with the sweetness of perfume that is of the springtime.

There was not a sigh of wind. The air was drowsy with its weight of perfume. It was a sweetness that would have been cloying had the air been heavy and humid. But the air was sharp and thin. It was as starlight transmuted into atmosphere, shot through and warmed by sunshine, and flower-drenched with sweetness.

An occasional butterfly drifted in and out through the

patches of light and shade. And from all about rose the low and sleepy hum of mountain bees—feasting Sybarites that jostled one another good-naturedly at the board, nor found time for rough discourtesy. So quietly did the little stream drip and ripple its way through the canyon that it spoke only in faint and occasional gurgles. The voice of the stream was as a drowsy whisper, ever interrupted by dozings and silences, ever lifted again in the awakenings.

The motion of all things was a drifting in the heart of the canyon. Sunshine and butterflies drifted in and out among the trees. The hum of the bees and the whisper of the stream were a drifting of sound. And the drifting sound and drifting color seemed to weave together in the making of a delicate and intangible fabric which was the spirit of the place. It was a spirit of peace that was not of death, but of smooth-pulsing life, of quietude that was not silence, of movement that was not action, of repose that was quick with existence without being violent with struggle and travail. The spirit of the place was the spirit of the peace of the living, somnolent with the easement and content of prosperity, and undisturbed by rumors of far wars.

The red-coated, many-antlered buck acknowledged the lordship of the spirit of the place and dozed knee-deep in the cool, shaded pool. There seemed no flies to vex him and he was languid with rest. Sometimes his ears moved when the stream awoke and whispered; but they moved lazily, with foreknowledge that it was merely the stream grown garrulous at discovery that it had slept.

But there came a time when the buck's ears lifted and tensed with swift eagerness for sound. His head was turned down the canyon. His sensitive, quivering nostrils scented the air. His eyes could not pierce the green screen through which the stream rippled away, but to his ears came the voice of a man. It was a steady, monotonous, singsong voice. Once the buck heard the harsh clash of metal upon rock. At the sound he snorted with a sudden start that jerked him through the air from water to meadow, and his feet sank into the young velvet while he pricked his ears and again scented the air. Then he stole across the tiny meadow, pausing once and again to listen, and faded away out of the canyon like a wraith, soft-footed and without sound.

The clash of steel-shod soles against the rocks began to be heard, and the man's voice grew louder. It was raised in a sort of chant and became distinct with nearness, so that the words could be heard.

> "Tu'n around an' tu'n yo' face
> Untoe them sweet hills of grace
>   (D' pow'rs of sin yo' am scornin'!).
> Look about an' look aroun'
> Fling yo' sin-pack on d' groun'
>   (Yo' will meet wid d' Lord in d'
>   mornin'!)."

A sound of scrambling accompanied the song, and the spirit of the place fled away on the heels of the red-coated buck. The green screen was burst asunder, and a man peered out at the meadow and the pool and the sloping side-hill. He was a deliberate sort of man. He took in the scene with one embracing glance, then ran his eyes over the details to verify the general impression.

Then, and not until then, did he open his mouth in vivid and solemn approval.

"Smoke of life an' snakes of purgatory! Will you just look at that! Wood an' water an' grass an' a side-hill! A pocket-hunter's delight an' a cayuse's paradise! Cool green for tired eyes! Pink pills for pale people ain't in it. A secret pasture for prospectors and a resting-place for tired burros. It's just booful!"

He was a sandy-complexioned man in whose face geniality and humor seemed the salient characteristics. It was a mobile face, quick-changing to inward mood and thought. Thinking was in him a visible process. Ideas chased across his face like wind flaws across the surface of a lake. His hair, sparse and unkempt of growth, was as indeterminate and colorless as his complexion. It would seem that all the color of his frame had gone into his eyes, for they were startlingly blue. Also, they were laughing and merry eyes, within them much of the naiveté and wonder of the child; and yet, in an unassertive way, they contained much of calm self-reliance and strength of purpose founded upon self-experience and experience of the world.

From out the screen of vines and creepers, he flung ahead of him a miner's pick and shovel and gold-pan. Then he crawled out himself into the open. He was clad in faded overalls and black cotton shirt, with hobnailed brogans on his feet, and on his head a hat whose shapelessness and stains advertised the rough usage of wind and rain and sun and camp smoke. He stood erect, seeing wide-eyed the secrecy of the scene and sensuously inhaling the warm, sweet breath of the canyon garden through nostrils that dilated and quivered with delight. His eyes narrowed to laughing slits of blue, his face wreathed itself in joy, and his mouth curled in a smile as he cried aloud, "Jumping dandelions and happy hollyhocks, but that smells good to me! Talk about your attar o' roses an' cologne factories! They ain't in it!"

He had the habit of soliloquy. His quick-changing facial expressions might tell every thought and mood, but the tongue, perforce, ran hard after, repeating, like a second Boswell.

The man lay down on the lip of the pool and drank long and deep of its water. "Tastes good to me," he murmured, lifting his head and gazing across the pool at the side-hill, while he wiped his mouth with the back of his hand. The side-hill attracted his attention. Still lying on his stomach, he studied the hill formation long and carefully. It was a practiced eye that traveled up the slope to the crumbling canyon wall and back and down again to the edge of the pool. He scrambled to his feet and favored the side-hill with a second survey.

"Looks good to me," he concluded, picking up his pick and shovel and gold-pan.

He crossed the stream below the pool, stepping agilely from stone to stone. Where the side-hill touched the water he dug up a shovelful of dirt and put it into the gold-pan. He squatted down, holding the pan in his two hands, and partly immersing it in the stream. Then he imparted to the pan a deft circular motion that sent the water sluicing in and out through the dirt and gravel. The larger and the lighter particles worked to the surface, and these, by a skillful dipping movement of the pan, he spilled out and over the edge. Occasionally, to expedite matters, he rested the pan and with his fingers raked out the large pebbles and pieces of rock.

The contents of the pan diminished rapidly until only

fine dirt and the smallest bits of gravel remained. At this stage he began to work very deliberately and carefully. It was fine washing, and he washed fine and finer, with a keen scrutiny and delicate and fastidious touch. At last the pan seemed empty of everything but water; but with a quick semicircular flirt that sent the water flying over the shallow rim into the stream, he disclosed a layer of black sand on the bottom of the pan. So thin was this layer that it was like a streak of paint. He examined it closely. In the midst of it was a tiny golden speck. He dribbled a little water in over the depressed edge of the pan. With a quick flirt he sent the water sluicing across the bottom, turning the grains of black sand over and over. A second tiny golden speck rewarded his effort.

The washing had now become very fine—fine beyond all need of ordinary placer mining. He worked the black sand, a small portion at a time, up the shallow rim of the pan. Each small portion he examined sharply, so that his eyes saw every grain of it before he allowed it to slide over the edge and away. Jealously, bit by bit, he let the black sand slip away. A golden speck, no larger than a pinpoint, appeared on the rim, and by his manipulation of the water it returned to the bottom of the pan. And in such fashion another speck was disclosed, and another. Great was his care of them. Like a shepherd he herded his flock of golden specks so that not one should be lost. At last, of the pan of dirt nothing remained but his golden herd. He counted it, and then, after all his labor, sent it flying out of the pan with one final swirl of water.

But his blue eyes were shining with desire as he rose to his feet. "Seven," he muttered aloud, asserting the sum of the specks for which he had toiled so hard and which he had so wantonly thrown away. "Seven," he repeated, with the emphasis of one trying to impress a number on his memory.

He stood still a long while, surveying the hillside. In his eyes was a curiosity, new-aroused and burning. There was an exultance about his bearing and a keenness like that of a hunting animal catching the fresh scent of game.

He moved down the stream a few steps and took a second panful of dirt.

Again came the careful washing, the jealous herding of the golden specks, and the wantonness with which he sent them flying into the stream. His golden herd diminished. "Four, five," he muttered, and repeated, "five."

He could not forbear another survey of the hill before filling the pan farther down the stream. His golden herds diminished. "Four, three, two, two, one," were his memory tabulations as he moved down the stream. When but one speck of gold rewarded his washing, he stopped and built a fire of dry twigs. Into this he thrust the gold-pan and burned it till it was blue black. He held up the pan and examined it critically. Then he nodded approbation. Against such a color-background he could defy the tiniest yellow speck to elude him.

Still moving down the stream, he panned again. A single speck was his reward. A third pan contained no gold at all. Not satisfied with this, he panned three times again, taking his shovels of dirt within a foot of one another. Each pan proved empty of gold, and the fact, instead of discouraging him, seemed to give him satisfaction. His elation increased with each barren washing, until he arose, exclaiming jubilantly:

"If it ain't the real thing, may God knock off my head with sour apples!"

Returning to where he had started operations, he began to pan up the stream. At first his golden herds increased—increased prodigiously. "Fourteen, eighteen, twenty-one, twenty-six," ran his memory tabulations. Just above the pool he struck his richest pan—thirty-five colors.

"Almost enough to save," he remarked regretfully as he allowed the water to sweep them away.

The sun climbed to the top of the sky. The man worked on. Pan by pan, he went up the stream, the tally of results steadily decreasing.

"It's just booful, the way it peters out," he exulted when a shovelful of dirt contained no more than a single speck of gold.

And when no specks at all were found in several pans, he straightened up and favored the hillside with a confident glance.

"Ah, ha! Mr. Pocket!" he cried out, as though to an auditor hidden somewhere above him beneath the surface of the slope.

"Ah, ha! Mr. Pocket! I'm a-comin', I'm a-comin', an' I'm shorely gwine to get yer! You heah me, Mr. Pocket? I'm gwine to get yer as shore as punkins ain't cauliflowers!"

He turned and flung a measuring glance at the sun poised above him in the azure of the cloudless sky. Then he went down the canyon, following the line of shovel holes he had made in filling the pans. He crossed the stream below the pool and disappeared through the green screen. There was little opportunity for the spirit of the place to return with its quietude and repose, for the man's voice, raised in ragtime song, still dominated the canyon with possession.

After a time, with a greater clashing of steel-shod feet on rock, he returned. The green screen was tremendously agitated. It surged back and forth in the throes of a struggle. There was a loud grating and clanging of metal. The man's voice leaped to a higher pitch and was sharp with imperativeness. A large body plunged and panted. There was a snapping and ripping and rending, and amid a shower of falling leaves a horse burst through the screen. On its back was a pack, and from this trailed broken vines and torn creepers. The animal gazed with astonished eyes at the scene into which it had been precipitated, then dropped its head to the grass and began contentedly to graze. A second horse scrambled into view, slipping once on the mossy rocks and regaining equilibrium when its hoofs sank into the yielding surface of the meadow. It was riderless, though on its back was a high-horned Mexican saddle, scarred and discolored by long usage.

The man brought up the rear. He threw off pack and saddle, with an eye to camp location, and gave the animals their freedom to graze. He unpacked his food and got out frying pan and coffeepot. He gathered an armful of dry wood, and with a few stones made a place for his fire.

"My!" he said, "but I've got an appetite. I could scoff ironfilings an' horseshoe nails an' thank you kindly, ma'am, for a second helpin'."

He straightened up, and while he reached for matches in the pocket of his overalls, his eyes traveled across the pool to the side-hill. His fingers had clutched the matchbox, but they relaxed their hold and the hand came out empty. The man wavered perceptibly. He looked at his preparations for cooking and he looked at the hill.

"Guess I'll take another whack at her," he concluded, starting to cross the stream.

"They ain't no sense in it, I know," he mumbled apologetically. "But keepin' grub back an hour ain't goin' to hurt none, I reckon."

A few feet back from his first of test pans he started a second line. The sun dropped down the western sky, the shadows lengthened, but the man worked on. He began a third line of test pans. He was crosscutting the hillside, line by line, as he ascended. The center of each line produced the richest pans, while the ends came where no colors showed in the pan. And as he ascended the hillside the lines grew perceptibly shorter. The regularity with which their length diminished served to indicate that somewhere up the slope the last line would be so short as to have scarcely length at all, and that beyond could come only a point. The design was growing into an inverted V. The converging sides of this V marked the boundaries of the gold-bearing dirt.

The apex of the V was evidently the man's goal. Often he ran his eye along the converging sides and on up the hill, trying to divine the apex, the point where the gold-bearing dirt must cease. Here resided Mr. Pocket—for so the man familiarly addressed the imaginary point above him on the slope, crying out, "Come down out o' that, Mr. Pocket! Be right smart an' agreeable, an' come down!

"All right," he would add later, in a voice resigned to determination. "All right, Mr. Pocket. It's plain to me I got to come right up an' snatch you out bald headed. An' I'll do it! I'll do it!" he would threaten still later.

Each pan he carried down to the water to wash, and as he went higher up the hill the pans grew richer, until he began to save the gold in an empty baking-powder can which he carried carelessly in his hip-pocket. So engrossed was he in his toil that he did not notice the long twilight of oncoming night. It was not until he tried vainly to see the gold colors in the bottom of the pan that he realized the passage of time. He straightened up abruptly. An expression of whimsical wonderment and awe overspread his face as he drawled, "Gosh darn my buttons! If I didn't plumb forget dinner!"

He stumbled across the stream in the darkness and lighted his long-delayed fire. Flapjacks and bacon and warmed-over beans constituted his supper. Then he smoked a pipe by the smoldering coals, listening to the night noises and watching the moonlight stream through the canyon. After that he unrolled his bed, took off his heavy shoes and pulled the blankets up to his chin. His face showed white in the moonlight, like the face of a corpse. But it was a corpse that knew its resurrection, for the man rose suddenly on one elbow and gazed across at his hillside.

"Good night, Mr. Pocket," he called sleepily. "Good night."

He slept through the early gray of morning until the direct rays of the sun smote his closed eyelids, when he awoke with a start and looked about him until he had established the continuity of his existence and identified his present self with the days previously lived.

To dress, he had merely to buckle on his shoes. He glanced at his fireplace and at his hillside, wavered, but fought down the temptation and started the fire.

"Keep yer shirt on, Bill; keep yer shirt on," he admonished himself. "What's the good of rushin'? No use in gettin' all het up an' sweaty. Mr. Pocket'll wait for you. He ain't a-runnin' away before you can get your breakfast. Now, what you want, Bill, is something fresh in yer bill o' fare. So it's up to you to go an' get it."

He cut a short pole at the water's edge and drew from one of his pockets a bit of line and a draggled fly that had once been a royal coachman.

"Mebbe they'll bite in the early morning," he muttered, as he made his first cast into the pool. And a moment later he was gleefully crying, "What'd I tell you, eh? What'd I tell you?"

He had no reel nor any inclination to waste time, and by main strength, and swiftly, he drew out of the water a flashing ten-inch trout. Three more, caught in rapid succession, furnished his breakfast. When he came to the stepping-stones on his way to his hillside, he was struck by a sudden thought, and paused.

"I'd just better take a hike downstream a ways," he said. "There's no tellin' who may be snoopin' around."

But he crossed over on the stones, and with a "I really oughter take that hike," the need of the precaution passed out of his mind, and he fell to work.

At nightfall he straightened up. The small of his back was stiff from stooping toil, and as he put his hand behind him to soothe the protesting muscles, he said; "Now what d'ye think of that? I clean forgot my dinner again! If I don't watch out, I'll sure be degeneratin' into a two-meal-a-day crank.

"Pockets is the hangedest things I ever see for makin' a man absent-minded," he communed that night, as he crawled into his blankets. Nor did he forget to call up the hillside, "Good night, Mr. Pocket! Good night!"

Rising with the sun, and snatching a hasty breakfast, he was early at work. A fever seemed to be growing in him, nor did the increasing richness of the test pans allay this fever. There was a flush in his cheek other than that made by the heat of the sun, and he was oblivious to fatigue and the passage of time. When he filled a pan with dirt, he ran down the hill to wash it; nor could he forbear running up the hill again, panting and stumbling profanely, to refill the pan.

He was now a hundred yards from the water, and the inverted V was assuming definite proportions. The width of the paydirt steadily decreased, and the man extended in his mind's eye the sides of the V to their meeting place far up the hill. This was his goal, the apex of the V, and he panned many times to locate it.

"Just about two yards above that manzanita bush an' a yard to the right," he finally concluded.

Then the temptation seized him. "As plain as the nose on your face," he said, as he abandoned his laborious crosscutting and climbed to the indicated apex. He filled a pan and carried it down the hill to wash. It contained no trace of gold. He dug deep, and he dug shallow, filling and washing a dozen pans, and was unrewarded even by the tiniest golden speck. He was enraged at having yielded to the temptation, and berated himself blasphemously and pridelessly. Then he went down the hill and took up the cross-cutting.

"Slow an' certain, Bill; slow an' certain," he crooned. "Shortcuts to fortune ain't in your line, an' it's about time you know it. Get wise, Bill; get wise. Slow an' certain's the only hand you can play; so get to it, an' keep to it, too."

As the crosscuts decreased, showing that the sides of

the V were converging, the depth of the V increased. The gold trace was dipping into the hill. It was only at thirty inches beneath the surface that he could get colors in his pan. The dirt he found at twenty-five inches from the surface, and at thirty-five inches, yielded barren pans. At the base of the V, by the water's edge, he had found the gold colors at the grass roots. The higher he went up the hill, the deeper the gold dipped. To dig a hole three feet deep in order to get one test pan was a task of no mean magnitude; while between the man and the apex intervened an untold number of such holes to be dug. "An' there's no tellin' how much deeper it'll pitch," he sighed in a moment's pause while his fingers soothed his aching back.

Feverish with desire, with aching back and stiffening muscles, with pick and shovel gouging and mauling the soft brown earth, the man toiled up the hill. Before him was the smooth slope, spangled with flowers and made sweet with their breath. Behind him was devastation. It looked like some terrible eruption breaking out on the smooth skin of the hill. His slow progress was like that of a slug, befouling beauty with a monstrous trail.

Though the dipping gold trace increased the man's work, he found consolation in the increasing richness of the pans. Twenty cents, thirty cents, fifty cents, sixty cents, were the values of the gold found in the pans, and at nightfall he washed his banner pan, which gave him a dollar's worth of gold dust from a shovelful of dirt.

"I'll just bet it's my luck to have some inquisitive one come buttin' in here on my pasture," he mumbled sleepily that night as he pulled the blankets up to his chin.

Suddenly he sat upright. "Bill!" he called sharply.

"Now, listen to me, Bill; d'ye hear! It's up to you, to-morrow mornin', to mosey round an' see what you can see. Understand? Tomorrow morning, an' don't you forget it!"

He yawned and glanced across at his side-hill. "Good night, Mr. Pocket," he called.

In the morning he stole a march on the sun, for he had finished breakfast when its first rays caught him, and he was climbing the wall of the canyon where it crumbled away and gave footing. From the outlook at the top he found himself in the midst of loneliness. As far as he could see, chain after chain of mountains heaved themselves into his vision. To the east his eyes, leaping the miles between range and range and between many ranges, brought up at last against the white-peaked Sierras—the main crest, where the backbone of the Western world reared itself against the sky! To the north and south he could see more distinctly the cross systems that broke through the main trend of the sea of mountains. To the west the ranges fell away, one behind the other, diminishing and fading into the gentle foothills that, in turn, descended into the great valley which he could not see.

And in all that mighty sweep of earth he saw no sign of man nor of the handiwork of man—save only the torn bosom of the hillside at his feet. The man looked long and carefully. Once, far down his own canyon, he thought he saw in the air a faint hint of smoke. He looked again and decided that it was the purple haze of the hills made dark by a convolution of the canyon wall at its back.

"Hey, you, Mr. Pocket!" he called down into the canyon. "Stand out from under! I'm a-comin', Mr. Pocket! I'm a-comin'!"

The heavy brogans on the man's feet made him appear clumsyfooted, but he swung down from the giddy height as lightly and airily as a mountain goat. A rock, turning under his foot on the edge of the precipice, did not disconcert him. He seemed to know the precise time required for the turn to culminate in disaster, and in the meantime he utilized the false footing itself for the momentary earth contact necessary to carry him on into safety. Where the earth sloped so steeply that it was impossible to stand for a second upright, the man did not hesitate. His foot pressed the impossible surface for but a fraction of the fatal second and gave him the bound that carried him onward. Again, where even the fraction of a second's footing was out of the question, he would swing his body past by a moment's handgrip on a jutting knob of rock, a crevice or a precariously rooted shrub. At last, with a wild leap and yell, he exchanged the face of the wall for an earthslide and finished the descent in the midst of several tons of sliding earth and gravel.

His first pan of the morning washed out over two dollars in coarse gold. It was from the center of the V. To either side the diminution in the values of the pans was swift. His lines of crosscutting holes were growing very short. The converging sides of the inverted V were only a few yards apart. Their meeting point was only a few yards above him. But the pay streak was dipping deeper and deeper into the earth. By early afternoon he was sinking the test holes five feet before the pans could show the gold trace.

For that matter, the gold trace had become something more than a trace; it was a placer mine in itself, and the man resolved to come back after he had found the pocket and work over the ground. But the increasing richness of the pans began to worry him. By late afternoon the worth of the pans had grown to three and four dollars. The man scratched his head perplexedly and looked a few feet up the hill at the manzanita bush that marked approximately the apex of the V. He nodded his head and said oracularly:

"It's one o' two things, Bill; one o' two things. Either Mr. Pocket's spilled himself all out an' down the hill, or else Mr. Pocket's so rich you maybe won't be able to carry him all away with you. And that'd be an awful shame, wouldn't it, now?" He chuckled at contemplation of so pleasant a dilemma.

Nightfall found him by the edge of the stream, his eyes wrestling with the gathering darkness over the washing of a five-dollar pan.

"Wisht I had an electric light to go on working," he said.

He found sleep difficult that night. Many times he composed himself and closed his eyes for slumber to overtake him; but his blood pounded with too strong desire, and as many times his eyes opened and he murmured wearily, "Wisht it was sunup."

Sleep came to him in the end, but his eyes were open with the first paling of the stars, and the gray of dawn caught him with breakfast finished and climbing the hillside in the direction of the secret abiding-place of Mr. Pocket.

The first crosscut the man made, there was space for only three holes, so narrow had become the pay streak and so close was he to the fountainhead of the golden stream he had been following for four days.

"Be ca'm, Bill; be ca'm," he admonished himself, as he broke ground for the final hole where the sides of the V had at last come together in a point.

"I've got the almighty cinch on you, Mr. Pocket, an' you can't lose me," he said many times as he sank the hole deeper and deeper.

Four feet, five feet, six feet, he dug his way down into the earth. The digging grew harder. His pick grated on broken rock. He examined the rock. "Rotten quartz" was his conclusion as, with the shovel, he cleared the bottom of the hole of loose dirt. He attacked the crumbling quartz with the pick, bursting the disintegrating rock asunder with every stroke.

He thrust his shovel into the loose mass. His eye caught a gleam of yellow. He dropped the shovel and squatted suddenly on his heels. As a farmer rubs the clinging earth from fresh-dug potatoes, so the man, a piece of rotten quartz held in both hands, rubbed the dirt away.

"Sufferin' Sardanopolis!" he cried. "Lumps an' chunks of it! Lumps an' chunks of it!"

It was only half rock he held in his hand. The other half was virgin gold. He dropped it into his pan and examined another piece. Little yellow was to be seen, but with his strong fingers he crumbled the rotten quartz away till both hands were filled with glowing yellow. He rubbed the dirt away from fragment after fragment, tossing them into the gold-pan. It was a treasure hole. So much had the quartz rotted away that there was less of it than there was of gold. Now and again he found a piece to which no rock clung—a piece that was all gold. A chunk where the pick had laid open the heart of the gold glittered like a handful of yellow jewels, and he cocked his head at it and slowly turned it around and over to observe the rich play of the light upon it.

"Talk about yer too-much-gold diggin's!" the man snorted contemptuously. "Why, this diggin' 'd make it look like thirty cents. This diggin' is all gold. An' right here an' now I name this yere canyon All Gold Canyon, b' gosh!"

Still squatting on his heels, he continued examining the fragments and tossing them into the pan. Suddenly there came to him a premonition of danger. It seemed a shadow had fallen upon him. But there was no shadow. His heart had given a great jump up into his throat and was choking him. Then his blood slowly chilled, and he felt the sweat of his shirt cold against his flesh.

He did not spring up nor look around. He did not move. He was considering the nature of the premonition he had received, trying to locate the source of the mysterious force that had warned him, striving to sense the imperative presence of the unseen thing that threatened him. There is an aura of things hostile, made manifest by messengers too refined for the senses to know; and this aura he felt, but knew not how he felt it. His was the feeling as when a cloud passes over the sun. It seemed that between him and life had passed something dark and smothering and menacing; a gloom, as it were, that swallowed up life and made for death—his death.

Every force of his being impelled him to spring up and confront the unseen danger, but his soul dominated the panic, and he remained squatting on his heels, in his hands a chunk of gold. He did not dare to look around, but he knew by now that there was something behind him and above him. He made believe to be interested in the gold in his hand. He examined it critically, turned it over and over, and rubbed the dirt from it. And all the time he knew that something behind him was looking at the gold over his shoulder.

Still feigning interest in the chunk of gold in his hand, he listened intently and he heard the breathing of the thing behind him. His eyes searched the ground in front of him for a weapon, but he saw only the uprooted gold, worthless to him now in his extremity. There was his pick, a handy weapon on occasion; but this was not such an occasion. The man realized his predicament. He was in a narrow hole that was seven feet deep. His head did not come to the surface of the ground. He was in a trap.

He remained squatting on his heels. He was quite cool and collected; but his mind, considering every factor, showed him only his helplessness. He continued rubbing the dirt from the quartz fragments and throwing the gold into the pan. There was nothing else for him to do. Yet he knew that he would have to rise up, sooner or later, and face the danger that breathed at his back. The minutes passed, and with the passage of each minute he knew that by so much he was nearer the time when he must stand up, or else—and his wet shirt went cold against his flesh again at the thought—or else he might receive death as he stooped there over his treasure.

Still he squatted on his heels, rubbing dirt from gold and debating in just what manner he should rise up. He might rise up with a rush and claw his way out of the hole to meet whatever threatened on the even footing above ground. Or he might rise up slowly and carelessly, and feign casually to discover the thing that breathed at his back. His instinct and every fighting fiber of his body favored the mad, clawing rush to the surface. His intellect, and the craft thereof, favored the slow and cautious meeting with the thing that menaced and which he could not see. And while he debated, a loud, crashing noise burst on his ear. At the same instant he received a stunning blow on the left side of his back, and from the point of impact felt a rush of flame through his flesh. He sprang up in the air but, halfway to his feet, collapsed. His body crumpled in like a leaf withered in sudden heat, and he came down, his chest across his pan of gold, his face in the dirt and rock, his legs tangled and twisted because of the restricted space at the bottom of the hole. His legs twitched convulsively several times. His body was shaken with a mighty ague. There was a slow expansion of the lungs, accompanied by a deep sigh. Then the air was slowly, very slowly, exhaled, and his body as slowly flattened itself down into inertness.

Above, revolver in hand, a man was peering down over the edge of the hole. He peered for a long time at the prone and motionless body beneath him. After a while the stranger sat down on the edge of the hole so that he could see into it, and rested the revolver on his knee. Reaching his hand into a pocket, he drew out a wisp of brown paper. Into this he dropped a few crumbs of tobacco. The combination became a cigarette, brown and squat, with the ends turned in. Not once did he take his eyes from the body at the bottom of the hole. He lighted the cigarette and drew its smoke into his lungs with a caressing intake of the breath. He smoked slowly. Once the cigarette went out and he relighted it. And all the while he studied the body beneath him.

In the end he tossed the cigarette stub away and rose to his feet. He moved to the edge of the hole. Spanning it, a hand resting on each edge, and with the revolver still in the right hand, he muscled his body down into the hole. While his feet were yet a yard from the bottom, he released his hands and dropped down.

At the instant his feet struck bottom he saw the pocket-miner's arm leap out, and his own legs knew a swift, jerking grip that overthrew him. In the nature of the jump his revolver-hand was above his head. Swiftly as the grip had flashed about his legs, just as swiftly he brought the revolver down. He was still in the air, his fall in process of completion, when he pulled the trigger. The explosion was deafening in the confined space. The smoke filled the hole so that he could see nothing. He struck the bottom on his back, and like a cat's the pocket-miner's body was on top of him. Even as the miner's body passed on top, the stranger crooked in his right arm to fire; and even in that instant the miner, with a quick thrust of elbow, struck his wrist. The muzzle was thrown up and the bullet thudded into the dirt of the side of the hole.

The next instant the stranger felt the miner's hand grip his wrist. The struggle was now for the revolver. Each man strove to turn it against the other's body. The smoke in the hole was clearing. The stranger, lying on his back, was beginning to see dimly. But suddenly he was blinded by a handful of dirt deliberately flung into his eyes by his antagonist. In that moment of shock his grip on the revolver was broken. In the next moment he felt a smashing darkness descend upon his brain, and in the midst of the darkness even the darkness ceased.

But the pocket miner fired again and again, until the revolver was empty. Then he tossed it from him and, breathing heavily, sat down on the dead man's legs.

The miner was sobbing and struggling for breath. "Measly skunk!" he panted, "a-campin' on my trail an' lettin' me do the work, an' then shootin' me in the back!''

He was half crying from anger and exhaustion. He peered at the face of the dead man. It was sprinkled with loose dirt and gravel, and it was difficult to distinguish the features.

"Never laid eyes on him before," the miner concluded his scrutiny. "Just a common an' ordinary thief, hang him! An' he shot me in the back! He shot me in the back!''

He opened his shirt and felt himself, front and back, on his left side.

"Went clean through, and no harm done!" he cried jubilantly. "I'll bet he aimed all right; but he drew the gun over when he pulled the trigger—the cur! But I fixed 'm! Oh, I fixed 'm!''

His fingers were investigating the bullet hole in his side, and a shade of regret passed over his face. "It's goin' to be stiffer'n hell," he said. "An' it's up to me to get mended an' get out o' here."

He crawled out of the hole and went down the hill to his camp. Half an hour later he returned, leading his packhorse. His open shirt disclosed the rude bandages with which he had dressed his wound. He was slow and awkward with his left-hand movements, but that did not prevent his using the arm.

The bight of the pack rope under the dead man's shoulders enabled him to heave the body out of the hole. Then he set to work gathering up his gold. He worked steadily for several hours, pausing often to rest his stiffening shoulder and to exclaim, "He shot me in the back, the measly skunk! He shot me in the back!''

When his treasure was quite cleaned up and wrapped

securely into a number of blanket-covered parcels, he made an estimate of its value.

"Four hundred pounds, or I'm a Hottentot," he concluded. "Say two hundred in quartz an' dirt—that leaves two hundred pounds of gold. Bill! Wake up! Two hundred pounds of gold! Forty thousand dollars! An' it's yourn—all yourn!"

He scratched his head delightedly and his fingers blundered into an unfamiliar groove. They quested along it for several inches. It was a crease through his scalp where the second bullet had ploughed.

He walked angrily over to the dead man.

"You would, would you?" he bullied. "You would, eh? Well, I fixed you good an' plenty, an' I'll give you a decent burial, too. That's more'n you'd have done for me."

He dragged the body to the edge of the hole and toppled it in. It struck the bottom with a dull crash, on its side, the face twisted up to the light. The miner peered down at it.

"An' you shot me in the back!" he said accusingly.

With pick and shovel he filled the hole. Then he loaded the gold on his horse. It was too great a load for the animal, and when he had gained his camp he transferred part of it to his saddle horse. Even so, he was compelled to abandon a portion of his outfit—pick and shovel and gold-pan, extra food and cooking utensils, and divers odds and ends.

The sun was at the zenith when the man forced the horses at the screen of vines and creepers. To climb the huge boulders the animals were compelled to uprear and struggle blindly through the tangled mass of vegetation. Once the saddle horse fell heavily and the man removed the pack to get the animal on its feet. After it started on its way again the man thrust his head out from among the leaves and peered up at the hillside.

"The measly skunk!" he said, and disappeared.

There was a ripping and tearing of vines and boughs. The trees surged back and forth, marking the passage of the animals through the midst of them. There was a clashing of steel-shod hoofs on stone, and now and again a sharp cry of command. Then the voice of the man was raised in song.

> "Tu'n around an' tu'n yo' face
> Untoe them sweet hills of grace
>   (D' pow'rs of sin you' am scornin'!).
> Look about an' look aroun'
> Fling yo' sin-pack on d' groun'
>   (Yo' will meet wid d' Lord in d'
>   mornin'!)."

The song grew faint and fainter, and through the silence crept back the spirit of the place. The stream once more drowsed and whispered; the hum of the mountain bees rose sleepily. Down through the perfume-weighted air fluttered the snowy fluffs of the cottonwoods. The butterflies drifted in and out among the trees, and over all blazed the quiet sunshine. Only remained the hoof marks in the meadow and the torn hillside to mark the boisterous trail of the life that had broken the peace of the place and passed on.

MAGO'S BRIDE

Loren D. Estleman

IN SAN HERMOSO there was always fiesta whenever Mago took a wife.

He had had two that year. One, a plump Castilian, had died during the trek across Chihuahua in August. The other, a dark and glowering *rustica* from one of the anonymous pueblos along the Bravo, had bored Mago before a month was out and been packed off to a convent in Mexico City. No one discussed his first bride, an American girl seized in Las Cruces who flung herself from the bell tower of the San Hermoso church on their wedding night years before; but all remembered the three days of fiesta that had preceded the ceremony.

So it was that when the Magistas learned of the bandit chief's approach with yet another prospective señora in tow, they hauled three long tables of unplaned pine from the cantina into the plaza, loaded them with delicacies liberated from pilgrims, butchered three fat heifers that

Don Alberto would never miss from his herd of twenty thousand, and laid the pits with mesquite. Tequila and *cerveza* were conjured up from hidden stores, and Otto von Streubing, Mago's lieutenant and a disgraced Hapsburg prince (or so he styled himself), went out with a party in search of antelope. These preparations were made with great solemnity; for marriage was serious business among the Christ-loving people of San Hermoso, and there was nothing frivolous about the way those who did *not* love Christ took their pleasure.

When the outriders returned to announce Mago, his men and their women gathered at the edge of the plaza to greet him. He was galloping his favorite mount, a glossy black gelding presented by the American president to an officer of Porfirio Díaz and claimed by Mago from between the dying officer's thighs at Veracruz. Riding behind the cantle, fingers laced tightly across the chief's middle to avoid falling, was an unknown woman with a face as dark as teak inside the sable tent of her hair.

"Yaqui," muttered the watchers; and those young enough to remember their catechisms crossed themselves, for her soiled blouse and dark skirts were certainly of Indian manufacture.

To Mago, of course, they would say nothing. Half Yaqui himself, with the black eyes and volcanic temperament of the breed, he also had the long memory for personal wrongs that came with his mother's Spanish blood. Even now he was coming hard as in wrath.

"The church!" he roared—and plunged, horse and rider, into the crowd without stopping.

Those with their wits about them flung themselves aside. Those without fell with broken bones and flesh torn by the gelding's steel-shod hoofs. Mago did not stop for them, nor even for the heavy laden tables in his path, but dug in his heels, and the gelding bounded screaming up and over all three, coming down on the other side with a heaving grunt and clawing for traction on the ground before the church.

Behind him, thunder rolled. Someone—the chief himself, perhaps, for he had continued without dismounting through the great, yawning, iron-banded doors of the church—swung the bell in the tower, clanging the alarm. Shouting, the Magistas and their women trailed him inside and managed with belated efficiency to draw the doors shut. Desperate fists hammered the bar into place.

The church had been designed as a fort in a land scarce in Christians. By the time the men took up their armed posts at the windows, the myriad heads of the enemy could be seen topping the eastern horizon like a black dawn. Here and there an ironwood lance swayed against the sky, bearing its inevitable human trophy. The word *Apache* sibilated like a telegraph current from window to window.

Mago, mounted still, was alone in the saddle. Of the woman there was no sign. He swept off his sombrero, allowing his dull black hair to tumble in its two famous locks across his temples, and barked orders in rapid dialect. Otto von Streubing, who comprehended little of it, asked what had happened. Mago smiled down at him.

"How close?" he inquired of the nearest sentry.

"Still outside rifle range, *mi jefe*. They have stopped, I think."

"The bastard thinks too much. It will kill him yet." Swinging down, the bandit chief started up the stone steps to the bell tower, jerking his head for Otto to follow.

At the top of the steep flight, Mago rapped on the low door. The pair were admitted by Juan Griz. Brown-eyed, wavy of hair, and built along the lines of a young cougar, Juan was easily the handsomest of those who followed Mago, as well as the most loyal and doglike. The simplest tasks were his great mission.

On the opposite side of the great iron bell, limned in the open arch by the sun, stood the loveliest woman the German had ever seen. Her hair was as dark as the Black Forest, her figure beneath the travel-stained clothes trim and fragile compared to the thick-waisted squaws he had known during his short time in the New World. Her eyes were wary. She seemed poised to fling herself into space. Otto thought—and immediately discarded it—of the fate of Mago's first wife. Instinctively he knew that this one would not make that same choice.

"Handsome baggage," he said finally. "Your fourth, I think. But what—"

Mago reached out and snatched the fine silver chain that hung around the woman's neck. She flinched, catching herself on the archway. Mago dangled the crucifix before his lieutenant's face.

"I know that piece," said Otto.

"You should, my friend. You have seen it around Nochebueno's neck often enough."

"*Lieber Gott*! What has she to do with that *verdammt* Christian Indian?"

"Cervata is her name. *Fawn* in the English you insist on using here instead of good Spanish. I found her bathing in a stream outside Nochebueno's camp. Mind you, had I known how she scratches, I would not have allowed her to dress before we left.'' He put a hand to the place where blood had dried on his cheek. ''It was not until I saw the crucifix that I knew she had until late been scratching that Apache bastard.''

''I do not imagine it occurred to you to return her.''

''My friend, it is foreign to my nature to return things.''

The woman spat a stream of mangled Spanish. The gist, if not the words, reached the German well enough. ''How did you manage to get this far?''

''Fortunately for my eyes, she hates the baptized savage more than she does me. I, however, am in love.''

A Magista with machete scars on both cheeks stormed through the open doorway, shoving aside Juan Griz. ''*Mi jefe!* The Apaches are attacking!'' A crackle of carbines from outside nearly drowned out the words.

Otto von Streubing was the finest marksman in San Hermoso. Mago stationed him in the tower with his excellent Mauser rifle, ordered Juan Griz to keep Cervata away from the openings, and accompanied the other Magista downstairs. For the next quarter hour the bandit chief busied himself with the fortress's defense, directing the men's fire and satisfying himself that the women were supplying them with loaded weapons as needed. The sun had begun to set. As shadows enveloped them, the Apaches withdrew, bearing their dead.

''What are our losses?'' demanded Mago of the man with the machete scars.

''Two dead, *mi jefe*; Paco Mendolo and the boy, Gonzales. Your cousin, Manuel, has lost an ear.''

''Which one?''

''The left, I think.''

Otto descended from the tower, where he had managed to pluck three savages off their mounts from three hundred yards. "It is not like Nochebueno to give up so easily," he said.

"A reprieve," said Mago. "It takes more than his Jesus to convince his braves their dead will find their way to the Happy Hunting Ground in the dark. At dawn the sun will be at their backs and in our eyes. Then they will throw everything they have at us."

"Not if we give them the woman tonight."

"I never give."

The bandits were quiet that night. If any of them wondered that their fates were caught up with Mago's marital aspirations, none spoke of it. As for the chief, he had retired to the rectory, which had become his quarters upon the departure of the mission's last padre. Otto entered without knocking and stood an unopened bottle of tequila on the great oak desk behind which his general sat eating rat cheese off the blade of his bowie.

"I confiscated it," the German explained. "I thought you might like some of them sober in the morning."

"*Gracias, amigo.* I shall consider it a wedding gift."

"Who will perform the ceremony this time?"

"That Dominican in Santa Carla has not done me a favor in a year."

"I suppose Manuel will stand up for you as always?"

"Manuel is infirm. I would ask you, but I imagine you are an infidel."

"Lutheran."

"As I said." Mago pulled the cork and tossed it over his shoulder. "Well, they can hardly excommunicate me again. To my best man." He lifted the bottle and drank.

Otto watched a drop trickle down his superior's stubbled chin. "I would take my pleasure now. You may not live to dance at your wedding."

"I do not bed women not my wives."

Someone battered the rectory door. Otto admitted a flat-faced Magista who was more Indian than Mexican and less man than animal, and who handed Mago a short-shafted arrow with the head broken off. The German could follow little of his speech but gathered that the arrow had narrowly missed a bandit dozing at a window and buried itself in the oaken altar. Mago untied a square of hide from the shaft and read the words burned into it.

"Curse an Indian who knows his letters," he said mildly. "He wishes to meet with me outside San Hermoso in an hour."

"Nochebueno?" said Otto. "What can he want to talk about?"

"We will know in an hour."

The site chosen was a patch of desert midway between the stronghold and the place where the Apaches had made camp. Nochebueno arrived first astride a blaze-faced sorrel, accompanied by two mounted warriors. Nearly as tall as his late, fabled grandfather, Mangas Coloradas, he was naked save for breechclout and moccasins and a rosary around his thick neck. His face was painted in halves of black and vermilion and resembled nothing so much as a particolored skull. Mago, who had selected a bay mare while his black gelding rested, halted beyond the light of the torches held by the two braves and turned to Otto.

"The ring on his finger, amigo. Do you see it?"

The German squinted. A large ring of what appeared

to be polished silver glittered on the Apache chief's right index finger. "A signal ring?"

"They are wizards with mirrors. You will remain here and fire your wonderful foreign rifle if he raises that hand."

Otto snaked his Mauser from the saddle scabbard. "Pray the torches do not flicker."

The bandit leader left him.

"Mago!" Nochebueno bared uncommonly fine teeth for an Indian. His Spanish was purer than the Mexican's. "I have not seen you these three years. You look well."

The other drew rein inside the torchlight. "Never better, Noche. I am preparing to marry."

Although the grin remained in place, something very like malice tautened the flat features beneath the war paint. "Step down, my friend," said he. "We have business."

"All of us?" Mago's gaze took in the two stony-faced braves at Nochebueno's elbows.

The Apache said something in his native tongue. The braves leaned over, jammed the pointed ends of the torches into the earth, wheeled their mounts, and cantered back the way they had come. The bandit leader and the Indian chief stepped down then, and squatted on their heels.

"You have a woman in San Hermoso," Nochebueno began.

"Amigo, I have had many women, in and out of San Hermoso."

"This one is a personal favorite, purchased at the expense of several very good horses from her father, who manages a coffee plantation near Chiapas. I would have her back."

Mago showed a gold tooth. "You would have her back, and I would have her stay, and that is how it will be all night and all day tomorrow. I waste my time." But he made no move to rise.

"You waste more than time, my friend. You waste the lives of every man, woman, and child in San Hermoso."

"I hear the lion's roar. I do not see his claws."

Nochebueno reached behind him and produced a knife from a sheath at his waist. It was of European manufacture, with a long, slender Sheffield blade and a heavily worked hilt fashioned after a cross.

"A souvenir from my former days of darkness, stolen from a cathedral in Acapulco," he said. "It dates back to the Crusades."

"Your invitation said no weapons, amigo."

"It did, and you may stop fingering that derringer in your pocket. I have not brought it as a weapon."

Mago waited.

"A game!" barked the Indian suddenly, making the torches waver. "You who know me so well know also my passion for sport. I suggest a contest to settle what would otherwise be a long and bloody fight, most unChristian. My friend, are you feeling strong this night?"

"What are the rules?"

"My question is answered." With a sudden movement Nochebueno sank the knife to its hilt in the hard earth between them. The haft threw a shadow in the shape of a crucifix. "We shall lie upon our stomachs facing each other, each with a hand on the handle of the knife. If you are the first to snap the blade, the woman is yours, and my warriors and I shall ride from this place in peace."

"And if you are first?"

"My friend, that is entirely up to you. Naturally I would prefer if in the spirit of sport you would surrender the woman, in which case we would still ride from this place in peace. Women—they are for pleasure, not war."

"And yet you are prepared to make war if I refuse this contest."

The Indian's grin was diabolical. "You will not refuse. I see in your eyes that you will not. Am I wrong?"

In response the bandit chief stretched out on his stomach and grasped the handle.

"So it is; so it has always been," said Nochebueno, assuming the same position, fingers interlaced with Mago's. "*El Indio y el conquistador*. To the end."

The Mexican was born strong and hardened from the saddle; the Apache, smaller and built along slighter lines, was as a hot wind with meanness and hatred for Mago and all his kind. Their hands quivered and grew slick with sweat. The torches burned low.

There was an earsplitting snap. Roaring triumphantly, Mago sprang to his knees waving the handle with its broken piece of blade.

"Congratulations, my friend." Nochebueno gathered his legs beneath him. His right hand shot up. It had no index finger.

As he gaped at the bleeding stump, the crack of Otto von Streubing's Mauser rifle reached the place where the two men knelt. The bullet had taken away finger and signal ring in one pass.

With a savage cry the Apache chief was on his feet, followed by Mago, clawing for the derringer in his pocket. Before the watching braves could react, Otto galloped between the pair. He threw the bay mare's reins to Mago, who vaulted into the saddle and swung toward San Hermoso just as the Apaches began firing. The bay mare screamed and fell. Mago landed on his feet, caught hold of the German's outstretched hand, and, riding double, the bandits fled through a hail of fire in the direction of the stronghold. Behind them, Nochebueno shrieked Christian obscenities in Spanish and shook his bloody fist, unwittingly spoiling his braves' aim.

"Fine shooting, amigo," Mago shouted over the hammering hooves.

"Not so fine," said the other sourly. "I was aiming for his throat."

The Magista with the machete scars opened the church door for them. Otto handed him his horse's reins. "Wake the others and tell them to prepare for siege," he said.

Mago said, "Let them sleep. The bastards will not attack before morning, if then. If I know Nochebueno, he is halfway back to his village, squawling for the medicine man to wrap his finger. Whatever bowels his people's god gave him, he surrendered them when he accepted Christ. Close the door, amigo. Why do you stand there?"

The Magista was peering into the darkness of the plaza. "Did not the others return with you, *jefe*?"

"What others?"

"Juan Griz and the Yaqui woman. He said you had left orders to join you with the woman and your black gelding. He sent me for his piebald."

Mago said a thing not properly spoken in church and charged up the stone steps to the bell tower, taking them two at a time. Otto seized the man's collar. "When?"

"Just after you and *el jefe* left, señor. Juan said—"

"Juan Griz never said a thing in his life not placed in his mouth by someone smarter. I knew this woman was a witch when I first laid eyes on her."

Mago came down as swiftly as he had gone up. He was buckling on a cartridge belt. "Fresh mounts, Otto, quickly! They cannot have gotten far in this darkness."

"There is no catching that gelding when it is rested. If we capture anyone, it will be Juan."

"Then I will have his testicles! Why do you laugh, amigo?"

Otto was astonished to find that he was indeed laughing. He had not done so since coming to this barbaric place where Christians fought Christians and men stabled their horses in church.

"I laugh because it is funny, Mago. Do you not see how funny it is? While you and Nochebueno were fighting like knights for Cervata's fine brown hand, Juan Griz was absconding with the rest of her. Not to mention your favorite mount. Or do I mix the two?" He was becoming silly in his mirth. It had spread to the scarred Magista, who cast frightened eyes upon his chief at first, then forgot him in his own helplessness.

Mago scowled. Madness had entered his camp. And then he, too, began to laugh. It was either that or slay two of his best men.

"Well," said he when they had begun to master themselves, "of what worth is a bride who chooses pleasing looks over intelligence and courage? Wake the men, Otto! We have won one victory this night, and a woman is a small enough price to pay for Nochebueno's finger."

That night San Hermoso rang with the din of fiesta.

COWBOY
BLUES

Lenore Carroll

WHEN I CAME out to the guest ranch I had this idea about finding a cowboy to be my boyfriend—every Eastern girl's dream. Broad-brimmed hat, boots, tattoo, Coors belt buckle, and a room-temperature IQ. I saved my money and sent references and drove three days; I was going to find me one and see what he was like. Did he wear a down vest indoors? Did he drive a pickup? With a gun rack? He had to have a dog named Bubba. I was looking for something like Joel McCrea in those old movies my dad watched, only modern. I called him Jim Bob.

After my girlfriend, Debbie, and I checked in at the place near Sheridan, I put on my jeans and my new boots and went out to the corral. There they were, lean and battered, with sun-squint eyes and neckerchiefs and Skoal tins in their back pockets. This was what I had dreamed about all winter, watching Busch commercials and reading travel brochures.

My girlfriend, Debbie—she's a word processor at Datatech like me—found one right away and I didn't see much of her. During the first few days I zeroed in on a tall, lean wrangler with battered chaps who kept looking at me when I waited at the fence for my mount. "How about you and me getting together after dinner?" I asked.

"You deserve something better than a cheap fling with an old saddle tramp like me."

I told him I liked *him*, but he just shook his head and said, "No, no, little lady."

I was so mad I wanted to scream, but I tried to maintain some dignity. I left him standing there by the fence, with the Big Horns behind him and a dirt smudge on his battered hat and a rope in his hands. He had the high plains pink over his year-round tan and hands as rough as a backcountry road. Instead of fun and games in the cabin, I was left with bridge in the lodge with old folks. Well, I wasn't going to sit around and feel sorry for myself. I fixed myself up after dinner and borrowed Deb's car and drove into town and walked into the first likely place.

When I stepped inside the Golden Spur, glittering eyes from twenty stuffed heads stared back; I felt like I was a prize mare, up before the judges. I wished Deb was with me. Why was I doing this? Then I remembered the wrangler. I'd find me a *real* cowboy and Not Think about that bastard.

The back bar was an elaborate mirrored affair that I'd seen in dozens of cowboy movies. It looked a hundred years old, with a carved deer head in the center of the mahogany.

The bartender nodded and I ordered a beer. I stood crowded in with a bunch of people my age and listened to the conversation. I swallowed a little Bud, gradually calmed down, and listened. Most of the people seemed to know each other and gossiped about who was doing what.

Besides the staring heads on the walls there was the heroic version of the Battle of the Little Big Horn— Custer was still winning. Bird and horse paintings. Crowded between the heads were beer mirrors, antlers, skulls, announcements for rodeos and a county fair and an art exhibit. And framed photographs of people on horseback doing weird things to cows.

I studied the clientele—local men and girls, dude men and girls, some other guys I couldn't quite figure out who looked more like Ralph Lauren cowboys than the real thing. But they were all friendly and started talking to me, asked me where I was from and hoped I liked it out here and could they buy me a beer?

I gradually relaxed and caught a whiff of something familiar. A guy stood by the jukebox with one hand in his Levi's pocket, fingers angled toward the zipper, thumb hooked over the edge of the pocket. Another young man carefully recentered his hat, revealing biceps as he raised his arms. Tourists and dudes like me were just watching, but the local kids exchanged telling looks, or casually brushed by each other in the crowded room. All of the guys watched one girl with a perfect tush as she maneuvered around the pool table. This wasn't a singles bar, with loud rock music like the places back home, but I recognized the longing and the horniness. That's the same anywhere.

Members of the three-piece combo played on a small platform at the back of the room. Couples crowded the dance floor, swinging each other to the drummer's steady beat. I took my beer and watched, then a guy in a pointy-yoke shirt asked me to dance. Sure. I would drink and have a good time and Not Think about that wrangler.

After a few dances, the guy led me back to the bar and said, "Hey, Curry, you had any accidents lately?" to a big, good-looking guy.

"Yeah, but that sumbitch ain't caught me yet."

"You burned yourself on the propane forge?"

"Naw, we've been putting up hay. I don't get many calls for shoeing this time of year."

Curry was crisply turned out in a laundry-creased shirt, spotless jeans, and a summer straw Stetson that looked riveted in place. Maybe it was the hat, pulled down to half an inch above his eyebrows, that gave him a dim look. Then it registered and I almost dropped my beer. This was my Jim Bob. I found out Curry worked on a ranch east of Ucross, came into town on weekends like a soldier on leave. He had that ground-in tan and muscles straining the plaid shirt and pale, innocent blue eyes.

"This cop stopped me," Curry said. "I was driving in this park in Denver. And when he looked in the pickup, there was this woman giving me a blow job."

People around Curry laughed. I usually ignore stories like that, but I kept listening. And Not Thinking.

"She never even stopped till we were done. And the cop said, 'I don't know what to write on the ticket.' Hell,

I didn't know what to say. I must have been driving funny. It was a miracle I kept the pickup on the road. Then the cop said, 'I'm going to put down obstructing the view of the driver.' So I said, 'Sounds okay to me.' "

Everybody laughed. Curry was feeling his Coors and he had an audience.

"It cost me thirty-eight hundred dollars to get my shoulder fixed," he said, "so I never did get my wrist taken care of. But except for that I was good at rodeoing." His listeners laughed and one reminded him of all the falls he had taken bull riding.

"Yeah," continued Curry. "But that wasn't how I got hurt. I'm acrobatic. I knew how to fall."

"Then why did you quit?" asked a blond girl.

"Got tired of bull snot in my back pocket," said Curry.

"What?" I asked.

"Bull snot. Dropping down on my backside when I was on the ground."

"What else did you do, rodeoing?" I asked.

"Roping, bronc riding, all that stuff."

"Why'd you quit?"

"Well, I got into trouble with that old sumbitch I was working for, at Arvada. It wasn't nothing. I didn't go to do it on purpose, but he got mean and called the cops on me."

"What'd you do?"

"I set his foreman's house on fire."

"Just like that?"

"Well, I was using this propane branding iron and I got too close to the siding and the next thing I knew, the house was on fire."

"Sounds like you're—"

"Accident-prone, that's what they say. Anyway, I had a choice and I went in the army and that was the end of rodeoing for me."

"What do you do now?"

"Whatever the boss tells me—fix fences, move cattle, put up hay, take care of the horses, shoe them."

"Sounds interesting," I said.

"Not as interesting as being here. Would you like to dance?"

"Sure, if you don't mind getting your feet stepped on."

Curry placed a hand lightly at my back and we walked onto the dance floor. The combo was doing a slow, non-Willie Nelson version of "Whiskey River" and Curry swung me in front of him and wrapped an arm around my waist and took my hand and gently started the steps. It wasn't very complicated, but when I tried to think of what I should be doing, I stumbled and lost the beat. I would Not Think. I would dance and drink enough to feel the edges soften and listen to Curry bullshit about his accidents. This was the warm cowboy I'd dreamed about all winter.

I laughed, mostly from nervousness, and he just kept steering me back and forth. He sang along with the band and it sounded kind of nice to have his voice soft in my ear, his cheek on mine. Occasionally, I'd knock his hat loose when I lifted my head, but he'd calmly screw it back in place.

The band went into a fast version of "Honkytonk Man" and I tried to keep up with Curry. For a beefy guy, he was light on his feet and tireless. My awkwardness didn't seem to bother him and he patiently got me back on the beat until I was more or less following him. His hand slipped down my back to my waist, then to my ass, and at first I didn't even notice. It seemed *normal* to have a hand there. Then I remembered I had just met him and pulled it back up.

After half a dozen dances, the band took a break and he led me back to the bar and bought me a beer. I asked him about his work and shoeing and he told me and joked about it.

We danced again and I felt a little drunk. It was easy to lean against Curry and let him lead me around the floor. He did a lot of "sugar, honey, baby, sweetie" stuff, told me I had a great body. He sang some more, his mouth close to my ear. After a while he stopped singing and started kissing and nuzzling my neck. I pulled away, but in a few minutes he was back again and it seemed like too much trouble to stop him. His hand slipped down to my ass again and I let it stay. I just wanted to sway and shuffle and Not Think.

After another round of beer and dancing, he asked, "Would you like to go home with me?"

"Where's home?" I asked. I had trouble concentrating.

"I got this little house outside Sheridan," he said. "Well, it's not mine, but my uncle is off on a pack trip over by Jackson and I stay there on weekends."

"What would we do at your uncle's?" I knew damned well what we'd do, but I wanted to hear what he'd say.

"Well, we could put a pizza in the microwave and turn on the late movie and then we'll *see* what we could do."

For some reason, that sounded appealing. I wouldn't

be able to think about the wrangler if I went. I wouldn't have to think at all. Curry was my Jim Bob. No Coors belt buckle, but all the other qualifications. I tried to think of reasons why I shouldn't, but I was foggy from beer. And I didn't want to talk myself out of it. I wondered if there was a gun rack in his pickup.

I left Deb's car in the parking lot and got in Curry's truck. The floor was littered with rust-red gravel, fast-food containers, and empty beer cans. A brown plaid bath towel covered the shredded upholstery. Curry said his dog tore it up. I looked for the seat belt, but it had disappeared and I wasn't in the mood to dig for it. I felt dizzy and I was riding without a safety belt anyway.

He drove south on the main drag out of Sheridan and turned off the highway at the edge of the city. We bounced down a long gravel drive and around some trees to a small frame house with a dog tied to the front porch. The dog, a sheepdog mix, went berserk, barking and leaping against the rope. I don't know if he was any good scaring away burglars, but he convinced me. Curry hollered, "Shut up, Igor," on his way past and the dog quieted.

Well, a dog named Bubba was too much to expect.

I stood in front of Curry's house and looked west. The moon hit the last of the snow on the peaks of the Big Horns and I expected theme music by Dmitri Tiomkin to swell in my head. It didn't seem possible that this crackerbox house and the mountains were in sight of each other. I wanted a developer to rezone the West and get rid of the trailers and trashy houses and non-photogenic farms and it would all look like an old B movie. Curry looked okay, but this wasn't turning out the way I'd planned.

I stood beside the pickup with the passenger door handle in a death grip. I couldn't go through with it. I felt sick and wondered if it was the beer, Curry, or myself. I scuffed gravel. I eyed the dog. I looked through the open door to the living room. Curry opened the screen, which didn't hang plumb, and walked out on the porch. He held two cans of Coors in one hand.

"Igor won't bite you. Come on up."

I wasn't afraid of the dog. He looked like a floppy dust mop, once he collapsed by the porch steps. I just wanted out. I didn't want a tussle with Curry, a little old roll in the hay. And I didn't know how I could get out of it. This was what I wanted, wasn't it?

Curry had talked steadily through half a dozen Coors and started repeating himself after two hours. In the pickup I'd heard about the ticket in Denver again. I'd been waiting for the rodeo stories to recycle.

I must have sobered up enough on the drive out to realize I was fooling myself. This warm cowboy wasn't really what I wanted. He'd called me "ma'am," and held the doors for me, and now I was being awful and I didn't care.

He'd been out on the ranch, working hard all week. He'd gotten cleaned up, come to town, petted me and danced, chatted and done all the right things and now I was walking out on the unspoken contract. Bitch. Tease. But I wasn't in love with him and there would be the whole routine with the lies and getting out of our clothes and figuring out what to do after. That wasn't part of my dream.

And there was something unmovable about him. People who work alone get strange. When they finally get out and start socializing, they want other people to be-

have as they expect, as they've imagined in their alone-
ness.

He sucked on a beer and I clutched the door handle.

"You gonna stay out there all night?" He sounded
stone-hard peeved.

"Take me back to town."

"What the hell? You wanted to come here. Now you
change your mind?"

"Yes."

"No you ain't."

"Take me back."

"Not when I had a hard-on for two hours."

"Tough," I said. He'd probably had a hard-on for a
week. I turned on my heel and started walking down the
long driveway. He caught up with me, grabbed my arm
and spun me around.

"You ain't leaving now."

"It's my period." I shook his hand off.

"No it ain't."

I took a couple of deep breaths. I was weaving a little
and things tried to spin, but I was soberer than Curry.
"I'm leaving."

I turned to walk away and Curry hit me hard below
the shoulder blades. I went off balance and hit the dusty
red gravel, grazed my chin, and the air whooshed out of
my lungs. I wrenched the hand I flung out to catch my
fall. I was jarred more than hurt. I got to my hands and
knees, then to my feet, wondering what he would do
next.

I started to say something and he backhanded me
across the mouth. I could taste salty blood and my face
hurt.

"What do you do for an encore?" I said. "Kick the dog?"

He stood with fists clenched, watching me. I stood facing him, weaving and half-drunk. He took a step toward me. I tensed up. The blood and saliva choked me. I took another breath and vomited. The spasms bent me double. Curry backed away. I heard him spit in disgust, but all I could do was stand there and heave till my stomach emptied itself.

When I could breathe without triggering a spasm, I straightened up and started down the driveway again. Curry stood with the dog beside the porch steps.

I was at least two miles out of town, then another mile to the Golden Spur. I hoped my new boots didn't rub a blister. I couldn't think straight. Several cars went by, but I was walking against traffic and nobody stopped.

I felt like I was choking, like I still wanted to throw up, but it wasn't beer. I was sick-disgusted with myself. I wanted a warm cowboy, but what was I going to do with him when I got him? I couldn't take him home. Was I going to wear his scalp on my belt for two weeks in Sheridan?

Walking that gravel shoulder back to town helped sort out what I'd done. It was John Wayne, apple pie, and the American flag—that's what my dream of making love to a warm cowboy was. I'd never once thought about the real person behind the pearly-snap shirt and the Stetson.

The Golden Spur was still open when I got there and I used the ladies' room. My face was starting to swell and ache. I felt awful. I rinsed my mouth over and over, but I couldn't wash the bad taste away.

By the time I got in Deb's car I was more or less sober, and maybe a little smarter. I fell into the driver's seat, headed for the highway, and drove back to the guest ranch.

Can't judge a book by its cover, so why did I try to fall in love with a dust jacket?

FENIMORE COOPER'S LITERARY OFFENSES

Mark Twain

The Pathfinder *and* The Deerslayer *stand at the head of Cooper's novels as artistic creations. There are others of his works which contain parts as perfect as are to be found in these, and scenes even more thrilling. Not one can be compared with either of them as a finished whole.*

The defects in both of these tales are comparatively slight. They were pure works of art.

—PROF. LOUNSBURY.

The five tales reveal an extraordinary fulness of invention. . . . One of the very greatest characters in fiction, "Natty Bumppo." . . .

The craft of the woodsman, the tricks of the trap-

117

*per, all the delicate art of the forest, were familiar
to Cooper from his youth up.*
                              —PROF. BRANDER MATTHEWS.

*Cooper is the greatest artist in the domain of ro-
mantic fiction yet produced by America.*
                              —WILKIE COLLINS.

IT SEEMS TO me that it was far from right for the Professor of English Literature in Yale, the Professor of
English Literature in Columbia, and Wilkie Collins, to
deliver opinions on Cooper's literature without having
read some of it. It would have been much more decorous
to keep silent and let persons talk who have read Cooper.

Cooper's art has some defects. In one place in *Deerslayer*, and in the restricted space of two-thirds of a
page, Cooper has scored 114 offences against literary art
out of a possible 115. It breaks the record.

There are nineteen rules governing literary art in the
domain of romantic fiction—some say twenty-two. In
Deerslayer Cooper violated eighteen of them. These
eighteen require:

1. That a tale shall accomplish something and arrive
somewhere. But the *Deerslayer* tale accomplishes nothing and arrives in the air.

2. They require that the episodes of a tale shall be
necessary parts of the tale, and shall help to develop it.
But as the *Deerslayer* tale is not a tale, and accomplishes
nothing and arrives nowhere, the episodes have no right-
ful place in the work, since there was nothing for them
to develop.

3. They require that the personages in a tale shall be

alive, except in the case of corpses, and that always the reader shall be able to tell the corpses from the others. But this detail has often been overlooked in the *Deerslayer* tale.

4. They require that the personages in a tale, both dead and alive, shall exhibit a sufficient excuse for being there. But this detail also has been overlooked in the *Deerslayer* tale.

5. They require that when the personages of a tale deal in conversation, the talk shall sound like human talk, and be talk such as human beings would be likely to talk in the given circumstances, and have a discoverable meaning, also a discoverable purpose, and a show of relevancy, and remain in the neighborhood of the subject in hand, and be interesting to the reader, and help out the tale, and stop when the people cannot think of anything more to say. But this requirement has been ignored from the beginning of the *Deerslayer* tale to the end of it.

6. They require that when the author describes the character of a personage in his tale, the conduct and conversation of that personage shall justify said description. But this law gets little or no attention in the *Deerslayer* tale, as "Natty Bumppo's" case will amply prove.

7. They require that when a personage talks like an illustrated, gilt-edged, tree-calf, hand-tooled, seven-dollar Friendship's Offering in the beginning of a paragraph, he shall not talk like a negro minstrel in the end of it. But this rule is flung down and danced upon in the *Deerslayer* tale.

8. They require that crass stupidities shall not be played upon the reader as "the craft of the woodsman,

the delicate art of the forest,'' by either the author or the people in the tale. But this rule is persistently violated in the *Deerslayer* tale.

9. They require that the personages of a tale shall confine themselves to possibilities and let miracles alone; or, if they venture a miracle, the author must so plausibly set it forth as to make it look possible and reasonable. But these rules are not respected in the *Deerslayer* tale.

10. They require that the author shall make the reader feel a deep interest in the personages of his tale and in their fate; and that he shall make the reader love the good people in the tale and hate the bad ones. But the reader of the *Deerslayer* tale dislikes the good people in it, is indifferent to the others, and wishes they would all get drowned together.

11. They require that the characters in a tale shall be so clearly defined that the reader can tell beforehand what each will do in a given emergency. But in the *Deerslayer* tale this rule is vacated.

In addition to these large rules there are some little ones. These require that the author shall

12. *Say* what he is proposing to say, not merely come near it.

13. Use the right word, not its second cousin.

14. Eschew surplusage.

15. Not omit necessary details.

16. Avoid slovenliness of form.

17. Use good grammar.

18. Employ a simple and straightforward style.

Even these seven are coldly and persistently violated in the *Deerslayer* tale.

Cooper's gift in the way of invention was not a rich

endowment; but such as it was he liked to work it, he was pleased with the effects, and indeed he did some quite sweet things with it. In his little box of stage properties he kept six or eight cunning devices, tricks, artifices for his savages and woodsmen to deceive and circumvent each other with, and he was never so happy as when he was working these innocent things and seeing them go. A favorite one was to make a moccasined person tread in the tracks of the moccasined enemy, and thus hide his own trail. Cooper wore out barrels and barrels of moccasins in working that trick. Another stage-property that he pulled out of his box pretty frequently was his broken twig. He prized his broken twig above all the rest of his effects, and worked it the hardest. It is a restful chapter in any book of his when somebody doesn't step on a dry twig and alarm all the reds and whites for two hundred yards around. Every time a Cooper person is in peril, and absolute silence is worth four dollars a minute, he is sure to step on a dry twig. There may be a hundred handier things to step on, but that wouldn't satisfy Cooper. Cooper requires him to turn out and find a dry twig; and if he can't do it, go and borrow one. In fact the Leather Stocking Series ought to have been called the Broken Twig Series.

I am sorry there is not room to put in a few dozen instances of the delicate art of the forest, as practiced by Natty Bumppo and some of the other Cooperian experts. Perhaps we may venture two or three samples. Cooper was a sailor—a naval officer; yet he gravely tells us how a vessel, driving toward a lee shore in a gale, is steered for a particular spot by her skipper because he knows of an *undertow* there which will hold her back against the gale and save her. For just pure woodcraft, or sailorcraft, or whatever it is, isn't that neat? For several years Cooper was daily in the society of artillery, and he ought to have noticed that when a cannon ball strikes the ground it either buries itself or skips a hundred feet or so; skips again a hundred feet or so—and so on, till it finally gets tired and rolls. Now in one place he loses some "females"—as he always calls women—in the edge of a wood near a plain at night in a fog, on purpose to give Bumppo a chance to show off the delicate art of the forest before the reader. These mislaid people are hunting for a fort. They hear a cannon-blast, and a cannonball presently comes rolling into the wood and stops at their feet. To the females this suggests nothing. The case is very different with the admirable Bumppo. I wish I may never know peace again if he doesn't strike out promptly and *follow the track* of that cannon-ball across the plain through the dense fog and find the fort. Isn't it a daisy? If Cooper had any real knowledge of Nature's ways of doing things, he had a most delicate art in concealing the fact. For instance: one of his acute Indian experts, Chingachgook (pronounced Chicago, I think), has lost the trail of a person he is tracking through the forest. Apparently that trail is hopelessly lost. Neither you nor I could ever have guessed out the way to find it. It was very different with Chicago. Chicago was not stumped for long. He turned a running stream out of its course, and there, in the slush in its old bed, were that person's moccasin-tracks. The current did not wash them away, as it would have done in all other like cases—no, even the eternal laws of Nature have to vacate when Cooper wants to put up a delicate job of woodcraft on the reader.

We must be a little wary when Brander Matthews tells

us that Cooper's books "reveal an extraordinary fulness of invention." As a rule, I am quite willing to accept Brander Matthews's literary judgements and applaud his lucid and graceful phrasing of them; but that particular statement needs to be taken with a few tons of salt. Bless your heart, Cooper hadn't any more invention than a horse; and I don't mean a high-class horse, either; I mean a clothes-horse. It would be very difficult to find a really clever "situation" in Cooper's books; and still more difficult to find one of any kind which he has failed to render absurd by his handling of it. Look at the episodes of "the caves"; and at the celebrated scuffle between Maqua and those others on the table-land a few days later; and at Hurry Harry's queer water-transit from the castle to the ark; and at Deerslayer's half hour with his first corpse; and at the quarrel between Hurry Harry and Deerslayer later; and at—but choose for yourself; you can't go amiss.

If Cooper had been an observer, his inventive faculty would have worked better, not more interestingly, but more rationally, more plausibly. Cooper's proudest creations in the way of "situations" suffer noticeably from the absence of the observer's protecting gift. Cooper's eye was splendidly inaccurate. Cooper seldom saw anything correctly. He saw nearly all things as through a glass eye, darkly. Of course a man who cannot see the commonest little everyday matters accurately is working at a disadvantage when he is constructing a "situation." In the *Deerslayer* tale Cooper has a stream which is fifty feet wide, where it flows out of a lake; it presently narrows to twenty as it meanders along for no given reason, and yet, when a stream acts like that it ought to be required to explain itself. Fourteen pages later the width of the brook's outlet from the lake has suddenly shrunk thirty feet, and become ''the narrowest part of the stream.'' This shrinkage is not accounted for. The stream has bends in it, a sure indication that it has alluvial banks, and cuts them; yet these bends are only thirty and fifty feet long. If Cooper had been a nice and punctilious observer he would have noticed that the bends were oftener nine hundred feet long than short of it.

Cooper made the exit of that stream fifty feet wide in the first place, for no particular reason; in the second place, he narrowed it to less than twenty to accommodate some Indians. He bends a ''sapling'' to the form of an arch over this narrow passage, and conceals six Indians in its foliage. They are ''laying'' for a settler's scow or ark which is coming up the stream on its way to the lake; it is being hauled against the stiff current by a rope whose stationary end is anchored in the lake; its rate of progress cannot be more than a mile an hour. Cooper describes the ark, but pretty obscurely. In the matter of dimensions ''it was little more than a modern canal boat.'' Let us guess, then, that it was about 140 feet long. It was of ''greater breadth than common.'' Let us guess, then, that it was about sixteen feet wide. This leviathan had been prowling down bends which were but a third as long as itself, and scraping between banks where it had only two feet of space to spare on each side. We cannot too much admire this miracle. A low-roofed log dwelling occupies ''two-third's of the ark's length''—a dwelling ninety feet long and sixteen feet wide, let us say—a kind of vestibule train. The dwelling has two rooms—each forty-five feet long and sixteen feet wide, let us guess. One of them is the bed-room of the Hutter girls, Judith and Hetty; the other is the parlor, in the day time, at night it is papa's bed chamber. The ark is arriving at the stream's exit, now, whose width has been reduced to less than twenty feet to accommodate the Indians—say to eighteen. There is a foot to spare on each side of the boat. Did the Indians notice that there was going to be a tight squeeze there? Did they notice that they could make money by climbing down out of that arched sapling and just stepping aboard when the ark scraped by? No; other Indians would have noticed these things, but Cooper's Indians never notice anything. Cooper thinks they are marvellous creatures for noticing, but he was almost always in error about his Indians. There was seldom a sane one among them.

The ark is 140 feet long; the dwelling is 90 feet long. The idea of the Indians is to drop softly and secretly from the arched sapling to the dwelling as the ark creeps along under it at the rate of a mile an hour, and butcher the family. It will take the ark a minute and a half to pass under. It will take the 90-foot dwelling a minute to pass under. Now, then, what did the six Indians do? It would take you thirty years to guess, and even then you would have to give it up, I believe. Therefore, I will tell you what the Indians did. Their chief, a person of quite extraordinary intellect for a Cooper Indian, warily watched the canal boat as it squeezed along under him, and when he had got his calculations fined down to exactly the right shade, as he judged, he let go and dropped. And *missed the house*! That is actually what he did. He missed the house and landed in the stern of the scow. It was not much of a fall, yet it knocked him silly. He lay there unconscious. If the house had been

97 feet long, he would have made the trip. The fault was Cooper's, not his. The error lay in the construction of the house. Cooper was no architect.

There still remained in the roost five Indians. The boat has passed under and is now out of their reach. Let me explain what the five did—you would not be able to reason it out for yourself. No. 1 jumped for the boat, but fell in the water astern of it. Then No. 2 jumped for the boat, but fell in the water still further astern of it. Then No. 3 jumped for the boat, and fell a good way astern of it. Then No. 4 jumped for the boat, and fell in the water *away* astern. Then even No. 5 made a jump for the boat—for he was a Cooper Indian. In the matter of intellect, the difference between a Cooper Indian and the Indian that stands in front of the cigar shop is not spacious. The scow episode is really a sublime burst of invention; but it does not thrill, because the inaccuracy of the details throws a sort of air of fictitiousness and general improbability over it. This comes of Cooper's inadequacy as an observer.

The reader will find some examples of Cooper's high talent for inaccurate observation in the account of the shooting match in *The Pathfinder*. "A common wrought nail was driven lightly into the target, its head having been first touched with paint." The color of the paint is not stated—an important omission, but Cooper deals freely in important omissions. No, after all, it was not an important omission; for this nail head is a *hundred yards* from the marksman and could not be seen by them at that distance no matter what its color might be. How far can the best eyes see a common house fly? A hundred yards? It is quite impossible. Very well, eyes that cannot see a house fly that is a hundred yards away cannot see an ordinary nail head at that distance, for the size of the two objects is the same. It takes a keen eye to see a fly or a nail head at fifty yards—one hundred and fifty feet. Can the reader do it?

The nail was lightly driven, its head painted, and game called. Then the Cooper miracles began. The bullet of the first marksman chipped an edge of the nail head; the next man's bullet drove the nail a little way into the target—and removed all the paint. Haven't the miracles gone far enough now? Not to suit Cooper; for the purpose of this whole scheme is to show off his prodigy, Deerslayer-Hawkeye-Long-Rifle-Leather-Stocking-Pathfinder-Bumppo before the ladies.

> *"Be all ready to clench it, boys!" cried out Pathfinder, stepping into his friend's tracks the instant they were vacant. "Never mind a new nail; I can see that, though the paint is gone, and what I can see, I can hit at a hundred yards, though it were only a mosquito's eye. Be ready to clench!"*
>
> *The rifle cracked, the bullet sped its way and the head of the nail was buried in the wood, covered by the piece of flattened lead.*

There, you see, is a man who could hunt flies with a rifle, and command a ducal salary in a Wild West show to-day, if we had him back with us.

The recorded feat is certainly surprising, just as it stands; but it is not surprising enough for Cooper. Cooper adds a touch. He has made Pathfinder do this miracle with another man's rifle, and not only that, but Pathfinder did not have even the advantage of loading it himself. He had everything against him, and yet he made that impossible shot, and not only made it, but did it with absolute confidence, saying, ''Be ready to clench.'' Now a person like that would have undertaken that same feat with a brickbat, and with Cooper to help he would have achieved it, too.

Pathfinder showed off handsomely that day before the ladies. His very first feat was a thing which no Wild West show can touch. He was standing with the group of marksmen, observing—a hundred yards from the target, mind: one Jasper raised his rifle and drove the centre of the bull's-eye. Then the quartermaster fired. The target exhibited no result this time. There was a laugh. ''It's a dead miss,'' said Major Lundie. Pathfinder waited an impressive moment or two, then said in that calm, indifferent, know-it-all way of his, ''No, Major— he has covered Jasper's bullet, as will be seen if any one will take the trouble to examine the target.''

Wasn't it remarkable! How *could* he see that little pellet fly through the air and enter that distant bullet-hole? Yet that is what he did; for nothing is impossible to a Cooper person. Did any of those people have any deep-seated doubts about this thing? No; for that would imply sanity, and these were all Cooper people.

The respect for Pathfinder's skill and for his quickness and accuracy of sight (the italics are mine) was so profound and general, that the instant he made this declaration the spectators began to distrust their own opinions, and a dozen rushed to the target in order to ascertain the fact. There, sure

*enough, it was found that the quartermaster's bullet
had gone through the hole made by Jasper's, and
that, too, so accurately as to require a minute examination to be certain of the circumstances,
which, however, was soon established by discov-
ering one bullet over the other in the stump against
which the target was placed.*

They made a "minute" examination; but never mind,
how could they know that there were two bullets in that
hole without digging the latest one out? for neither probe
nor eyesight could prove the presence of any more than
one bullet. Did they dig? No; as we shall see. It is the
Pathfinder's turn now; he steps out before the ladies,
takes aim, and fires.

But alas! here is a disappointment; an incredible, an
unimaginable disappointment—for the target's aspect is
unchanged; there is nothing there but that same old bullet hole!

*"If one dared to hint at such a thing," cried Major
Duncan, "I should say that the Pathfinder has also
missed the target."*

As nobody had missed it yet, the "also" was not necessary; but never mind about that, for the Pathfinder is
going to speak.

*"No, no, Major," said he, confidently, "that would
be a risky declaration. I didn't load the piece, and
can't say what was in it, but if it was lead, you will
find the bullet driving down those of the Quarter-*

master and Jasper, else is not my name Path-finder.''

A shout from the target announced the truth of this assertion.

Is the miracle sufficient as it stands? Not for Cooper. The Pathfinder speaks again, as he ''now slowly advances towards the stage occupied by the females'':

''That's not all, boys, that's not all; if you find the target touched at all, I'll own to a miss. The Quartermaster cut the wood, but you'll find no wood cut by the last messenger.''

The miracle is at last complete. He knew—doubtless *saw*—at the distance of a hundred yards—that his bullet had passed into the hole *without fraying the edges*. There were now three bullets in that one hole—three bullets imbedded processionally in the body of the stump back of the target. Everybody knew this—somehow or other—and yet nobody had dug any of them out to make sure. Cooper is not a close observer, but he is interesting. He is certainly always that, no matter what happens. And he is more interesting when he is not noticing what he is about than when he is. This is a considerable merit.

The conversations in the Cooper books have a curious sound in our modern ears. To believe that such talk really ever came out of people's mouths would be to believe that there was a time when time was of no value to a person who thought he had something to say; when a man's mouth was a rolling-mill, and busied itself all day long in turning four-foot pigs of thought into thirty-foot bars of conversational railroad iron by attenuation;

when subjects were seldom faithfully stuck to, but the talk wandered all around and arrived nowhere; when conversations consisted mainly of irrelevances, with here and there a relevancy, a relevancy with an embarrassed look, as not being able to explain how it got there.

Cooper was certainly not a master in the construction of dialogue. Inaccurate observation defeated him here as it defeated him in so many other enterprises of his. He even failed to notice that the man who talks corrupt English six days in the week must and will talk it on the seventh, and can't help himself. In the *Deerslayer* story he lets Deerslayer talk the showiest kind of book talk sometimes, and at other times the basest of base dialects. For instance, when some one asks him if he has a sweetheart, and if so, where she abides, this is his majestic answer:

> *"She's in the forest—hanging from the boughs of the trees, in a soft rain—in the dew on the open grass—the clouds that float about in the blue heavens—the birds that sing in the woods—the sweet springs where I slake my thirst—and in all the other glorious gifts that come from God's Providence!"*

And he preceded that, a little before, with this:

> *"It consarns me as all things that touches a fri'nd consarns a fri'nd."*

And this is another of his remarks:

"If I was Injin born, now, I might tell of this, or carry in the scalp and boast of the expl'ite afore the whole tribe; or if my inimy had only been a bear"—and so on.

We cannot imagine such a thing as a veteran Scotch Commander-in-Chief comporting himself in the field like a windy melodramatic actor, but Cooper could. On one occasion Alice and Cora were being chased by the French through a fog in the neighborhood of their father's fort:

"Point de quartier aux coquins!" *cried an eager pursuer, who seemed to direct the operations of the enemy.*

"Stand firm and be ready, my gallant 60ths!" suddenly exclaimed a voice above them; "wait to see the enemy: fire low, and sweep the glacis."

"Father! father!" exclaimed a piercing cry from out the mist; "it is I! Alice! thy own Elsie! spare, O! save your daughters!"

"Hold!" shouted the former speaker, in the awful tones of parental agony, the sound reaching even to the woods, and rolling back in solemn echo. "Tis she! God has restored me my children! Throw open the sally-port; to the field, 60ths, to the field; pull not a trigger, lest ye kill my lambs! Drive off these dogs of France with your steel."

Cooper's word-sense was singularly dull. When a person has a poor ear for music he will flat and sharp right along without knowing it. He keeps near the tune, but it is *not* the tune. When a person has a poor ear for words, the result is a literary flatting and sharping; you perceive what he is intending to say, but you also perceive that he doesn't *say* it. This is Cooper. He was not a word-musician. His ear was satisfied with the *approximate* word. I will furnish some circumstantial evidence in support of this charge. My instances are gathered from half a dozen pages of the tale called *Deerslayer*. He uses "verbal," for "oral"; "precision," for "facility"; "phenomena," for "marvels"; "necessary," for "predetermined"; "unsophisticated," for "primitive"; "preparation," for "expectancy"; "rebuked," for "subdued"; "dependent on," for "resulting from"; "fact," for "condition"; "fact," for "conjecture"; "precaution," for "caution"; "explain," for "determine"; "mortified," for "disappointed"; "meretricious," for "factitious"; "materially," for "considerably"; "decreasing," for "deepening"; "increasing," for "disappearing"; "embedded," for "enclosed"; "treacherous," for "hostile"; "stood," for "stooped"; "softened," for "replaced"; "rejoined," for "remarked"; "situation," for "condition"; "different," for "differing"; "insensible," for "unsentient"; "brevity," for "celerity"; "distrusted," for "suspicious"; "mental imbecility," for "imbecility"; "eyes," for "sight"; "counteracting," for "opposing"; "funeral obsequies," for "obsequies."

There have been daring people in the world who claimed that Cooper could write English, but they are all dead now—all dead but Lounsbury. I don't remember that Lounsbury makes the claim in so many words, still he makes it, for he says that *Deerslayer* is a "pure work of art." Pure, in that connection, means faultless—faultless in all details—and language is a detail. If Mr.

Lounsbury had only compared Cooper's English with the English which he writes himself—but it is plain that he didn't; and so it is likely that he imagines until this day that Cooper's is as clean and compact as his own. Now I feel sure, deep down in my heart, that Cooper wrote about the poorest English that exists in our language, and that the English of *Deerslayer* is the very worst than even Cooper ever wrote.

I may be mistaken, but it does seem to me that *Deerslayer* is not a work of art in any sense; it does seem to me that it is destitute of every detail that goes to the making of a work of art; in truth, it seems to me that *Deerslayer* is just simply a literary *delirium tremens*.

A work of art? It has no invention; it has no order, system, sequence, or result, it has no lifelikeness, no thrill, no stir, no seeming of reality; its characters are confusedly drawn, and by their acts and words they prove that they are not the sort of people the author claims that they are; its humor is pathetic; its pathos is funny; its conversations are—oh! indescribable; its love-scenes odious; its English a crime against the language.

Counting these out, what is left is Art. I think we must all admit that.

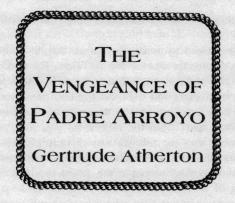

THE VENGEANCE OF PADRE ARROYO

Gertrude Atherton

PILAR, FROM HER little window just above the high wall surrounding the big adobe house set apart for the women neophytes of the Mission of Santa Ines, watched, morning and evening, for Andreo, as he came and went from the rancheria. The old women kept the girls busy, spinning, weaving, sewing; but age nods and youth is crafty. The tall young Indian who was renowned as the best huntsman of all the neophytes, and who supplied Padre Arroyo's table with deer and quail, never failed to keep his ardent eyes fixed upon the grating so long as it lay within the line of his vision. One day he went to Padre Arroyo and told him that Pilar was the prettiest girl behind the wall—the prettiest girl in all the Californias—and that she should be his wife. But the kind stern old padre shook his head.

"You are both too young. Wait another year, my son,

and if thou art still in the same mind, thou shalt have her.''

Andreo dared to make no protest, but he asked permission to prepare a home for his bride. The padre gave it willingly, and the young Indian began to make the big adobes, the bright red tiles. At the end of a month he had built him a cabin among the willows of the rancheria, a little apart from the others; he was in love, and association with his fellows was distasteful. When the cabin was builded his impatience slipped from its curb, and once more he besought the priest to allow him to marry.

Padre Arroyo was sunning himself on the corridor of the mission, shivering in his heavy brown robes, for the day was cold.

''Orion,'' he said sternly—he called all his neophytes after the celebrities of earlier days, regardless of the names given them at the font—''have I not told thee thou must wait a year? Do not be impatient, my son. She will keep. Women are like apples: when they are too young, they set the teeth on edge; when ripe and mellow, they please every sense; when they wither and turn brown, it is time to fall from the tree into a hole. Now go and shoot a deer for Sunday: the good padres from San Luis Obispo and Santa Barbara are coming to dine with me.''

Andreo, dejected, left the padre. As he passed Pilar's window and saw a pair of wistful black eyes behind the grating, his heart took fire. No one was within sight. By a series of signs he made his lady understand that he would place a note beneath a certain adobe in the wall.

Pilar, as she went to and fro under the fruit trees in the garden, or sat on the long corridor weaving baskets, watched that adobe with fascinated eyes. She knew that Andreo was tunnelling it, and one day a tiny hole proclaimed that his work was accomplished. But how to get the note? The old women's eyes were very sharp when the girls were in front of the gratings. Then the civilizing development of Christianity upon the heathen intellect triumphantly asserted itself. Pilar, too, conceived a brilliant scheme. That night the padre, who encouraged any evidence of industry, no matter how eccentric, gave her a little garden of her own—a patch where she could raise sweet peas and Castilian roses.

"That is well, that is well, my Nausicaa," he said, stroking her smoky braids. "Go cut the slips and plant them where thou wilt. I will send thee a package of sweet pea seeds."

Pilar spent every spare hour bending over her "patch"; and the hole, at first no bigger than a pin's point, was larger at each setting of the sun behind the mountain. The old women, scolding on the corridor, called to her not to forget vespers.

On the third evening, kneeling on the damp ground, she drew from the little tunnel in the adobe a thin slip of wood covered with the labour of sleepless nights. She hid it in her smock—that first of California's love-letters—then ran with shaking knees and prostrated herself before the altar. That night the moon streamed through her grating, and she deciphered the fact that Andreo had loosened eight adobes above her garden, and would await her every midnight.

Pilar sat up in bed and glanced about the room with terrified delight. It took her but a moment to decide the question; love had kept her awake too many nights. The neophytes were asleep; as they turned now and again, their narrow beds of hide, suspended from the ceiling, swung too gently to awaken them. The old women snored loudly. Pilar slipped from her bed and looked through the grating. Andreo was there, the dignity and repose of primeval man in his bearing. She waved her hand and pointed downward to the wall; then, throwing on the long coarse gray smock that was her only garment, crept from the room and down the stair. The door was protected against hostile tribes by a heavy iron bar, but Pilar's small hands were hard and strong, and in a moment she stood over the adobes which had crushed her roses and sweet peas.

As she crawled through the opening, Andreo took her hand bashfully, for they had never spoken. "Come," he said; "we must be far away before dawn."

They stole past the long mission, crossing themselves as they glanced askance at the ghostly row of pillars; past the guard-house, where the sentries slept at their post; past the rancheria; then, springing upon a waiting mustang, dashed down the valley. Pilar had never been on a horse before, and she clung in terror to Andreo, who bestrode the unsaddled beast as easily as a cloud rides the wind. His arm held her closely, fear vanished, and she enjoyed the novel sensation. Glancing over Andreo's shoulder she watched the mass of brown and white buildings, the winding river, fade into the mountain. Then they began to ascend an almost perpendicular steep. The horse followed a narrow trail; the crowding trees and shrubs clutched the blankets and smocks of the riders; after a time trail and scene grew white; the snow lay on the heights.

"Where do we go?" she asked.

"To Zaca Lake, on the very top of the mountain,

miles above us. No one has ever been there but myself. Often I have shot deer and birds beside it. They never will find us there."

The red sun rose over the mountains of the east. The crystal moon sank in the west. Andreo sprang from the weary mustang and carried Pilar to the lake.

A sheet of water, round as a whirlpool but calm and silver, lay amidst the sweeping willows and pine-forested peaks. The snow glittered beneath the trees, but a canoe was on the lake, a hut on the marge.

Padre Arroyo tramped up and down the corridor, smiting his hands together. The Indians bowed lower than usual, as they passed, and hastened their steps. The soldiers scoured the country for the bold violators of mission law. No one asked Padre Arroyo what he would do with the sinners, but all knew that punishment would be sharp and summary: the men hoped that Andreo's mustang had carried him beyond its reach; the girls, horrified as they were, wept and prayed in secret for Pilar.

A week later, in the early morning, Padre Arroyo sat on the corridor. The mission stood on a plateau over-looking a long valley forked and sparkled by the broad river. The valley was planted thick with olive trees, and their silver leaves glittered in the rising sun. The mountain peaks about and beyond were white with snow, but the great red poppies blossomed at their feet. The padre, exiled from the luxury and society of his dear Spain, never tired of the prospect: he loved his mission children, but he loved Nature more.

Suddenly he leaned forward on his staff and lifted the heavy brown hood of his habit from his ear. Down the road winding from the eastern mountains came the echo of galloping footfalls. He rose expectantly and waddled out upon the plaza, shading his eyes with his hand. A half-dozen soldiers, riding closely about a horse bestridden by a stalwart young Indian supporting a woman, were rapidly approaching the mission. The padre returned to his seat and awaited their coming.

The soldiers escorted the culprits to the corridor; two held the horse while they descended, then led it away, and Andreo and Pilar were alone with the priest. The bridegroom placed his arm about the bride and looked defiantly at Padre Arroyo, but Pilar drew her long hair about her face and locked her hands together.

Padre Arroyo folded his arms and regarded them with lowered brows, a sneer on his mouth.

"I have new names for you both," he said, in his thickest voice. "Antony, I hope thou hast enjoyed the honeymoon. Cleopatra, I hope thy little toes did not get frost-bitten. You both look as if food had been scarce. And your garments have gone in good part to clothe the brambles, I infer. It is too bad you could not wait a year and love in your cabin at the rancheria, by a good fire, and with plenty of frijoles and tortillas in your stomachs." He dropped his sarcastic tone, and, rising to his feet, extended his right arm with a gesture of malediction. "Do you comprehend the enormity of your sin?" he shouted. "Have you not learned on your knees that the fires of hell are the rewards of unlawful love? Do you not know that even the year of sackcloth and ashes I shall impose here on earth will not save you from those flames a million times hotter than the mountain fire, than the roaring pits in which evil Indians torture one another? A hundred years of their scorching breath, of roasting flesh, for a week of love! Oh, God of my soul!"

Andreo looked somewhat staggered, but unrepentant. Pilar burst into loud sobs of terror.

The padre stared long and gloomily at the flags of the corridor. Then he raised his head and looked sadly at his lost sheep.

"My children," he said solemnly, "my heart is wrung for you. You have broken the laws of God and of the Holy Catholic Church, and the punishments thereof are awful. Can I do anything for you, excepting to pray? You shall have my prayers, my children. But that is not enough; I cannot—ay! I cannot endure the thought that you shall be damned. Perhaps"—again he stared meditatively at the stones, then, after an impressive silence, raised his eyes. "Heaven vouchsafes me an idea, my children. I will make your punishment here so bitter that Almighty God in His mercy will give you but a few years of purgatory after death. Come with me."

He turned and led the way slowly to the rear of the mission buildings. Andreo shuddered for the first time, and tightened his arm about Pilar's shaking body. He knew that they were to be locked in the dungeons. Pilar, almost fainting, shrank back as they reached the narrow spiral stair which led downward to the cells. "Ay! I shall die, my Andreo!" she cried. "Ay! my father, have mercy!"

"I cannot, my children," said the padre, sadly. "It is for the salvation of your souls."

"Mother of God! When shall I see thee again, my Pilar?" whispered Andreo. "But, ay! the memory of that week on the mountain will keep us both alive."

Padre Arroyo descended the stair and awaited them at its foot. Separating them, and taking each by the hand, he pushed Andreo ahead and dragged Pilar down the narrow passage. At its end he took a great bunch of keys from his pocket, and raising both hands commanded them to kneel. He said a long prayer in a loud monotonous voice which echoed and re-echoed down the dark hall and made Pilar shriek with terror. Then he fairly hurled the marriage ceremony at them, and made the couple repeat after him the responses. When it was over, ''Arise,'' he said.

The poor things stumbled to their feet, and Andre caught Pilar in a last embrace.

. ''Now bear your incarceration with fortitude, my children; and if you do not beat the air with your groans, I will let you out in a week. Do not hate your old father, for love alone makes him severe, but pray, pray, pray.''

And then he locked them both in the same cell.

THE BLUE HOTEL

Stephen Crane

1

THE PALACE HOTEL at Fort Romper was painted a light blue, a shade that is on the legs of a kind of heron, causing the bird to declare its position against any background. The Palace Hotel, then, was always screaming and howling in a way that made the dazzling winter landscape of Nebraska seem only a gray swampish hush. It stood alone on the prairie, and when the snow was falling, the town two hundred yards away was not visible. But when the traveler alighted at the railway station, he was obliged to pass the Palace Hotel before he could come upon the company of low clapboard houses which composed Fort Romper, and it was not to be thought that any traveler could pass the Palace Hotel without looking at it. Pat Scully, the proprietor, had proved himself a master of strategy when he chose his

paints. It is true that on clear days, when the great trans-
continental expresses, long lines of swaying Pullmans,
swept through Fort Romper, passengers were overcome
at the sight, and the cult that knows the brown reds and
the subdivisions of the dark greens of the East expressed
shame, pity, horror, in a laugh. But to the citizens of
this prairie town and to the people who would naturally
stop there, Pat Scully had performed a feat. With this
opulence and splendor, these creeds, classes, egotisms,
that streamed through Romper on the rails day after day,
they had no color in common.

As if the displayed delights of such a blue hotel were
not sufficiently enticing, it was Scully's habit to go every
morning and evening to meet the leisurely trains that
stopped at Romper and work his seductions upon any
man that he might see wavering, gripsack in hand.

One morning, when a snow-crusted engine dragged
its long string of freight cars and its one passenger coach
to the station, Scully performed the marvel of catching
three men. One was a shaky and quick-eyed Swede, with
a great shining cheap valise; one was a tall bronzed cowboy, who was on his way to a ranch near the Dakota
line; one was a little silent man from the East, who
didn't look it and didn't announce it. Scully practically
made them prisoners. He was so nimble and merry and
kindly that each probably felt it would be the height of
brutality to try to escape. They trudged off over the
creaking board sidewalks in the wake of the eager little
Irishman. He wore a heavy fur cap squeezed tightly
down on his head. It caused his two red ears to stick out
stiffly, as if they were made of tin.

At last, Scully, elaborately, with boisterous hospitality, conducted them through the portals of the blue hotel.

The room which they entered was small. It seemed to be merely a proper temple for an enormous stove, which, in the center, was humming with godlike violence. At various points on its surface, the iron had become luminous and glowed yellow from the heat. Beside the stove Scully's son Johnnie was playing high-five with an old farmer who had whiskers both gray and sandy. They were quarreling. Frequently the old farmer turned his face toward a box of sawdust—colored brown from tobacco juice—that was behind the stove, and spat with an air of great impatience and irritation. With a loud flourish of words, Scully destroyed the game of cards and bustled his son upstairs with part of the baggage of the new guests. He himself conducted them to three basins of the coldest water in the world. The cowboy and the Easterner burnished themselves fiery red with this water, until it seemed to be some kind of metal polish. The Swede, however, merely dipped his fingers gingerly and with trepidation. It was notable that throughout this series of small ceremonies, the three travelers were made to feel that Scully was very benevolent. He was conferring great favors upon them. He handed the towel from one to another with an air of philanthropic impulse.

Afterward they went to the first room, and, sitting about the stove, listened to Scully's officious clamor at his daughters, who were preparing the midday meal. They reflected in the silence of experienced men who tread carefully amid new people. Nevertheless, the old farmer, stationary, invincible in his chair near the warmest part of the stove, turned his face from the sawdust box frequently and addressed a glowing commonplace to the strangers. Usually he was answered in short but adequate sentences by either the cowboy or the Easterner. The Swede said nothing. He seemed to be occupied in making furtive estimates of each man in the room. One might have thought that he had the sense of silly suspicion which comes to guilt. He resembled a badly frightened man.

Later, at dinner, he spoke a little, addressing his conversation entirely to Scully. He volunteered that he had come from New York where for ten years he had worked as a tailor. These facts seemed to strike Scully as fascinating, and afterward he volunteered that he had lived at Romper for fourteen years. The Swede asked about the crops and the price of labor. He seemed barely to listen to Scully's extended replies. His eyes continued to rove from man to man.

Finally, with a laugh and a wink, he said that some of these Western communities were very dangerous; and after his statement he straightened his legs under the table, tilted his head and laughed again, loudly. It was plain that the demonstration had no meaning to the others. They looked at him wondering and in silence.

2

As the men trooped heavily back into the front room, the two little windows presented views of a turmoiling sea of snow. The huge arms of the wind were making attempts—mighty, circular, futile—to embrace the flakes as they sped. A gatepost like a still man with a blanched face stood aghast amid this profligate fury. In a hearty voice Scully announced the presence of a blizzard. The guests of the blue hotel, lighting their pipes, assented with grunts of lazy masculine contentment. No island of the sea could be exempt in the degree of this little room with its humming stove. Johnnie, son of Scully, in a tone which defined his opinion of his ability as a cardplayer, challenged the old farmer of both gray and sandy whiskers to a game of high-five. The farmer agreed with a contemptuous and bitter scoff. They sat close to the stove, and squared their knees under a wide board. The cowboy and the Easterner watched the game with interest. The Swede remained near the window, aloof, but with a countenance that showed signs of an inexplicable excitement.

The play of Johnnie and the graybeard was suddenly ended by another quarrel. The old man arose while casting a look of heated scorn at his adversary. He slowly buttoned his coat, and then stalked with fabulous dignity from the room. In the discreet silence of all the other men, the Swede laughed. His laughter rang somehow childish. Men by this time had begun to look at him askance, as if they wished to inquire what ailed him.

A new game was formed jocosely. The cowboy volunteered to become the partner of Johnnie, and they all then turned to ask the Swede to throw in his lot with the little Easterner. He asked some questions about the game, and, learning that it wore many names, and that he had played it when it was under an alias, he accepted the invitation. He strode toward the men nervously, as if he expected to be assaulted. Finally, seated, he gazed from face to face and laughed shrilly. This laugh was so strange that the Easterner looked up quickly, the cowboy sat intent and with his mouth open, and Johnnie paused, holding the cards with still fingers.

Afterward there was a short silence. Then Johnnie said, ''Well, let's get at it. Come on, now!'' They pulled their chairs forward until their knees were bunched under the board. They began to play, and their interest in the game caused the others to forget the manner of the Swede.

The cowboy was a board-whacker. Each time that he held superior cards he whanged them, one by one, with exceeding force, down upon the improvised table, and took the tricks with a glowing air of prowess and ride that sent thrills of indignation into the hearts of his opponents. A game with a board-whacker in it is sure to become intense. The countenances of the Easterner and the Swede were miserable whenever the cowboy thundered down his aces and kings, while Johnnie, his eyes gleaming with joy, chuckled and chuckled.

Because of the absorbing play none considered the strange ways of the Swede. They paid strict heed to the game. Finally, during a lull caused by a new deal, the Swede suddenly addressed Johnnie. "I suppose there have been a good many men killed in this room." The jaws of the others dropped and they looked at him.

"What in hell are you talking about?" said Johnnie.

The Swede laughed again his blatant laugh, full of a kind of false courage and defiance. "Oh, you know what I mean all right," he answered.

"I'm a liar if I do!" Johnnie protested. The card was halted, and the men stared at the Swede. Johnnie evidently felt that as the son of the proprietor he should make a direct inquiry. "Now, what might you be drivin' at, mister?" he asked. The Swede winked at him. It was a wink full of cunning. His fingers shook on the edge of the board. "Oh, maybe you think I have been to nowheres. Maybe you think I'm a tenderfoot?"

"I don't know nothin' about you," answered Johnnie,

"and I don't give a damn where you've been. All I got to say is that I don't know what you're driving at. There hain't never been nobody killed in this room."

The cowboy, who had been steadily gazing at the Swede, then spoke. "What's wrong with you, mister?"

Apparently it seemed to the Swede that he was formidably menaced. He shivered and turned white near the corners of his mouth. He sent an appealing glance in the direction of the little Easterner. During these moments he did not forget to wear his air of advanced pot-valor. "They say they don't know what I mean," he remarked mockingly to the Easterner.

The latter answered after prolonged and cautious reflection. "I don't understand you," he said impassively.

The Swede made a movement then which announced that he thought he had encountered treachery from the only quarter where he had expected sympathy, if not help. "Oh, I see you are all against me. I see—"

The cowboy was in a state of deep stupefaction. "Say," he cried, as he tumbled the deck violently down upon the board, "say, what are you gittin' at, hey?"

The Swede sprang up with the celerity of a man escaping from a snake on the floor. "I don't want to fight!" he shouted. "I don't want to fight!"

The cowboy stretched his long legs indolently and deliberately. His hands were in his pockets. He spat into the sawdust box. "Well, who the hell thought you did?" he inquired.

The Swede backed rapidly toward a corner of the room. His hands were out protectingly in front of his chest, but he was making an obvious struggle to control his fright. "Gentlemen," he quavered, "I suppose I am going to be killed before I can leave this house! I suppose I am going to be killed before I can leave this house!'' In his eyes was the dying-swan look. Through the windows could be seen the snow turning blue in the shadow of dusk. The wind tore at the house, and some loose thing beat regularly against the clapboards like a spirit tapping.

A door opened, and Scully himself entered. He paused in surprise as he noted the tragic attitude of the Swede. Then he said, ''What's the matter here?''

The Swede answered him swiftly and eagerly, ''These men are going to kill me.''

''Kill you!'' ejaculated Scully. ''Kill you! What are you talkin'?''

The Swede made the gesture of a martyr.

Scully wheeled sternly upon his son. ''What is this, Johnnie?''

The lad had grown sullen. ''Damned if I know,'' he answered. ''I can't make no sense to it.'' He began to shuffle the cards, fluttering them together with an angry snap. ''He says a good many men have been killed in this room, or something like that. And he says he's goin' to be killed here too. I don't know what ails him. He's crazy, I shouldn't wonder.''

Scully then looked for explanation to the cowboy, but the cowboy simply shrugged his shoulders.

''Kill you?'' said Scully again to the Swede. ''Kill you? Man, you're off your nut.''

''Oh, I know,'' burst out the Swede. ''I know what will happen. Yes, I'm crazy—yes. Yes, of course, I'm crazy—yes. But I know one thing—'' There was a sort of sweat of misery and terror upon his face. ''I know I won't get out of here alive.''

The cowboy drew a deep breath, as if his mind was

passing into the last stages of dissolution. "Well, I'm doggoned," he whispered to himself.

Scully wheeled suddenly and faced his son. "You've been troublin' this man!"

Johnnie's voice was loud with its burden of grievance. "Why, good Gawd, I ain't done nothin' to 'im."

The Swede broke in. "Gentlemen, do not disturb yourselves. I will leave this house. I will go away, because"—he accused them dramatically with his glance—"because I do not want to be killed."

Scully was furious with his son. "Will you tell me what is the matter, you young devil? What's the matter, anyhow? Speak out!"

"Blame it!" cried Johnnie in despair, "don't I tell you I don't know? He—he says we want to kill him, and that's all I know. I can't tell what ails him."

The Swede continued to repeat, "Never mind, Mr. Scully; never mind. I will leave this house. I will go away, because I do not wish to be killed. Yes, of course, I am crazy—yes. But I know one thing! I will go away. I will leave this house. Never mind, Mr. Scully; never mind. I will go away."

"You will not go 'way," said Scully. "You will not go 'way until I hear the reason of this business. If anybody has troubled you, I will take care of him. This is my house. You are under my roof, and I will not allow any peaceable man to be troubled here." He cast a terrible eye upon Johnnie, the cowboy and the Easterner.

"Never mind, Mr. Scully; never mind. I will go away. I do not wish to be killed." The Swede moved toward the door which opened upon the stairs. It was evidently his intention to go at once for his baggage.

"No, no," shouted Scully peremptorily; but the

white-faced man slid by him and disappeared. "Now," said Scully severely, "what does this mean?"

Johnnie and the cowboy cried together, "Why, we didn't do nothin' to 'im!"

Scully's eyes were cold. "No," he said, "you didn't?"

Johnnie swore a deep oath. "Why, this is the wildest loon I ever see. We didn't do nothin' at all. We were just sittin' here playin' cards, and he—"

The father suddenly spoke to the Easterner. "Mr. Blanc," he asked, "what has these boys been doin'?"

The Easterner reflected again. "I didn't see anything wrong at all," he said at last slowly.

Scully began to howl. "But what does it mane?" He stared ferociously at his son. "I have a mind to lather you for this, me boy."

Johnnie was frantic. "Well, what have I done?" he bawled at his father.

3

"I think you are tongue-tied," said Scully finally to his son, the cowboy and the Easterner; and at the end of this scornful sentence, he left the room.

Upstairs the Swede was swiftly fastening the straps of his great valise. Once his back happened to be half turned toward the door, and, hearing a noise there, he wheeled and sprang up, uttering a loud cry. Scully's wrinkled visage showed grimly in the light of the small lamp he carried. This yellow effulgence, streaming upward, colored only his prominent features, and left his eyes, for instance, in mysterious shadow. He resembled a murderer.

"Man! man!" he exclaimed, "have you gone daffy?"

"Oh, no! Oh, no!" rejoined the other. "There are people in this world who know pretty nearly as much as you do—understand?"

For a moment they stood gazing at each other. Upon the Swede's deathly pale cheeks were two spots brightly crimson and sharply edged, as if they had been carefully painted. Scully placed the light on the table and sat himself on the edge of the bed. He spoke ruminatively. "By cracky, I never heard of such a thing in my life. It's a complete muddle. I can't, for the soul of me, think how you ever got this idea into your head." Presently he lifted his eyes and asked, "And did you sure think they were going to kill you?"

The Swede scanned the old man as if he wished to see into his mind. "I did," he said at last. He obviously suspected that this answer might precipitate an outbreak. As he pulled on a strap his whole arm shook, the elbow wavering like a bit of paper.

Scully banged his hand impressively on the footboard of the bed. "Why, man, we're goin' to have a line of ilictric streetcars in this town next spring."

" 'A line of electric streetcars,' " repeated the Swede stupidly.

"And," said Scully, "there's a new railroad goin' to be built down from Broken Arm to here. Not to mention the four churches and the smashin' big brick schoolhouse. Then there's the big factory, too. Why, in two years Romper'll be a met-tro-*pol*-is."

Having finished the preparation of his baggage, the Swede straightened himself. "Mr. Scully," he said, with sudden hardihood, "how much do I owe you?"

"You don't owe me anythin'," said the old man, angrily.

"Yes, I do," retorted the Swede. He took seventy-five cents from his pocket and tendered it to Scully; but the latter snapped his fingers in disdainful refusal. However, it happened that they both stood gazing in a strange fashion at three silver pieces on the Swede's open palm.

"I'll not take your money," said Scully at last. "Not after what's been goin' on here." Then a plan seemed to strike him. "Here," he cried, picking up his lamp and moving toward the door. "Here! Come with me a minute."

"No," said the Swede, in overwhelming alarm.

"Yes," urged the old man. "Come on! I want you to come and see a picter—just across the hall—in my room."

The Swede must have concluded that his hour was come. His jaw dropped and his teeth showed like a dead man's. He ultimately followed Scully across the corridor, but he had the step of one hung in chains.

Scully flashed the light high on the wall of his own chamber. There was revealed a ridiculous photograph of a little girl. She was leaning against a balustrade of gorgeous decoration, and the formidable bang to her hair was prominent. The figure was as graceful as an upright sled-stake, and, withal, it was of the hue of lead. "There," said Scully, tenderly, "that's the picter of my little girl that died. Her name was Carrie. She had the purtiest hair you ever saw. I was that fond of her, she—"

Turning then, he saw that the Swede was not contemplating the picture at all, but, instead, was keeping keen watch on the gloom in the rear.

"Look, man!" cried Scully, heartily. "That's the picter of my little gal that died. Her name was Carrie. And then here's the picter of my oldest boy, Michael. He's a lawyer in Lincoln, an' doin' well. I gave that boy a grand eddication, and I'm glad for it now. He's a fine boy. Look at 'im now. Ain't he bold as blazes, him there in Lincoln, an honored an' respicted gintleman! An honored and respected gintleman," concluded Scully with a flourish. And, so saying, he smote the Swede jovially on the back.

The Swede faintly smiled.

"Now," said the old man, "there's only one more thing." He dropped suddenly to the floor and thrust his hand beneath the bed. The Swede could hear his muffled voice. "I'd keep it under me piller if it wasn't for that boy Johnnie. Then there's the old woman—Where is it now? I never put it twice in the same place. Ah, now come out with you!"

Presently he backed clumsily from under the bed, dragging with him an old coat rolled into a bundle. "I've fetched him," he muttered. Kneeling on the floor, he unrolled the coat and extracted from its heart a large yellow brown whisky bottle.

His first maneuver was to hold the bottle up to the light. Reassured, apparently, that nobody had been tampering with it, he thrust it with a generous movement toward the Swede.

The weak-kneed Swede was about to eagerly clutch this element of strength, but he suddenly jerked his hand away and cast a look of horror upon Scully.

"Drink," said the old man affectionately. He had

risen to his feet, and now stood facing the Swede.

There was a silence. Then again Scully said, "Drink!"

The Swede laughed wildly. He grabbed the bottle, put it to his mouth; and as his lips curled absurdly around the opening and his throat worked, he kept his glance, burning with hatred, upon the old man's face.

4

After the departure of Scully the three men, with the cardboard still upon their knees, preserved for a long time an astounded silence. Then Johnnie said, "That's the daddangedest Swede I ever see."

"He ain't no Swede," said the cowboy scornfully.

"Well, what is he then?" cried Johnnie. "What is he then?"

"It's my opinion," replied the cowboy deliberately, "he's some kind of a Dutchman." It was a venerable custom of the country to entitle as Swedes all light-haired men who spoke with a heavy tongue. In consequence the idea of the cowboy was not without its daring. "Yes, sir," he repeated. "It's my opinion this feller is some kind of a Dutchman."

"Well, he says he's a Swede, anyhow," muttered Johnnie, sulkily. He turned to the Easterner. "What do you think, Mr. Blanc?"

"Oh, I don't know," replied the Easterner.

"Well, what do you think makes him act that way?" asked the cowboy.

"Why, he's frightened." The Easterner knocked his

pipe against a rim of the stove. "He's clear frightened out of his boots."

"What at?" cried Johnnie and the cowboy together.

The Easterner reflected over his answer.

"What at?" cried the others again.

"Oh, I don't know, but it seems to me this man has been reading dime novels, and he thinks he's right out in the middle of it—the shootin' and stabbin' and all."

"But," said the cowboy, deeply scandalized, "this ain't Wyoming, ner none of them places. This is Nebrasker."

"Yes," added Johnnie, "an' why don't he wait till he gits *out West*?"

The traveled Easterner laughed. "It isn't different there even—not in these days. But he thinks he's right in the middle of hell."

Johnnie and the cowboy mused long.

"It's awful funny," remarked Johnnie at last.

"Yes," said the cowboy. "This is a queer game. I hope we don't git snowed in, because then we'd have to stand this here man bein' around with us all the time. That wouldn't be no good."

"I wish pop would throw him out," said Johnnie.

Presently they heard a loud stamping on the stairs, accompanied by ringing jokes in the voice of old Scully, and laughter, evidently from the Swede. The men around the stove stared vacantly at each other. "Gosh!" said the cowboy. The door flew open, and old Scully, flushed and anecdotal, came into the room. He was jabbering at the Swede, who followed him, laughing bravely. It was the entry of two roisterers from a banquet hall.

"Come now," said Scully sharply to the three seated men, "move up and give us a chance at the stove." The cowboy and the Easterner obediently sidled their chairs to make room for the newcomers. Johnnie, however, simply arranged himself in a more indolent attitude, and then remained motionless.

"Come! Git over there," said Scully.

"Plenty of room on the other side of the stove," said Johnnie.

"Do you think we want to sit in the draught?" roared the father.

But the Swede here interposed with a grandeur of confidence. "No, no. Let the boy sit where he likes," he cried in a bullying voice to the father.

"All right! All right!" said Scully, deferentially. The cowboy and the Easterner exchanged glances of wonder.

The five chairs were formed in a crescent about one side of the stove. The Swede began to talk; he talked arrogantly, profanely, angrily. Johnnie, the cowboy and the Easterner maintained a morose silence, while old Scully appeared to be receptive and eager, breaking in constantly with sympathetic ejaculations.

Finally the Swede announced that he was thirsty. He moved in his chair, and said that he would go for a drink of water.

"I'll git it for you," cried Scully at once.

"No," said the Swede, contemptuously. "I'll get it for myself." He arose and stalked with the air of an owner off into the executive parts of the hotel.

As soon as the Swede was out of hearing, Scully sprang to his feet and whispered intensely to the others, "Upstairs he thought I was tryin' to poison 'im."

"Say," said Johnnie, "this makes me sick. Why don't you throw 'im out in the snow?"

"Why, he's all right now," declared Scully. "It was

only that he was from the East, and he thought this was a tough place. That's all. He's all right now."

The cowboy looked with admiration upon the Easterner. "You were straight," he said. "You were on to that there Dutchman."

"Well," said Johnnie to his father, "he may be all right now, but I don't see it. Other time he was scared, but now he's too fresh."

Scully's speech was always a combination of Irish brogue and idiom, Western twang and idiom, and scraps of curiously formal diction taken from the storybooks and newspapers. He now hurled a strange mass of language at the head of his son. "What do I keep? What do I keep? What do I keep?" he demanded, in a voice of thunder. He slapped his knee impressively, to indicate that he himself was going to make reply, and that all should heed. "I keep a hotel," he shouted. "A hotel, do you mind? A guest under my roof has sacred privileges. He is to be intimidated by none. Not one word shall he hear that would prijudice him in favor of goin' away. I'll not have it. There's no place in this here town where they can say they iver took in a guest of mine because he was afraid to stay here." He wheeled suddenly upon the cowboy and the Easterner. "Am I right?"

"Yes, Mr. Scully," said the cowboy, "I think you're right."

"Yes, Mr. Scully," said the Easterner, "I think you're right."

5

At six o'clock supper, the Swede fizzed like a fire wheel. He sometimes seemed on the point of bursting into riotous song, and in all his madness he was encouraged by old Scully. The Easterner was encased in reserve; the cowboy sat in wide-mouthed amazement, forgetting to eat, while Johnnie wrathily demolished great plates of food. The daughters of the house, when they were obliged to replenish the biscuits, approached as warily as Indians, and, having succeeded in their purpose, fled with ill-concealed trepidation. The Swede domineered the whole feast, and he gave it the appearance of a cruel bacchanal. He seemed to have grown suddenly taller; he gazed, brutally disdainful, into every face. His voice rang through the room. Once when he jabbed out harpoon-fashion with his fork to pinion a biscuit, the weapon nearly impaled the hand of the Easterner, which had been stretched quietly out for the same biscuit.

After supper, as the men filed toward the other room, the Swede smote Scully ruthlessly on the shoulder. "Well, old boy, that was a good, square meal." Johnnie looked hopefully at his father; he knew that shoulder was tender from an old fall; and, indeed, it appeared for a moment as if Scully was going to flame out over the matter, but in the end he smiled a sickly smile and remained silent. The others understood from his manner that he was admitting his responsibility for the Swede's new viewpoint.

Johnnie, however, addressed his parent in an aside. "Why don't you license somebody to kick you downstairs?'' Scully scowled darkly by way of reply.

When they were gathered about the stove, the Swede insisted on another game of high-five. Scully gently deprecated the plan at first, but the Swede turned a wolfish glare upon him. The old man subsided, and the Swede canvased the others. In his tone there was always a great threat. The cowboy and the Easterner both remarked indifferently that they would play. Scully said that he would presently have to go to meet the 6:58 train, and so the Swede turned menacingly upon Johnnie. For a moment their glances crossed like blades, and then Johnnie smiled and said, ''Yes, I'll play.''

They formed a square, with the little board on their knees. The Easterner and the Swede were again partners. As the play went on, it was noticeable that the cowboy was not board-whacking as usual. Meanwhile, Scully, near the lamp, had put on his spectacles and, with an appearance curiously like an old priest, was reading a newspaper. In time he went out to meet the 6:58 train, and, despite his precautions, a gust of polar wind whirled into the room as he opened the door. Besides scattering the cards, it chilled the players to the marrow. The Swede cursed frightfully. When Scully returned, his entrance disturbed a cozy and friendly scene. The Swede again cursed. But presently they were once more intent, their heads bent forward and their hands moving swiftly. The Swede had adopted the fashion of board-whacking.

Scully took up his paper and for a long time remained immersed in matters which were extraordinarily remote from him. The lamp burned badly, and once he stopped to adjust the wick. The newspaper, as he turned from page to page, rustled with a slow and comfortable sound.

Then suddenly he heard three terrible words. "You are cheatin'!"

Such scenes often prove that there can be little of dramatic import in environment. Any room can present a tragic front; any room can be comic. This little den was now hideous as a torture chamber. The new faces of the men themselves had changed it upon the instant the Swede held a huge fist in front of Johnnie's face, while the latter looked steadily over it into the blazing orbs of his accuser. The Easterner had grown pallid; the cowboy's jaw had dropped in that expression of bovine amazement which was one of his important mannerisms. After the three words, the first sound in the room was made by Scully's paper as it floated forgotten to his feet. His spectacles had also fallen from his nose, but by a clutch he had saved them in air. His hand, grasping the spectacles, now remained poised awkwardly and near his shoulder. He stared at the cardplayers.

Probably the silence was while a second elapsed. Then, if the floor had been suddenly twitched out from under the men, they could not have moved quicker. The five had projected themselves headlong toward a common point. It happened that Johnnie, in rising to hurl himself upon the Swede, had stumbled slightly because of his curiously instinctive care for the cards and the board. The loss of the moment allowed time for the arrival of Scully, and also allowed the cowboy time to give the Swede a great push which sent him staggering back. The men found tongue together, and hoarse shouts of rage, appeal or fear burst from every throat. The cowboy pushed and jostled feverishly at the Swede, and the East-erner and Scully clung wildly to Johnnie; but through the smoky air, above the swaying bodies of the peace-compellers, the eyes of the two warriors ever sought each other in glances of challenge that were at once hot and steely.

Of course the board had been overturned, and now the whole company of cards was scattered over the floor, where the boots of the men trampled the fat and painted kings and queens as they gazed with their silly eyes at the war that was waging above them.

Scully's voice was dominating the yells. "Stop now! Stop, I say! Stop, now—"

Johnnie, as he struggled to burst through the rank formed by Scully and the Easterner, was crying, "Well, he says I cheated! He says I cheated! I won't allow no man to say I cheated! If he says I cheated, he's a———!"

The cowboy was telling the Swede, "Quit, now! Quit, d'ye hear—"

The screams of the Swede never ceased. "He did cheat! I saw him! I saw him—"

As for the Easterner, he was importuning in a voice that was not heeded, "Wait a moment, can't you? Oh, wait a moment. What's the good of a fight over a game of cards? Wait a moment—"

In this tumult no complete sentences were clear. "Cheat"—"quit"—"he says"—these fragments pierced the uproar and rang out sharply. It was remarkable that, whereas Scully undoubtedly made the most noise, he was the least heard of any of the riotous band.

Then suddenly there was a great cessation. It was as if each man had paused for breath; and although the room was still lighted with the anger of men, it could be seen that there was no danger of immediate conflict, and at once Johnnie, shouldering his way forward, almost succeeded in confronting the Swede. "What did you say I cheated for? What did you say I cheated for? I don't cheat, and I won't let no man say I do!"

The Swede said, "I saw you! I saw you!"

"Well," cried Johnnie, "I'll fight any man what says I cheat!"

"No, you won't," said the cowboy. "Not here."

"Ah, be still, can't you?" said Scully, coming between them.

The quiet was sufficient to allow the Easterner's voice to be heard. He was repeating, "Oh, wait a moment, can't you? What's the good of a fight over a game of cards? Wait a moment!"

Johnnie, his red face appearing above his father's shoulder, hailed the Swede again. "Did you say I cheated?"

The Swede showed his teeth. "Yes."

"Then," said Johnnie, "we must fight."

"Yes, fight," roared the Swede. He was like a demoniac. "Yes, fight! I'll show you what kind of a man I am! I'll show you who you want to fight! Maybe you think I can't fight! Maybe you think I can't! I'll show you, you skin, you cardsharp. Yes, you cheated! You cheated! You cheated!"

"Well, let's go at it, then, mister," said Johnnie coolly.

The cowboy's brow was beaded with sweat from his efforts in intercepting all sorts of raids. He turned in despair to Scully. "What are you goin' to do now?"

A change had come over the Celtic visage of the old man. He now seemed all eagerness; his eyes glowed.

"We'll let them fight," he answered, stalwartly. "I

can't put up with it any longer. I've stood this damned Swede till I'm sick. We'll let them fight.''

6

The men prepared to go out of doors. The Easterner was so nervous that he had great difficulty in getting his arms into the sleeves of his new leather coat. As the cowboy drew his fur cap down over his ears, his hands trembled. In fact, Johnnie and old Scully were the only ones who displayed no agitation. These preliminaries were conducted without words.

Scully threw open the door. ''Well, come on,'' he said. Instantly a terrific wind caused the flame of the lamp to struggle at its wick, while a puff of black smoke sprang from the chimney top. The stove was in midcurrent of the blast, and its voice swelled to equal the roar of the storm. Some of the scarred and bedabbled cards were caught up from the floor and dashed helplessly against the farther wall. The men lowered their heads and plunged into the tempest as into a sea.

No snow was falling, but great whirls and clouds of flakes, swept up from the ground by the frantic winds, were streaming southward with the speed of bullets. The covered land was blue with the sheen of an unearthly satin, and there was no other hue save where, at the low black railway station—which seemed incredibly distant— one light gleamed like a tiny jewel. As the men floundered into a thigh-deep drift, it was known that the Swede was bawling out something. Scully went to him, put a hand on his shoulder and projected an ear. ''What's that you say?'' he shouted.

"I say," bawled the Swede again, "I won't stand much show against this gang. I know you'll all pitch on me."

Scully smote him reproachfully on the arm. "Tut, man!" he yelled. The wind tore the words from Scully's lips and scattered them far alee.

"You are all a gang of—" boomed the Swede, but the storm also seized the remainder of this sentence.

Immediately turning their backs upon the wind, the men had swung around a corner to the sheltered side of the hotel. It was the function of the little house to preserve here, amid this great devastation of snow, an irregular V-shape of heavily encrusted grass, which crackled beneath the feet. One could imagine the great drifts piled against the windward side. When the party reached the comparative peace of this spot, it was found that the Swede was still bellowing.

"Oh, I know what kind of a thing this is! I know you'll all pitch on me. I can't lick you all!"

Scully turned upon him panther-fashion. "You'll not have to whip all of us. You'll have to whip my son Johnnie. An' the man what troubles you durin' that time will have me to deal with."

The arrangements were swiftly made. The two men faced each other, obedient to the harsh commands of Scully, whose face, in the subtly luminous gloom, could be seen set in the austere impersonal lines that are pictured on the countenances of the Roman veterans. The Easterner's teeth were chattering, and he was hopping up and down like a mechanical toy. The cowboy stood rocklike.

The contestants had not stripped off any clothing. Each was in his ordinary attire. Their fists were up, and they eyed each other in a calm that had the elements of leonine cruelty in it.

During this pause, the Easterner's mind, like a film, took lasting impressions of three men—the iron-nerved master of the ceremony; the Swede, pale, motionless, terrible; and Johnnie, serene yet ferocious, brutish yet heroic. The entire prelude had in it a tragedy greater than the tragedy of action, and this aspect was accentuated by the long, mellow cry of the blizzard as it sped the tumbling and wailing flakes into the black abyss of the south.

"Now!" said Scully.

The two combatants leaped forward and crashed together like bullocks. There was heard the cushioned sound of blows, and of a curse squeezing out from between the tight teeth of one.

As for the spectators, the Easterner's pent-up breath exploded from him with a pop of relief, absolute relief from the tension of the preliminaries. The cowboy bounded into the air with a yowl. Scully was immovable as from supreme amazement and fear at the fury of the fight which he himself had permitted and arranged.

For a time the encounter in the darkness was such a perplexity of flying arms that it presented no more detail than would a swiftly revolving wheel. Occasionally, a face, as if illumined by a flash of light, would shine out, ghastly and marked with pink spots. A moment later, the men might have been known as shadows if it were not for the involuntary utterance of oaths that came from them in whispers.

Suddenly a holocaust of warlike desire caught the cowboy, and he bolted forward with the speed of a bronco. "Go it, Johnnie! Go it! Kill him! Kill him!"

Scully confronted him. ''Kape back,'' he said; and by his glance the cowboy could tell that this man was Johnnie's father.

To the Easterner there was a monotony of unchangeable fighting that was an abomination. This confused mingling was eternal to his sense, which was concentrated in a longing for the end, the priceless end. Once the fighters lurched near him, and as he scrambled hastily backward he heard them breathe like men on the rack.

''Kill him, Johnnie! Kill him! Kill him! Kill him!'' The cowboy's face was contorted like one of those agony masks in museums.

''Keep still,'' said Scully icily.

Then there was a sudden loud grunt, incomplete, cut short, and Johnnie's body swung away from the Swede and fell with sickening heaviness to the grass. The cowboy was barely in time to prevent the mad Swede from flinging himself upon his prone adversary. ''No, you don't,'' said the cowboy, interposing an arm. ''Wait a second.''

Scully was at his son's side. ''Johnnie! Johnnie, me boy!'' His voice had a quality of melancholy tenderness. ''Johnnie! Can you go on with it?'' He looked anxiously down into the bloody, pulpy face of his son.

There was a moment of silence, and then Johnnie answered in his ordinary voice. ''Yes, I—it—yes.''

Assisted by his father he struggled to his feet. ''Wait a bit now till you git your wind,'' said the old man.

A few paces away the cowboy was lecturing the Swede. ''No, you don't! Wait a second!''

The Easterner was plucking at Scully's sleeve. ''Oh,

this is enough,'' he pleaded. "This is enough! Let it go as it stands. This is enough!''

"Bill,'' said Scully, "git out of the road.'' The cowboy stepped aside. "Now.'' The combatants were actuated by a new caution as they advanced toward collision. They glared at each other, and then the Swede aimed a lightning blow that carried with it his entire weight. Johnnie was evidently half stupid from weakness, but he miraculously dodged, and his fist sent the overbalanced Swede sprawling.

The cowboy, Scully and the Easterner burst into a cheer that was like a chorus of triumphant soldiery, but before its conclusion the Swede had scuffed agilely to his feet and come in berserk abandon at his foe. There was another perplexity of flying arms, and Johnnie's body again swung away and fell, even as a bundle might fall from a roof. The Swede instantly staggered to a little wind-waved tree and leaned upon it, breathing like an engine, while his savage and flame-lit eyes roamed from face to face as the men bent over Johnnie. There was a splendor of isolation in his situation at this time which the Easterner felt once when, lifting his eyes from the man on the ground, he beheld that mysterious and lonely figure, waiting.

"Are you any good yet, Johnnie?'' asked Scully in a broken voice.

The son gasped and opened his eyes languidly. After a moment he answered, "No—I ain't—any good—any—more.'' Then from shame and bodily ill, he began to weep, the tears furrowing down through the blood stains on his face. "He was too—too—heavy for me.''

Scully straightened and addressed the waiting figure. "Stranger,'' he said, evenly, "it's all up with our side.''

Then his voice changed into that vibrant huskiness which is commonly the tone of the most simple and deadly announcements. "Johnnie is whipped."

Without replying, the victor moved off on the route to the front door of the hotel.

The cowboy was formulating new and unspellable blasphemies. The Easterner was startled to find that they were out in a wind that seemed to come direct from the shadowed arctic floes. He heard again the wail of the snow as it was flung to its grave in the south. He knew now that all this time the cold had been sinking into him deeper and deeper, and he wondered that he had not perished. He felt indifferent to the condition of the vanquished man.

"Johnnie, can you walk?" asked Scully.

"Did I hurt—hurt him any?" asked the son.

"Can you walk, boy? Can you walk?"

Johnnie's voice was suddenly strong. There was a robust impatience in it. "I asked you whether I hurt him any!"

"Yes, yes, Johnnie," answered the cowboy, consolingly, "he's hurt a good deal."

They raised him from the ground, and as soon as he was on his feet, he went tottering off, rebuffing all attempts at assistance. When the party rounded the corner, they were fairly blinded by the pelting of the snow. It burned their faces like fire. The cowboy carried Johnnie through the drift to the door. As they entered, some cards rose from the floor and beat against the wall.

The Easterner rushed to the stove. He was so profoundly chilled that he almost dared to embrace the glowing iron. The Swede was not in the room. Johnnie sank into a chair and, folding his arms on his knees, buried his face in them. Scully, warming one foot and then the other at the rim of the stove, muttered to himself with Celtic mournfulness. The cowboy had removed his fur cap, and with a dazed and rueful air he was running one hand through his tousled locks. From overhead they could hear the creaking of boards as the Swede tramped here and there in his room.

The sad quiet was broken by the sudden flinging open of a door that led toward the kitchen. It was instantly followed by an onrush of women. They precipitated themselves upon Johnnie amid a chorus of lamentation. Before they carried their prey off to the kitchen, there to be bathed and harangued with that mixture of sympathy and abuse which is a feat of their sex, the mother straightened herself and fixed old Scully with an eye of stern reproach. "Shame be upon you, Patrick Scully!" she cried. "Your own son, too. Shame be upon you!"

"There, now! Be quiet, now!" said the old man weakly to this slogan, sniffed disdainfully in the direction of those trembling accomplices, the cowboy and the Easterner. Presently they bore Johnnie away, and left the three men to dismal reflection.

7

"I'd like to fight this here Dutchman myself," said the cowboy, breaking a long silence.

Scully wagged his head sadly. "No, that wouldn't do. It wouldn't be right. It wouldn't be right."

"Well, why wouldn't it?" argued the cowboy. "I don't see no harm in it."

"No," answered Scully, with mournful heroism. "It

wouldn't be right. It was Johnnie's fight, and now we mustn't whip the man just because he whipped Johnnie.''

''Yes, that's true enough,'' said the cowboy, ''but— he better not get fresh with me, because I couldn't stand no more of it.''

''You'll not say a word to him,'' commanded Scully, and even then they heard the tread of the Swede on the stairs. His entrance was made theatric. He swept the door back with a bang and swaggered to the middle of the room. No one looked at him. ''Well,'' he cried, insolently, at Scully,''I s'pose you'll tell me now how much I owe you?''

The old man remained stolid. ''You don't owe me nothin'.''

''Huh!'' said the Swede, ''huh! Don't owe 'im nothin'.''

The cowboy addressed the Swede. ''Stranger, I don't see how you come to be so gay around here.''

Old Scully was instantly alert. ''Stop!'' he shouted, holding his hand forth, fingers upward. ''Bill, you shut up!''

The cowboy spat carelessly into the sawdust box. ''I didn't say a word, did I?'' he asked.

''Mr. Scully,'' called the Swede, ''how much do I owe you?'' It was seen that he was attired for departure, and that he had his valise in his hand.

''You don't owe me nothin','' repeated Scully in the same imperturbable way.

''Huh!'' said the Swede. ''I guess you're right. I guess if it was any way at all, you'd owe me somethin'. That's what I guess.'' He turned to the cowboy. '' 'Kill him! Kill him! Kill him!' '' he mimicked, and then guffawed victoriously. " 'Kill him!' " He was convulsed with ironical humor.

But he might have been jeering the dead. The three men were immovable and silent, staring with glassy eyes at the stove.

The Swede opened the door and passed into the storm, giving one derisive glance backward at the still group.

As soon as the door was closed, Scully and the cowboy leaped to their feet and began to curse. They trampled to and fro, waving their arms and smashing into the air with their fists. "Oh, but that was a hard minute!" wailed Scully. "That was a hard minute! Him there leerin' and scoffin'! One bang at his nose was worth forty dollars to me that minute! How did you stand it, Bill?"

"How did I stand it?" cried the cowboy in a quivering voice. "How did I stand it? Oh!"

The old man burst into sudden brogue. "I'd loike to take that Swade," he wailed, "and hould 'im down on a shtone flure and bate 'im to a jelly wid a shtick!"

The cowboy groaned in sympathy. "I'd like to git him by the neck and ha-ammer him"—he brought his hand down on a chair with a noise like a pistol shot—"hammer that there Dutchman until he couldn't tell himself from a dead coyote!"

"I'd bate 'im until he—"

"I'd show *him* some things—"

And then together they raised a yearning, fantastic cry—"Oh-o-oh! if we only could—"

"Yes!"

"Yes!"

"And then I'd—"

"O-o-oh!"

8

The Swede, tightly gripping his valise, tacked across the face of the storm as if he carried sails. He was following a line of little naked, grasping trees which, he knew, must mark the way of the road. His face, fresh from the pounding of Johnnie's fists, felt more pleasure than pain in the wind and the driving snow. A number of square shapes loomed upon him finally, and he knew them as the houses of the main body of the town. He found a street and made travel along it, leaning heavily upon the wind whenever, at a corner, a terrific blast caught him.

He might have been in a deserted village. We picture the world as thick with conquering and elate humanity, but here, with the bugles of the tempest pealing, it was hard to imagine a peopled earth. One viewed the existence of man then as a marvel, and conceded a glamour of wonder to these lice which were caused to cling to a whirling, fire-smitten, ice-locked, disease-stricken, space-lost bulb. The conceit of man was explained by this storm to be the very engine of life. One was a coxcomb not to die in it. However, the Swede found a saloon.

In front of it an indomitable red light was burning, and the snowflakes were made blood color as they flew through the circumscribed territory of the lamp's shining. The Swede pushed open the door of the saloon and entered. A sanded expanse was before him, and at the end of it four men sat about a table drinking. Down one side of the room extended a radiant bar, and its guardian was leaning upon his elbows listening to the talk of the men at the table. The Swede dropped his valise upon the floor and, smiling fraternally upon the barkeeper, said, "Gimme some whisky, will you?" The man placed a bottle, a whisky glass, and a glass of ice-thick water upon the bar. The Swede poured himself an abnormal portion of whisky and drank it in three gulps. "Pretty bad night," remarked the bartender indifferently. He was making the pretension of blindness which is usually a distinction of his class; but it could have been seen that he was furtively studying the half-erased bloodstains on the face of the Swede. "Bad night," he said again.

"Oh, it's good enough for me," replied the Swede hardily as he poured himself some more whisky. The barkeeper took his coin and maneuvered it through its reception by a highly nickeled cash-machine. A bell rang; a card labeled "20 cts." had appeared.

"No," continued the Swede, "this isn't too bad weather. It's good enough for me."

"So?" murmured the barkeeper languidly.

The copious drams made the Swede's eyes swim, and he breathed a trifle heavier. "Yes, I like this weather. I like it. It suits me." It was apparently his design to impart a deep significance to these words.

"So?" murmured the bartender again. He turned to gaze dreamily at the scroll-like birds and birdlike scrolls which had been drawn with soap upon the mirrors in back of the bar.

"Well, I guess I'll take another drink," said the Swede presently. "Have something?"

"No, thanks; I'm not drinkin'," answered the bartender. Afterward he asked, "How did you hurt your face?"

The Swede immediately began to boast loudly.

"Why, in a fight. I thumped the soul out of a man down here at Scully's hotel."

The interest of the four men at the table was at last aroused.

"Who was it?" said one.

"Johnnie Scully," blustered the Swede. "Son of the man what runs it. He will be pretty near dead for some weeks, I can tell you. I made a nice thing of him, I did. He couldn't get up. They carried him in the house. Have a drink?"

Instantly the men in some subtle way encased themselves in reserve. "No, thanks," said one. The group was of curious formation. Two were prominent local business men; one was the district attorney; and one was a professional gambler of the kind known as "square." But a scrutiny of the group would not have enabled an observer to pick the gambler from the men of more reputable pursuits. He was, in fact, a man so delicate in manner when among people of fair class, and so judicious in his choice of victims, that in the strictly masculine part of the town's life he had come to be explicitly trusted and admired. People called him a thoroughbred. The fear and contempt with which his craft was regarded were undoubtedly the reason why his quiet dignity shone conspicuous above the quiet dignity of men who might be merely hatters, billiard markers or grocery clerks. Beyond an occasionally unwary traveler who came by rail, this gambler was supposed to prey solely upon reckless and senile farmers, who, when flush with good crops, drove into town in all the pride and confidence of an absolutely invulnerable stupidity. Hearing at times in circuitous fashion of the despoilment of such a farmer, the important men of Romper invariably laughed in contempt of the victim, and if they thought of the wolf at all, it was with a kind of pride at the knowledge that he would never dare think of attacking their wisdom and courage. Besides, it was popular that this gambler had a real wife and two real children in a neat cottage in a suburb, where he led an exemplary home life; and when any one even suggested a discrepancy in his character, the crowd immediately vociferated descriptions of this virtuous family circle. Then men who led exemplary home lives, and men who did not lead exemplary home lives, all subsided in a bunch, remarking that there was nothing more to be said.

However, when a restriction was placed upon him—as, for instance, when a strong clique of members of the new Polywog Club refused to permit him, even as a spectator, to appear in the rooms of the organization—the candor and gentleness with which he accepted the judgment disarmed many of his foes and made his friends more desperately partisan. He invariably distinguished between himself and a respectable Romper man so quickly and frankly that his manner actually appeared to be a continual broadcast compliment.

And one must not forget to declare the fundamental fact of his entire position in Romper. It is irrefutable that in all affairs outside his business, in all matters that occur eternally and commonly between man and man, this thieving cardplayer was so generous, so just, so moral, that in a contest he could have put to flight the consciences of nine-tenths of the citizens of Romper.

And so it happened that he was seated in this saloon with the two prominent local merchants and the district attorney.

The Swede continued to drink raw whisky, meanwhile

babbling at the barkeeper and trying to induce him to indulge in potations. "Come on. Have a drink. Come on. What—no? Well, have a little one, then. By gawd, I've whipped a man tonight, and I want to celebrate. I whipped him good, too. Gentlemen," the Swede cried to the men at the table. "Have a drink?"

"Ssh!" said the barkeeper.

The group at the table, although furtively attentive, had been pretending to be deep in talk, but now a man lifted his eyes toward the Swede and said shortly, "Thanks. We don't want any more."

At this reply the Swede ruffled out his chest like a rooster. "Well," he exploded, "it seems I can't get anybody to drink with me in this town. Seems so, don't it? Well!"

"Ssh!" said the barkeeper.

"Say," snarled the Swede, "don't you try to shut me up. I won't have it. I'm a gentleman, and I want people to drink with me. And I want 'em to drink with me now. *Now*—do you understand?" He rapped the bar with his knuckles.

Years of experience had calloused the bartender. He merely grew sulky. "I hear you," he answered.

"Well," cried the Swede, "listen hard then. See those men over there? Well, they're going to drink with me, and don't you forget it. Now you watch."

"Hi!" yelled the barkeeper, "this won't do!"

"Why won't it?" demanded the Swede. He stalked over to the table, and by chance laid his hand upon the shoulder of the gambler. "How about this?" he asked wrathfully. "I asked you to drink with me."

The gambler simply twisted his head and spoke over his shoulder. "My friend, I don't know you."

"Oh, hell!" answered the Swede, "come and have a drink."

"Now, my boy," advised the gambler kindly, "take your hand off my shoulder and go 'way and mind your own business." He was a little, slim man, and it seemed strange to hear him use this tone of heroic patronage to the burly Swede. The other men at the table said nothing.

"What! You won't drink with me, you little dude? I'll make you, then! I'll make you!" The Swede had grasped the gambler frenziedly at the throat, and was dragging him from his chair. The other men sprang up. The barkeeper dashed around the corner of his bar. There was a great tumult, and then was seen a long blade in the hand of the gambler. It shot forward, and a human body, this citadel of virtue, wisdom, power, was pierced as easily as if it had been a melon. The Swede fell with a cry of supreme astonishment.

The prominent merchants and the district attorney must have at once tumbled out of the place backward. The bartender found himself hanging limply to the arm of a chair and gazing into the eyes of a murderer.

"Henry," said the latter as he wiped his knife on one of the towels that hung beneath the bar rail, "you tell 'em where to find me. I'll be home, waiting for 'em." Then he vanished. A moment afterward the barkeeper was in the street, dinning through the storm for help and, moreover, companionship.

The corpse of the Swede, alone in the saloon, had its eyes fixed upon a dreadful legend that dwelt atop of the cash-machine: "This registers the amount of your purchase."

9

Months later the cowboy was frying pork over the stove of a little ranch near the Dakota line when there was a quick thud of hoofs outside, and presently the Easterner entered with the letters and the papers.

"Well," said the Easterner at once, "the chap that killed the Swede has got three years. Wasn't much, was it?"

"He has? Three years?" The cowboy poised his pan of pork while he ruminated upon the news. "Three years. That ain't much."

"No. It was a light sentence," replied the Easterner as he unbuckled his spurs. "Seems there was a good deal of sympathy for him in Romper."

"If the bartender had been any good," observed the cowboy thoughtfully, "he would have gone in and cracked that there Dutchman on the head with a bottle in the beginnin' of it and stopped all this here murderin'."

"Yes, a thousand things might have happened," said the Easterner tartly.

The cowboy returned his pan of pork to the fire, but his philosophy continued. "It's funny, ain't it? If he hadn't said Johnnie was cheatin', he'd be alive this minute. He was an awful fool. Game played for fun, too. Not for money. I believe he was crazy."

"I feel sorry for that gambler," said the Easterner.

"Oh, so do I," said the cowboy. "He don't deserve none of it for killin' who he did."

"The Swede might not have been killed if everything had been square."

"Might not have been killed?" exclaimed the cowboy. "Everythin' square? Why, when he said that Johnnie was cheatin' and acted like such a jackass? And then in the saloon he fairly walked up to git hurt?" With these arguments the cowboy browbeat the Easterner and reduced him to rage.

"You're a fool!" cried the Easterner, viciously. "You're a bigger jackass than the Swede by a million majority. Now let me tell you one thing. Let me tell you something. Listen! Johnnie *was* cheating!"

" 'Johnnie,' " said the cowboy, blankly. There was a minute of silence, and then he said, robustly, "Why, no. The game was only for fun."

"Fun or not," said the Easterner, "Johnnie was cheating. I saw him. I know it. I saw him. And I refused to stand up and be a man. I let the Swede fight it out alone. And you—you were simply puffing around the place and wanting to fight. And then old Scully himself! We are all in it! This poor gambler isn't even a noun. He is kind of an adverb. Every sin is the result of a collaboration. We, five of us, have collaborated in the murder of this Swede. Usually there are from a dozen to forty women really involved in every murder, but in this case it seems to be only men—you, I, Johnnie, old Scully and that fool of an unfortunate gambler came merely as a culmination, the apex of a human movement, and gets all the punishment."

The cowboy, injured and rebellious, cried out blindly into this fog of mysterious theory, "Well, I didn't do anythin', did I ?"

THE NAKED GUN

John Jakes

GEORGE BODIE SAT smoking a cigar in the parlor of Chinese Annie's house on Nebraska Street when the message came.

Bodie had his dusty boots propped on a stool and his heavy woolen coat open to reveal the single holster with the Navy Colt on his hip. He might have been thirty or forty.

His cheeks in the lamplight were shadowy with pox scars. He was ugly, but hard and capable looking. His smile had a crooked, sarcastic quality as the cigar smoke drifted past his face.

Maebelle Tait, owner of the establishment—Chinese Annie had died; her name was kept for reasons of good will—hitched up the bodice of her faded ball gown and poured a drink.

"Lu ought to be down before too long," she said. From somewhere above came a man's laugh.

"Good. I've only been in this town an hour, but I've seen everything there is worth seeing, except Lu. Things don't change much."

Maebelle sat with her drink and lit a black cheroot. "Where you been, George?"

Bodie shrugged. "Hays City, mostly." His smile widened and his hand touched his holster.

"How many is it now?" Maebelle asked with a kind of disgusted curiosity.

"Eleven." Bodie walked over and poured a hooker for himself. "One more and I got me a dozen." He glanced irritably at the ceiling. "What's she doin'? Customer?"

Maebelle shook her head. "Straightening up the second-floor parlor. We got a group of railroad men stopping over around two in the morning." Maebelle's tone lingered halfway between cynicism and satisfaction.

The front door opened and a blast of chill air from the early winter night swept across the floor. Bodie craned his neck as Tad, Maebelle's seven-year-old boy, came in, wiping his nose with his muffler. Maebelle's other child, three, sat quietly in a chair in the corner, fingering a page in an Eastern ladies' magazine, her eyes round and silently curious.

"Where you been, Tad?" Maebelle demanded.

He glanced at Bodie. "Over at Simms' livery stable. I . . . I saw Mr. Wyman there."

Bodie caught the frowning glance Maebelle directed at him. "New law in town?" he asked.

Maebelle nodded. "Lasted six months, so far. Quiet gent. He carries a shotgun."

Bodie touched the oiled Colt's hammer. "This can beat it, anytime."

Maebelle's frown deepened. "George, I don't want you to go hunting for your dozenth while you're on my property. I'm glad for you to come, but I don't want any shooting in this house. I got a reputation to protect."

Bodie poured another drink. The boy Tad drew a square of paper from his pocket and looked at his mother.

"Mr. Wyman gave me this."

He held it out to Bodie, with hesitation.

"He said for me to give it to you right away."

Bodie's brows knotted together. He unfolded the paper, and with effort read the carefully blocked letters. The words formed a delicate bond between two men who nearly did not know how to read. Bodie's mouth thinned as he digested the message:

WE DO NOT WANT A MAN LIKE YOU IN THIS TOWN. YOU HAVE TIL MIDNIGHT TO RIDE OUT. (SIGNED) DALE WYMAN, TOWN MARSHAL.

Bodie laughed and crumpled the note and threw it into the crackling fire in the grate.

"I guess the word travels," he said with a trace of pride. "Maybe I will collect my dozenth." He raised one hand. "But not on your property, Maebelle. I'll do it in the street, when this marshal comes to run me out. So's everybody can see." His hand went toward the liquor bottle.

Maebelle pushed Tad in the direction of the hall. "Go to the kitchen and get something to eat. And take sister Emma with you."

Grumbling, the boy took the tiny girl's hand and

dragged her toward the darkened, musty-smelling hallway.

The girl disengaged her hand, and stopped. Curious, she lifted Bodie's hat from where it rested on a chair.

Maebelle slapped her hand smartly. "Go along, Tad. You follow him, Emma. Honest to heaven, that child is the picking-up-est thing I ever knew. Born bank robber; I guess, if she was a boy."

"Where the hell's Lu?" Bodie wanted to know.

"Don't get your dander up, George," Maebelle said quickly. "I'll go see."

She went to the bottom of the staircase and bawled the girl's name several times. A girlish "Coming!" echoed from somewhere above. A knock sounded at the door and Maebelle opened it. She talked with the man for a moment, and then his heavy boots clomped up the stairway. As she returned to the parlor Bodie looked at the clock.

"Quarter to eleven, Maebelle. An hour and fifteen minutes before I get me number twelve." He chuckled.

Maebelle busied herself straightening a doily on the sofa, not looking at him.

Bodie helped himself to still another drink, and swallowed it hastily. "Don't worry about the whiskey," he said over his shoulder. "I'm even faster when I got an edge on."

Light footsteps sounded on the stair. Bodie turned as the girl Lu came into the room. She ran to Bodie and kissed him, throwing her arms around his neck. She was young beneath the shiny hardness of her face. Her lips were heavily painted, and her white breast above the gown smelled of dusting powder.

"Oh, George, I'm glad you got here."

"I came just to see you, honey. Two hundred miles."
His arm crept around her waist, his hand touched her
breast. He kissed her lightly.

"Well, I'm not running this for charity, you know,"
Maebelle said.

"I'll settle up," Bodie replied. "Don't worry. Right
now though . . ."

He and Lu began to walk toward the stairway.

Another knock came at the door. Maebelle went to
open it, and Bodie heard a voice say out of the frosty
dark, "Evening, Miz Tait. Lu here?"

Bodie dropped his arm.

Maebelle started to protest, but the man came on into
the lighted parlor. The cowboy was thin. His cheeks
were red from wind and liquor, and he blinked at Bodie,
with suspicion. Lu gaped at the floor, flustered.

"Hello, Lu. Did you forgit I was comin' tonight?"

"Maybe she did forget," Bodie said. "She's busy."

"Come on, Fred," Maebelle said urgently. She pulled
the cowboy's arm. "I know Bertha'd be glad to see
you."

"Bertha, hell," the cowboy complained. "I rode in
sixty miles, like I do every month, just to see Lu. It's
all set up." He stepped forward and grabbed Lu's wrist.
Bodie's fingers touched leather, like a caress.

"You're out of luck, friend," Bodie said. "I told you
Lu's busy tonight."

"Like hell," the cowboy insisted, pulling Lu. "Come
on, sweetie. I come sixty miles, and it's mighty
cold . . ."

"Get your hands off her," Bodie said.

Lu jerked away, retreated and stared, round-eyed, like a worn doll, pretty but empty.

"Don't you prod me," the cowboy said, weaving a little. His blue eyes snapped in the lamplight. "Who are you, anyway, acting so big? The governor or somebody?"

"I'm George Bodie. Didn't you hear about me tonight?"

"George Bo . . ."

The cowboy's eyes whipped frantically to the side. He licked his lips and his hand crawled down toward the hem of his jacket.

"Not in here, George, for God's sakes," Maebelle protested.

"Keep out of it," Bodie said softly. His eyes had a hard, predatory shine. "Now, mister cowboy, you got anything more to say about not bein' satisfied with Bertha?"

The cowboy looked at Lu. Bodie and Maebelle could read his face easily: fear clawed, and fought with the idea of what would happen if he backed down before Lu.

His sharp, scrawny-red Adam's apple bobbed.

His hand dropped.

Bodie's eyes glistened as the Navy cleared and roared.

The cowboy's gun slipped out of his fingers unfired. He dropped to his knees, cursed, shut his eyes, bleeding from the chest. Then he pitched forward and lay coughing. In a few seconds the coughing had stopped.

Bodie smiled easily and put the Navy away.

"One dozen," he said, like a man uttering a benediction.

"You damned fool," Maebelle raged. "Abraham!

Abraham!'' she shouted. ''Get yourself in here.''

In a moment an old arthritic black man hobbled into the room from the back of the house.

''Get that body out of here. Take the rig and dump him on the edge of town. Jump to it.''

Abraham began laboriously dragging the corpse out of the parlor by the rear door. Boots, then feminine titters, sounded on the stairs.

Maebelle held down her rage, whirled and stalked into the hall.

''It's all right, folks,'' she said, vainly trying to block the view. People craned forward on the steps. Abraham didn't move fast enough. ''Nothing's happened,'' Maebelle insisted. ''The man's just hurt a little. Just a friendly argument.''

''He's dead,'' a reedy male voice said. ''Any fool kin see that.''

Bodie stood in the doorway, his arm around Lu once more, complacently smirking at the confusion of male and female bodies at the bottom of the stairs. He heard his name whispered.

The thin voice popped up, ''I'm getting out of here, Maebelle. This is too much for my blood.'' A spindly shape darted toward the door.

''Now wait a minute, Hiram,'' Maebelle protested.

The door slammed on the breath of chill air from the street.

Maebelle walked back toward Bodie, her eyes angry. ''Now you've done it for fair. That yellow pipsqueak will spread it all over town that George Bodie just killed a man in my house.''

''Let him,'' Bodie said. He glanced back at the clock.

"In an hour I got an engagement with the marshal anyway. But that's in an hour."

Lu snuggled against him as he started up the stairs. The crowd parted respectfully. Maebelle scratched her head desperately, then spoke up in a voice that had a false boom to it:

"Come on into the parlor, folks. I'll pour a drink for those with bad nerves."

Abraham had removed the body, but she still noticed a greasy black stain on the carpet. Her eyes flew to the clock, which ticked steadily.

Bodie awoke suddenly, chilly in the dark room. His hand shot out for the Navy, but drew back when he recognized the boy Tad in the thin line of lamplight falling through the open door. He yawned and rolled over. Lu had gone, and he had dozed.

"What is it, boy?" he asked.

"Mr. Wyman's in the street, asking for you."

Bodie swung his legs off the bed, laughed, and lit the lamp. The holster hung on the bedpost, with the Colt in it.

"What time is it?" Bodie wanted to know.

"Quarter of twelve. Mr. Wyman hasn't got his shotgun. Said he wanted to talk to you about something."

Bodie frowned. "What sort of an hombre is this Mr. Wyman? Would he be hiding a gun on him?"

The boy shook his head. "He belongs to the Methodist Church. Everybody says he's real honest," the boy answered, pronouncing the last word with faint suspicion.

Bodie's eyes slitted down in the lamplight. Then he stood, scratched his belly and laughed. "I imagine it wouldn't do no harm to talk to the marshal. And let him know what's going to happen to him.''

Bodie drew on his shirt, pants, and boots. He pointed to the holster on the bedpost. ''I'll come back for that, if this marshal still wants to hold me to the midnight deadline. Thanks for telling me, boy.''

He went out of the room and down the stairs, a smile of anticipation on his face.

The house was strangely quiet. No one was in the parlor. But Bodie had a good idea that Maebelle, and others, would be watching from half a dozen darkened windows. Bodie put his hand on the doorknob, pulled, and stepped out into the biting air.

Wyman stood three feet from the hitchrack.

He had both hands raised to his face, one holding a flaring match, the other shielding it from the wind as he lit his pipe. Bodie recognized the gesture for what it was: a means of showing that the town marshal kept his word. Wyman flicked the match away and the bowl of the pipe glowed.

Bodie walked forward and leaned on the hitchrack, grinning. The cold air stung his cheeks. Across the way, at Aunt Gert's, a girl in a spangled green dress drank from a whiskey bottle behind a window.

''You Wyman?''

''That's right.''

''Well, I'm Bodie. Speak your piece.''

Bodie saw a slender man, thirty, with a high-crowned hat, fur-collared coat, and drooping mustache. His face was pale in the starlight.

''I started out to see if I could talk you into leaving town,'' Wyman said slowly. ''I figure I don't want to kill anybody in my job if I don't have to.''

"I'll say you got a nerve, Marshal," Bodie said, laughter in his words. "Ain't you scared? I got me my dozenth man tonight."

"I know."

"You still want to talk me into riding without a fight?"

Wyman shook his head. "I said that's why I came, why I started out. On the way I heard about the killing. Hiram Riggs ran through the streets yelling his head off about it. I can't let you go now. But I can ask you to come along without a fight. Otherwise you might wind up dead, Bodie."

"I doubt it, Marshal. I just purely doubt that."

Bodie scratched the growth of whiskers along the line of his jaw. He lounged easily, but he saw Wyman shift his feet as the rasp-rasp of the scratching sounded loudly in the night street.

"You know, you didn't answer my question about being scared."

"Of course I am, if that makes you feel better," Wyman said, without malice.

"Nobody ever told me that before, Marshal. Of course, most didn't have time."

"Why should I lie? I'm not a professional."

"Then why are you in the job, Marshal? I'm sort of curious."

"I don't know. People figured I'd try, I imagine." Sharply he raised his heel and knocked glimmering sparks from his pipe. "Hell, I'm not here to explain to you why I don't want to fight. I'm telling you I will, if you won't come with me."

• • • •

Bodie hesitated, tasting the moment like good liquor. "Now, Marshal, did you honestly think when you walked over here that you'd get me to give up?"

Starlight shone in Wyman's bleak eyes for a moment. "No."

"Then why don't you go on home to bed? You haven't got a chance."

In a way Bodie admired the marshal's cheek, fool though he was.

Wyman turned his head slightly, indicating the opposite side of the street. For the first time Bodie noticed a shadowy rider on one of the horses at Aunt Gert's rack.

"When I come, Bodie, I'll have my deputy. He carries a shotgun too."

Bodie scowled into the night, then stepped down off the sidewalk, trembling with anger.

"That's not a very square shake, Marshal."

"Don't talk to me about square shakes. I knew that cowboy you shot. He couldn't have matched you with a gun. And there've been others. If you're trying to tell me two against one isn't fair, all I've got to say is, if I had a big cat killing my beef, I wouldn't worry whether I had two or twenty men after him." Hardness edged Wyman's words now. "I don't worry about how I kill an animal, Bodie. If you'd given that cowboy a chance, maybe I'd feel different. But I've got to take you one way or another. You wrecked the square shake, not me."

Bodie's fingers crawled along the hip of his jeans.

"Can't do it by yourself?" he said contemptuously.

"I won't do it by myself."

"Why not? You can't trust your own gun?"

"Maybe that's where you made your mistake, Bodie. I'd rather trust another man than a gun."

"I don't need nobody or nothing but my gun. I never have," Bodie said softly. "Where's your shotgun, Marshal?"

Wyman nodded toward the silent deputy on the horse. "He's got it."

"I'll put my gun up against you two," Bodie said with seething savagery. "You just wait."

Bodie started back for the entrance, and from the shadows before Aunt Gert's came a sharp voice calling:

"He might run out the back, Dale."

And Wyman's answer, "No, he won't . . ." was cut off by Bodie's vicious slam of the door.

Maebelle stuck her head out of the parlor as he bounded up the stairs, his teeth tight together and a thick angry knot in his belly. He had murder on his face.

He stomped into the bedroom, was halfway across, when the sight of the bedpost in the lamplight registered on his mind.

His holster—and the Navy—were gone.

Bodie crashed back against the wall, a strangled cry choking up out of his throat, his eyes frantically searching the room.

He lunged forward and ripped away the bedclothes. He pulled the scarred chest from the wall, threw the empty drawers on the floor, then overturned the chest with a curse and a crash. He raised the window, and the glass whined faintly.

He stood staring out for a moment at the collection of star-washed shanties stretching down the hill behind the house. Then he sat down on the edge of the bed, laced his fingers together. His shoulders began to tremble.

He let out a string of obscenities like whimpers, his eyes wide. He jumped to his feet and began to tear at the mattress cover. Then he stopped again, shaking.

He felt Wyman laughing at him, and he heard Wyman's words once more. Black unreason boiled up through him, making him tremble all the harder. With an animal growl he ran out of the room, stopped in the hall, and looked frantically up and down.

He kicked in the door across the room. The girl shrieked softly, her hand darting for the coverlet.

"What the hell, amigo..." began the man, half-timidly.

Like an animal in a trap, Bodie scanned the room, turned and went racing down the staircase. He breathed hard. His chest hurt. He felt a sick cold in his stomach like he'd never known before. Hearing his heavy tread, Maebelle came out of the parlor. Before she could speak, he threw her against the wall and held her. Words caught in her throat when she saw his face.

"Where is it?" he yelled. "Where's my Navy?" His voice went keening up on a shrill note. "Tell me where it is, Maebelle, or I'll kill you!"

"George, George... Lord, I don't know," she protested, frightened, writhing under his hands.

He hit her, slamming her head against the wall, turning her face toward the top of the stairs. She choked. The fingers of one hand twitched feebly against the wall, the nails pecking a signal on the wallpaper.

"Emma...," she said.

She sagged as he released her. He cleared the stairs in threes to where the round-eyed, curious little girl stood at the landing in her nightdress, shuffling slowly forward as if to find the commotion, and holding the

Navy in one hand, upside-down, by the grip, while her other finger ran along the barrel, feeling the metal. Bodie tore it away from her and struck her across the face with the barrel.

Then he turned, lunging down the stairs again, muttering and cursing and smiling, past Maebelle. She watched him with a look of madness creeping across her face.

At the top of the staircase, the girl Emma, as if accustomed to such treatment, picked herself up and started down, dragging the leather holster she had picked up near the baseboard. She came down a step at a time, the welt on her cheek angry red but her eyes still childish and round . . .

Bodie peered through the curtains.

He could see Wyman and his deputy in the center of the street, waiting, their shotguns shiny in the starlight. He had never wanted to kill any men so badly before.

He snatched the door open, slipped through, and flattened his back against the wall, the Navy rising with its old, smooth feel, and a hot red laugh on his lips as he squeezed.

Wyman stepped forward, feet planted wide, and the shotgun flowered red in the night.

Then the deputy fired. Bodie felt a murderous weight against his chest.

The Navy clattered on the plank sidewalk, unfired.

Bodie fell across the hitchrack, his stomach warm and bleeding, the shape of Wyman coming toward him but growing dimmer each second. Bodie felt for the Navy as he slipped to a prone position, and one short shriek of betrayal came tearing off his lips.

Wyman pushed back his hat and cradled the shotgun in the crook of his arm.

Across the street window blinds flew up, and then the windows themselves, clattering.

Maebelle stuck her head out the front door.

Lu came down the stairs, crying and hugging a shabby dressing gown to her breasts, bumping the girl Emma.

With round, curious eyes, Emma righted herself, drawn by the sound of the shots.

She started down more rapidly, one step at a time, toward the voices there on the wintry porch, and as she hurried, first the holster slipped from her fingers and then the bright shells from the other tiny, white, curious hand. They fell, and Emma worked her way purposefully down to the next step, leaving the playthings forgotten on the garish, somewhat faded carpet.

WAR PARTY

Louis L'Amour

WE BURIED PA on a sidehill out west of camp, buried him high up so his ghost could look down the trail he'd planned to travel.

We piled the grave high with rocks because of the coyotes, and we dug the grave deep, and some of it I dug myself, and Mr. Sampson helped, and some others.

Folks in the wagon train figured ma would turn back, but they hadn't known ma so long as I had. Once she set her mind to something she wasn't about to quit.

She was a young woman and pretty, but there was strength in her. She was a lone woman with two children, but she was of no mind to turn back. She'd come through the Little Crow massacre in Minnesota and she knew what trouble was. Yet it was like her that she put it up to me.

"Bud," she said, when we were alone, "we can turn back, but we've nobody there who cares about us, and it's of you and Jeanie that I'm thinking. If we go west you will have to be the man of the house, and you'll have to work hard to make up for pa."

"We'll go west," I said. A boy those days took it for granted that he had work to do, and the men couldn't do it all. No boy ever thought of himself as only twelve or thirteen or whatever he was, being anxious to prove himself a man, and take a man's place and responsibilities.

Ryerson and his wife were going back. She was a complaining woman and he was a man who was always ailing when there was work to be done. Four or five wagons were turning back, folks with their tails betwixt their legs running for the shelter of towns where their own littleness wouldn't stand out so plain.

When a body crossed the Mississippi and left the settlements behind, something happened to him. The world seemed to bust wide open, and suddenly the horizons spread out and a man wasn't cramped any more. The pinched-up villages and the narrowness of towns, all that was gone. The horizons simply exploded and rolled back into enormous distance, with nothing around but prairie and sky.

Some folks couldn't stand it. They'd cringe into themselves and start hunting excuses to go back where they came from. This was a big country needing big men and women to live in it, and there was no place out here for the frightened or the mean.

The prairie and sky had a way of trimming folks down to size, or changing them to giants to whom nothing seemed impossible. Men who had cut a wide swath back in the States found themselves nothing out here. They were folks who were used to doing a lot of talking who suddenly found that no one was listening any more, and things that seemed mighty important back home, like family and money, they amounted to nothing alongside character and courage.

There was John Sampson from our town. He was a man used to being told to do things, used to looking up to wealth and power, but when he crossed the Mississippi he began to lift his head and look around. He squared his shoulders, put more crack to his whip and began to make his own tracks in the land.

Pa was always strong, an independent man given to reading at night from one of the four or five books we had, to speaking up on matters of principle and to straight shooting with a rifle. Pa had fought the Comanche and lived with the Sioux, but he wasn't strong enough to last more than two days with a Kiowa arrow through his lung. But he died knowing ma had stood by the rear wheel and shot the Kiowa whose arrow it was.

Right then I knew that neither Indians nor country was going to get the better of ma. Shooting that Kiowa was the first time ma had shot anything but some chicken-killing varmint—which she'd done time to time when pa was away from home.

Only ma wouldn't let Jeanie and me call it home. "We came here from Illinois," she said, "but we're going home now."

"But, ma," I protested, "I thought home was where we came from?"

"Home is where we're going now," ma said, "and we'll know it when we find it. Now that pa is gone we'll have to build that home ourselves."

She had a way of saying "home" so it sounded like a rare and wonderful place and kept Jeanie and me looking always at the horizon, just knowing it was over there, waiting for us to see it. She had given us the dream, and even Jeanie, who was only six, she had it too.

She might tell us that home was where we were going, but I knew home was where ma was, a warm and friendly place with biscuits on the table and fresh-made butter. We wouldn't have a real home until ma was there and we had a fire going. Only I'd build the fire.

Mr. Buchanan, who was captain of the wagon train, came to us with Tryon Burt, who was guide. "We'll help you," Mr. Buchanan said. "I know you'll be wanting to go back, and—"

"But we are not going back." Ma smiled at them. "And don't be afraid we'll be a burden. I know you have troubles of your own, and we will manage very well."

Mr. Buchanan looked uncomfortable, like he was trying to think of the right thing to say. "Now, see here," he protested, "we started this trip with a rule. There has to be a man with every wagon."

Ma put her hand on my shoulder. "I have my man. Bud is almost thirteen and accepts responsibility. I could ask for no better man."

Ryerson came up. He was thin, stooped in the shoulder, and whenever he looked at ma there was a greasy look to his eyes that I didn't like. He was a man who looked dirty even when he'd just washed in the creek. "You come along with me, ma'am," he said. "I'll take good care of you."

"Mr. Ryerson"—ma looked him right in the eye—"you have a wife who can use better care than she's getting, and I have my son."

"He's nothin' but a boy."

"You are turning back, are you not? My son is going on. I believe that should indicate who is more the man. It is neither size nor age that makes a man, Mr. Ryerson, but something he has inside. My son has it."

Ryerson might have said something unpleasant only Tryon Burt was standing there wishing he would, so he just looked ugly and hustled off.

"I'd like to say you could come," Mr. Buchanan said, "but the boy couldn't stand up to a man's work."

Ma smiled at him, chin up, the way she had. "I do not believe in gambling, Mr. Buchanan, but I'll wager a good Ballard rifle there isn't a man in camp who could follow a child all day, running when it runs, squatting when it squats, bending when it bends and wrestling when it wrestles and not be played out long before the child is."

"You may be right, ma'am, but a rule is a rule."

"We are in Indian country, Mr. Buchanan. If you are killed a week from now, I suppose your wife must return to the States?"

"That's different! Nobody could turn back from there!"

"Then," ma said sweetly, "it seems a rule is only a rule within certain limits, and if I recall correctly no such limit was designated in the articles of travel. Whatever limits there were, Mr. Buchanan, must have been passed sometime before the Indian attack that killed my husband."

"I can drive the wagon, and so can ma," I said. "For the past two days I've been driving, and nobody said anything until pa died."

Mr. Buchanan didn't know what to say, but a body

could see he didn't like it. Nor did he like a woman who talked up to him the way ma did.

Tryon Burt spoke up. "Let the boy drive. I've watched this youngster, and he'll do. He has better judgment than most men in the outfit, and he stands up to his work. If need be, I'll help."

Mr. Buchanan turned around and walked off with his back stiff the way it is when he's mad. Ma looked at Burt, and she said, "Thank you, Mr. Burt. That was nice of you."

Try Burt, he got all red around the gills and took off like somebody had put a burr under his saddle.

Come morning our wagon was the second one ready to take its place in line, with both horses saddled and tied behind the wagon, and me standing beside the off ox.

Any direction a man wanted to look there was nothing but grass and sky, only sometimes there'd be a buffalo wallow or a gopher hole. We made eleven miles the first day after pa was buried, sixteen the next, then nineteen, thirteen and twenty-one. At no time did the country change. On the sixth day after pa died I killed a buffalo.

It was a young bull, but a big one, and I spotted him coming up out of a draw and was off my horse and bellied down in the grass before Try Burt realized there was game in sight. That bull came up from the draw and stopped there, staring at the wagon train, which was a half-mile off. Setting a sight behind his left shoulder, I took a long breath, took in the trigger slack, then squeezed off my shot so gentle-like the gun jumped in my hands before I was ready for it.

The bull took a step back like something had surprised him, and I jacked another shell into the chamber and was sighting on him again when he went down on his knees and rolled over on his side.

"You got him, Bud!" Burt was more excited than me. "That was shootin'!"

Try got down and showed me how to skin the bull, and lent me a hand. Then we cut out a lot of fresh meat and toted it back to the wagons.

Ma was at the fire when we came up, a wisp of brown hair alongside her cheek and her face flushed from the heat of the fire, looking as pretty as a bay pony.

"Bud killed his first buffalo," Burt told her, looking at ma like he could eat her with a spoon.

"Why, Bud! That's wonderful!" Her eyes started to dance with a kind of mischief in them, and she said, "Bud, why don't you take a piece of that meat along to Mr. Buchanan and the others?"

With Burt to help, we cut the meat into eighteen pieces and distributed it around the wagons. It wasn't much, but it was the first fresh meat in a couple of weeks.

John Sampson squeezed my shoulder and said, "Seems to me you and your ma are folks to travel with. This outfit needs some hunters."

Each night I staked out that buffalo hide, and each day I worked at curing it before rolling it up to pack on the wagon. Believe you me, I was some proud of that buffalo hide. Biggest thing I'd shot until then was a cottontail rabbit back in Illinois, where we lived when I was born. Try Burt told folks about that shot. "Two hundred yards," he'd say, "right through the heart."

Only it wasn't more than a hundred and fifty yards the way I figured, and pa used to make me pace off distances, so I'd learn to judge right. But I was nobody to argue with Try Burt telling a story—besides, two hundred yards makes an awful lot better sound than one hundred and fifty.

After supper the menfolks would gather to talk plans. The season was late, and we weren't making the time we ought if we hoped to beat the snow through the passes of the Sierras. When they talked I was there because I was the man of my wagon, but nobody paid me no mind. Mr. Buchanan, he acted like he didn't see me, but John Sampson would not, and Try Burt always smiled at me.

Several spoke up for turning back, but Mr. Buchanan said he knew of an outfit that made it through later than this. One thing was sure. Our wagon wasn't turning back. Like ma said, home was somewhere ahead of us, and back in the States we'd have no money and nobody to turn to, nor any relatives, anywhere. It was the three of us.

"We're going on," I said at one of these talks. "We don't figure to turn back for anything."

Webb gave me a glance full of contempt. "You'll go where the rest of us go. You an' your ma would play hob gettin' by on your own."

Next day it rained, dawn to dark it fairly poured, and we were lucky to make six miles. Day after that, with the wagon wheels sinking into the prairie and the rain still falling, we camped just two miles from where we started in the morning.

Nobody talked much around the fires, and what was said was apt to be short and irritable. Most of these folks had put all they owned into the outfits they had, and if they turned back now they'd have nothing to live on and nothing left to make a fresh start. Except a few like Mr. Buchanan, who was well off.

"It doesn't have to be California," ma said once. "What most of us want is land, not gold."

"This here is Indian country," John Sampson said, "and a sight too open for me. I'd like a valley in the hills, with running water close by."

"There will be valleys and meadows," ma replied, stirring the stew she was making, "and tall trees near running streams, and tall grass growing in the meadows, and there will be game in the forest and on the grassy plains, and places for homes."

"And where will we find all that?" Webb's tone was slighting.

"West," ma said, "over against the mountains."

"I suppose you've been there?" Webb scoffed.

"No, Mr. Webb, I haven't been there, but I've been told of it. The land is there, and we will have some of it, my children and I, and we will stay through the winter, and in the spring we will plant our crops."

"Easy to say."

"This is Sioux country to the north," Burt said. "We'll be lucky to get through without a fight. There was a war party of thirty or thirty-five passed this way a couple of days ago."

"Sioux?"

"Uh-huh—no women or children along, and I found where some war paint rubbed off on the brush."

"Maybe," Mr. Buchanan suggested, "we'd better turn south a mite."

"It is late in the season," ma replied, "and the straightest way is the best way now."

"No use to worry," White interrupted; "those Indians

went on by. They won't likely know we're around."

"They were riding southeast," ma said, "and their home is in the north, so when they return they'll be riding northwest. There is no way they can miss our trail."

"Then we'd best turn back," White said.

"Don't look like we'd make it this year, anyway," a woman said, "the season is late."

That started the argument, and some were for turning back and some wanted to push on, and finally White said they should push on, but travel fast.

"Fast?" Webb asked disparagingly. "An Indian can ride in one day the distance we'd travel in four."

That started the wrangling again and ma continued with her cooking. Sitting there watching her, I figured I never did see anybody so graceful or quick on her feet as ma, and when we used to walk in the woods back home I never knew her to stumble or step on a fallen twig or branch.

The group broke up and returned to their own fires with nothing settled, only there at the end Mr. Buchanan looked to Burt. "Do you know the Sioux?"

"Only the Utes and Shoshonis, and I spent a winter on the Snake with the Nez Percés one time, but I've had no truck with the Sioux. Only they tell me they're bad medicine. Fightin' men from way back and they don't cotton to white folks in their country. If we run into Sioux, we're in trouble."

After Mr. Buchanan had gone Tryon Burt accepted a plate and cup from ma and settled down to eating. After a while he looked up at her and said, "Beggin' your pardon, ma'am, but it struck me you knew a sight about trackin' for an Eastern woman. You'd spotted those

Sioux your own self, an' you figured it right that they'd pick up our trail on the way back.''

She smiled at him. "It was simply an observation, Mr. Burt. I would believe anyone would notice it. I simply put it into words.''

Burt went on eating, but he was mighty thoughtful, and it didn't seem to me he was satisfied with ma's answer. Ma said finally, "It seems to be raining west of here. Isn't it likely to be snowing in the mountains?''

Burt looked up uneasily. "Not necessarily so, ma'am. It could be raining here and not snowing there, but I'd say there was a chance of snow.'' He got up and came around the fire to the coffeepot. "What are you gettin' at, ma'am?''

"Some of them are ready to turn back or change their plans. What will you do then?''

He frowned, placing his cup on the grass and starting to fill his pipe. "No idea—might head south for Santa Fe. Why do you ask?''

"Because we're going on," ma said. "We're going to the mountains, and I am hoping some of the others decide to come with us.''

"You'd go alone?'' He was amazed.

"If necessary.''

We started on at daybreak, but folks were more scary than before, and they kept looking at the great distances stretching away on either side, and muttering. There was an autumn coolness in the air, and we were still short of South Pass by several days with the memory of the Donner party being talked up around us.

There was another kind of talk in the wagons, and some of it I heard. The nightly gatherings around ma's fire had started talk, and some of it pointed to Tryon Burt, and some were saying other things.

We made seventeen miles that day, and at night Mr. Buchanan didn't come to our fire; and when White stopped by, his wife came and got him. Ma looked at her and smiled, and Mrs. White sniffed and went away beside her husband.

"Mr. Burt"—ma wasn't one to beat around a bush—"is there talk about me?"

Try Burt got red around the ears and he opened his mouth, but couldn't find the words he wanted. "Maybe—well, maybe I shouldn't eat here all the time. Only—well, ma'am, you're the best cook in camp."

Ma smiled at him. "I hope that isn't the only reason you come to see us, Mr. Burt."

He got redder than ever then and gulped his coffee and took off in a hurry.

Time to time the men had stopped by to help a little, but next morning nobody came by. We got lined out about as soon as ever, and ma said to me as we sat on the wagon seat, "Pay no attention, Bud. You've no call to take up anything if you don't notice it. There will always be folks who will talk, and the better you do in the world the more bad things they will say of you. Back there in the settlement you remember how the dogs used to run out and bark at our wagons?"

"Yes, ma."

"Did the wagons stop?"

"No, ma."

"Remember that, son. The dogs bark, but the wagons go on their way, and if you're going some place you haven't time to bother with barking dogs."

We made eighteen miles that day, and the grass was

better, but there was a rumble of distant thunder, whimpering and muttering off in the canyons, promising rain.

Webb stopped by, dropped an armful of wood beside the fire, then started off.

"Thank you, Mr. Webb," ma said, "but aren't you afraid you'll be talked about?"

He looked angry and started to reply something angry, and then he grinned and said, "I reckon I'd be flattered, Mrs. Miles."

Ma said, "No matter what is decided by the rest of them, Mr. Webb, we are going on, but there is no need to go to California for what we want."

Webb took out his pipe and tamped it. He had a dark, devil's face on him with eyebrows like you see on pictures of the devil. I was afraid of Mr. Webb.

"We want land," ma said, "and there is land around us. In the mountains ahead there will be streams and forests, there will be fish and game, logs for houses and meadows for grazing."

Mr. Buchanan had joined us. "That's fool talk," he declared. "What could anyone do in these hills? You'd be cut off from the world. Left out of it."

"A man wouldn't be so crowded as in California," John Sampson remarked. "I've seen so many go that I've been wondering what they all do there."

"For a woman," Webb replied, ignoring the others, "you've a head on you, ma'am."

"What about the Sioux?" Mr. Buchanan asked dryly.

"We'd not be encroaching on their land. They live to the north," ma said. She gestured toward the mountains. "There is land to be had just a few days further on, and that is where our wagon will stop."

A few days! Everybody looked at everybody else. Not

months, but days only. Those who stopped then would have enough of their supplies left to help them through the winter, and with what game they could kill—and time for cutting wood and even building cabins before the cold set in.

Oh, there was an argument, such argument as you've never heard, and the upshot of it was that all agreed it was fool talk and the thing to do was keep going. And there was talk I overheard about ma being no better than she should be, and why was that guide always hanging around her? And all those men? No decent woman—I hurried away.

At break of day our wagons rolled down a long valley with a small stream alongside the trail, and the Indians came over the ridge to the south of us and started our way—tall, fine-looking men with feathers in their hair.

There was barely time for a circle, but I was riding off in front with Tryon Burt, and he said, ''A man can always try to talk first, and Injuns like a palaver. You get back to the wagons.''

Only I rode along beside him, my rifle over my saddle and ready to hand. My mouth was dry and my heart was beating so's I thought Try could hear it, I was that scared. But behind us the wagons were making their circle, and every second was important.

Their chief was a big man with splendid muscles, and there was a scalp not many days old hanging from his lance. It looked like Ryerson's hair, but Ryerson's wagons should have been miles away to the east by now.

Burt tried them in Shoshoni, but it was the language of their enemies and they merely stared at him, understanding well enough, but of no mind to talk. One young buck kept staring at Burt with a taunt in his eye, daring

Burt to make a move; then suddenly the chief spoke, and they all turned their eyes toward the wagons.

There was a rider coming, and it was a woman. It was ma.

She rode right up beside us, and when she drew up she started to talk, and she was speaking their language. She was talking Sioux. We both knew what it was because those Indians sat up and paid attention. Suddenly she directed a question at the chief.

"Red Horse," he said, in English.

Ma shifted to English. "My husband was blood brother to Gall, the greatest warrior of the Sioux nation. It was my husband who found Gall dying in the brush with a bayonet wound in his chest, who took Gall to his home and treated the wound until it was well."

"Your husband was a medicine man?" Red Horse asked.

"My husband was a warrior," ma replied proudly, "but he made war only against strong men, not women or children or the wounded."

She put her hand on my shoulder. "This is my son. As my husband was blood brother to Gall, his son is by blood brotherhood the son of Gall, also."

Red Horse stared at ma for a long time, and I was getting even more scared. I could feel a drop of sweat start at my collar and crawl slowly down my spine. Red Horse looked at me. "Is this one a fit son for Gall?"

"He is a fit son. He has killed his first buffalo."

Red Horse turned his mount and spoke to the others. One of the young braves shouted angrily at him, and Red Horse replied sharply. Reluctantly, the warriors trailed off after their chief.

"Ma'am," Burt said, "you just about saved our bacon. They were just spoilin' for a fight."

"We should be moving," ma said.

Mr. Buchanan was waiting for us. "What happened out there? I tried to keep her back, but she's a difficult woman."

"She's worth any three men in the outfit," Burt replied.

That day we made eighteen miles, and by the time the wagons circled there was talk. The fact that ma had saved them was less important now than other things. It didn't seem right that a decent woman could talk Sioux or mix in the affairs of men.

Nobody came to our fire, but while picking the saddle horses I heard someone say, "Must be part Injun. Else why would they pay attention to a woman?"

"Maybe she's part Injun and leadin' us into a trap."

"Hadn't been for her," Burt said, "you'd all be dead now."

"How do you know what she said to 'em? Who savvies that lingo?"

"I never did trust that woman," Mrs. White said; "too high and mighty. Nor that husband of hers, either, comes to that. Kept to himself too much."

The air was cool after a brief shower when we started in the morning, and no Indians in sight. All day long we moved over grass made fresh by new rain, and all the ridges were pineclad now, and the growth along the streams heavier. Short of sundown I killed an antelope with a running shot, dropped him mighty neat—and looked up to see an Indian watching from a hill. At the distance I couldn't tell, but it could have been Red Horse.

Time to time I'd passed along the train, but nobody waved or said anything. Webb watched me go by, his face stolid as one of the Sioux, yet I could see there was a deal of talk going on.

"Why are they mad at us?" I asked Burt.

"Folks hate something they don't understand, or anything seems different. Your ma goes her own way, speaks her mind, and of an evening she doesn't set by and gossip."

He topped out on a rise and drew up to study the country, and me beside him. "You got to figure most of these folks come from small towns where they never knew much aside from their families, their gossip and their church. It doesn't seem right to them that a decent woman would find time to learn Sioux."

Burt studied the country. "Time was, any stranger was an enemy, and if anybody came around who wasn't one of yours, you killed him. I've seen wolves jump on a wolf that was white or different somehow—seems like folks and animals fear anything that's unusual."

We circled, and I staked out my horses and took the oxen to the herd. By the time ma had her grub-box lid down, I was fixing at a fire when here come Mr. Buchanan, Mr. and Mrs. White and some other folks, including that Webb.

"Ma'am"—Mr. Buchanan was mighty abrupt—"we figure we ought to know what you said to those Sioux. We want to know why they turned off just because you went out there."

"Does it matter?"

Mr. Buchanan's face stiffened up. "We think it does. There's some think you might be an Indian your own self."

"And if I am?" ma was amused. "Just what is it you have in mind, Mr. Buchanan?"

"We don't want no Injuns in this outfit!" Mr. White shouted.

"How does it come you can talk that language?" Mrs. White demanded. "Even Tryon Burt can't talk it."

"I figure maybe you want us to keep goin' because there's a trap up ahead!" White declared.

I never realized folks could be so mean, but there they were facing ma like they hated her, like those witch-hunters ma told me about back in Salem. It didn't seem right that ma, who they didn't like, had saved them from an Indian attack, and the fact that she talked Sioux like any Indian bothered them.

"As it happens," ma said, "I am not an Indian, although I should not be ashamed of it if I were. They have many admirable qualities. However, you need worry yourselves no longer, as we part company in the morning. I have no desire to travel further with you— *gentlemen.*"

THE KILLING AT
TRIPLE TREE

Evan Hunter

I SAW THE RIDER appear over the brow of the hill, coming at a fast gallop. He loomed black against the scrub oak lining the trail, dropped into a small gulley, and splashed across the narrow creek. I lost sight of him behind an outcropping of gray boulders, and when he appeared again it was right between the ears of the sorrel I was riding, like a target resting on the notched sight of a rifle.

The sorrel lifted her head, blocking the rider from view for a moment. She twitched her ears and snorted, and I laid my hand on her neck and said, "Easy, girl. Easy now."

The rider kept coming, dust pluming up around him. He was mounted on a roan, and the lather on the horse's flanks told me he'd been riding hard for a long time. He came closer, and then yelled, "Johnny! Hey, Johnny!"

I spurred the sorrel and galloped down the road to

meet him. He'd reined in, and he stood in his stirrups now, the sweat beading his brow and running down his nose in a thin trickle.

"Johnny! Christ, I thought I'd never find you."

The rider was Rafe Dooley, one of my deputies, a young kid of no more than nineteen. He'd been tickled to death to get the badge, and he wore it proudly, keeping it polished bright on his vest.

"What's the matter, Rafe?"

He swallowed hard and passed the back of his hand over his forehead. He shook the sweat from his hand, then ran his tongue over the dryness of his lips. It took him a long time to start speaking.

"What the hell is it, Rafe?"

"Johnny, it's . . . it's . . ." He stopped again, a pained expression on his face.

"Trouble? Is it trouble?"

He nodded wordlessly.

"What kind of trouble? For God's sake, Rafe, start . . ."

"It's May, Johnny. She . . ."

"May?" My hands tightened on on the reins. "What's wrong? What happened?"

"She's . . . she's dead, Johnny."

For a second, it didn't register. I was staring at the drop of sweat working its way down Rafe's nose, and I kept staring at it, almost as if I hadn't heard what he'd said. It began to seep in then, not with sudden shock, but a sort of slow comprehension, building inside me, the way thunderheads build over the mountains.

"What?" I asked. "What did you say, Rafe?"

"She's dead," he said, and he almost began crying. His face screwed up, and he began shaking his head from side to side. "I didn't want to tell you. I wanted them to send someone else. Johnny, I didn't want to be the one. She's dead, Johnny. She's dead."

I nodded, and then I shook my head, and then I nodded again. "What . . . what happened? How . . ."

"You'll see her, Johnny," he said. "Please, don't make me talk about it. Please, Johnny. Please."

"Where?"

"In town. Johnny, I didn't want to tell . . ."

"Come on, Rafe."

Doc Talmadge had pulled a sheet over her.

I stared at the white fabric outlining her body, and I almost knew it was her before I'd seen her face. Doc stood near the table and reached for the sheet.

"It's May, Johnny," he said. "You sure you want to see her?"

"I'm sure."

"Johnny . . ."

"Pull back the sheet, Doc."

Doc Talmadge shrugged, let out his breath, and pulled his brows together in a frown. He took the end of the sheet in careful fingers, gently pulled it back over her face.

Her hair lay beneath her head like a nest of black feathers, cushioning the softness of her face. Her eyes were closed, and her skin was like snow, white and cold. Her lips were pressed together into a narrow line, and a trickle of blood was drying at one corner of her mouth.

"I . . . I didn't wash her off," Doc said. "I wanted you to . . ."

Her shoulders were bare, and I saw the purple bruises just above the hollow of her throat. I took the sheet from

Doc's hands and pulled it all the way down. She was wearing a skirt, but it had been torn to tatters. She was barefoot, and there were scratches on the long curve of her legs. She wore no blouse. The bruises above her waist were ugly against the swell of her breasts.

I pulled the sheet over her and turned away.

"Where'd they find her?" I asked.

"The woods. Just outside of town. She had a basket with her, Johnny, and some flowers in it. I guess she was just . . ." He took another deep breath, "picking flowers."

"Who did it?" He turned to me.

"I don't know, Johnny."

"A posse out?"

"We were waiting for you. We figured . . ."

"Waiting? Why? Why in Christ's name were you waiting?"

Doc seemed to pull his neck into his collar. "She . . . she's your wife, Johnny. We thought . . ."

"Thought, hell! The sonovabitch who did this is roaming around loose, and you all sat around on your fat duffs! What the hell kind of thinking is that?"

"Johnny . . ."

"Johnny, Johnny, Johnny! Shut up! Shut up and get out in the street and get some riders for me. Get some riders for me, Doc. Get some riders . . ." I bunched my fists into balls, and I turned my face away from Doc because it had hit me all of a sudden and I didn't want him to see his town marshal behaving like a baby. "Get me some riders," I said, and then I choked and didn't say anything else.

"Sure, Johnny. Sure."

•   •   •

They showed me the spot where May had been attacked.

A few scattered flowers were strewn over the ground. Some of the flowers were stamped into the dirt, where the attacker's boots had trod on them. May's blouse was on the ground, too, the buttons gone from it, and some of the material torn when the blouse had been ripped.

We followed her tracks to where the attacker must have first spotted her. There was a patch of daisies on a green hillock near the edge of the woods. The trail ran past the hillock, and any rider on the trail would have had no difficulty in spotting a girl picking flowers there. Beyond the hillock, we found the rider's sign. The sign was easy to read, with the horse's right hind leg carrying a cracked shoe. We saw the spot some fifty feet from the hillock, where the rider had reined in and sat his saddle for a while, it seemed. The dead ashes of a cigarette lay in the dust of the trail, and it was easy to get the picture. The rider had come around the bend, seen May on the hillock, and pulled in his horse. He had watched her while he smoked a cigarette, and then started for the hillock. The tracks led around the daisy patch, with clods of earth and grass pulled out of the hill where the horse had started to climb. May must have broken away at about that time and started into the woods, with the rider after her. We found both her shoes a little ways from the hillock, and the rider's tracks following across the floor of the forest. He'd jumped from his horse, it looked like, and grabbed her then, taking what he wanted, and then strangling her to death.

We followed the tracks to the edge of the forest, the sign of the cracked hind shoe standing out like an elephant's print. When they reached the trail again, they blended with a hundred other hoofprints to form a dusty, tangled puzzle.

I looked at the muddled trail.

"It don't look good, Johnny," Rafe said.

"No."

"What are we going to do?"

"Split up. You come with me, Rafe. We'll head away from town. The rest of you head back to town and on through toward Rock Falls. Stop anyone you meet on the trail. If you find a rider on a horse with a cracked shoe, bring him in."

"Bring him in, Johnny?" one of the possemen asked.

"You heard me."

"Sure. I just thought . . ."

"Bring him in. Let's go, Rafe."

We turned our mounts and started riding away from the woods, and away from the scene of May's attack. There was an emptiness inside me, and a loneliness, as if someone had deliberately drained all feeling from me, as if someone had taken away my life and left only my body. We rode in silence because there was nothing to say. Rafe looked at me from time to time, uneasy in my company, the way a man would be in a funeral parlor when the corpse was someone he knew.

We'd been riding for an hour when Rafe said, "Up ahead, Johnny."

We reined in, and I looked at the cloud of dust in the distance.

"A rider."

"Going like hell afire," Rafe said.

"I'll take him, Rafe," I said softly. "Get back to town."

"Huh?"

"Get back to town. I'll bring him in."

"But, Johnny, I thought you wanted my . . ."

"I don't want anything, Rafe. Just get the hell back to town and leave me alone. I'll take care of this."

"Sure. I'll see you, Johnny."

Rafe turned his mount, and I waited until he was out of sight before I started after the rider. I gave the sorrel the spurs, and I rode hard because the rider was out to break all records for speed. The distance between us closed, and when I was close enough, I fired a shot over my head. I saw the rider's head turn, but he didn't stop, so I poured on a little more, closing the gap until I was some thirty feet behind him.

"Hey!" I yelled. "Hey, you!"

The rider pulled up this time, and I brought my horse up close to his, wheeling around to get a good look at him.

"What's your hurry, mister?" I asked.

He was tall and rangy, and he sat his saddle with the practiced ease of years of experience. He wore a gray hat pulled low over his eyes, and a shock of unruly brown hair spilled from under his hat onto his forehead. A blue bandana was knotted around his throat, and his shirt and trousers were covered with dust and lather.

"What's it to you?" he asked. His voice was soft, mildly inquisitive, not in the least offensive.

"I'm the marshal of Triple Tree."

"So?"

"You been through town lately?"

"Don't even know where your town is," he said.

"No?"

"Nope. Why? Somebody rob a bank or something?"

"Something," I said. "Want to get off your mount?"

He was riding a sorrel that could have been a twin to my own horse.

"Nope, can't say that I do. Suppose you tell me what's on your mind, marshal?"

"Suppose I don't."

The rider shrugged. He wasn't a bad-looking fellow, and a half-smile lurked at the corners of his mouth and in the depths of his blue eyes. "Marshal," he said, "this here's a free country. You don't want to tell me what you're all het up about, that's fine with me. Me, I'll just mosey along and forget I ever . . ."

"Just a second, mister."

"Yes, marshal?" He moved his hands to his saddle horn, crossed them there. He wore a single Colt.44 strapped to his waist, the holster tied to his thigh with a leather thong.

"Where are you bound?"

"Nowheres in particular. Down the road a piece, I suppose. Might be able to pick up some work there. If not, I'll ride on a little more."

"What kind of work?"

"Punching. Cattle drive. Shoveling horse manure or cow dung. I ain't particular."

"How come you didn't ride through Triple Tree?"

"I crossed over the mountains yonder," he said. "Spotted the trail and headed for it. Any law against that?"

"What's your name?"

The rider smiled. "Jesse James. My brother Frank's right behind that tree there."

"Don't get funny," I told him. "I'm in no mood for jokes."

"You *are* in a pretty sour mood, ain't you, marshal?"

He wagged his head sorrowfully. "Something you et, maybe?"

"What's your name, mister?"

"Jack," he said simply, drawling the word.

"Jack what?"

"Hawkins. Jack Hawkins."

"Get off your horse, Hawkins."

"Why?"

I was through playing games. I cleared leather and rested the barrel of my gun on my saddle horn. "Because I say so. Come on, swing down."

Hawkins eyed the .44 with respect. "My, my," he said. He swung his long legs over the saddle, and looked at the gun again. "My!"

"You better drop your gun belt, Hawkins."

Hawkins's eyes widened a bit. "I'll bet a bank *was* robbed," he said. "Hell, marshal, I ain't a bank robber." He loosened his belt and dropped the holstered .44 to the road.

"Back away a bit."

"How far, marshal?"

"Listen . . ."

"I just asked . . ."

I fired two shots in quick succession, both plowing up dirt a few inches from his toe boots.

"Hey!"

"Do as I say, goddamnit!"

"Sure, sure." A frown replaced the smile on his face, and he stood watching me tight-lipped.

I walked around the side of his horse and lifted the right hind hoof. I stared at it for a few seconds, and then dropped it to the dust again.

"Where's her shoe?" I asked.

"On her hoof," Hawkins replied. "Where the hell do you suppose it would be?"

"She's carrying no shoe on that hoof, Hawkins."

He seemed honestly surprised. "No? Must have lost it. I'll be damned if everything doesn't happen to me."

"Was the shoe cracked? Is that why she lost it?"

"Hell, no. Not that I know of."

I looked at him, trying to read meaning in the depths of his eyes. I couldn't tell. I couldn't be sure. A horse could lose a shoe anytime. That didn't mean it was carrying a cracked shoe, before the shoe got lost.

"You better mount up," I said.

"Why?"

"We're taking a little ride back to Triple Tree."

"You intent on pinning that bank job on me, ain't you? Marshal, I ain't been in a bank in five years."

"How long is it since you've been in the woods?"

"What?"

"Mount up!"

Hawkins cursed under his breath and reached for his gun belt in the dust.

"I'll take care of that," I said. I hooked it with my toe and pulled it toward me, lifting it and looping it over my saddle horn.

Hawkins stared at me for a few seconds, then shook his head and swung into his saddle. "Here goes another day shot up the behind," he said. "All right, marshal, let's get this goddamned farce over with."

The town was deserted.

The afternoon sun beat down on the dusty street with fierce intensity. The street was lonely, and we rode past the blacksmith shop in silence, past the saloon, past the post office, past my office, up the street with the sound of our horses' hooves the only thing to break the silence.

"Busy little town you got here," Hawkins said.

"Shut up, Hawkins."

He shrugged. "Whatever you say, marshal."

The silence was strange and forbidding. It was like walking in on someone who'd been talking about you. It magnified the heat, made the dust swirling up around us seem more intolerable.

When the voice came, it shattered the silence into a thousand brittle shards.

"Marshal! Hey, marshal!"

I wheeled the sorrel and spotted old Jake Trilby pushing open the batwings on the saloon. He waved and I walked the horse over to him, waiting while he put his crutch under his arm and stepped out onto the boardwalk.

"Where is everyone, Jake?"

"They got him, marshal," he said. "The feller killed your wife."

"What?"

"Yep, they got him. Caught him just outside of Rock Falls. Ridin' a horse with a cracked right hind shoe. Had blood on his clothes, too. He's the one, all right, marshal. He's the one killed May, all right."

"Where? Where is he?"

"They didn't wait for you this time, marshal. They knowed you wanted action."

"Where are they?"

"Out hangin' him. If he ain't hanged already by this time." Old Jake chuckled. "They're givin' it to him, marshal. They're showin' him."

"Where, Jake?"

"The oak down by the fork. You know where. Heck, marshal, he's dancin' on air by now."

I turned the sorrel and raked my spurs over her belly. She gave a leap forward, and as we rode past Hawkins, I tossed him his gun belt. A surprised look covered his face, and then I didn't see him any more because he was behind me, and I was heading for the man who killed her.

I saw the tree first, reaching for the sky with heavy branches. A rope had been thrown over one of those branches, and it hung limply now, its ends lost in the milling crowd beneath the tree. The crowd was silent, a tight knot of men and women forming the nucleus, a loose unraveling of kids on the edges. I couldn't see the man the crowd surrounded until I got a little closer. I pushed the sorrel right into the crowd and it broke apart like a rotten apple, and then I saw the man sitting the bay under the tree, his hands tied behind him, the rope knotted around his neck.

"Here's Johnny," someone shouted, and then the cry seemed to sweep over the crowd like a small brush fire. "Here's Johnny."

"Hey, Johnny!"

"We got him, Johnny!"

"Just in time, Johnny!"

I swung off the horse and walked over to where Doc Talmadge was pulling the rope taut.

"Hello, Johnny," he said, greeting me affably. "We got the bastard, and this time we didn't wait for you. Another few minutes and you'd have missed it all."

"Put that rope down, Doc," I said.

Doc's eyes widened and then blinked. "Huh? What, Johnny?"

"What the hell do you think you're doing?"

"I was just fixin' to tie the rope around the trunk here. After that, we going to take that horse from underneath this sonova . . ."

"What's the matter, Johnny?" someone called.

"Come on, Johnny," another voice prodded. "Let's get on with this."

The sky overhead was a bright blue, and the sun gleamed in it like a fiery eye. It was a beautiful day, with a few clouds trailing wisps of cotton close to the horizon. I glanced up at the sky and then back to the man sitting the bay.

He was narrow faced, with slitted brown eyes and jaws that hadn't been razor-scraped in days. His mouth was expressionless. Only his eyes spoke, and they told of silent hatred. His clothes were dirty, and his shirt was spattered with blood.

I walked away from Doc, leaving him to knot the rope around the tree trunk. The crowd fell silent as I approached the man on the bay.

"What's your name?" I asked.

"Dodd," he said.

"This your horse?"

"Yep."

I walked around behind the horse and checked the right hind hoof. The shoe was cracked down the center. I dropped the hoof and walked back to face Dodd.

I stared at him for a few minutes, our eyes locked. Then I turned to the crowd and said, "Go on home. Go on. There'll be no hanging here today."

Rafe stepped out of the crowd and put his hands on

his hips. "You nuts, Johnny? This is the guy who killed May. He killed your wife!"

"We don't know that," I said.

"We don't know it? Jesus, you just saw the broken shoe. What the hell more do you want?"

"He's got blood all over his shirt, Johnny," Doc put in. "Hell, he's our man."

"Even if he is, he doesn't hang," I said tightly.

An excited murmur went up from the crowd and then Jason Bragg shouldered his way through and stood in front of me, one hand looped in his gun belt. He was a big man, with corn yellow hair and pale blue eyes. He was a farmer with a wife and three grown daughters. When he spoke now, it was in slow and measured tones.

"Johnny, you are not doing right."

"No, Jason?"

Jason shook his massive head, and pointed up to Dodd. "This man is a killer. We know he's a killer. You're the marshal here. It's your job to . . ."

"It's my job to do justice."

"Yes, it's your job to do justice. It's your job to see that this man is hanged!" He looked at me as if he thought I was some incredible kind of insect. "Johnny, he killed *your own wife*!"

"That doesn't mean we take the law into our own hands."

"Johnny . . ."

"It doesn't mean that this town will get blood on its hands, either. If you hang this man, you'll all be guilty of murder. You'll be just as much a killer as he is. Every last one of you! You'll be murdering in a group, but you'll still be murdering. You've got no right to do that."

"The hell we ain't!" someone shouted.

"Come on, Johnny, quit the goddamned stalling!"

"What is this, a tea party?"

"We got our man, now string him up!"

"That's the man killed your wife, Johnny."

Jason Bragg cleared his throat. "Johnny, I got a wife and three girls. You remember my daughters when they were buttons. They're young ladies now. We let this one get away with what he's done, and this town won't be safe for anyone any more. My daughters . . ."

"He won't get away with anything," I said. "But you're not going to hang him."

"He killed your wife!" someone else shouted.

"He's ridin' the horse that made the tracks."

"Shut up!" I yelled. "Shut up, all of you!"

There was an immediate silence, and then, cutting through the silence like a sharp-edged knife, a voice asked, "You backin' out, marshal?"

The heads in the crowd turned, and I looked past them to see Hawkins sitting his saddle on the fringe of the crowd.

"Keep out of this, stranger," I called. "Just ride on to wherever the hell you were going."

"Killed your wife, did he?" Hawkins said. He looked over to Dodd, and then slowly began rolling a cigarette. "No wonder you were all het up back there on the trail."

"Listen, Hawkins . . ."

"You seemed all ready to raise six kinds of hell a little while ago. What's the matter, a hangin' turn your stomach?"

The crowd began to murmur again, and Hawkins grinned.

"Hawkins," I started, but he raised his voice above mine and shouted, "Are you sure this is the man?"

"Yes!" the crowd yelled. "Yes!"

"Ain't no two ways about it. He's the one! Even got scratches on his neck where May grabbed at him."

I glanced quickly at Dodd, saw his face pale, and saw the deep fresh scratches on the side of his neck at the same time.

"Then string him up!" Hawkins shouted. "String him higher'n the sun! String him up so your wives and your daughters can walk in safety. String him up even if you've got a yellow-livered marshal who . . ."

"String him up!" the cry rose.

The crowd surged forward and Doc Talmadge brought his hand back to slap at the bay's rump. I took a step backward and pulled my .44 at the same time. Without turning my back to the crowd, I swung the gun down, chopping the barrel onto Doc's wrist. He pulled back his hand and let out a yelp.

"First man moves a step," I said, "gets a hole in his gut!"

Jason Bragg took a deep breath. "Johnny, don't try to stop us. You should be ashamed of yourself. You should . . ."

"I like you, Jason," I said. "Don't let it be you." I cocked the gun, and the click was loud in the silence.

"Johnny," Rafe said, "you don't know what you're doing. You're upset, you're . . ."

"Stay where you are, Rafe. Don't move an inch."

"You going to let him stop you?" Hawkins called.

No one answered him.

"You going to let him stop justice?" he shouted.

I waited for an answer, and when there was none, I

said, "Go home. Go back to your homes. Go back to your shops. Go on, now. Go on."

The crowd began to mumble, and then a few kids broke away and began running back to town. Slowly, the women followed, and then Jason Bragg turned his back to me and stumped away silently. Rafe looked at me sneeringly and followed the rest. Doc Talmadge was the last to go, holding his wrist against his chest.

Hawkins sat his sorrel and watched the crowd walking back to town. When he turned, there was a smile on his face.

"Thought we were going to have a little excitement," he said.

"You'd better get out of town, Hawkins. You'd better get out damned fast."

"I was just leavin', marshal." He raised his hand in a salute, wheeled his horse, and said, "So long, chum."

I watched while the horse rode up the dusty trail, parting the walkers before it. Then the horse was gone, and I kept watching until the crowd turned the bend in the road and was gone, too.

I walked over to Dodd.

He sat on the bay with his hands tied behind him, his face noncommittal.

"Did you kill her?" I asked.

He didn't answer.

"Come on," I said. "You'll go before a court anyway, and there's no one here but me to hear a confession. Did you?"

He hesitated for a moment, and then he nodded briefly.

"Why?" I asked.

He shrugged his thin shoulders.

I looked into his eyes, but there was no answer there, either.

"I appreciate what you done, marshal," he said suddenly, his lips pulling back to expose narrow teeth. "Considering everything . . . well, I just appreciate it."

"Sure," I said. "I'm paid to see that justice is done."

"Well, I appreciate it."

I stepped behind him and untied his hands, and then I loosened the noose around his neck.

"That feels good," he said, massaging his neck.

"I'll bet it does." I reached into my pocket for the makings. "Here," I said, "roll yourself a cigarette."

"Thanks. Say, thanks."

His manner grew more relaxed. He sat in the saddle and sprinkled tobacco into the paper. He knew better than to try a break, because I was still holding my .44 in my hand. He worked on the cigarette, and he asked, "Do you think . . . do you think it'll go bad for me?"

I watched him wet the paper and put the cigarette into his mouth.

"Not too bad," I said.

He nodded, and the cigarette bobbed, and he reached into his pocket for a match.

I brought the .44 up quickly and fired five fast shots, watching his face explode in soggy red chunks.

He dropped out of the saddle.

The cigarette falling to the dust beside him.

Then I mounted up and rode back to town.

The Hanging Man

Bill Pronzini

IT WAS SAM McCullough who found the hanging man, down on the river bank behind his livery stable.

Straightaway he went looking for Ed Bozeman and me, being as we were the local sheriff's deputies. Tule River didn't have any fulltime law officers; just volunteers like Boze and me to keep the peace, and a fat-bottomed sheriff who came through from the county seat two or three days a month to look things over and to stuff himself on pig's knuckles at the Germany Café.

Time was just past sunup, on one of those frosty mornings Northern California gets in late November, and Sam found Boze already to work inside his mercantile. But they had to come fetch me out of my house, where I was just sitting down to breakfast. I never did open up my place of business—Miller's Feed and Grain—until 8:30 of a weekday morning.

I had some trouble believing it when Sam first told

235

about the hanging man. He said, ''Well, how in hell do you think *I* felt.'' He always has been an excitable sort and he was frothed up for fair just then. ''I like to had a hemorrhage when I saw him hanging there on that black oak. Damnedest sight a man ever stumbled on.''

''You say he's a stranger?''

''Stranger to me. Never seen him before.''

''You make sure he's dead?''

Sam made a snorting noise. ''I ain't even going to answer that. You just come along and see for yourself.''

I got my coat, told my wife Ginny to ring up Doc Petersen on Mr. Bell's invention, and then hustled out with Sam and Boze. It was mighty cold that morning; the sky was clear and brittle-looking, like blue-painted glass, and the sun had the look of a two-day-old egg yolk above the tule marshes east of the river. When we came in alongside the stable I saw that there was silvery frost all over the grass on the river bank. You could hear it crunch when you walked on it.

The hanging man had frost on him, too. He was strung up on a fat old oak between the stable and the river, opposite a high board fence that separated Sam's property from Joel Pennywell's fixit shop next door. Dressed mostly in black, he was—black denims, black boots, a black cutaway coat that had seen better days. He had black hair, too, long and kind of matted. And a black tongue pushed out at one corner of a black-mottled face. All that black was streaked in silver, and there was silver on the rope that stretched between his neck and the thick limb above. He was the damnedest sight a man ever stumbled on, all right. Frozen up there, silver and black, glistening in the cold sunlight, like something cast up from the Pit.

We stood looking at him for a time, not saying anything. There was a thin wind off the river and I could feel it prickling up the hair on my neck. But it didn't stir that hanging man, nor any part of him or his clothing.

Boze cleared his throat, and he did it loud enough to make me jump. He asked me, "You know him, Carl?"

"No," I said. "You?"

"No. Drifter, you think?"

"Got the look of one."

Which he did. He'd been in his thirties, smallish, with a clean-shaven fox face and pointy ears. His clothes were shabby, shirt cuffs frayed, button missing off his cutaway coat. We got us a fair number of drifters in Tule River, up from San Francisco or over from the mining country after their luck and their money ran out—men looking for farm work or such other jobs as they could find. Or sometimes looking for trouble. Boze and I had caught one just two weeks before and locked him up for chicken stealing.

"What I want to know," Sam said, "is what in the name of hell he's doing *here*?"

Boze shrugged and rubbed at his bald spot, like he always does when he's fuddled. He was the same age as me, thirty-four, but he'd been losing his hair for the past ten years. He said, "Appears he's been hanging a while. When'd you close up last evening, Sam?"

"Six, like always."

"Anybody come around afterwards?"

"No."

"Could've happened any time after six, then. It's kind of a lonely spot back here after dark. I reckon there's not much chance anybody saw what happened."

"Joel Pennywell, maybe," I said. "He stays open late some nights."

"We can ask him."

Sam said, "But why'd anybody string him up like that?"

"Maybe he wasn't strung up. Maybe he hung himself."

"Suicide?"

"It's been known to happen," Boze said.

Doc Petersen showed up just then, and a couple of other townsfolk with him; word was starting to get around. Doc, who was sixty and dyspeptic, squinted up at the hanging man, grunted, and said, "Strangulation."

"Doc?"

"Strangulation. Man strangled to death. You can see that from the way his tongue's out. Neck's not broken; you can see that too."

"Does that mean he could've killed himself?"

"All it means," Doc said, "is that he didn't jump off a high branch or get jerked hard enough off a horse to break his neck."

"Wasn't a horse involved anyway," I said. "There'd be shoe marks in the area; ground was soft enough last night, before the freeze. Boot marks here and there, but that's all."

"I don't know anything about that," Doc said. "All I know is, that gent up there died of strangulation. You want me to tell you anything else, you'll have to cut him down first."

Sam and Boze went to the stable to fetch a ladder. While they were gone I paced around some, to see if there was anything to find in the vicinity. And I did find something, about a dozen feet from the oak where the boot tracks were heaviest in the grass. It was a circlet of bronze, about three inches in diameter, and when I picked it up, I saw that it was one of those presidential medals the government used to issue at the Philadelphia Mint. On one side it had a likeness of Benjamin Harrison, along with his name and the date of his inauguration, 1889, and on the other were a tomahawk, a peace pipe and a pair of clasped hands.

There weren't many such medals in California; mostly they'd been supplied to army officers in other parts of the West, who handed them out to Indians after peace treaties were signed. But this one struck a chord in my memory: I recollected having seen it or one like it some months back. The only thing was, I couldn't quite remember where.

Before I could think any more on it, Boze and Sam came back with the ladder, a plank board and a horse blanket. Neither of them seemed inclined to do the job at hand, so I climbed up myself and sawed through that half-frozen rope with my pocket knife. It wasn't good work; my mouth was dry when it was done. When we had him down we covered him up and laid him on the plank. Then we carried him out to Doc's wagon and took him to the Spencer Funeral Home.

After Doc and Obe Spencer stripped the body, Boze and I went through the dead man's clothing. There was no identification of any kind; if he'd been carrying any before he died, somebody had filched it. No wallet or purse, either. All he had in his pockets was the stub of a lead pencil, a half-used book of matches, a short-six seegar, a nearly empty Bull Durham sack, three wheat-straw papers, a two-bit piece, an old Spanish *real* coin and a dog-eared and stained copy of a Beadle dime novel called *Captain Dick Talbot, King of the Road; Or, The Black-Hoods of Shasta*.

"Drifter, all right," Boze said when we were done. "Wouldn't you say, Carl?"

"Sure seems that way."

"But even drifters have more belongings than this. Shaving gear, extra clothes—at least that much."

"You'd think so," I said. "Might be he had a carpetbag or the like and it's hidden somewhere along the river bank."

"Either that or it was stolen. But we can go take a look when Doc gets through studying on the body."

I fished out the bronze medal I'd found in the grass earlier and showed it to him. "Picked this up while you and Sam were getting the ladder," I said.

"Belonged to the hanging man, maybe."

"Maybe. But it seems familiar, somehow. I can't quite place where I've seen one like it."

Boze turned the medal over in his hand. "Doesn't ring any bells for me," he said.

"Well, you don't see many around here, and the one I recollect was also a Benjamin Harrison. Could be coincidence, I suppose. Must be if that fella died by his own hand."

"If he did."

"Boze, you think it *was* suicide?"

"I'm hoping it was," he said, but he didn't sound any more convinced than I was. "I don't like the thought of a murderer running around loose in Tule River."

"That makes two of us," I said.

Doc didn't have much to tell us when he came out. The hanging man had been shot once a long time ago— he had bullet scars on his right shoulder and back—and one foot was missing a pair of toes. There was also a fresh bruise on the left side of his head, above the ear.

Boze asked, "Is it a big bruise, Doc?"

"Big enough."

"Could somebody have hit him hard enough to knock him out?"

"And then hung him afterward? Well, it could've happened that way. His neck's full of rope burns and lacerations, the way it would be if somebody hauled him up over that tree limb."

"Can you reckon how long he's been dead?"

"Last night some time. Best I can do."

Boze and I headed back to the livery stable. The town had come awake by this time. There were plenty of people on the boardwalks and Main Street was crowded with horses and farm wagons; any day now I expected to see somebody with one of those newfangled motor cars. The hanging man was getting plenty of lip service, on Main Street and among the crowd that had gathered back of the stable to gawk at the black oak and trample the grass.

Nothing much goes on in a small town like Tule River, and such as a hanging was bound to stir up folks' imaginations. There hadn't been a killing in the area in four or five years. And damned little mystery since the town was founded back in the days when General Vallejo owned most of the land hereabouts and it was the Mexican flag, not the Stars and Stripes, that flew over California.

None of the crowd had found anything in the way of evidence on the river bank; they would have told us if they had. None of them knew anything about the hanging man, either. That included Joel Pennywell, who had come over from his fixit shop next door. He'd closed up around 6:30 last night, he said, and gone straight on home.

After a time Boze and I moved down to the river's edge and commenced a search among the tule grass and trees that grew along there. The day had warmed some; the wind was down and the sun had melted off the last of the frost. A few of the others joined in with us, eager and boisterous, like it was an Easter egg hunt. It was too soon for the full impact of what had happened to settle in on most folks; it hadn't occurred to them yet that maybe they ought to be concerned.

A few minutes before ten o'clock, while we were combing the west-side bank up near the Main Street Basin, and still not finding anything, the Whipple youngster came running to tell us that Roberto Ortega and Sam McCullough wanted to see us at the livery stable. Roberto owned a dairy ranch just south of town and claimed to be a descendant of a Spanish conquistador. He was also an honest man, which was why he was in town that morning. He'd found a saddled horse grazing on his pastureland and figured it for a runaway from Sam's livery, so he'd brought it in. But Sam had never seen the animal, an old swaybacked roan, until Roberto showed up with it. Nor had he ever seen the battered carpetbag that was tied behind the cantle of the cheap Mexican saddle.

It figured to be the drifter's horse and carpetbag, sure enough. But whether the drifter had turned the animal loose himself, or somebody else had, we had no way of knowing. As for the carpetbag, it didn't tell us any more about the hanging man than the contents of his pockets. Inside it were some extra clothes, an old Colt Dragoon revolver, shaving tackle, a woman's garter, and nothing at all that might identify the owner.

Sam took the horse, and Boze and I took the carpetbag over to Obe Spencer's to put with the rest of the hanging man's belongings. On the way we held a conference. Fact was, a pair of grain barges were due upriver from San Francisco at eleven, for loading and return. I had three men working for me, but none of them handled the paperwork; I was going to have to spend some time at the feed mill that day, whether I wanted to or not. Which is how it is when you have part-time deputies who are also full-time businessmen. It was a fact of small-town life we'd had to learn to live with.

We worked it out so that Boze would continue making inquiries while I went to work at the mill. Then we'd switch off at one o'clock so he could give his wife Ellie, who was minding the mercantile, some help with customers and with the drummers who always flocked around with Christmas wares right after Thanksgiving.

We also decided that if neither of us turned up any new information by five o'clock—or even if we did— we would ring up the county seat and make a full report to the sheriff. Not that Joe Perkins would be able to find out anything we couldn't. He was a fat-cat political appointee, and about all he knew how to find was pig's knuckles and beer. But we were bound to do it by the oath of office we'd taken.

We split up at the funeral parlor and I went straight to the mill. My foreman, Gene Kleinschmidt, had opened up; I'd given him a set of keys and he knew to go ahead and unlock the place if I wasn't around. The barges came in twenty minutes after I did, and I had to hustle to get the paperwork ready that they would be carrying back down to San Francisco—bills of lading, requisitions for goods from three different companies.

I finished up a little past noon and went out onto the dock to watch the loading. One of the bargemen was talking to Gene. And while he was doing it, he kept flipping something up and down in his hand—a small gold nugget. It was the kind of thing folks made into a watch fob, or kept as a good-luck charm.

And that was how I remembered where I'd seen the Benjamin Harrison presidential medal. Eight months or so back a newcomer to the area, a man named Jubal Parsons, had come in to buy some sacks of chicken feed. When he'd reached into his pocket to pay the bill he had accidentally come out with the medal. "Good-luck charm," he'd said, and let me glance at it before putting it away again.

Back inside my office I sat down and thought about Jubal Parsons. He was a tenant farmer—had taken over a small farm owned by the Siler brothers out near Willow Creek about nine months ago. Big fellow, over six feet tall, and upwards of two hundred twenty pounds. Married to a blonde woman named Greta, a few years younger than him and pretty as they come. Too pretty, some said; a few of the womenfolk, Ellie Bozeman included, thought she had the look and mannerisms of a tramp.

Parsons came into Tule River two or three times a month to trade for supplies, but you seldom saw the wife. Neither of them went to church on Sunday, nor to any of the social events at the Odd Fellows Hall. Parsons kept to himself mostly, didn't seem to have any friends or any particular vices. Always civil, at least to me, but taciturn and kind of broody-looking. Not the sort of fellow you find yourself liking much.

But did the medal I'd found belong to him? And if it did, had he hung the drifter? And if he had, what was his motive?

I was still puzzling on that when Boze showed up. He was a half-hour early, and he had Floyd Jones with him. Floyd looked some like Santa Claus—fat and jolly and white-haired—and he liked it when you told him so. He was the night bartender at the Elkhorn Bar and Grill.

Boze said, "Got some news, Carl. Floyd here saw the hanging man last night. Recognized the body over to Obe Spencer's just now."

Floyd bobbed his head up and down. "He came into the Elkhorn about eight o'clock, asking for work."

I said, "How long did he stay?"

"Half-hour, maybe. Told him we already had a swamper and he spent five minutes trying to convince me he'd do a better job of cleaning up. Then he gave it up when he come to see I wasn't listening, and bought a beer and nursed it over by the stove. Seemed he didn't much relish going back into the cold."

"He say anything else to you?"

"Not that I can recall."

"Didn't give his name, either," Boze said. "But there's something else. Tell him, Floyd."

"Well, there was another fella came in just after the drifter," Floyd said. "Ordered a beer and sat watching him. Never took his eyes off that drifter once. I wouldn't have noticed except for that and because we were near empty. Cold kept most everybody to home last night."

"You know this second man?" I asked.

"Sure do. Local farmer. Newcomer to the area, only been around for—"

"Jubal Parsons?"

Floyd blinked at me. "Now how in thunder did you know that?"

"Lucky guess. Parsons leave right after the drifter?"

"He did. Not more than ten seconds afterward."

"You see which direction they went?"

"Downstreet, I think. Toward Sam McCullough's livery."

I thanked Floyd for his help and shooed him on his way. When he was gone Boze asked me, "Just how did you know it was Jubal Parsons?"

"I finally remembered where I'd seen that presidential medal I found. Parsons showed it when he was here one day several months ago. Said it was his good-luck charm."

Boze rubbed at his bald spot. "That and Floyd's testimony make a pretty good case against him, don't they?"

"They do. Reckon I'll go out and have a talk with him."

"We'll both go," Boze said. "Ellie can mind the store the rest of the day. This is more important. Besides, if Parsons *is* a killer, it'll be safer if there are two of us."

I didn't argue; a hero is something I never was nor wanted to be. We left the mill and went and picked up Boze's buckboard from behind the mercantile. On the way out of town we stopped by his house and mine long enough to fetch our rifles. Then we headed west on Willow Creek Road.

It was a long cool ride out to Jubal Parsons's tenant

farm, through a lot of rich farmland and stands of willows and evergreens. Neither of us said much. There wasn't much to say. But I was tensed up and I could see that Boze was, too.

A rutted trail hooked up to the farm from Willow Creek Road, and Boze jounced the buckboard along there some past three o'clock. It was pretty modest acreage. Just a few fields of corn and alfalfa, with a cluster of ramshackle buildings set near where Willow Creek cut through the northwest corner. There was a one-room farmhouse, a chicken coop, a barn, a couple of lean-tos, and a pole corral. That was all except for a small windmill—a Fairbanks, Morse Eclipse—that the Siler brothers had put up because the creek was dry more than half the year.

When we came in sight of the buildings I could tell that Jubal Parsons had done work on the place. The farmhouse had a fresh coat of whitewash, as did the chicken coop, and the barn had a new roof.

There was nobody in the farmyard, just half a dozen squawking leghorns, when we pulled in and Boze drew rein. But as soon as we stepped down, the front door of the house opened and Greta Parsons came out on the porch. She was wearing a calico dress and high-button shoes, but her head was bare; that butter-yellow hair of hers hung down to her hips, glistening like the bargeman's gold nugget in the sun. She was some pretty woman, for a fact. It made your throat thicken up just to look at her, and funny ideas start to stir around in your head. If ever there was a woman to tempt a man to sin, I thought, it was this one.

Boze stayed near the buckboard, with his rifle held loose in one hand, while I went over to the porch steps

and took off my hat. "I'm Carl Miller, Mrs. Parsons,"
I said. "That's Ed Bozeman back there. We're from
Tule River. Maybe you remember seeing us?"

"Yes, Mr. Miller. I remember you."

"We'd like a few words with your husband. Would
he be somewhere nearby?"

"He's in the barn," she said. There was something
odd about her voice—a kind of dullness, as if she was
fatigued. She moved that way, too, loose and jerky. She
didn't seem to notice Boze's rifle, or to care if she did.

I said, "Do you want to call him out for us?"

"No, you go on in. It's all right."

I nodded to her and rejoined Boze, and we walked on
over to the barn. Alongside it was a McCormick & Deer-
ing binder-harvester, and further down, under a lean-to,
was an old buggy with its storm curtains buttoned up.
A big gray horse stood in the corral, nuzzling a pile of
hay. The smell of dust and earth and manure was ripe
on the cool air.

The barn doors were shut. I opened one half, stood
aside from the opening, and called out, "Mr. Parsons?
You in there?"

No answer.

I looked at Boze. He said, "We'll go in together,"
and I nodded. Then we shouldered up and I pulled the
other door half open. And we went inside.

It was shadowed in there, even with the doors open;
those parts of the interior I could make out were empty.
I eased away from Boze, toward where the corn crib
was. There was sweat on me; I wished I'd taken my
own rifle out of the buckboard.

"Mr. Parsons?"

Still no answer. I would have tried a third time, but

right then Boze said, "Never mind, Carl," in a way that made me turn around and face him.

He was a dozen paces away, staring down at something under the hayloft. I frowned and moved over to him. Then I saw it too, and my mouth came open and there was a slithery feeling on my back.

Jubal Parsons was lying there dead on the sod floor, with blood all over his shirtfront and the side of his face. He'd been shot. There was a .45-70 Springfield rifle beside the body, and when Boze bent down and struck a match, you could see the black-powder marks mixed up with the blood.

"My God," I said, soft.

"Shot twice," Boze said. "Head and chest."

"Twice rules out suicide."

"Yeah," he said.

We traded looks in the dim light. Then we turned and crossed back to the doors. When we came out Mrs. Parsons was sitting on the front steps of the house, looking past the windmill at the alfalfa fields. We went over and stopped in front of her. The sun was at our backs, and the way we stood put her in our shadow. That was what made her look up; she hadn't seen us coming, or heard us crossing the yard.

She said, "Did you find him?"

"We found him," Boze said. He took out his badge and showed it to her. "We're county sheriff's deputies, Mrs. Parsons. You'd best tell us what happened in there."

"I shot him," she said. Matter-of-fact, like she was telling you the time of day. "This morning, just after breakfast. Ever since I've wanted to hitch up the buggy and drive in and tell about it, but I couldn't seem to find the courage. It took all the courage I had to fire the rifle.''

"But why'd you do a thing like that?''

"Because of what he did in Tule River last night.''

"You mean the hanging man?''

"Yes. Jubal killed him.''

"Did he tell you that?''

"Yes. Not long before I shot him.''

"Why did he do it—hang that fellow?''

"He was crazy jealous, that's why.''

I asked her, "Who was the dead man?''

"I don't know.''

"You mean to say he was a stranger?''

"Yes,'' she said. "I only saw him once. Yesterday afternoon. He rode in looking for work. I told him we didn't have any, that we were tenant farmers, but he wouldn't leave. He kept following me around, saying things. He thought I was alone here—a woman alone.''

"Did he—make trouble for you?''

"Just with words. He kept saying things, ugly things. Men like that—I don't know why, but they think I'm a woman of easy virtue. It has always been that way, no matter where we've lived.''

"What did you do?'' Boze asked.

"Ignored him at first. Then I begged him to go away. I told him my husband was wild jealous, but he didn't believe me. I thought I was alone too, you see; I thought Jubal had gone off to work in the fields.''

"But he hadn't?''

"Oh, he had. But he came back while the drifter was here and he overheard part of what was said.''

"Did he show himself to the man?''

"No. He would have if matters had gone beyond

words, but that didn't happen. After a while he got tired of tormenting me and went away. The drifter, I mean.''

''Then what happened?''

''Jubal saddled his horse and followed him. He followed that man into Tule River and when he caught up with him he knocked him on the head and he hung him.''

Boze and I traded another look. I said what both of us were thinking: ''Just for deviling you? He hung a man for that?''

''I told you, Jubal was crazy jealous. You didn't know him. You just—you don't know how he was. He said that if a man thought evil, and spoke evil, it was the same as doing evil. He said if a man was wicked, he deserved to be hung for his wickedness and the world would be a better place for his leaving it.''

She paused, and then made a gesture with one hand at her bosom. It was a meaningless kind of gesture, but you could see where a man might take it the wrong way. Might take *her* the wrong way, just like she'd said. And not just a man, either; women, too. Everybody that didn't keep their minds open and went rooting around after sin in other folks.

''Besides,'' she went on, ''he worshipped the ground I stand on. He truly did, you know. He couldn't bear the thought of anyone sullying me.''

I cleared my throat. The sweat on me had dried and I felt cold now. ''Did you hate him, Mrs. Parsons?''

''Yes, I hated him. Oh, yes. I feared him, too—for a long time I feared him more than anything else. He was so big. And so strong-willed. I used to tremble sometimes, just to look at him.''

"Was he cruel to you?" Boze asked. "Did he hurt you?"

"He was and he did. But not the way you mean; he didn't beat me, or once lay a hand to me the whole nine years we were married. It was his vengeance that hurt me. I couldn't stand it, I couldn't take any more of it."

She looked away from us again, out over the alfalfa fields—and a long ways beyond them, at something only she could see. "No roots," she said, "that was part of it, too. No roots. Moving here, moving there, always moving—three states and five homesteads in less than ten years. And the fear. And the waiting. This was the last time, I couldn't take it ever again. Not one more minute of his jealousy, his cruelty . . . *his* wickedness."

"Ma'am, you're not making sense—"

"But I am," she said. "Don't you see? He was Jubal Parsons, the Hanging Man."

I started to say something, but she shifted position on the steps just then—and when she did that her face came out of shadow and into the sunlight, and I saw in her eyes a kind of terrible knowledge. It put a chill on my neck like the night wind does when it blows across a graveyard.

"That drifter in Tule River wasn't the first man Jubal hung on account of me," she said. "Not even the first in California. That drifter was the Hanging Man's eighth."

SWEET CACTUS WINE

Marcia Muller

THE RAIN STOPPED as suddenly as it had begun, the way it always does in the Arizona desert. The torrent had burst from a near-cloudless sky, and now it was clear once more, the land nourished. I stood in the doorway of my house, watching the sun touch the stone wall, the old buckboard and the twisted arms of the giant saguaro cacti.

The suddenness of these downpours fascinated me, even though I'd lived in the desert for close to forty years, since the day I'd come here as Joe's bride in 1866. They'd been good years, not exactly bountiful, but we'd lived here in quiet comfort. Joe had the instinct that helped him bring the crops—melons, corn, beans—from the parched soil, an instinct he shared with the Papago Indians who were our neighbors. I didn't possess the knack, so now that he was gone I didn't farm. I did share one gift with the Papagos, however—the ability to make sweet cactus wine from the fruit of the saguaro. That wine was my livelihood now—as well as, I must admit, a source of Saturday-night pleasure—and the giant cacti scattered around the ranch were my fortune.

I went inside to the big rough-hewn table where I'd been shelling peas when the downpour started. The bowl sat there half full, and I eyed the peas with distaste. Funny what age will do to you. For years I'd had an overly hearty appetite. Joe used to say, "Don't worry, Katy. I like big women." Lucky for him he did, because I'd carried around enough lard for two such admirers, and I didn't believe in divorce anyway. Joe'd be surprised if he could see me now, though. I was tall, yes, still tall. But thin. I guess you'd call it gaunt. Food didn't interest me any more.

I sat down and finished shelling the peas anyway. It was market day in Arroyo, and Hank Gardner, my neighbor five miles down the road, had taken to stopping in for supper on his way home from town. Hank was widowed too. Maybe it was his way of courting. I didn't know and didn't care. One man had been enough trouble for me and, anyway, I intended to live out my days on these parched but familiar acres.

Sure enough, right about suppertime Hank rode up on his old bay. He was a lean man, browned and weathered by the sun like folks get in these parts, and he rode stiffly. I watched him dismount, then went and got the whiskey bottle and poured him a tumblerful. If I knew Hank, he'd had a few drinks in town and would be wanting another. And a glassful sure wouldn't be enough for old Hogsbreath Hank, as he was sometimes called.

He came in and sat at the table like he always did. I stirred the iron pot on the stove and sat down too. Hank was a man of few words, like my Joe had been. I'd heard tales that his drinking and temper had pushed his wife into an early grave. Sara Gardner had died of pneumonia, though, and no man's temper ever gave that to you.

Tonight Hank seemed different, jumpy. He drummed his fingers on the table and drank his whiskey.

To put him at his ease, I said, "How're things in town?"

"What?"

"Town. How was it?"

"Same as ever."

"You sure?"

"Yeah, I'm sure. Why do you ask?" But he looked kind of furtive.

"No reason," I said. "Nothing changes out here. I don't know why I asked." Then I went to dish up the stew. I set it and some corn bread on the table, poured more whiskey for Hank and a little cactus wine for me. Hank ate steadily and silently. I sort of picked at my food.

After supper I washed up the dishes and joined Hank on the front porch. He still seemed jumpy, but this time I didn't try to find out why. I just sat there beside him, watching the sun spread its redness over the mountains in the distance. When Hank spoke, I'd almost forgotten he was there.

"Kathryn"—he never called me Katy; only Joe used that name—"Kathryn, I've been thinking. It's time the two of us got married."

So that was why he had the jitters. I turned to stare. "What put an idea like that into your head?"

He frowned. "It's natural."

"Natural?"

"Kathryn, we're both alone. It's foolish you living here and me living over there when our ranches sit next to each other. Since Joe went, you haven't farmed the place. We could live at my house, let this one go, and I'd farm the land for you."

Did he want me or the ranch? I know passion is supposed to die when you're in your sixties, and as far as Hank was concerned mine had, but for form's sake he could at least pretend to some.

"Hank," I said firmly, "I've got no intention of marrying again—or of farming this place."

"I said I'd farm it for you."

"If I wanted it farmed, I could hire someone to do it. I wouldn't need to acquire another husband."

"We'd be company for one another."

"We're company now."

"What're you going to do—sit here the rest of your days scratching out a living with your cactus wine?"

"That's exactly what I plan to do."

"Kathryn . . ."

"No."

"But . . ."

"No. That's all."

Hank's jaw tightened and his eyes narrowed. I was afraid for a minute that I was going to be treated to a display of his legendary temper, but soon he looked placid as ever. He stood, patting my shoulder.

"You think about it," he said. "I'll be back tomorrow and I want a yes answer."

I'd think about it, all right. As a matter of fact, as he rode off on the bay I was thinking it was the strangest marriage proposal I'd ever heard of. And there was no way old Hogsbreath was getting any yesses from me.

He rode up again the next evening. I was out gathering cactus fruit. In the springtime, when the desert nights are still cool, the tips of the saguaro branches are covered with waxy white flowers. They're prettiest in the hours around dawn, and by the time the sun hits its peak, they close. When they die, the purple fruit begins to grow, and now, by midsummer, it was splitting open to show its bright red pulp. That pulp was what I turned into wine.

I stood by my pride and joy—a fifty-foot giant that was probably two hundred years old—and watched Hank come toward me. From his easy gait, I knew he was sure I'd changed my mind about his proposal. Probably figured he was irresistible, the old goat. He had a surprise coming.

"Well, Kathryn," he said, stopping and folding his arms across his chest, "I'm here for my answer."

"It's the same as it was last night. No. I don't intend to marry again."

"You're a foolish woman, Kathryn."

"That may be. But at least I'm foolish in my own way."

"What does that mean?"

"If I'm making a mistake, it'll be one I decide on, not one you decide for me."

The planes of his face hardened, and the wrinkles around his eyes deepened. "We'll see about that." He turned and strode toward the bay.

I was surprised he had backed down so easy, but relieved. At least he was going.

Hank didn't get on the horse, however. He fumbled at his saddle scabbard and drew his shotgun. I set down the basket of cactus fruit. Surely he didn't intend to shoot me!

He turned, shotgun in one hand.

"Don't be a fool, Hank Gardner."

He marched toward me. I got ready to run, but he kept going, past me. I whirled, watching. Hank went up to a nearby saguaro, a twenty-five footer. He looked at it, turned and walked exactly ten paces. Then he turned again, brought up the shotgun, sighted on the cactus, and began to fire. He fired at its base over and over.

I put my hand to my mouth, shutting off a scream.

Hank fired again, and the cactus toppled.

It didn't fall like a man would if he were shot. It just leaned backwards. Then it gave a sort of sigh and leaned farther and farther. As it leaned it picked up momentum, and when it hit the ground there was an awful thud.

Hank gave the cactus a satisfied nod and marched back toward his horse.

I found my voice. "Hey, you! Just what do you think you're doing?"

Hank got on the bay. "Cactuses are like people, Kathryn. They can't do anything for you once they're dead. Think about it."

"You bet I'll think about it! That cactus was valuable to me. You're going to pay!"

"What happens when there're no cactuses left?"

"What? What?"

"How're you going to scratch out a living on this miserable ranch if someone shoots all your cactuses?"

"You wouldn't dare!"

He smirked at me. "You know, there's one way cactuses *aren't* like people. Nobody ever hung a man for shooting one."

Then he rode off.

I stood there speechless. Did the bastard plan to shoot up my cacti until I agreed to marry him?

I went over to the saguaro. It lay on its back, oozing water. I nudged it gently with my foot. There were a few round holes in it—entrances to the caves where the Gila woodpeckers lived. From the silence, I guessed the birds hadn't been inside when the cactus toppled. They'd be mighty surprised when they came back and found their home on the ground.

The woodpeckers were the least of my problems, however. They'd just take up residence in one of the other giants. Trouble was, what if Hank carried out his veiled threat? Then the woodpeckers would run out of nesting places—and I'd run out of fruit to make my wine from.

I went back to the granddaddy of my cacti and picked up the basket. On the porch I set it down and myself in my rocking chair to think. What was I going to do?

I could go to the sheriff in Arroyo, but the idea didn't please me. For one thing, like Hank had said, there was no law against shooting a cactus. And for another, it was embarrassing to be in this kind of predicament at my age. I could see all the locals lined up at the bar of the saloon, laughing at me. No, I didn't want to go to Sheriff Daly if I could help it.

So what else? I could shoot Hank, I supposed, but that was even less appealing. Not that he didn't deserve shooting, but they could hang you for murdering a man, unlike a cactus. And then, while I had a couple of Joe's old rifles, I'd never been comfortable with them, never really mastered the art of sighting and pulling the trigger.

With my luck, I'd miss Hank and kill off yet another cactus.

I sat on the porch for a long time, puzzling and listening to the night sounds of the desert. Finally I gave up and went to bed, hoping the old fool would come to his senses in the morning.

He didn't, though. Shotgun blasts on the far side of the ranch brought me flying out of the house the next night. By the time I got over there, there was nothing around except a couple of dead cacti. The next night it happened again, and still the next night. The bastard was being cagey, too. I had no way of proving it actually was Hank doing the shooting. Finally I gave up and decided I had no choice but to see Sheriff Daly.

I put on my good dress, fixed my hair and hitched up my horse to the old buckboard. The trip into Arroyo was hot and dusty, and my stomach lurched at every bump in the road. It's no fun knowing you're about to become a laughingstock. Even if the sheriff sympathized with me, you can bet he and the boys would have a good chuckle afterwards.

I drove up Main Street and left the rig at the livery stable. The horse needed shoeing anyway. Then I went down the wooden sidewalk to the sheriff's office. Naturally, it was closed. The sign said he'd be back at two, and it was only noon now. I got out my list of errands and set off for the feed store, glancing over at the saloon on my way.

Hank was coming out of the saloon. I ducked into the shadow of the covered walkway in front of the bank and watched him, hate rising inside me. He stopped on the sidewalk and waited, and a moment later a stranger joined him. The stranger wore a frock coat and a broad-brimmed black hat. He didn't dress like anyone from these parts. Hank and the man walked toward the old adobe hotel and shook hands in front of it. Then Hank ambled over to where the bay was tied, and the stranger went inside.

I stood there, frowning. Normally I wouldn't have been curious about Hank Gardner's private business, but when a man's shooting up your cacti you develop an interest in anything he does. I waited until he had ridden off down the street, then crossed and went into the hotel.

Sonny, the clerk, was a friend from way back. His mother and I had run church bazaars together for years, back when I still had the energy for that sort of thing. I went up to him and we exchanged pleasantries.

Then I said, "Sonny, I've got a question for you, and I'd just as soon you didn't mention me asking it to anybody."

He nodded.

"A man came in here a few minutes ago. Frock coat, black hat."

"Sure. Mr. Johnson."

"Who is he?"

"You don't know?"

"I don't get into town much these days."

"I guess not. Everybody's talking about him. Mr. Johnson's a land developer. Here from Phoenix."

Land developer. I began to smell a rat. A rat named Hank Gardner.

"What's he doing, buying up the town?"

"Not the town. The countryside. He's making offers on all the ranches." Sonny eyed me thoughtfully. "Maybe you better talk to him. You've got a fair-sized spread there. You could make good money. In fact, I'm surprised he hasn't been out to see you.''

''So am I, Sonny. So am I. You see him, you tell him I'd like to talk to him.''

''He's in his room now. I could . . .''

''No.'' I held up my hand. ''I've got a lot of errands to do. I'll talk to him later.''

But I didn't do any errands. Instead I went home to sit in my rocker and think.

That night I didn't light my kerosene lamp. I kept the house dark and waited at the front door. When the evening shadows had fallen, I heard a rustling sound. A tall figure slipped around the stone wall into the dooryard.

I watched as he approached one of the giant saguaros in the dooryard. He went right up to it, like he had the first one he'd shot, turned and walked exactly ten paces, then blasted away. The cactus toppled, and Hank ran from the yard.

I waited. Let him think I wasn't to home. After about fifteen minutes, I got undressed and went to bed in the dark, but I didn't rest much. My mind was too busy planning what I had to do.

The next morning I hitched up the buckboard and drove over to Hank's ranch. He was around back, mending a harness. He started when he saw me. Probably figured I'd come to shoot him. I got down from the buckboard and walked up to him, a sad, defeated look on my face.

''You're too clever for me, Hank. I should have known it.''

''You ready to stop your foolishness and marry me?''

"Hank," I lied, "there's something more to my refusal than just stubbornness."

He frowned. "Oh?"

"Yes. You see, I promised Joe on his deathbed that I'd never marry again. That promise means something to me."

"I don't believe in . . ."

"Hush. I've been thinking, though, about what you said about farming my ranch. I've got an idea. Why *don't* you farm it for me? I'll move in over here, keep house and feed you. We're old enough everyone would know there weren't any shenanigans going on."

Hank looked thoughtful, pleased even. I'd guessed right; it wasn't my fair body he was after.

"That might work. But what if one of us died? Then what?"

"I don't see what you mean."

"Well, if you died, I'd be left with nothing to show for all that farming. And if I died, my son might come back from Tucson and throw you off the place. Where would you be then?"

"I see." I looked undecided, fingering a pleat in my skirt. "That *is* a problem." I paused. "Say, I think there's a way around it."

"Yeah?"

"Yes. We'll make wills. I'll leave you my ranch in mine. You do the same in yours. That way we'd both have something to show for our efforts."

He nodded, looking foxy. "That's a good idea, Kathryn. Very good."

I could tell he was pleased I'd thought of it myself.

"And, Hank, I think we should do it right away. Let's

go into town this afternoon and have the wills drawn up.''

"Fine with me." He looked even more pleased. "Just let me finish with this harness."

The will signing, of course, was a real solemn occasion. I even sniffed a little into my handkerchief before I put my signature to the document. The lawyer, Will Jones, was a little surprised by our bequests, but not much. He knew I was alone in the world, and Hank's son John was known to be more of a ne'er-do-well than his father. Probably Will Jones was glad to see the ranch wouldn't be going to John.

I had Hank leave me off at my place on his way home. I wanted, I said, to cook him one last supper in my old house before moving to his in the morning. I went about my preparations, humming to myself. Would Hank be able to resist rushing back into town to talk to Johnson, the land developer? Or would he wait a decent interval, say a day?

Hank rode up around sundown. I met him on the porch, twisting my handkerchief in my hands.

"Kathryn, what's wrong?"

"Hank, I can't do it."

"Can't do what?"

"I can't leave the place. I can't leave Joe's memory. This whole thing's been a terrible mistake."

He scowled. "Don't be foolish. What's for supper?"

"There isn't any."

"What?"

"How could I fix supper with a terrible mistake like this on my mind?"

"Well, you just get in there and fix it. And stop talking this way."

I shook my head. "No, Hank, I mean it. I can't move to your place. I can't let you farm mine. It wouldn't be right. I want you to go now, and tomorrow I'm going into town to rip up my will."

"You what?" His eyes narrowed.

"You heard me, Hank."

He whirled and went toward his horse. "You'll never learn, will you?"

"What are you going to do?"

"What do you think? Once your damned cactuses are gone, you'll see the light. Once you can't make any more of that wine, you'll be only too glad to pack your bags and come with me."

"Hank, don't you dare!"

"I do dare. There won't be a one of them standing."

"Please, Hank! At least leave my granddaddy cactus." I waved at the fifty-foot giant in the outer dooryard. "It's my favorite. It's like a child to me."

Hank grinned evilly. He took the shotgun from the saddle and walked right up to the cactus.

"Say good-bye to your child."

"Hank! Stop!"

He shouldered the shotgun.

"Say good-bye to it, you foolish woman."

"Hank, don't you pull that trigger!"

He pulled it.

Hank blasted at the giant saguaro—one, two, three times. And, like the others, it began to lean.

Unlike the others, though, it didn't lean backwards. It gave a great sigh and leaned and leaned and leaned forwards. And then it toppled. As it toppled, it picked up momentum. And when it fell on Hank Gardner, it made an awful thud.

I stood quietly on the porch. Hank didn't move. Finally I went over to him. Dead. Dead as all the cacti he'd murdered.

I contemplated his broken body a bit before I hitched up the buckboard and went to tell Sheriff Daly about the terrible accident. Sure was funny, I'd say, how that cactus toppled forwards instead of backwards. Almost as if the base had been partly cut through and braced so it would do exactly that.

Of course, the shotgun blasts would have destroyed any traces of the cutting.

THE RETURN
OF A PRIVATE

Hamlin Garland

THE NEARER THE train drew toward La Crosse, the soberer the little group of "vets" became. On the long way from New Orleans they had beguiled tedium with jokes and friendly chaff; or with planning with elaborate detail what they were going to do now, after the war. A long journey, slowly, irregularly, yet persistently pushing northward. When they entered on Wisconsin territory they gave a cheer, and another when they reached Madison, but after that they sank into a dumb expectancy. Comrades dropped off at one or two points beyond, until there were only four or five left who were bound for La Crosse County.

Three of them were gaunt and brown, the fourth was gaunt and pale, with signs of fever and ague upon him. One had a great scar down his temple, one limped, and they all had unnaturally large, bright eyes, showing emaciation. There were no hands greeting them at the station, no banks of gayly dressed ladies waving handkerchiefs and shouting "Bravo!" as they came in on the caboose of a freight train into the towns that had cheered and blared at them on their way to war. As they looked out or stepped upon the platform for a moment, while the train stood at the station, the loafers looked at them indifferently. Their blue coats, dusty and grimy, were too familiar now to excite notice, much less a friendly word. They were the last of the army to return, and the loafers were surfeited with such sights.

The train jogged forward so slowly that it seemed likely to be midnight before they should reach La Crosse. The little squad grumbled and swore, but it was no use; the train would not hurry, and, as a matter of fact, it was nearly two o'clock when the engine whistled "down brakes."

All of the group were farmers, living in districts several miles out of the town, and all were poor.

"Now, boys," said Private Smith, he of the fever and ague, "we are landed in La Crosse in the night. We've got to stay somewhere till mornin'. Now I ain't got no two dollars to waste on a hotel. I've got a wife and children, so I'm goin' to roost on a bench and take the cost of a bed out of my hide."

"Same here," put in one of the other men. "Hide'll grow on again, dollars'll come hard. It's going to be mighty hot skirmishin' to find a dollar these days."

"Don't think they'll be a deptuation of citizens waitin' to 'scort us to a hotel, eh?" said another. His sarcasm was too obvious to require an answer.

Smith went on, "Then at daybreak we'll start for home—at least, I will."

"Well, I'll be dummed if I'll take two dollars out o'

my hide,'' one of the younger men said. "I'm goin' to a hotel, ef I don't never lay up a cent.''

"That'll do f'r you,'' said Smith; "but if you had a wife an' three young uns dependin' on yeh—''

"Which I ain't, thank the Lord! and don't intend havin' while the court knows itself.''

The station was deserted, chill, and dark, as they came into it at exactly a quarter to two in the morning. Lit by the oil lamps that flared a dull red light over the dingy benches, the waiting room was not an inviting place. The younger man went off to look up a hotel, while the rest remained and prepared to camp down on the floor and benches. Smith was attended to tenderly by the other men, who spread their blankets on the bench for him, and, by robbing themselves, made quite a comfortable bed, though the narrowness of the bench made his sleeping precarious.

It was chill, though August, and the two men, sitting with bowed heads, grew stiff with cold and weariness, and were forced to rise now and again and walk about to warm their stiffened limbs. It did not occur to them, probably, to contrast their coming home with their going forth, or with the coming home of the generals, colonels, or even captains—but to Private Smith, at any rate there came a sickness at heart almost deadly as he lay there on his hard bed and went over his situation.

In the deep of the night, lying on a board in the town where he had enlisted three years ago, all elation and enthusiasm gone out of him, he faced the fact that with the joy of home-coming was already mingled the bitter juice of care. He saw himself sick, worn out, taking up the work on his half-cleared farm, the inevitable mortgage standing ready with open jaw to swallow half his earnings. He had given three years of his life for a mere pittance of pay, and now!—

Morning dawned at last, slowly, with a pale yellow dome of light rising silently above the bluffs, which stand like some huge storm-devasted castle, just east of the city. Out to the left the great river swept on its massive yet silent way to the south. Blue-jays called across the water from hillside to hillside through the clear, beautiful air, and hawks began to skim the tops of the hills. The older men were astir early, but Private Smith had fallen at last into a sleep, and they went out without waking him. He lay on his knapsack, his gaunt face turned toward the ceiling, his hands clasped on his breast, with a curious pathetic effect of weakness and appeal.

An engine switching near woke him at last, and he slowly sat up and stared about. He looked out of the window and saw that the sun was lightening the hills across the river. He rose and brushed his hair as well as he could, folded his blankets up, and went out to find his companions. They stood gazing silently at the river and at the hills.

"Looks natcher'l, don't it?" they said, as he came out.

"That's what it does," he replied. "An' it looks good. D' yeh see that peak?" He pointed at a beautiful symmetrical peak, rising like a slightly truncated cone, so high that it seemed the very highest of them all. It was touched by the morning sun and it glowed like a beacon, and a light scarf of gray morning fog was rolling up its shadowed side.

"My farm's just beyond that. Now, if I can only ketch a ride, we'll be home by dinner-time."

"I'm talkin' about breakfast," said one of the others.

"I guess it's one more meal o'hardtack f'r me," said Smith.

They foraged around, and finally found a restaurant with a sleepy old German behind the counter, and procured some coffee, which they drank to wash down their hardtack.

"Time'll come," said Smith, holding up a piece by the corner, "when this'll be a curiosity."

"I hope to God it will! I bet I've chawed hardtack enough to shingle every house in the coolly. I've chawed it when my lampers was down, and when they wasn't. I've took it dry, soaked, and mashed. I've had it wormy, musty, sour, and blue-mouldy. I've had it in little bits and big bits; 'fore coffee an' after coffee. I'm ready f'r a change. I'd like t' git holt jest about now o'some of the hot biscuits my wife c'n make when she lays herself out f'r company."

"Well, if you set there gabblin', you'll never *see* yer wife."

"Come on," said Private Smith. "Wait a moment, boys; less take suthin'. It's on me." He led them to the rusty tin dipper which hung on a nail beside the wooden water-pail, and they grinned and drank. Then shouldering their blankets and muskets, which they were "takin' home to the boys," they struck out on their last march.

"They called that coffee Jayvy," grumbled one of them, "but it never went by the road where government Jayvy resides. I reckon I know coffee from peas."

They kept together on the road along the turnpike, and up the winding road by the river, which they followed for some miles. The river was very lovely, curving down along its sandy beds, pausing now and then under broad basswood trees, or running in dark, swift, silent currents under tangles of wild grapevines, and drooping alders, and haw trees. At one of these lovely spots the three vets sat down on the thick green sward to rest, "on Smith's account." The leaves of the trees were as fresh and green as in June, the jays called cheery greetings to them, and kingfishers darted to and fro with swooping, noiseless flight.

"I tell yeh, boys, this knocks the swamps of Loueesiana into kingdom come."

"You bet. All they c'n raise down there is snakes, niggers, and p'rticler hell."

"An' fighting men," put in the older man.

"An' fightin' men. If I had a good hook an' line I'd sneak a pick'rel out o' that pond. Say, remember that time I shot that alligator—"

"I guess we'd better be crawlin' along," interrupted Smith, rising and shouldering his knapsack, with considerable effort, which he tried to hide.

"Say, Smith, lemme give you a lift on that."

"I guess I c'n manage," said Smith, grimly.

"Course. But, yo' see, I may not have a chance right off to pay yeh back for the times you've carried my gun and hull caboodle. Say, now, gimme that gun, anyway."

"All right, if yeh feel like it, Jim," Smith replied, and they trudged along doggedly in the sun, which was getting higher and hotter each half-mile.

"Ain't it queer there ain't no teams comin' along," said Smith, after a long silence.

"Well, no, seein's it's Sunday."

"By jinks, that's a fact. It *is* Sunday. I'll git home in time f'r dinner, sure!" he exulted. "She don't hev dinner usially till about *one* on Sundays.'' And he fell into a muse, in which he smiled.

''Well, I'll git home jest about six o'clock, jest about when the boys are milkin' the cows,'' said old Jim Cranby. ''I'll step into the barn, an' then I'll say: '*Heah!* why ain't this milkin' done before this time o' day?' An' then won't they yell!'' he added, slapping his thigh in great glee.

Smith went on. ''I'll jest go up the path. Old Rover'll come down the road to meet me. He won't bark; he'll know me, an' he'll come down waggin' his tail an' showin' his teeth. That's his way of laughin'. An' so I'll walk up to the kitchen door, an' I'll say, '*Dinner* f'r a hungry man!' An' then she'll jump up, an'—''

He couldn't go on. His voice choked at the thought of it. Saunders, the third man, hardly uttered a word, but walked silently behind the others. He had lost his wife the first year he was in the army. She died of pneumonia, caught in the autumn rains while working in the fields in his place.

They plodded along till at last they came to a parting of the ways. To the right the road continued up the main valley; to the left it went over the big ridge.

''Well, boys,'' began Smith, as they grounded their muskets and looked away up the valley, ''here's where we shake hands. We've marched together a good many miles, an' now I s'pose we're done.''

''Yes, I don't think we'll do any more of it f'r a while. I don't want to, I know.''

''I hope I'll see yeh once in a while, boys, to talk over old times.''

''Of course,'' said Saunders, whose voice trembled a

little, too. "It ain't *exactly* like dyin'." They all found it hard to look at each other.

"But we'd ought'r go home with you," said Cranby. "You'll never climb that ridge with all them things on yer back."

"Oh, I'm all right! Don't worry about me. Every step takes me nearer home, yeh see. Well, good-by, boys."

They shook hands. "Good-by. Good luck!"

"Same to you. Lemme know how you find things at home."

"Good-by."

"Good-by."

He turned once before they passed out of sight, and waved his cap, and they did the same, and all yelled. Then all marched away with their long, steady, loping, veteran step. The solitary climber in blue walked on for a time, with his mind filled with the kindness of his comrades, and musing upon the many wonderful days they had had together in camp and field.

He thought of his chum, Billy Tripp. Poor Billy! A "Minié" ball fell into his breast one day, fell wailing like a cat, and tore a great ragged hole in his heart. He looked forward to a sad scene with Billy's mother and sweetheart. They would want to know all about it. He tried to recall all that Billy had said, and the particulars of it, but there was little to remember, just that wild wailing sound high in the air, a dull slap, a short, quick, expulsive groan, and the boy lay with his face in the dirt in the ploughed field they were marching across.

That was all. But all the scenes he had since been through had not dimmed the horror, the terror of that moment, when his boy comrade fell, with only a breath between a laugh and a death-groan. Poor handsome

Billy! Worth millions of dollars was his young life.

These sombre recollections gave way at length to more cheerful feelings as he began to approach his home coolly. The fields and houses grew familiar, and in one or two he was greeted by people seated in the doorways. But he was in no mood to talk, and pushed on steadily, though he stopped and accepted a drink of milk once at the well-side of a neighbor.

The sun was burning hot on that slope, and his step grew slower, in spite of his iron resolution. He sat down several times to rest. Slowly he crawled up the rough, reddish-brown road, which wound along the hillside, under great trees, through dense groves of jack oaks, with tree-tops far below him on his left hand, and the hills far above him on his right. He crawled along like some minute, wingless variety of fly.

He ate some hardtack, sauced with wild berries, when he reached the summit of the ridge, and sat there for some time, looking down into his home coolly.

Sombre, pathetic figure! His wide, round, gray eyes gazing down into the beautiful valley, seeing and not seeing, the splendid cloud-shadows sweeping over the western hills and across the green and yellow wheat far below. His head drooped forward on his palm, his shoulders took on a tired stoop, his cheek-bones showed painfully. An observer might have said, "He is looking down upon his own grave."

2

Sunday comes in a Western wheat harvest with such sweet and sudden relaxation to man and beast that it would be holy for that reason, if for no other, and Sundays are usually fair in harvest-time. As one goes out into the field in the hot morning sunshine, with no sound abroad save the crickets and the indescribably pleasant silken rustling of the ripened grain, the reaper and the very sheaves in the stubble seem to be resting, dreaming.

Around the house, in the shade of the trees, the men sit, smoking, dozing, or reading the papers, while the women, never resting, move about at the housework. The men eat on Sundays about the same as on other days, and breakfast is no sooner over and out of the way than dinner begins.

But at the Smith farm there were no men dozing or reading. Mrs. Smith was alone with her three children, Mary, nine, Tommy, six, and little Ted, just past four. Her farm, rented to a neighbor, lay at the head of a coolly or narrow gully, made at some far-off post-glacial period by the vast and angry floods of water which gullied these tremendous furrows in the level prairie—furrows so deep that undisturbed portions of the original level rose like hills on either side, rose to quite considerable mountains.

The chickens wakened her as usual that Sabbath morning from dreams of her absent husband, from whom she had not heard for weeks. The shadows drifted over the hills, down the slopes, across the wheat, and up the opposite wall in a leisurely way, as if, being Sunday, they could take it easy also. The fowls clustered about the housewife as she went out into the yard. Fuzzy little chickens swarmed out from the coops, where their clucking and perpetually disgruntled mothers tramped about, petulantly thrusting their heads through the spaces between the slats.

A cow called in a deep, musical bass, and a calf answered from a little pen near by, and a pig scurried guiltily out of the cabbages. Seeing all this, seeing the pig in the cabbages, the tangle of grass in the garden, the broken fence which she had mended again and again—the little woman, hardly more than a girl, sat down and cried. The bright Sabbath morning was only a mockery without him!

A few years ago they had bought this farm, paying part, mortgaging the rest in the usual way. Edward Smith was a man of terrible energy. He worked "nights and Sundays," as the saying goes, to clear the farm of its brush and of its insatiate mortgage! In the midst of his Herculean struggle came the call for volunteers, and with the grim and unselfish devotion to his country which made the Eagle Brigade able to "whip its weight in wild-cats," he threw down his scythe and grub-axe, turned his cattle loose, and became a blue-coated cog in a vast machine for killing men, and not thistles. While the millionaire sent his money to England for safe-keeping, this man, with his girl-wife and three babies, left them on a mortgaged farm, and went away to fight for an idea. It was foolish, but it was sublime for all that.

That was three years before, and the young wife, sitting on the well-curb on this bright Sabbath harvest morning, was righteously rebellious. It seemed to her that she had borne her share of the country's sorrow. Two brothers had been killed, the renter in whose hands her husband had left the farm had proved a villain; one year the farm had been without crops, and now the over-ripe grain was waiting the tardy hand of the neighbor who had rented it, and who was cutting his own grain first.

About six weeks before, she had received a letter saying, "We'll be discharged in a little while." But no other word had come from him. She had seen by the papers that his army was being discharged, and from day to day other soldiers slowly percolated in blue streams back into the State and county, but still *her* hero did not return.

Each week she had told the children that he was coming, and she had watched the road so long that it had become unconscious; and as she stood at the well, or by the kitchen door, her eyes were fixed unthinkingly on the road that wound down the coolly.

Nothing wears on the human soul like waiting. If the stranded mariner, searching the sun-bright seas, could once give up hope of a ship, that horrible grinding on his brain would cease. It was this waiting, hoping, on the edge of despair, that gave Emma Smith no rest.

Neighbors said, with kind intentions: "He's sick, maybe, an' can't start north just yet. He'll come along one o' these days."

"Why don't he write?" was her question, which silenced them all. This Sunday morning it seemed to her as if she could not stand it longer. The house seemed intolerably lonely. So she dressed the little ones in their best calico dresses and home-made jackets, and, closing up the house, set off down the coolly to old Mother Gray's.

"Old Widder Gray" lived at the "mouth of the coolly." She was a widow woman with a large family of stalwart boys and laughing girls. She was the visible incarnation of hospitality and optimistic poverty. With

Western open-heartedness she fed every mouth that asked food of her, and worked herself to death as cheerfully as her girls danced in the neighborhood harvest dances.

She waddled down the path to meet Mrs. Smith with a broad smile on her face.

"Oh, you little dears! Come right to your granny. Gimme me a kiss! Come right in, Mis' Smith. How are yeh, anyway? Nice mornin', ain't it? Come in an' set down. Everything's in a clutter, but that won't scare you any."

She led the way into the best room, a sunny, square room, carpeted with a faded and patched rag carpet, and papered with white-and-green wall-paper, where a few faded effigies of dead members of the family hung in variously sized oval walnut frames. The house resounded with singing, laughter, whistling, tramping of heavy boots, and riotous scufflings. Half-grown boys came to the door and crooked their fingers at the children, who ran out, and were soon heard in the midst of the fun.

"Don't s'pose you've heard from Ed?" Mrs. Smith shook her head. "He'll turn up some day, when you ain't lookin' for 'm." The good old soul had said that so many times that poor Mrs. Smith derived no comfort from it any longer.

"Liz heard from Al the other day. He's comin' some day this week. Anyhow, they expect him."

"Did he say anything of—"

"No, he didn't," Mrs. Gray admitted. "But then it was only a short letter, anyhow. Al ain't much for writin', anyhow.—But come out and see my new cheese. I tell yeh, I don't believe I ever had better luck in my life.

If Ed should come, I want you should take him up a piece of this cheese."

It was beyond human nature to resist the influence of that noisy, hearty, loving household, and in the midst of the singing and laughing the wife forgot her anxiety, for the time at least, and laughed and sang with the rest.

About eleven o'clock a wagon-load more drove up to the door, and Bill Gray, the widow's oldest son, and his whole family, from Sand Lake Coolly, piled out amid a good-natured uproar. Every one talked at once, except Bill, who sat in the wagon with his wrists on his knees, a straw in his mouth, and an amused twinkle in his blue eyes.

"Ain't heard nothin' o' Ed, I s'pose?" he asked in a kind of bellow. Mrs. Smith shook her head. Bill, with a delicacy very striking in such a great giant, rolled his quid in his mouth, and said:

"Didn't know but you had. I hear two or three of the Sand Lake boys are comin'. Left New Orleans some time this week. Didn't write nothin' about Ed, but no news is good news in such cases, mother always says."

"Well, go put out yer team," said Mrs. Gray, "an' go'n bring me in some taters, an', Sim, you go see if you c'n find some corn. Sadie, you put on the water to bile. Come now, hustle yer boots, all o' yeh. If I feed this yer crowd, we've got to have some raw materials. If y' think I'm goin' to feed yeh on pie—you're just mightily mistaken."

The children went off into the field, the girls put dinner on to boil, and then went to change their dresses and fix their hair. "Somebody might come," they said.

"Land sakes, I *hope* not! I don't know where in time

I'd set 'em, 'less they'd eat at the second table," Mrs. Gray laughed, in pretended dismay.

The two older boys, who had served their time in the army, lay out on the grass before the house, and whittled and talked desultorily about the war and the crops, and planned buying a threshing-machine. The older girls and Mrs. Smith helped enlarge the table and put on the dishes, talking all the time in that cheery, incoherent, and meaningful way a group of such women have,—a conversation to be taken for its spirit rather than for its letter, though Mrs. Gray at last got the ear of them all and dissertated at length on girls.

"Girls in love ain' no use in the whole blessed week," she said. "Sundays they're a-lookin' down the road, expectin' he'll *come*. Sunday afternoons they can't think o'nothin' else, 'cause he's *here*. Monday mornin's they're sleepy and kind o' dreamy and slimpsy, and good f'r nothin' on Tuesday and Wednesday. Thursday they git absent-minded, an' begin to look off toward Sunday agin, an' mope aroun' and let the dishwater git cold, right under their noses. Friday they break dishes, an' go off in the best room an' snivel, an' look out o' the winder. Saturdays they have queer spurts o' workin' like all p'ssessed, an' spurts o' frizzin' their hair. An' Sunday they begin it all over agin."

The girls giggled and blushed, all through this tirade from their mother, their broad faces and powerful frames anything but suggestive of lackadaisical sentiment. But Mrs. Smith said:

"Now, Mrs. Gray, I hadn't ought to stay to dinner. You've got—"

"Now you set right down! If any of them girls' beaus comes, they'll have to take what's left, that's all. They ain't s'posed to have much appetite, nohow. No, you're goin' to stay if they starve, an' they ain't no danger o' that.''

At one o'clock the long table was piled with boiled potatoes, cords of boiled corn on the cob, squash and pumpkin pies, hot biscuit, sweet pickles, bread and butter, and honey. Then one of the girls took down a conchshell from a nail, and going to the door, blew a long, fine, free blast, that showed there was no weakness of lungs in her ample chest.

Then the children came out of the forest of corn, out of the creek, out of the loft of the barn, and out of the garden.

''They come to their feed f'r all the world jest like the pigs when y' holler 'poo-ee!' See 'em scoot!'' laughed Mrs. Gray, every wrinkle on her face shining with delight.

The men shut up their jack-knives, and surrounded the horse-trough to souse their faces in the cold, hard water, and in a few moments the table was filled with a merry crowd, and a row of wistful-eyed youngsters circled the kitchen wall, where they stood first on one leg and then on the other, in impatient hunger.

''Now pitch in, Mrs. Smith,'' said Mrs. Gray, presiding over the table. ''You know these men critters. They'll eat every grain of it, if yeh give 'em a chance. I swan, they're made o' India-rubber, their stomachs is, I know it.''

''Haf to eat to work,'' said Bill, gnawing a cob with a swift, circular motion that rivalled a corn-sheller in results.

''More like workin' to eat,'' put in one of the girls, with a giggle. ''More eat'n work with you.''

"*You* needn't say anything, Net. Any one that'll eat seven ears——"

"I didn't, no such thing. You piled your cobs on my plate."

"That'll do to tell Ed Varney. It won't go down here where we know yeh."

"Good land! Eat all yeh want! They's plenty more in the fiel's, but I can't afford to give you young uns tea. The tea is for us women-folks, and 'specially f'r Mis' Smith an' Bill's wife. We're a-goin' to tell fortunes by it."

One by one the men filled up and shoved back, and one by one the children slipped into their places, and by two o'clock the women alone remained around the débris-covered table, sipping their tea and telling fortunes.

As they got well down to the grounds in the cup, they shook them with a circular motion in the hand, and then turned them bottom-side-up quickly in the saucer, then twirled them three or four times one way, and three or four times the other, during a breathless pause. Then Mrs. Gray lifted the cup, and, gazing into it with profound gravity, pronounced the impending fate.

It must be admitted that, to a critical observer, she had abundant preparation for hitting close to the mark, as when she told the girls that "somebody was comin'."

"It's a man," she went on gravely. "He is cross-eyed——"

"Oh, you hush!" cried Nettie.

"He has red hair, and is death on b'iled corn and hot biscuit."

The others shrieked with delight.

"But he's goin' to get the mitten, that red-headed feller is, for I see another feller comin' up behind him."

"Oh, lemme see, lemme see!" cried Nettie.

"Keep off," said the priestess, with a lofty gesture. "His hair is black. He don't eat so much, and he works more."

The girls exploded in a shriek of laughter, and pounded their sister on the back.

At last came Mrs. Smith's turn, and she was trembling with excitement as Mrs. Gray again composed her jolly face to what she considered a proper solemnity of expression.

"Somebody is comin' to *you*," she said, after a long pause. "He's got a musket on his back. He's a soldier. He's almost here. See?"

She pointed at two little tea-stems, which really formed a faint suggestion of a man with a musket on his back. He had climbed nearly to the edge of the cup. Mrs. Smith grew pale with excitement. She trembled so she could hardly hold the cup in her hand as she gazed into it.

"It's Ed," cried the old woman. "He's on the way home. Heavens an' earth! There he is now!" She turned and waved her hand out toward the road. They rushed to the door to look where she pointed.

A man in a blue coat, with a musket on his back, was toiling slowly up the hill on the sun-bright, dusty road, toiling slowly, with bent head half hidden by a heavy knapsack. So tired it seemed that walking was indeed a process of falling. So eager to get home he would not stop, would not look aside, but plodded on, amid the cries of the locusts, the welcome of the crickets, and the rustle of the yellow wheat. Getting back to God's country, and his wife and babies!

Laughing, crying, trying to call him and the children

at the same time, the little wife, almost hysterical, snatched her hat and ran out into the yard. But the soldier had disappeared over the hill into the hollow beyond, and, by the time she had found the children, he was too far away for her voice to reach him. And, besides, she was not sure it was her husband, for he had not turned his head at their shouts. This seemed so strange. Why didn't he stop to rest at his old neighbor's house? Tortured by hope and doubt, she hurried up the coolly as fast as she could push the baby wagon, the blue-coated figure just ahead pushing steadily, silently forward up the coolly.

When the excited, panting little group came in sight of the gate they saw the blue-coated figure standing, leaning upon the rough rail fence, his chin on his palms, gazing at the empty house. His knapsack, canteen, blankets, and musket lay upon the dusty grass at his feet.

He was like a man lost in a dream. His wide, hungry eyes devoured the scene. The rough lawn, the little unpainted house, the field of clear yellow wheat behind it, down across which streamed the sun, now almost ready to touch the high hill to the west, the crickets crying merrily, a cat on the fence near by, dreaming, unmindful of the stranger in blue—

How peaceful it all was. O God! How far removed from all camps, hospitals, battle lines. A little cabin in a Wisconsin coolly, but it was majestic in its peace. How did he ever leave it for those years of tramping, thirsting, killing?

Trembling, weak with emotion, her eyes on the silent figure, Mrs. Smith hurried up to the fence. Her feet made no noise in the dust and grass, and they were close upon him before he knew of them. The oldest boy ran a little ahead. He will never forget that figure, that face. It will always remain as something epic, that return of the private. He fixed his eyes on the pale face covered with a ragged beard.

"Who *are* you, sir?" asked the wife, or, rather, started to ask, for he turned, stood a moment, and then cried:

"Emma!"

"Edward!"

The children stood in a curious row to see their mother kiss this bearded, strange man, the elder girl sobbing sympathetically with her mother. Illness had left the soldier partly deaf, and this added to the strangeness of his manner.

But the youngest child stood away, even after the girl had recognized her father and kissed him. The man turned then to the baby, and said in a curiously unpaternal tone:

"Come here, my little man; don't you know me?" But the baby backed away under the fence and stood peering at him critically.

"My little man!" What meaning in those words! This baby seemed like some other woman's child, and not the infant he had left in his wife's arms. The war had come between him and his baby—he was only a strange man to him, with big eyes; a soldier, with mother hanging to his arm, and talking in a loud voice.

"And this is Tom," the private said, drawing the oldest boy to him. "*He'll* come and see me. *He* knows his poor old pap when he comes home from the war."

The mother heard the pain and reproach in his voice and hastened to apologize.

"You've changed so, Ed. He can't know yeh. This is papa, Teddy; come and kiss him—Tom and Mary do.

Come, won't you?'' But Teddy still peered through the fence with solemn eyes, well out of reach. He resembled a half-wild kitten that hesitates, studying the tones of one's voice.

''I'll fix him,'' said the soldier, and sat down to undo his knapsack, out of which he drew three enormous and very red apples. After giving one to each of the older children, he said:

''*Now* I guess he'll come. Eh, my little man? Now come see your pap.''

Teddy crept slowly under the fence, assisted by the overzealous Tommy, and a moment later was kicking and squalling in his father's arms. Then they entered the house, into the sitting room, poor, bare, art-forsaken little room, too, with its rag carpet, its square clock, and its two or three chromos and pictures from *Harper's Weekly* pinned about.

''Emma, I'm all tired out,'' said Private Smith, as he flung himself down on the carpet as he used to do, while his wife brought a pillow to put under his head, and the children stood about munching their apples.

''Tommy, you run and get me a pan of chips, and Mary, you get the tea-kettle on, and I'll go and make some biscuit.''

And the soldier talked. Question after question he poured forth about the crops, the cattle, the renter, the neighbors. He slipped his heavy government brogan shoes off his poor, tired, blistered feet, and lay out with utter, sweet relaxation. He was a free man again, no longer a soldier under a command. At supper he stopped once, listened and smiled. ''That's old Spot. I know her voice. I s'pose that's her calf out there in the pen. I can't milk her to-night, though. I'm too tired. But I tell you,

I'd like a drink of her milk. What's become of old Rove?''

"He died last winter. Poisoned, I guess." There was a moment of sadness for them all. It was some time before the husband spoke again, in a voice that trembled a little.

"Poor old feller! He'd 'a' known me half a mile away. I expected him to come down the hill to meet me. It 'ud 'a' been more like comin' home if I could 'a' seen him comin' down the road an' waggin' his tail, an' laughin' that way he has. I tell yeh, it kind o' took hold o' me to see the blinds down an' the house shut up.''

"But, yeh see, we—expected you'd write again 'fore you started. And then we thought we'd see you if you *did* come," she hastened to explain.

"Well, I ain't worth a cent on writin'. Besides, it's just as well yeh didn't know when I was comin'. I tell you, it sounds good to hear them chickens out there, an' turkeys, an' the crickets. Do you know they don't have just the same kind o' crickets down South? Who's Sam hired t' help cut yer grain?''

"The Ramsey boys.''

"Looks like a good crop; but I'm afraid I won't do much gettin' it cut. This cussed fever an' ague has got me down pretty low. I don't know when I'll get rid of it. I'll bet I've took twenty-five pounds of quinine if I've taken a bit. Gimme another biscuit. I tell yeh, they taste good, Emma. I ain't had anything like it—Say, if you'd 'a' hear'd me braggin' to th' boys about your butter 'n' biscuits I'll bet your ears 'ud' 'a' burnt.''

The private's wife colored with pleasure. "Oh, you're always a-braggin' about your things. Everybody makes good butter.''

"Yes; old lady Snyder, for instance."

"Oh, well, she ain't to be mentioned. She's Dutch."

"Or old Mis' Snively. One more cup o' tea, Mary. That's my girl! I'm feeling better already. I just b'lieve the matter with me is, I'm *starved*."

This was a delicious hour, one long to be remembered. They were like lovers again. But their tenderness, like that of a typical American family, found utterance in tones, rather than in words. He was praising her when praising her biscuit, and she knew it. They grew soberer when he showed where he had been struck, one ball burning the back of his hand, one cutting away a lock of hair from his temple, and one passing through the calf of his leg. The wife shuddered to think how near she had come to being a soldier's widow. Her waiting no longer seemed hard. This sweet, glorious hour effaced it all.

Then they rose, and all went out into the garden and down to the barn. He stood beside her while she milked old Spot. They began to plan fields and crops for next year.

His farm was weedy and encumbered, a rascally renter had run away with his machinery (departing between two days), his children needed clothing, the years were coming upon him, he was sick and emaciated, but his heroic soul did not quail. With the same courage with which he had faced his Southern march he entered upon a still more hazardous future.

Oh, that mystic hour! The pale man with big eyes standing there by the well, with his young wife by his side. The vast moon swinging above the eastern peaks, the cattle winding down the pasture slopes with jangling bells, the crickets singing, the stars blooming out sweet and far and serene; the katydids rhythmically calling, the little turkeys crying querulously, as they settled to roost in the poplar tree near the open gate. The voices at the well drop lower, the little ones nestle in their father's arms at last, and Teddy falls asleep there.

The common soldier of the American volunteer army had returned. His war with the South was over, and his fight, his daily running fight with nature and against the injustice of his fellowmen, was begun again.

SINGING SAND

Erle Stanley Gardner

1

Whiskey—Neat

EVERY PLACE A man lives leaves its stamp upon that man.

The city dweller differs from the desert man. It ain't always easy to tell just where the difference comes in, but you can tell it. I knew that Harry Karg was from the city the minute I saw him, and I knew he was hard.

It wasn't his body that was hard. It was his mind.

He was in a saloon in Mexicali, and he was drinking whisky. The more he drank the harder his eyes got, the more he watched himself.

Lots of people take a few drinks and relax. Their muscles slacken, their lips get loose, and they laugh when there's nothing to laugh at. But it wasn't that way with

Karg. Every time he hoisted his elbow he got more cautious, more wary in his glance, more tight about the lips.

I've seen a few desert men that way, but Karg was the first city man I'd ever seen that was like that.

I watched him, then I looked at the bartender.

The bartender was a Mexican lad that I'd known for some time. He made a motion with his right hand, then jerked his head toward the man I was watching.

I stiffened up a bit and got back into the shadows.

After a while, the bartender sidled over toward me.

"He's looking for you, Señor Zane," he said.

"What's he want?"

"*Señor*, I do not know, but he wants to see you, and he is impatient."

I get along with those Mexicans pretty well because I can speak their language well enough to savvy their psychology. I knew the bartender for a tough egg, but he professed to be my friend, and now he seemed to be proving it.

"If he is impatient," I said, "let him wait until I come in again."

And I sat back in the shadows of a corner and watched him.

He drank ten whiskies inside of twenty minutes, and he complained about the quality of the stuff. I watched him drink, and waited for him to get a little loose about the mouth, waited for the eyes to get watery.

Nothing happened.

His eyes were as hard as ever, and his mouth was a thin line over a bony jaw.

I tipped the bartender the wink and went out the back door.

Back doors in Mexicali open onto some funny places,

and I walked through a cement courtyard that had little doors opening on either side, and then swung to the right, into a sun-swept street, turned the corner and walked in the front door.

"Here," said the bartender, speaking English in a voice loud enough for me to hear, "is Señor Zane."

The tall man with the brittle eyes dropped the elbow that was halfway to the mouth and looked me over. I walked up to the bar.

"Humph," said the tall man.

I ordered a beer.

The tall man set his glass of whisky on the bar, turned to face me, and then walked over.

"Bob Zane?" he asked.

I nodded.

He shot out his hand.

"Karg's my name, Harry Karg."

I took his hand. He hunched his shoulder, tried to squeeze my bones flat, just to show me how hard he was. I knew then he was strong, awfully strong.

I arched my hand, sort of cupping the knuckles, and let him squeeze until he was tired. Let your knuckles stay straight, and pressure may get one of 'em in and another out and hurt like the devil. Arch your hand, and a man can squeeze until his muscles ache.

Karg squeezed.

When he got tired he let go of the hand, swung his left over to the whisky glass, raised it, downed the whisky, slid the wet glass across the top of the mahogany bar and snapped an order at the bartender.

"Fill it up again and fill up Mr. Zane's glass. Then we'll drink."

I drank my beer.

The bartender filled the glass, then he filled Karg's whisky glass, and he shot me a flickering glance out of his smoky eyes.

It was a warning glance.

Some of those bartenders get pretty wise at sizing up character quick.

"Finish this, and have another and we'll talk," said Karg.

"I don't drink over two in succession, and I don't talk," I told him. "I listen."

He tossed off the whisky.

Lord knows how many he'd had, and it was hot. But he didn't show it. He looked cold sober, beyond just a faint flush of color that darkened his face with a sinister look.

"Come over here to a table," he said. "Bartender, bring me the bottle and a glass. It's rotten stuff, but it kills germs, and I had a drink of water a while ago. The water wasn't boiled."

I sat down at the table with him.

He tilted the bottle until the glass was full, and leaned toward me.

"I'm a hard man," he said.

He wasn't telling me anything. I'd known that as soon as I saw him.

"And I don't like to be monkeyed with," he went on.

I didn't even nod. I was listening.

He waited for a minute, and then flashed his hard, gray eyes into mine.

"That's why it didn't make any hit with me to have the bartender tip you off I was looking for you," he said.

He waited for me to color up, or deny it, or explain.

If he'd kept on waiting until I turned color he'd have been waiting yet. Harry Karg was nothing to me, and if he didn't like my style he could go to hell.

When he saw it was falling flat, he let his eyes shift.

"I knew he tipped you off, and I knew you were studying me," he said.

I kept right on listening. I didn't say a thing.

And his eyes slithered away from my face, over the top of the table, and then stared at the floor for a minute.

Right then I had him classified.

He was from the city, and his hardness was the hardness of the city. If he could get another man on the defensive, he'd ride him to death. But when the other man didn't squirm, Harry Karg felt uncomfortable inside.

"Well," I said slowly. "You wanted to see me. Now you're here, and I'm here."

He laughed uneasily, took a big breath, and got hard again.

It had just been a minute that he'd squirmed around uncomfortably, but that had been enough to show me the weakness that was in him. I remembered it, and let it go at that.

"They tell me you know the desert," he said.

"I'm listening," I told him.

"Like no other man knows it, that you can get by in the desert where another man would starve to death and die of thirst," he said, and his tones were insinuating.

I shrugged my shoulders.

"People will tell you lots of things, if you'll listen," I said.

He reached into an inside pocket and pulled out a map.

It was a page that had been torn from an atlas, and it showed the desert southwest of the United States and a part of Mexico. There was one little spot on it that was sort of greasy, as though somebody had been rubbing it with a moist finger.

He put his finger on the spot.

It was down over the border, in the Yaqui country of Mexico.

"Could you go there?" he asked.

I studied the spot.

"Yes," I said. "Lots of men have gone to that section of the country."

He looked surprised.

"Lots of men?" he asked.

I nodded. "Quite a few, anyway."

"Then I wouldn't need you to guide me to get there?"

"You'd need someone that knew the desert country."

"But I could get there?"

"Yes, I think you could."

"And back?"

I shook my head.

"No," I told him. "I didn't say anything about coming back. Lots of men have been there, but I only know of one who came back."

"Who," he asked, "was that?"

"Myself," I said.

He spread the map on the sticky surface of the dirty table. Outside the blare of drowsy music sounded through the sun-swept street. Inside it was darker and the flies buzzed around in circles. He tapped the spot on the map impressively.

"You've been *there*?"

I nodded.

"And back?"

I nodded again.

"What did you find?"

I leaned a little toward him.

"I found a section of the country that the Yaqui Indians want to keep people out of. I found thirst and suffering, and guns that popped off from concealed nests in the rocks, and sent silver bullets humming through the air.

"I found a man, dead. Someone had driven a sharp stake in the ground, leaving about four feet of it sticking up. Then they had sharpened the point and hardened it in fire. After they'd done that, they'd sat the man down on the stake. The sharpened point was sticking out, just back of his neck.

"And I found a rock slab with an iron chain, and the embers of a fire around it, an old fire, and there were bones, and the chain was wrapped around the bones, and the bones were blackened by fire, and bleached by sun. And I found a man who had had the soles of his feet peeled off with a skinning knife, and then been told to walk back over the hot sand.

"It's a country where the Yaqui Indians don't want any one to go. They say it's where they get the gold that they do their trading with."

"Trading?" he asked, and he had to wet his thin lips with the tip of his tongue before the word would come out.

"Yes," I said. "They work up along the ridge of the Sierra Madre Mountains, come down into some of the Arizona towns and buy gunpowder."

"Bullets?" he asked.

"They cast 'em out of silver. They don't need to worry about lead."

He was silent for several seconds.

Finally, he reached in a coat pocket and took out a little bag of buckskin. The buckskin was glazed with dirt and sweat, all smooth, dark and shiny. He opened it up.

It was filled with gold.

There wasn't a lot of it, but it was a coarse gold, about the size of wheat grains, and it looked good.

"That gold came from right here," he said, and he tapped the greasy spot on the map with his forefinger. "If you'd go there with me you'd find all you wanted."

His voice was smooth, seductive.

"Did you ever see a placer where the gold was like that?" he asked. "Just to be had for the taking?"

He was trying to arouse my greed.

I let my eyes lock with his.

"Did you ever see a man stuck on a pointed stake?" I asked.

Despite himself there was a little shudder that ran along his spine. I smiled to myself when I saw it. He was hard, but it was the hardness of the city. I didn't think he'd be hard long in the desert.

"I can offer you much money," he said, "a guarantee of success. You can be rich. You can go to the best hotels, eat at the best restaurants, take in the best shows, have the most beautiful women."

I smiled at that. His idea of luxury was the city man's idea.

"Did you ever see a man with the soles of his feet skinned off?" I asked him.

And then he got down to business.

"Listen," he said, and he lowered his voice until it

was almost a whisper, "I've got to go there. I'm administrator of an estate. The sole heir is a girl. That girl went there and didn't come back. I've got to find her and bring her out."

I was interested now.

"People who go there seldom come out," I said.

"No," he told me, "she's alive. I've heard from her. She's a prisoner there, and she's inherited a fortune. I've got to find her to keep the fortune from going to another branch of the family that's hostile."

I knew, even then, that there was a chance he was lying, a big chance. But I kept thinking of a white woman, trapped in that country, held a prisoner.

I looked squarely into his gray eyes.

"I'll go," I said, "on one condition."

"That is?"

"That you go along."

He let his eyes turn watery. His lips drooped. His face blanched. He tried to look away from me, and couldn't. I was holding his eyes with my own.

He heaved a deep sigh.

"I'll go," he said.

It wasn't exactly the answer I had expected, and, perhaps, he read that in my eyes.

He laughed, and the laugh was hard.

"Don't think I'm a fool," he said. "I've got an ace up my sleeve you haven't heard about, yet."

He just let his laugh fade into a smile, then the smile was wiped out and his face was hard as rock, hard with a thin-lipped expression of cruelty.

"Yes," he said. "We can go—and we can come back."

And he looked at me.

"There will be four in the party," he said.

"Four?"

"Yourself, myself, and two others."

"The others?"

"A man named Pedro Murietta, and Phil Brennan."

I stared at him. To get a Mexican to go into the Yaqui country was like getting a superstitious Negro to walk through a graveyard at midnight.

"Pedro Murietta?" I asked.

"A Yaqui Indian," he said. "Pure blood."

Then he laughed.

"I told you I had an ace up my sleeve," he said.

I rolled a cigarette.

"When do we start?"

"How soon can we start?"

I flipped away the cigarette.

"Right now," I told him and got up from the table.

2

A Mystery Package

It was the third day that the desert gripped us with its full strength.

The desert is a wonderful place. It's cruel, the cruelest enemy man ever had. And it's the kindest friend. Probably it's kind because it's so cruel. It's the cruelty that makes a man—or breaks him.

Phil Brennan was one of these delicate, retiring individuals. He was always in the background. Pedro Murietta had something wrong with him. I couldn't find out what. He was thin, and he was nervous, and his eyes were like those of a hunted animal.

Harry Karg was hard. He was cruel.

And on the third day the desert blazed into our faces, white hot with reflected sunlight, glaring, dazzling, shimmering, shifting. The horizons did a devil dance in the heat. The air writhed under the torture of the sun. All about us was a white furnace.

I'd had the two white men keep their skins oiled and covered with a red preparation that kept out some of the sunlight, letting them get accustomed to it by degrees.

But the sun was broiling their skins right through all the protective coverings.

A hot wind blew the stinging sand into little blistering pellets.

"How much longer?" asked Karg.

"Of what?" I inquired.

"Of this awful heat?"

It was the query I'd been waiting for. I faced him.

"You'll have it so long that you'll get accustomed to it," I told him. "Until your body dries out like a mummy; until you get so you know it's there but don't mind it; until you get so you quit sweating, and can go all day on a cup of water."

He cursed.

"Do you know what I heard?" he demanded.

"What did you hear?" I asked.

"That we could have come this far, and fifty miles farther by automobile, and started from there, gaining over five days in time and sparing us all this agony."

"You could," I said.

"Well, you're a hell of a guide," he stormed. "What's the idea in taking us through this hell hole?"

His face was writhing with rage, and his eyes, that had kept so clear all through his whisky drinking, were red now, so red it was hard to see any white in them.

The other two gathered around, made a little ring.

I wanted them to hear my answer, so I waited to make it impressive.

"The object in taking you on this trip was to toughen you up," I said. "If we'd taken the first lap by automobile, you'd have had to drink water on the last lap just like you're drinking it now. You're going to walk through the heat of this desert until you get so you can have one drink in the morning and one drink at night—and no more.

"You're going to walk through this desert until you quit thinking it's a hell hole and think it's one of the most beautiful places a man ever lived in.

"Then you'll be ready to start on the real part of the trip."

And I pushed him to one side and started on.

He· was hard, and he was strong, and the heat had frazzled his nerves, and he was accustomed to all sorts of little tricks of domination. It was inevitable that we should clash sooner or later. We clashed then.

He grabbed for me.

I swung my right to his jaw in a blow that was a full-arm swing, timed perfectly. It lifted him off his feet. He flung back his hands and then stretched his length on the sand that was so hot it would have cooked an egg.

The Yaqui said nothing.

Phil Brennan muttered an exclamation of disgust—for me.

I didn't care. I sat down on my heels and rolled a

cigarette, waiting for Harry Karg to get back to consciousness.

We have to do things in the desert so that they're done with the least waste of time.

The sand burned into the man's back. The sun tortured his eyelids. He groaned and twisted like an ant on a hot rock. I waited until he had opened his red eyes and realization dawned in them. Then I talked to him.

"You've been hard," I told him, "with men you could dominate. You've avoided those you couldn't. That's been all right in the city. You're in a different place now. You're in the desert. You can't bluff the desert, and you can't four-flush. You're going to tackle a real fight. I'm getting you ready for it.

"Now do you want to go on, or do you want to turn back? Do you want to take that one punch as settling things, or do you want to try a little more of the same?"

He squirmed about like a fresh trout in a hot frying pan. He tried to avoid meeting my eyes. But I held my gaze on him until he had to look at me.

We stared at each other for a full five seconds.

I read hatred and futility in his eyes.

But I knew the desert. I was doing things the only way possible for our own good. His eyes turned away.

"All right," he said. "I guess you know best."

I got up and walked to the burros then, and left him to plod along after he'd got up and scraped the hot sand out of his sweaty hair.

That night I cut down on their water supply. We had plenty, and we were coming to a country where there were springs. But I was giving them a taste of what was to come.

They had about half a pint of water apiece. It was

warm water, flat and insipid, and it tasted of tin from the canteen, but they'd have to get used to it.

Pedro Murietta, the Yaqui, took his water.

He didn't seem to care what happened. His devotion to Harry Karg was absolute, and yet it seemed to me to be founded on a hatred. He seemed constantly trying to break away from Karg's dominating influence, yet he couldn't.

Phil Brennan took his water, and he started to protest. Then he averted his eyes.

He wanted to fight, but he hated to oppose his will against that of another man. It wasn't that he was submitting. It was simply that he wasn't fighting. I didn't like it.

Harry Karg started to throw his water in my face.

I guess he'd have done it, too, if it hadn't been for the showdown we'd had earlier in the day.

He finally took the water, gulped it down in two big swallows and held out the empty cup for more.

I turned on my heel and walked away, leaving him with the empty cup. He had to learn his lesson sooner or later. It might as well be sooner.

That night the desert started to talk.

Deserts will do that. They'll be hot and silent, sometimes for days at a time. Then, at night, they'll begin to whisper.

Of course, it's just the sand that comes slithering along on the wings of the night winds that spring up from nowhere with great force, and die down as suddenly and mysteriously as they come up. But it sounds as though the sand is whispering as it slides along, hissing against the rocks, against the stems of the sage, the big barrels of the cacti, and finally, when the wind gets just right, against the sand itself.

But all the desert dwellers know those sand whispers, and, just before they drop off to sleep, they get the idea the desert is whispering to them, trying to tell them some age-old secret.

Some of the old-timers will admit it, and claim they can understand the desert. Some of them don't admit feeling that way. But they all have heard the song of the sand.

We lay in our blankets. The stars blazed down, and the sand talked. The spell of the desert gripped us.

I saw a shadow lurch against the stars, and someone came over toward my blankets. I stuck my hand on the butt of my six-gun, and slid back the trigger.

But it was only Phil Brennan.

He paused, then when I sat up, he came over toward me.

"I wasn't sure you were awake," he said.

I didn't say anything. I knew he had something he wanted to talk about.

"The sand seems to be hissing little whispers," he said.

I nodded. He hadn't come over to me to tell me the sand was whispering.

"Of course," he said, "it's nothing but the wind."

I just sat there, listening.

"You said the desert was a beautiful place," he said.

I nodded.

"You meant the sunsets and the colors, the sunrises and the purple shadows?" he asked uneasily.

"No," I said. "That's not real beauty. That's just an illusion. I meant the desert was beautiful because it strips a man's soul stark naked, because it rips off the veneer and blasts right down to the real soul. I meant it was beautiful because it's so cruel. It makes a man fight. It constantly threatens him. It'll kill you if you make a mistake. It'll kill off four-flushers and cowards and make a man find himself.

"Man learns the lesson of life from fighting. Some men are afraid to fight. The desert lures them into itself with its soft colors and its beautiful sunsets and lights and shadows, and then, before they know it, they're fighting, fighting for their lives.

"That's been your trouble. You've been too damned sensitive to fight. Now wait and see what the desert does."

And I dropped back in my light blanket, pillowed my head on the saddle, and let him see I'd talked all I was going to.

I heard him tossing in his blankets. And I heard the desert whispering to him. The sand whispers were soft and furtive that night, sand whispering to sand, mostly, and there was something as full of promise about them as a woman crooning whispers to the man she loves.

Some time after midnight the wind died away, all at once, and the desert became calm and silent, a great big aching void, empty of noise, menacing.

The desert knows the true philosophy of life. Man lives and suffers, and he learns through his suffering.

We plodded on.

The second day found us at the base of a big butte.

I rubbed it in a little.

"Here is where we could have come by machine," I said.

The party was silent. The Yaqui, because he was always silent. Phil Brennan, because he was thinking. Harry Karg, because he was afraid to trust himself to speech. He was fighting something now that he couldn't dominate, and it bothered him.

"We'd have reached it in a half a day by auto," I said.

That made Karg's heat-tortured face writhe.

But he kept silent.

I turned, and led the way into the desert that could only be traveled on foot, and my three companions were almost hard enough to stand a chance—if nothing went wrong. They weren't tough enough yet but what a dry water hole would have spelled disaster—but that's part of the game one plays in the desert.

We marched into the shimmering heat until the shadows closed about us. Then we had a little tea, and pushed on until it got too dark to see where we were going.

We made camp. The desert was silent, ominously silent.

The next day was an inferno with mountains that grimaced at us from the distance, rocky, hot mountains that writhed and wriggled all over the horizon.

That was the Yaqui country.

That afternoon I noticed the Yaqui.

After we'd spread our blankets and unsaddled the burros, I went to Harry Karg.

"I don't know what sort of a hold you've got on that Indian," I said, "but watch him."

He laughed at me.

"Leave that Indian to me," he said.

He seemed confident, sure of himself.

I shrugged my shoulders and turned away. I'd told him.

About midnight I woke up. Some one was crawling over the sand, and the sand made little crunching noises under his weight. I got my hand around the butt of my six-gun and rolled over.

The shadow was working its way toward Karg's blankets, and it was filled with menace.

I slid my six-gun around into a good position and thumbed back the hammer.

The shadow raised an arm. The starlight glinted on steel.

I let the hammer down on the shell.

I'd sort of pointed in the general direction of the knife, but I hadn't expected to hit it. It was too close shooting, to blaze away by the feel of the weapon alone. But I guess I didn't miss very far.

The shadow rolled over with a howl.

Karg jumped up out of his blankets, and he screamed as he came awake, which showed how taut his nerves were, and what the country had done to him.

I ran forward, keeping my gun on the squirming shadow.

It was the Indian. I'd missed the knife, but the bullet had ripped off the end of his thumb, right at the first joint.

I kicked the knife into the sand, searched the Indian for a gun, and then made a fire. It was a hard thing to do, but I limited the water for dressing the wound. One cup and no more.

Karg let it boil.

I knew as I watched him that he was a doctor. He took out a little chest of instruments, a folding leather affair of glittering instruments, and sterilized the tips in the water. Then he cleaned out the wound, did something to an artery that was giving little spurts of blood, and bandaged it up.

The Indian said nothing.

Karg took me to one side.

"What do we do with him?"

"Take the guns away, and watch him as best we can. We can't call a cop and have him arrested, and we can't turn him out in the desert, not unless he tries it again."

"Why did he use a knife instead of a gun?"

"Because he wanted all three of us. A gun would have only been good for one."

"How'd you happen to wake up?" he asked next.

I grunted.

"By the time you've lived as long as I have in the desert, you'll wake up when any one crawls around near your bed, or else you'll be asleep permanently."

He nodded.

"All right, then," he said, "you take it."

"Take what?" I asked.

"This," he said, and slid something into my hand. "I'll want it every day, sometimes twice a day. When I do, I'll come to you and get it. Guard it with your life. Don't let any one know you've got it. And don't ever try to look inside of it. It's locked."

I laughed at him; he was mixing in insults and compliments.

"Afraid to keep it yourself?" I asked him.

And there was a look of futility and of fear in his eyes, which showed what the desert was doing to him.

"Yes," he said, "I am afraid to keep it."

So I took it.

The next day the Yaqui was running a fever from the wound, and I took it easy. We didn't dare to stop. We had to keep on toward the next water hole. That's the desert; it's hard.

We came to bones that day. That was when we knew we were in Yaqui country.

The bones were bleached and white, and the skull grinned at us with the eye sockets looming startlingly black against the white brilliance of the sun-whitened bones.

I looked around the bones for signs of clothes. There should have been a few shreds of fiber, but there weren't any.

"Died of thirst," I told Karg. "They always rip their clothes off in the last frenzied run they make. Then they shred the flesh of their fingers into bloody ribbons digging into the sand. Then they die."

Phil Brennan turned sick at the stomach and walked away. Karg's face winced.

The Yaqui glanced at the bones with his smoky, desertwise eyes, and said nothing.

"And you said the desert was beautiful!" snapped Brennan.

I looked him over.

"Yes," I said, "it's beautiful."

3

A Traitor Returns

We started our march again, leaving the white bones out in the clean sunlight, the skull grinning at us. The party was silent. I noticed something gleaming off in the distance, and swung around so the sun glinted from it, then I headed toward the glint.

It turned out to be a burro packsaddle with the cinches cut through, and there were two canteens on the saddle.

I lifted one of them; it was empty. I lifted the other, and grunted my surprise.

It was full.

"Belonged to that dead man, I guess," I told them, "but he died of thirst, and this canteen is full."

It had been there in the sun for a long time, and the top was screwed on tight. The blanket covering was ripped and worn away, and the sun glinted from the metal that was so hot it would have blistered ungloved hands.

I unscrewed the cap and tilted the canteen.

Sand flowed out. It was sand that was so fine and dry that it flowed out just like water.

I laughed.

"What is it?" asked Karg.

"A pleasant little Yaqui trick," I said. "A man comes to a water hole, fills his canteen. The Yaquis follow him and find out what canteen he is using. Then they sneak into camp and pour the water out of the other canteen and fill it with sand.

"That's all they need to do. No rough stuff, nothing violent. The man simply goes out into the desert, not knowing anything's wrong. He travels until he's used up one canteen of water, then he starts on the other canteen—and nothing flows out but sand.

"He's one canteen's distance from his last water hole, usually one canteen's distance from the next. The Yaquis haven't had to follow him out into the desert.

They've simply left him and the desert together.

"And the answer is a pile of bones, such as we see every once in a while on the desert."

Brennan stared at me, soul sick, his eyes horror-stricken.

Hard Harry Karg was shivering as with the ague.

"Want to go back?" I asked him.

"Yes," he said, all at once, blurting out the word.

I nodded.

"Thought you would. Well, you can't. You may be in this thing for gold, or for a big fee for closing an estate, or because of some other reason. But there's a white woman held captive at the other end of the trail, and we're going to her. You might as well know it now as later."

I don't know what he would have said just then. I was hoping the shock of it all, and the surprise of my words, would force the truth out of him. The man wasn't a lawyer at all; he was a doctor. And he was a liar.

But the Yaqui had wandered off while I was examining the canteen. I looked up as I finished with my ultimatum to Karg, and saw the Yaqui silhouetted against the blue of the hot sky, on a hill, and he had a pile of green sage in front of him and some dry wood.

It was too far for a revolver shot. I ran for my rifle, and got there too late.

"What is it? What's he doing?" yelled Karg.

He got his answer as I flung the rifle around.

The Indian struck a match to the tinder dry wood. It crackled into flame. Then he flung himself over the crest of the hill as my bullet zinged through the hot air.

The dry wood sent flames into the oily leaves of the desert plants and a white smoke went up. I smashed bullets into the pile, knocking it into fragments of burning embers, but the damage was done.

The pillar of smoke went swirling up into the air, and ascended high into the blue before little wisps of wind scattered it.

I put fresh shells into the rifle.

Ten minutes later there were answering columns of smoke coming up from the mountains ahead of us.

Karg's face was chalky.

"Yes," he said, "I want to turn back."

Phil Brennan clamped his lips.

"No," he said. "We're going forward."

His face was as white as Karg's, but he was standing straight and his head was back.

The desert was commencing to leave its mark on Phil Brennan.

"Brennan wins. We go forward," I said.

I let them believe that it was because Brennan had made the decision. As a matter of fact, it was too late to go back.

"No, no!" rasped Karg. "I'm paying for this little expedition, and what I say goes. We're going back. Turn back, Zane."

I shrugged my shoulders and pointed back.

"If you want the back trail, there it is, shimmering in the heat. We're pushing forward."

And the thought of being alone in the desert sent Karg huddling close to us.

We marched on.

"The Yaqui?" asked Karg.

"Should be killed, but we can't waste time on him. He's burrowed into a shelter somewhere, and we'd be all day locating him."

"No," said Karg, "he'll be back, and he'll come asking for friendship." He spoke with calm confidence.

"You don't know the first damned thing about Indian character," I told him.

"Wait and see," he said.

I let it go at that.

But he was right.

It was the next afternoon, late. I could see that someone was running toward us, stumbling, holding his right hand up with the palm out, a gesture of peace.

I got out the gun.

The figure grew in size. It was the Yaqui.

He was haggard. His face was pale underneath its dusky color. His eyes were all red, and his lips were twitching. Little spasms seemed to ripple his skin.

I thought he wanted water, which was strange, because he had undoubtedly seen those answering smoke signals and been able to join his friends.

But it wasn't water he wanted.

And he'd met up with his friends, and deserted them again. For he had a canteen over his shoulder, and a gun at his hip. He'd left us empty handed.

I strode toward him.

But he avoided me. He dodged past and ran straight to Karg, and he was like a dog finding its master.

Karg motioned me to keep back, and then he walked out in the desert for fifty or sixty yards and had quite a little talk with the Yaqui.

The Indian was fawning on him, slavering for something, begging. Karg was hard. That was the way Karg could be his hardest, when some one was coming to him for something.

After a while Karg got up and came toward me.

The Indian remained on the desert, hunched over in a huddled heap.

"Give me the black package," said Karg.

I took it out from under my shirt.

He fitted a key to the lock, snapped it open, walked back toward the Yaqui. They went together down a little depression, walking along slowly.

They just walked through the depression, taking but little more time to it than they would have taken if they'd been walking steadily; but, somehow or other, I had an idea they had stopped for a few seconds.

They came back into sight, and the Indian had stopped talking. Karg motioned to him, and the Indian surrendered the gun. Karg came toward me.

"The Yaquis have got behind us, and they're closing in," he said.

"Don't think you're telling me any news." I said.

"You knew it?"

"Of course. After that smoke signal, there was nothing to it."

"Murietta betrayed us," said Karg. I laughed.

"That ain't news. It's history."

"And was to lead the attack," he said.

I nodded. "He led you here to lead you into a trap," I told him. "He'd been intending to betray you all along. You've got some hold on him, but he hates you."

He made an impatient gesture with his hand, as though he was brushing something aside, something that was unimportant.

"All men that I have a hold on hate me," he said.

"But Pedro's going to lead us through their lines. There's just a chance we can get through. There's a water hole to the south that Pedro knows about. No one else knows of it. If we can win our way through, then we won't be surrounded."

"They'll trail us," I told him.

"Of course. But we'll have the advantage of them. We get into a rocky country."

"And Murietta's probably betraying you again."

He shook his head positively.

"No," he said, "never again. Murietta knows he has to save me now. He wants to save my life."

I laughed at him, but he was right. I found it out when I got to talking with the Indian. He was frantically, hysterically anxious to see that we went through, and then he wanted us to go back. He wanted to leave.

I knew that if he'd double-crossed his own people and come over to us to get us through, he'd never dare to be caught alive. They reserve their most fiendish tortures for those who turn traitors, those Yaquis.

But I couldn't figure out just what it was that was holding Murietta to Karg.

4

Into Ambush

We started out after night, on a course at right angles, and we pushed through little passes, down little coulees, along dry stream beds, over little rocky ridges. The Indian seemed to know every foot of the way.

Then a dog barked.

Someone muttered something in a hoarse voice and the rocks began to spit little tongues of fire.

The bullets rained around us. Karg wanted to return

the shots, but I held his hand. They outnumbered us about ten to one, and the flashes of our guns would have shown them exactly where we were. But, pushing forward in the darkness, keeping under cover, we had them shooting with only a general idea of what they were shooting at.

We lost one of the burros, and, as we were winning clear, I felt something slam into my side with a force that spun me around, jerked me off my feet.

I figured it was the end, but I dropped and didn't say anything. I wanted the others to win through if they could. No use waiting for me.

It was Phil Brennan who came running back.

I tried to send him on, but I couldn't get my breath, couldn't manage to say a word. I made motions with my hands, but he stuck to me, lifted me to my feet.

Then I began to get so I could breathe. I put my hand to my side to see how badly I was hit. I could feel moisture trickling down my side, and my hand came away all sticky. I felt that my side was ripped wide open.

But, when I finally located the place, I found that it wasn't a wound at all. The bullet had ripped into the black leather case that Karg had given me to keep for him, and had slammed it into my side with the force of a mule's kick.

I could talk then, and explained to Brennan, but I couldn't walk, and the Indians were milling around over the country, calling to each other, lighting torches, trying to pick up our trail.

I persuaded Brennan to run on ahead and join the others and tell them I was waiting behind to act as sort of a rear guard, that I was all right, and would join them as soon as I found out just what the Indians would do.

He went on.

After a while I forced my legs into action, and forged ahead as best I could, but I'd lost the others. There was no moon, and the starlight was deceptive. I plugged along in the direction the Indian had said to take, but I couldn't find any trace of the others.

The Indians had the trail by this time, but a trail in rocky country by torchlight isn't easy to follow, and there were mountains off to the left that were great slabs of rock and timber. I figured they'd have to ditch the burros, but they stood some chance of getting through.

I could tell from the noise and the flicker of the red torchlight that I was off to the left of the trail the others had left.

I didn't have any burros, and I was taking time, so I wasn't leaving any trail. On the other hand, I only had a light canteen of water, a little salt, and a small packet of flour.

I got up on a rocky pinnacle, saw the east beginning to turn color, found a place where I could burrow in out of the heat of the sun, and decided to hole up a while.

After this, it would be a case of travel at night.

I was tired, and my side was sore and bruised. I dropped off to sleep.

When I woke up the sun was up.

I was careful to keep from getting so much as the tip of my head against the sky line. I made a survey of the country. It was rocky, a tumbled mass of blistering hot rocks piled in twisted confusion, and stretching from foothills up to high mountains that had timber.

I knew the general run of the country.

There'd be water in those mountains.

But I couldn't see a sign of life, either Indian or white.

I knew the Indians would be perched up on the rocky crests, waiting and watching. And I hoped Murietta would be true enough to keep the others from moving around in daylight. To move was to invite sure death.

I made sure my hiding place was pretty safe, and crawled back in the shade of the overhanging rock. The sun crept up, and the heat began to turn my little hiding place into an oven.

I thought of the leather packet that had saved my life.

I took it out from underneath my shirt. The bullet was of the type I knew it would be, almost pure silver. It had ripped into the leather and smashed some bottles, and it was the liquid from those bottles that I had felt trickling down my side.

I looked at the bottles, and then I knew the truth—knew the reason the Yaqui had been such a slave to Harry Karg. Karg had made him a dope fiend, and the leather case contained lots of little vials of dope, ready mixed for hypodermic use. And then, in case that wasn't enough, there were some bottles of morphia, heroin, cocaine, all in little powders and tablets.

Most of the mixed stuff had broken under the impact of the bullet and had soaked through the case, but the upper end of the case that had the tablets in it was uninjured.

There was a letter wadded in there, a letter written in a feminine hand.

I saw Brennan's name scrawled on a margin.

Some people may be hesitant about reading letters that are written to other people. I'm not—not when the other person has got me out in the Yaqui country with an Indian that he's made a dope fiend out of, and it's beginning to look as though he lied to get me there.

I spread out the letter.

The bullet had torn off one corner, but the writing was intact. It started out: "Harry," not "Dear Harry" or "Friend Harry" or any of that mushy stuff, just "Harry."

The message was the kind that showed just how the woman felt. She didn't mince words.

Harry:

I know now that you tricked father into coming here. You knew he would. You didn't count on his taking me with him.

I know now that you tricked me, through father, into promising that I would marry you. You knew I loved Phil Brennan, and I think he loves me. But he's too retiring to fight.

I give you the credit of really loving me, and think that my money doesn't enter into it. But, as you said, so frequently, "a Kettler never goes back on a promise." And you got my promise, both to you and to father.

Father came here after specimens, and the Indians killed him. I'm inclosing a bit of map torn from his atlas which shows where I am. I won't tell you how I'm managing to keep from being killed, whether or not I'm a prisoner.

I've promised I'd marry you, but you've got to come for your bride. If you want me badly enough to come and get me, and bring Phil Brennan with you to see fair play, I'll remember the promise I made father. If you don't come within three months after this message is delivered I'll consider you don't want your bride badly enough to come for her.

I'm sending this by a Yaqui I can trust. You remember telling me a hundred times that you liked me well enough to come to the ends of the earth for me. Well, this isn't exactly the end of the earth, but it will be a good test of whether or not I'm to be released from my promise.

SALLY KETTLER

I read the note and knew a lot more than I had before. Evidently Harry Karg had used some sort of pressure to get a promise from the woman, but he had to come to her to get her to keep that promise. He was now at almost the exact spot on the map the woman had marked, the spot from which the mark she had made had been obliterated by the oil of many fingers smearing over the colored surface of the paper as they pressed down on it. I wondered how many guides Karg had tried to engage before he had hit on me, had thought of making a dope fiend out of the Indian messenger.

I wondered what the Indian would do when he realized Karg had no more dope for him. Apparently he had been a slave to Karg until he got within striking distance of an Indian doctor. Then he had gone to the Indian medicine man, told the story, been treated.

But the herbs of the Yaquis had been of no avail against the gnawing of the drug hunger. And the Yaqui had realized, too late, that he had only one chance for satisfying that terrible craving—to find the man he had betrayed.

But now . . .

It was just the faintest suggestion of sound, the bare hint of a pebble rattling down a rock, but I grasped my weapon and rolled swiftly to the little rim of rock.

I determined I was going to make them buy my life at a dear price.

But it wasn't an Indian.

Down below me, toiling along, carrying a rifle and a heavy canteen, was Phil Brennan, working his way with what he thought was great caution.

I couldn't imagine how the Indians could have passed him up. He hadn't even figured out the advantage of areas of low visibility sufficiently to keep in the patches of shade. He was trying to walk quietly, but the keen senses of the Yaquis would hear sounds that I couldn't, and I had heard him from seventy yards up the slope.

I was afraid to signal to him, afraid he would give a shout or betray himself still further through a scramble up the slope. I slid the rifle forward and concentrated on his back trail, ready to pick off any one who followed.

But no one seemed to be following, which was a mystery to me.

Then I caught a flicker of motion and the sights of my rifle snapped into line. I had the hot stock pressed to my cheek, and was ready to squeeze the trigger, when the person stepped out from between two boulders, and I got a brief glimpse.

It was a woman, slender, graceful as a deer, clad in a garment made out of tanned skins, and the flesh which was disclosed over the top of the skins, and down below the hem of the short skirt, was as sun-tanned and bronzed as old ivory.

She was following him, and she was moving with the lithe grace of a wild animal.

Phil Brennan sat down on a hot rock. He mopped his forehead, gazed apprehensively about him. But he didn't see the girl. For that matter, I couldn't see her any longer. There had been just that one brief, flashing glimpse. She was as intangible as a deer slipping up a brush-covered slope.

Brennan unscrewed the cap of the canteen, raised it.

I frowned, considered flinging him a low word of caution. This was no time to be wasting water.

But I held my speech. After all, there were more important things than water.

I saw Brennan fling back his head, throw the canteen from him. His fingers clawed at his mouth. He looked as though the water from the canteen had been some deadly acid that burned its way into his flesh.

For a second I couldn't understand, and my eye flashed to the canteen.

Then I understood.

A white stream was slipping silently from the mouth of the canteen, a stream, not of water, but of sand.

5

"Isn't It Beautiful?"

I thought panic was going to grip the man when he realized that he was in the midst of a hostile desert without water, that there were enemies surrounding him.

He got to his feet, swung around, took a running step or two, and came to a dead stop as he heard my voice raised in a low command.

It took him a little while to locate me, and, in that

interval, I knew he was getting himself under control.

"Here I am, up here. That's it. Now work up here towards me, and take it slow. Keep to the shadows. Don't get impatient and try to come too fast. Take it easy."

He came up to me, then, listening for my commands.

I kept him well under cover, as well as I could. The sunlight was beating pitilessly down on the rocky slope of the hill, but that made the darkness of the shadows the more intense, and I hoped there was a chance, perhaps one in ten, that he could make it without betraying himself to watching eyes.

I couldn't understand why those eyes hadn't seen him before this, didn't understand it until the sound of a rifle shot, thin and thready in the hot air, came to my ears. Then there was another shot and another, a rattle of swift fire and then silence.

Then I knew, knew even before I heard words of confirmation from Brennan. He and Karg had separated. Karg had been thinking over the Yaqui trick of putting sand in a canteen and getting a man trapped into going into the desert country. It had been just the sort of scheme he liked. He had tried it on Brennan.

They had separated, Brennan tricked into taking the canteen of sand, and Karg had forged ahead with the water. But his cleverness had been his undoing; the Yaquis had spotted him. They had signaled their discovery, concentrated on Karg, and then—torture.

I greeted Brennan. He was mouthing curses against Karg and his trickery.

I interrupted them.

"We stand a chance," I told him. "The mountains. The Yaquis have been spread out, doing scout work, searching for us. But when they found Karg they all swung in together for an attack. That leaves us unguarded, and if we can get to the mountains there's a chance.''

He was interested, looking up at the white-hot slopes of the rocky mountains, then back at the tumbled mass of foothills.

"How about Karg?" he asked.

I shrugged my shoulders.

He sighed, got to his feet. "Let's go," he said.

I said nothing about the form of the girl I had seen on his back trail, nor did I say anything about the letter in the bullet-ripped leather packet.

We gained the mountains, kept to the hot rocks, leaving but little trail. From time to time, I paused to search the back trail, but I could see no one. And yet I had the feeling that we were being followed. I wondered if it was the girl, or something more sinister.

The afternoon shadows lengthened. I proposed a rest. We'd have to travel long into the night.

"In which direction?" asked Brennan.

"Back, of course."

He shook his head.

"No; I haven't got what I came here for, yet."

I said nothing.

We waited. I watched the back trail. We could hear the distant barking of a dog, an hour or so after sunset.

"How about Karg?" asked Brennan.

"That's the second time you've asked about him," I said.

"It's the hundredth time I've thought about him."

"Don't worry about not being revenged. The Indians will take care of that."

He shuddered.

"That's exactly it. Think of the stake in the ground . . . Ugh!"

I looked at the stars, steady, bright, giving lots of light.

"There's perhaps a village out where that dog is barking," I told him.

"They'd take him there?"

"Yes."

He got to his feet uncertainly.

"Okay. Let's go back. I've got to save him. I hate the sight of him. After I rescue him I'll beat him to a pulp. But I can't run away and leave him."

I warned him.

"You don't stand any chance. They will hear us. They will simply capture us, too."

"Us?" he said. "You're going?"

"Of course, if you go."

He wet his lips.

"I'm going," he said, and took a stride forward.

I've lived in the desert for a long time. I think I know something about woodcraft and the way men stalk in the open. I'd have sworn no one could have crawled up within listening distance without my hearing. But I'd have been wrong.

A slender shape rose from the rocks like a wraith.

Brennan recoiled.

"Phil!" she said.

"Sally!" was torn from his throat, and the word, as he said it, was an exclamation, a prayer, a benediction, and a great longing.

I dropped back, down behind the rocks.

I heard her voice.

"It's too late," she was saying. "He dug his own pitfall. The Yaqui murdered him when he found there was no more of the drug. It was the sound of that shot that brought the others."

They came to me later on.

The woman had established herself with the natives. They considered her as something of a priestess. The desert had done something to her, brought out something of the lithe grace which is inherent in youth and beauty. She had become as a wild thing, perfect in strength, poise, figure.

The Indians considered her a goddess and the priestess of the godhead. She came and she went as she saw fit. And she was promised to a man she didn't love; wanted the love of a man who loved her, but who would not speak.

So she had brought them into the crucible of the desert.

"If Harry had come," she told me privately, "openly and fairly, the Indians would have given him safe passage. But he came by trickery and deception. He tried to enslave to the dope habit the guide I sent, so there could be no question of treachery, and, by that treachery of his own, he brought about his own destruction."

"If he was to have come in safety," I asked, "why did you make him come at all? What was to be gained?"

She looked at the stars.

"Perhaps it was just to postpone things," she said softly, "perhaps it was a woman's intuition. But I have come to know the desert places. I thought that if I could get those two men together out into the desert . . ."

And I thought of what the desert had done, of how the man who had thought he was hard had had the surface hardness cut away by the hissing sand and the melting heat, until the craven soul beneath that surface had stood forth for all to see.

And I thought of how the tempering fire of the desert heat had fused the character of the other, melted away the surface weakness, and brought to light the inner strength of character.

And I continued to think, long after the two had left me, long after the desert had begun to talk, a wind hissing the sand against the rocks of the mountainside.

They were off to one side, sitting close, talking in low tones, and the desert whispers were sending an undercurrent of whispering sand against the crooning tones of their voices.

I was lulled into a doze.

I awakened with Phil Brennan's hand on my shoulder.

"Isn't it beautiful?" he asked softly.

I looked at the grayish white of the desert sand, at the inverted bowl of golden stars, blazing steadily.

"Isn't what beautiful?" I asked.

"The desert, of course!" he said.

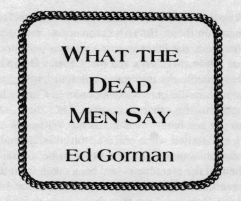

WHAT THE
DEAD
MEN SAY

Ed Gorman

THE NEWSPAPER ACCOUNT told it this way:

On the sunny morning of June 27, 1898, a thirteen-year-old girl named Clarice Ryan walked into the First Trust Bank of Council Bluffs, Iowa.

Out of school for the summer, Clarice was helping her father Septemus, one of the town's leading merchants, by taking the morning deposit to the bank.

Ordinarily, Clarice always stopped by the office of bank president Charles Dolan. The banker is said to have kept a drawerful of mints for the express purpose of giving one to his "lady friend," Clarice, each working morning.

On this particular morning, however, Clarice was unable to visit her friend Dolan. As soon as she walked into the bank, she saw immediately that a robbery was in progress.

Against the east wall, four customers stood with their

hands up as a man with a red bandana over his face held a shotgun on them. His two companions, one wearing a blue bandana, the other wearing a green one, stood near the safe while two clerks and Mr. Charles Dolan himself emptied greenbacks into three sailcloth bags.

The man in the blue bandana ordered Clarice to stand over next to the other customers. Like them, she was told to put her hands over her head. Witnesses said the young girl smiled when she was told this. Scared as she was, she obviously found the order to be a little silly.

When all the greenbacks had been taken from the safe, the three thieves gathered in the middle of the bank. At this point Dolan and the two clerks were moved over to join Clarice and the other customers.

It was then that policeman Michael Walden, who had seen what was going on from the window on the board-walk outside, came through the door with his own shot-gun, ordering the men to lay down their arms.

The rest of the story remains confused, Deputy Walden insisting that he fired only because one of the thieves opened fire on him. Two of the customers insisted that it was Walden who fired first.

At some point in the minute-long exchange of gunfire, one of the adult customers was shot in the shoulder. One of the thieves was also wounded, though all three managed to escape. Clarice Ryan, shot in the heart, was killed instantly.

Several rewards have been offered for the capture of the thieves. "I guess I don't need to say dead or alive," Council Bluffs police chief Dennis Foster told assembled reporters. "And a lot of folks would just as soon see them slung over horses and brought in dead as otherwise."

Investigation into the death of thirteen-year-old Clarice Ryan continues.

Chapter One

1

From the second-floor hotel veranda he could look down into the dusty street and see the women twirling their parasols and hurrying about in their bustles. These were town women with sweet Christian faces and sweet Christian souls. Carlyle, six years out of prison at Fort Madison, wanted such a woman. He imagined that their juices were tastier, their love by turns gentler and wilder, and their soft words in the darkness afterward balming like a cool breeze on a hot July afternoon. He would never know. Sweet Christian women had never taken to Carlyle. He had put his seed only in whores and long ago his seed had turned to poison.

Right now, though, Carlyle wasn't worrying about women, sweet or otherwise. He was looking at the two riders who were coming down the middle of the street, one astride a roan, one on a dun. A water wagon followed them, cutting the dust with sprays of silver water. Behind the wagon ran some noisy town kids waving and jumping and laughing and carrying on the way kids always did when they were three days out of school and just beginning summer vacation.

The two riders didn't seem to notice the kids. They didn't seem to notice much, in fact. The small Midwestern town was a showcase hereabouts, what with electricity, telephones, and a depot that President Harrison himself had once told the local Odd Fellows club was "most singularly impressive." Anyone could tell, therefore, that the two riders came from a city. Country folks always gawked when they came to Myles. City folks, who'd seen it all already, were too cynical and spoiled to gawk.

One of the riders was a boy, probably sixteen or so, tall and lanky, with a handsome rugged face. But it was on the other rider that Carlyle settled his attention. The man was short, somewhat chunky, packed into a dark vested suit far too hot for an afternoon like this. He wore a derby and carried a Winchester in his scabbard.

Carlyle knew the man. Oh, didn't know him in the sense that they'd spoken or anything, but knew him in the sense that the man was in some way familiar.

Carlyle raised his beer mug and sipped from it just as, sprawled in a chair behind him, the whore yawned again. She was too wide and too white. It was for the latter reason that she liked to sit out on the veranda, so the sun would tan her arms and bare legs. In her petticoats she was damned near naked and it seemed she could care less. Her name was Jenna and she and Carlyle had been living in the same hotel room for the past eight months. Last night she'd started talking marriage again and Carlyle, just drunk enough and not impressed by her threats of leaving him if he ever slapped her again, doubled his fist and poked it once straight and hard into her eye. Her shiner this morning was a beauty. Of course, he'd had to offer her something in compensation. Not marriage, he said; but teeth. Store-bought teeth. Hers were little brown stubs that made her mouth smell so bad he had to down two buckets of beer before he could bring himself to kiss her.

"What the hell you lookin' at so hard?" Jenna wanted to know.

"Man."

"What man?"

"Man on a dun."

"You never saw a man on no dun before?"

"Wonder why he came here."

"Came where?"

"To town. Myles."

"Free country."

"Yeah, but he wants somethin' special."

"How you know that?"

"You can see by the way he rides. Like he's just waitin' for somethin' to happen."

"That's how I was last night," Jenna laughed. "Waitin' for somethin' to happen."

He looked back at her. "You don't like it, you whore, you can always move out."

"Just a joke, Henry. Jus' teasin'. Too much beer affects most men that way."

But Carlyle was no longer listening. He had turned his attention back to the street and the two riders. Halfway down the block, and across the street, they were dismounting in front of the McAlester Hotel. Unlike the place where Carlyle and the whore lived, the McAlester didn't have cockroaches and colored maids who went through your room trying to steal stuff.

"Sonofabitch," Carlyle said.

"What?"

"I just recognized who he is."

"Who is he?"

"Sonofabitch," Carlyle said again.

He went back to the whore and tried to hand her his beer mug.

"I don't want that thing. I ain't your maid," she said. She could get real bitchy, this one.

Carlyle threw the beer in her face.

"You ain't got no right to do that," she said, spitting out suds.

"Hell if I don't," Carlyle said. "Long as I pay the rent on that room, I got a right to do any god damn thing I please."

Then he was gone, inside to his room and then into the hallway and then down the stairs to the lobby. He took two steps at a time.

He had suddenly remembered, from all the pictures in the newspapers right after it happened, who the man was.

He did not stop hurrying until he was two blocks from the downtown area, and running down a side street so fast people stopped to look at him.

2

The kid's name was James Patrick George Hogan, George being his confirmation name, taken for the saint who slew dragons. In his Catholic school book there had been an illustration of George in armor and mail standing triumphant with his huge battle sword near a slain dragon. The dragon's scales and reptilian snout had captivated James.

Looking at illustrations of dragons and dinosaurs was his favorite pastime. He could stare at them for hours, imagining himself living back then. The only thing wrong with this was that back then there would have been no Marietta Courtney, this being the fourteen-year-old public-school girl James had been steadfastly stuck on since he'd seen her a year ago riding her bicycle, her red hair gorgeous in the sunlight, her smile in equal parts impish and unknowable.

These were some of the things James had thought about on the last part of the journey to Myles. His uncle Septemus Ryan had fallen into one of his silences. Of course, James knew what the silence was about: a few years back his uncle's girl—and James's favorite cousin—Clarice, had been shot and killed in a bank robbery back in their hometown. This had been particularly hard on Septemus, because only two years previously his wife had died from whooping cough.

Since these deaths there had been a lot of talk in Council Bluffs about "poor Septemus not being quite right upstairs." He was given to violent tempers, unending days and nights of brooding, and talking to himself. The latter seemed particularly troubling to Council Bluffians. Here was a leading merchant, and a darned handsome one at that, walking down the streets of town quite obviously carrying on some kind of conversation with himself. What he was saying or to whom was a mystery, of course, and a disturbing one to those who cared about him.

In the dusty street, James and Septemus dismounted. They took the carpetbags from their saddles and carried them inside the hotel.

James appreciated the cooling shade of the fine hotel lobby. Gentlemen in percale shirts and straw boaters and cheery red sleeve garters sat in leather chairs smoking cigars, sipping lemonade, and reading newspapers and magazines. A few yellowbacks were even in evidence. James wondered if any of them were reading *The Train Boy*, which next to the works of Sir Walter Scott was the best thing he'd ever read.

The lobby had mahogany wainscoting and genuine brass cuspidors and great green ferns. The mustached man behind the registration desk looked as snappy as a man in a Sears catalog.

"Good afternoon, sir," the clerk said in a splendid manly voice.

"Afternoon," Septemus said. "One room, two beds. And we'll be wanting baths this afternoon."

"Cool ones, I trust, sir," the clerk said, smiling.

Septemus didn't smile back. The clerk, something dying in his eyes, looked mortally offended.

Up in their room, they emptied the carpetbags on their beds and then sat in the two chairs next to the window to sip their complimentary lemonade.

"You glad you came along?" Septemus said. Here it was three degrees hotter than down on the street, but here they could feel the breeze better, too. Septemus had taken his jacket and his vest off. At forty-five he was balding and getting fat, but he still looked muscular and his hard, angular face attracted women and made men wary. He didn't look at all like a haberdasher.

"Yessir."

"There you go again."

James blushed. "I'm sorry."

"No need to apologize, James. You've just got to remember the things I'm trying to teach you."

James nodded.

"You know why I took you on this trip?"

"Because you wanted to take me to the state fair." The fair was in Des Moines, some one hundred miles away. There would be amusement rides and prize live-stock and bearded ladies and magicians and probably two hundred girls who were as cute as Marietta Court-ney. Or at least James hoped so.

"The fair is part of the reason but it's not all of the reason."

"It's not?"

Septemus looked at James very hard. "I wanted to get you away from your mother's influence."

"You did?"

"I did."

"You don't like my mom?"

"I like your mom fine but she's not the best influence you could have."

"She's not?"

"Nope. Your father was."

"But he is dead."

"I'm well aware of that."

"And my mom has done a good job of raisin' us three kids ever since."

Septemus still looked solemn. "Your mother is my sister and a woman I respect no end. But she's a lot better mother to your two sisters than she is to you."

"She is?"

Septemus nodded, then sipped some lemonade. "Think about it, James."

"About what?"

"About what your life has been like since your father died. Without a proper male influence, that is."

"I don't understand."

"Violin lessons. Always wearing knickers and a clean

dress shirt. Spending most of your time on studies instead of being outside playing baseball. Do you honestly think this is a natural state of affairs for any young man? And that's what you are, James, whether your mother chooses to acknowledge it or not. You're sixteen and that makes you a young man.''

''I guess I never thought of it that way.''

''When your father was your age, he was supporting a family of three and going to work for the Union Central Life Insurance Company. By the time he was twenty, he had his own office.''

''That's right, Uncle Septemus.''

''And he was a man known to take a drink who could hold a drink, and a man known to hunt who had respect for the rifle and the prey alike, and a man known to please the ladies just by the manliness of his stride and the confidence of his smile. He was one hell of a real man.''

James couldn't help it. Hearing his father recalled so lovingly—Septemus and James's father had been best friends for many years—James got tears in his eyes and had a hard time swallowing.

''Your father wouldn't have approved of the violin lessons. Or the musicals in your parlor every Tuesday night. Or all those luncheons your mother takes you to.''

''He wouldn't have?''

Septemus shook his head. ''No, he wouldn't have. And that's why I brought you along on this trip.''

James looked perplexed.

''To start teaching you about manly things,'' Septemus said. ''Away from the influence of your mother.''

''Oh.''

''So stop being so deferential. Stop always 'Yessiring'

me. A gentlemen is always polite, but that doesn't mean
he has to be bowing and scraping. You understand
that?''

James almost said ''Yessir.'' Instead, he caught himself in time and simply nodded.

''Good. Now why don't you take a bath. I've got to
go do a little business. I'll be back to take my own bath
and then we can get something to eat.''

Septemus got up and stood over James and mussed
his hair with thick fingers. ''You look more like your
father all the time. You should be proud of that.''

''I am.''

For the first time since they'd left Council Bluffs, Septemus smiled. ''This trip'll be good for you, James. You
wait and see.''

Then, his boots loud on the linoleum floor in the
drowsy quiet of the afternoon, he went over and put his
vest and coat back on.

James couldn't help but notice that Septemus also
picked up his Winchester.

''See you in an hour or so, James,'' Septemus said.

Then he was gone.

3

Golden dust motes rolled in the sunlight angling through
a hat-sized hole in the roof of the barn. Griff was always
meaning to fix it but that would happen only if the Rochester Wagon Works opened its doors again and rehired
the eighty-six men they had laid off four and a half years
ago. Griff was a big man, blond and open, and in the
old days had always been laughing. He had a wife who'd

loved him since they'd been kids on adjoining farms, and two little girls who never seemed to tire of running up to him with their arms spread wide, having him pick them up and pretend he was dancing with them.

But one day Mr. Rochester himself had come to the plant and said, with genuine dismay, ''Men, the bank won't loan me no more money and our bills are just too far backed up; I'm gonna have to lay you all off. I'm sorry, men.'' There had been real tears in Mr. Rochester's eyes, and the men knew the tears were not fake because Mr. Rochester was just like them, a workingman who'd got lucky with his invention for building surreys a certain way, and who then, like most workingmen, got unlucky, too. He knew a hell of a lot about surreys, did Mr. Rochester, but he didn't know a damn about money; his pride and fear were such that he wouldn't listen to anybody either, even the well-intentioned bankers who'd meant to help him. So he'd gone bust with a bad hand, and his eighty-odd employees had gone bust right along with him.

There followed those events that always seem to follow men losing good jobs. Drink turned some of them mean and they beat their loving wives, and some even beat their children. At workingmen's taverns blood spilled all the time now, not just during the occasional Saturday brawl. The best of the men, the ones who didn't turn to drink and violence, tried to get other jobs; but, prosperous as the town was, there were no other jobs, not good ones anyway, not ones that could replace what they'd earned (and the kind of self-esteem they'd felt) as employees of the Rochester Wagon Works. These men took to serving the gentry, for there was a large class of rich people in the town. They became gardeners and handymen and drivers and housepainters; they learned how to say yes ma'm and yessir so sweet you almost couldn't hear the contempt in their voices for the spoiled, pushy, inconsiderate rich folks who employed them. They had no choice. They had families to feed.

It was sometime during this period when the happy Griff became the sorrowful Griff. He worked half a dozen jobs that first year after Rochester closed down, the worst of them being as a helper to one of the town's three morticians. He had hated seeing how the blood ran in the gutters of the undertaker's table and he had hated the white fishbelly look to the flesh of corpses and most especially the high fetid smell of the dead that he could never quite get clean of his nostrils. He tried getting back to farming somehow, but this was a time of many bank failures in the Midwest, currency shaky as hell, and so he could find nobody to stake him.

It was then that he evolved the idea of robbing banks. It would be simple enough. He would take two of the men he had worked with at Rochester—Kittredge, because he had good nerves and was intelligent; Carlyle, because he had the kind of Saturday night beery courage you needed in tight spots—and together they would travel in a three-hundred-mile semicircular radius (he had this drawn out on a map) and hold up banks three times a year. Kittredge and Carlyle were happy to be invited in. They had agreed to two inviolate propositions: Griff had the final say in any dispute, and there was to be no violence. No violence whatsoever. It was in the course of their very first robbery that either Kittredge or Carlyle (Griff could never be sure) panicked and the little girl got killed. It had been purely an accident—my God, nobody would shoot a little girl—but that didn't make her any less dead. The three men had been so sickened by the sight of the little girl lying in blood and dead on the floor that they forgot to grab the money. They left with guns blazing, empty-handed. They were lucky to escape.

So now he stood in the dusty sunlight of the long July afternoon in a barn that smelled of wood and tarpaper and hay and dogshit from the girls' collie. It smelled most especially of the grease and oil he used to work on his top grade surrey, the one expensive thing he'd ever bought in his forty-one years, bought at a forty-percent employee discount from Rochester back in the good working days. The surrey was fringed and built on elliptic end springs, and had axles of fifteen-sixteenths of an inch, wheels of seven-eighths of an inch and quarter-inch steel tires. The gear was made of second-growth timber ironed with genuine Norway iron and the upholstery was Evans leather. How nice it had been to take this spanking new surrey out for a Sunday drive behind a powerful dun, the girls sitting between Griff and his wife, the neighbors smiling and waving. Down Main Street they'd go every sunny Sunday, church done and a beef roast on the stove, past the Southern Hotel and the big stone bank building, the telegraph office and the telephone office, and McDougall the dentist's. Even a workingman could feel respectable in such circumstances.

Griff was just oiling the axle when he heard the collie, standing in the sunlight just outside the shade of the barn, start to bark. He looked over his shoulder and saw Carlyle. Carlyle looked upset. He also looked drunk. Ever since the little girl had died, Carlyle had spent most of his time on whores and whiskey. Griff no longer liked the man. "Told you I'd just as soon not have you come on my property."

"Don't give a good god damn what you told me."

Griff put down the oil can and turned around. He made fists of his hands. Because he was big and blond and fair, most people mistook him for a Swede, but he was Irish and had an Irish temper. "Don't appreciate you talking to me that way on my own property."

Carlyle didn't seem to hear. "He's here."

"Who's here?"

"Right in town."

Griff could see that Carlyle was caught up in his fear and his drunkenness. He reached out and took the gawky man by the shoulder. Carlyle smelled of sweat and heat and soured beer. Griff turned his face away as he said, "I want you to get hold of yourself."

"I got hold of myself."

"No, you don't."

"I'm tryin' to tell you, Griff, he's god damn here."

"And I'm tryin' to ask you, Carlyle, who's god damn here?"

"Her father."

"Whose father?"

"The little girl's."

"Jesus Christ," Griff said. He almost never took the Lord's name in vain. To him that was a significant sin— even a mortal sin that had to be confessed as such to Father Malloy—but right now he didn't care. "How do you know it's him?"

"We've seen his picture, ain't we, a hunnerd times."

"You're sure?"

"Griff, I'm positive."

"Maybe it's just a coincidence."

"Could be, but I doubt it."

Griff wiped sweat from his brow with his forearm. "How the hell could he have found us?"

"Maybe he never quit lookin'."

Griff came out from the cool shadows of the barn to stand in the sunlight with Carlyle. Carlyle looked old now. He had a couple of days' worth of beard and some of his hairs were black and some of them were white. His nose was kind of running and he hadn't cleaned the morning dirt from the corners of his eyes.

"What we gonna do?" Carlyle said.

"Nothing we can do. Not right now. Not till we see what he wants."

"Oh, I can tell you quick and proper what he wants, Griff."

"And what would that be?" Griff said. He felt calmer now, more in control of himself, the way he usually did.

"He wants us dead. All three of us."

"Can you blame him? We killed his little girl."

"Not on purpose."

"That don't bring her back to life."

Carlyle looked as if he were about to cry. "What the hell we gonna do, Griff? You're supposed to be the boss. You tell me."

"You go back to the hotel and relax."

"Yeah, sure, Griff. I sure can relax knowin' some sonofabitch is lookin' for me."

"Get ahold of Kittredge."

"And tell him what?"

"Tell him to meet us at nine tonight at the west end of the Second Avenue bridge."

"You know what he's like, Griff. He won't be able to handle this."

Griff stared at him hard. "He won't have much choice, Carlyle. None of us do." He nodded to the street. "Now go tell him and then stay in your room till you go to the bridge."

"You sure like givin' orders, don't you?"

Griff smiled without much humor. "If you want me to play boss then you better get used to me givin' orders. You understand me?"

Carlyle looked sulky. "I don't like none of this."

"Get going. And get going *now*."

Carlyle shook his head, wiped some sweat from his face, and then set off down the driveway to the street.

Griff watched the man go. Then his girls came up and jumped up and down around him in their faded gingham dresses. If good times ever rolled around again, the first thing Griff planned to do was buy the girls some new clothes. Now they wore hand-me-downs from in-laws and Griff, a proud man, just hated to see it.

Kneeling on his haunches, he drew the two girls close to him and hugged them tight with his eyes closed.

"Boy, it sure is hot, Daddy," Eloise said.

"It sure is," Tess agreed.

But that was the funny thing to Griff. Hot as it was—the afternoon ablaze now at three o'clock—he felt so cold he was shivering.

He hugged the girls even tighter, and tried not to think of how the little girl in the bank had looked that morning, bloody and dead on the linoleum floor.

Chapter Two

1

Just off the sidewalk there was a huge oak, one with roots like claws, and beneath it stood Ryan. On so hot a day he appreciated the shade, though curiously he left his vest and suitcoat on. Hanging loose from his left hand was his Winchester.

For the past ten minutes, Ryan had kept his brown eyes fixed on the small, white cottagelike house and the large barn that loomed over it directly behind. Griff and Carlyle were back there now, talking.

Ryan set the Winchester against the tree then took out a cigar and lighted it. Even on a day this hot, the fifty-cent Cuban tasted good, heady as wine the first few puffs.

A small boy pulling a small red wooden wagon inside of which sat an even smaller girl came by, followed by a yipping puppy. Ryan said hello to the boy and smiled at the puppy. The girl, even though she said hello, received nothing from Ryan, not even a glance. He knew better than to look at pretty girls.

As the kids and the wagon and the dog rolled past, Ryan looked down the street and saw Carlyle coming up the walk, moving fast. He looked agitated.

Carlyle didn't seem to see Ryan until he was a few feet from the tree.

Ryan hefted the Winchester then stepped out into the middle of the walk.

Carlyle, sensing rather than seeing somebody moving

into his way, stopped abruptly and raised his head. "Shit," he said when he saw who it was.

"Kind of a hot day to be moving so fast, Mr. Carlyle," Ryan said.

Carlyle's eyes had dropped to the new Winchester slung across Ryan's chest.

Ryan said, "You know who I am, don't you?"

"Yessir."

"And you know why I'm here."

"Yessir."

Ryan patted the Winchester. "And you know why I brought this."

Carlyle said, "It was an accident, sir, what happened to your daughter."

"You know, I've tried to console myself with that notion every once in a while. But then I start to thinking—if those three men hadn't gone to the bank that day, then the accident would never have happened. My little Clarice would have gone in there and made her deposit and Mr. Dolan would have given her a mint and then she would have walked back to my store and it would have been a regular, normal day." Now the tears came, but more in his voice than in his eyes. "She would have graduated from school this past spring, Mr. Carlyle. Her mother and I would have been so proud."

"We didn't mean for it to happen, Mr. Ryan. Honest."

"You know what happened to her mother?"

"No."

Ryan drew himself up and sighed. "Whooping cough."

Carlyle's eyes dropped back to the Winchester.

Ryan said, "You can always go to the sheriff here, Mr. Carlyle."

"Yessir."

"You can always tell him you were the men who robbed that bank and killed that little girl."

"Yessir."

"Because if you don't—" Now it was Ryan who looked at the Winchester. "Because if you don't, you're going to have to worry about me."

"Yessir."

"And you know something?"

"What, sir?"

"I'd sure as hell rather have to worry about the law than worry about me. Because maybe in a court of law you'll convince a jury that what you did was an accident—but you'll never convince me. You understand that?"

Carlyle didn't even have time to respond before Ryan raised the Winchester and slammed the butt of it into Carlyle's mouth.

Carlyle moaned, putting his hands to his mouth. He sounded as if he didn't know whether to puke or cry or what.

Ryan said. "That's just the start of things, Mr. Carlyle. Just the beginning."

But Carlyle wasn't paying any attention. He was looking at the tiny white stubs of teeth he'd just spit out bloodily into the palm of his right hand. He looked shocked and confused and terrified.

"Just the beginning," Ryan said, and walked off down the street toward town again.

2

James Hogan lay on his bed thinking of what he was going to say to his uncle Septemus as soon as he saw him. Septemus had no right to speak so slightingly of either James or his mother. She'd done a good job of raising all the kids and if she wasn't quite as good a father as she'd been a mother, well, you still couldn't blame her because she was a refined lady whose tastes just naturally gravitated to violin musicals in the parlor and the study of classical thinkers such as Plato and Socrates. Nothing wrong with that at all.

But of course it was Septemus's aspersions on James's own character that really had the boy angry. Hinting that James was a pantywaist and a mother's boy; hinting that at this rate he'd never grow up to be a man.

He lay shirtless on his back, a black fly crawling around on his red freckled face. Maybe he should tell Septemus about the time he got drunk on beer that Fourth of July night when everybody thought he'd gone up to bed; or maybe he should tell him about how many times he'd loaded cornsilk into a pipe bowl and smoked till he'd turned green; or maybe he should tell him about the time, a spring moon making him slightly mad, he'd nearly kissed Marietta right on the lips. Boy, wouldn't these things surprise Uncle Septemus? Wouldn't he then look at James in a very different way?

A pantywaist; a mama's boy. Just wait till he saw Septemus.

The knock startled him. He turned his head to face

the door so quickly that a line of warm pain shot up the side of his neck.

"That you, Uncle Septemus?" he called, uneasy about opening the door unless he knew who it was. His mother had given him explicit instructions about not putting himself in a position where he'd ever be alone with a stranger.

And then he heard Septemus inside his head: see how she's turning you into a sissy, son? Somebody knocks on your door and you won't even go open it. Now is that how a real man would act, son? Is it?

He fairly flung himself off the bed, making loose fists of his hands, striding to the door. To heck with what his mother said. He was sixteen; he was on his way to becoming a man. He would open the door and—

Halfway there, he realized he didn't have his shirt on. He was sure he shouldn't open the door half naked.

Feeling foolish and vulnerable, he dashed to the chair on the back of which was his shirt. He snapped it up and put it on and buttoned it. Then he went back to the door.

James had seen few men this tall. Even without a hat, the top of the man's head touched the top of the door frame. In addition to that, he was fleshy in a middle-aged sort of way, somewhat jowly and with a loose belly pinched tight by a huge silver buckle on which the initials DD had been sculpted. He wore a western-style white shirt, a brown leather vest, dark brown trousers, and Texas-toed black boots. He looked a little sweaty from the heat and a little sour around his large, wry mouth. James couldn't read his eyes at all.

His grin was somewhat surprising. "I take it you're not Septemus, son."

"No, sir," James said, then immediately recalled what his uncle had said about being too deferential. "I'm sure not." He tried to make the last sound hard-bitten, but his voice had soared too high for that. He'd just spotted the six-pointed star that the man wore tucked half under his vest.

"You'd be—"

"His nephew."

"I see." The man put out a huge hand. James slid his own into the other man's grasp. When they shook, James felt like a pump handle that somebody was jostling mercilessly. When he returned his hand to his side, James tried not to feel the pain the big man's hand had inflicted on him. "I'm Dodds."

"Dodds?"

"The sheriff."

"And you want to see my uncle Septemus?"

"If I could."

"He's not here."

The grin again. "I kinda figured that out for myself, son, I mean, I can see the whole room from here and I can see that it's empty except for you."

James flushed, knowing he'd been gently but absolutely shown his place.

"Any idea where I could find him?"

"Huh-uh."

"Any idea when he'll be back?"

"He said a couple of hours."

"How long ago was that?"

"'Bout an hour, I guess."

"Will you remember to tell him that Sheriff Dodds is lookin' for him?"

"Doesn't seem like the kind of thing I'd forget to mention."

This time the grin was accompanied by a whiskey laugh. "Say, you were bound and determined to pay me back for that crack I made, weren't you?"

James felt himself flush again. That's just what he'd been doing. Trying to show Dodds that he was a lot smarter than the lawman might think. "Guess so."

Dodds lifted the white Stetson he'd been keeping in his hand and cuffed James on the shoulder. "Damn straight, son. I've got a smart mouth on me and every once in a while somebody needs to put me in my place." He grinned again. "Damn straight."

Then he nodded and was gone.

James closed the door. He thought about lying down but he was too stirred up now. What would a sheriff want with Uncle Septemus?

He went over to the window and the billowing sheer curtain and stuck his head out. It was like leaning into an oven. Even though the water wagon had been over the dusty main street once today, dust devils rose in the still, chalky air. A crow sitting on the gable to James's right looked over at the boy with sleepy curiosity. The bird looked too tired to move.

There was no sign of Uncle Septemus.

James looked in every direction this particular window afforded. Then he looked again and saw nothing.

What the hell would a lawman want with his uncle?

He took his shirt off and went back and lay on the bed. There was no possibility of a nap now. He was too churned up.

Nor was he any longer angry with his uncle about the

man implying he was a mama's boy. They could settle that particular matter later.

He lay on the bed. Another black fly started walking around on his red freckles.

What the hell would a lawman want with Uncle Septemus, anyway?

3

"You telling me you don't believe in a divine being?"

"No. I'm just telling you that I'm tired of a prayer that goes on for five minutes."

"It's not just another prayer, Dennis. It's grace. It's thanking the Lord for all his wonderful gifts."

"And just what gifts would those be?" Dennis Kittredge asked his wife.

They were at the dining room table, the festive one with the red and white oilcloth spread over it, a small blue blown-glass butter dish the shape of a diamond, and a pair of salt and pepper shakers got up to look like stalks of sweet corn.

His wife Mae was a small and fine-boned woman who was given to excessively high collars and excessively long skirts and excessively stern looks. In her youth she'd been high fine company, a tireless attender of county fairs and ice cream socials, and a somewhat daring lover. While they had never committed the ultimate sin in the time before their vows, they had many nights come very, very close: especially downriver near the dam where fireflies glowed like jewels against the ebony sky, and there was music to be heard in the silver water splashing down on the sharp rocks below.

Then two years after their marriage Mae had become pregnant, but she'd lost the child in a bloody puddle in the middle of the night, on a white sleeping sheet she'd later burned.

Ever since then she'd been lost to God. Her juices had seemed to dry up till she was an old and indifferent woman about sex, and even worse about festivities. Nights, after Kittredge was home from the farms where he worked for twenty-three cents an hour, she played the saw as her mother had taught her, and in the soft fitful glow of the kerosene lamp read him the Bible, the only part of which he cared anything for being the Book of Job. Oh, yes; Job was a man Kittredge could believe, all pain and rage and dashed expectations. The rest of the biblical prophets struck him as stupid and they bored him silly. But Job . . .

"You ready now?" she said, as if he were a little boy she had only to wait out.

He sighed, a scarecrow of a man with a long, angular face and furious black brows and dead cornflower blue eyes. "Yeah, I'm ready."

"Then proceed."

Why the hell did he stay here anymore? It was like living with your maiden aunt. But where else could he go?

He said grace and he said it the way he knew she wanted him to. No mumbling, no sloppy posture. He sat up bolt straight and he spoke in clear, loud words, with his head bowed: "Bless us O Lord for these our gifts . . ."

There was one sure way to irritate her; to keep your head up or spend your time eating up the food with your eyes.

"God likes it better when you bow your head," she'd told him once. So that was that. Ever since then he'd bowed his head. It just wasn't worth the grief he'd have gotten otherwise.

"You say it nice," she said when he'd finished and was already helping himself to the boiled potatoes and tomatoes and chicken. "You've got such a strong, manly voice and the Lord appreciates that."

He glanced up at her for a dangerous moment. He almost asked: And just how do you know all these things the Lord wants so much? Does he come and visit you at night after I'm asleep? Or maybe he comes during the day while I'm working; comes in and helps himself to the teakettle and sits in the wooden rocker next to the window and tells you exactly what he wants me and you to do. It must be something like that, Mae, because there's no other way you could possibly know so much about his likes and dislikes. No other possible way.

But he couldn't ever bring himself to do this because then he'd remember the horror he'd seen in her the night she'd miscarried on the bed in there, and the way her skinny white fingers had so reverently touched the bloody puddle, as if that itself were her child. Even after the doctor left she'd been unable to talk, and then he'd held her on his lap in the darkness in the rocker by the moonlit window. She'd surprised him by staying still, no tears and no words, just the rocker creaking until the crows and the roosters woke at dawn, and every once in a while he'd look at her face, at the wornout girl of her and the birdy but pretty woman she'd become. And he'd realized then that he was holding a woman so sorrowful she was beyond any human solace, beyond it for the rest of their lives. Oh, in the spring they'd tried to have another child but it hadn't worked, nor had the attempt a year later. It was sometime then that she'd become so religious and it was around then that he'd lost his job over at Rochester and it was after that that the bank robbery went so wrong and the little girl was killed.

"Thank you," he said.

She looked up from cutting her chicken. "Thank you?"

"For saying that about my voice."

"Oh." She offered him one of her rare smiles, and he saw in the smile the girl she'd been, the girl he'd fallen in love with. "Well, you know it's true. All my friends used to say they wished their men had voices like yours."

He stopped eating. "Maybe it'd do you good to see them."

"Who?"

"Your old friends. Susan and Irma and Jane Marie."

She shrugged. "Oh, I see them every once in a while but I embarrass them." She shook her head. "They think I'm too religious. A fanatic." She looked straight at him and broke his heart with her madness. "They don't seem to know that the Lord is walking right alongside them and judging everything they do. Why, if we hadn't sinned before we were married, we'd probably have us three fine young children today."

This was another point in the conversation when he had to stop himself from speaking. Maybe it was the only way she could understand not being able to bear a child—through something she'd done wrong. But to him it was just sad foolishness, a judgment on them both, and just one more way in which he felt separated from her.

She patted his bony hand with her bony hand. It felt funny, like the cold touch of a stranger. "You're a good man, Dennis. The Lord's going to reward you on Judgment Day. You wait and see if he don't."

She had just settled into eating again, when they heard the neighbor dog yip and saw a shadow fall on the grass outside the kitchen window. Somebody was knocking on the back door.

"You finish eating," Kittredge said. "I'll get it."

He did not like who he saw framed in the door.

"Who is it?" Mae asked.

He decided to lie. Mae was harsh on the few friends he could claim. He'd convinced her he'd long ago given up the likes of Carlyle. "Kid from the smithy. I'll step outside. Want a smoke anyway."

She nodded to his plate. "You ain't finished yet, Dennis. You know how I worry about you."

And that was the terrible hell of it. She did love him and did worry about him just as he loved her and worried about her. But it was passionless. They might as well have been sister and brother.

He went outside into the fading day, into the fading heat of the fading day, and the first thing he did, right there on the stoop where his pa and grandpa had stood generations before him, was slap Carlyle right across the mouth.

"You know better than this," Kittredge said.

More humiliated than hurt, Carlyle touched the spot where the slap still burned and looked at Kittredge out of his poorshanty hurt and his poorshanty pain and said, "Onliest reason I did it was 'cause Griff told me to."

"Griff told you to come here?"

"That's exactly what he told me."

"I don't believe it."

"You go ask him."

"You know what my missus still thinks of the likes of you."

"Well, maybe I don't think a whole hell of a lot more of her, truth be told. You ever think of that? She gets flies on her shit the same way I do."

Kittredge looked back at the door, through the glass to where Mae had her head down eating. She never gained weight; there was a rawness to her skinniness. He looked back at Carlyle. "You don't use language like that in this house." Carlyle smirked. That was how Kittredge always thought of Carlyle—that poorshanty smirk over a dirty joke or a jibe that hurt somebody's feelings. "You know better than to push it with me, Carlyle. Least you should."

"Griff wants to see us. Tonight."

"Why?"

"West end of the Second Avenue bridge. Nine o'clock."

"You heard what I asked. Why?"

Carlyle shook his head. The smirk reappeared. He liked to smirk when he told you something that was going to scare you. He said, "That little girl's father came to town this afternoon."

"You're crazy, Carlyle. How could he track us down?"

"I don't know how he done it; but he done it. He's here and he's got a Winchester and he means to kill us." Carlyle ran a trembling hand over his sweaty head. "He was waitin' for me when I left Griff's."

"He tell you he means to kill us?"

"Pretty much."

"Pretty much doesn't mean that's what he's got in mind."

Carlyle shrugged. "You wasn't there. You didn't see his eyes, Kittredge."

"Your food's getting cold, dear," Mae called from the table.

Carlyle smirked. "Must be nice havin' a little lady call you 'dear' like that all the time."

"I'm not going to believe any of this till it's proven to me," Kittredge said.

"You better be there tonight or Griff's gonna be mad."

"I didn't know that Griff had become my boss."

"You better," Carlyle said, sounding like a little kid. "You better."

Then he turned and started away, into a path made golden by the fading rays of sunlight. When he was nothing more than a silhouette of flame, he turned back to Kittredge and said, "You shoulda seen his eyes, Kittredge. You shoulda seen 'em."

Then he was gone.

Chapter Three

1

When Uncle Septemus came back into the hotel room, he took off his hat, vest, and coat, set the Winchester against the bureau, and came over and lay down on the bed across from James.

James was reading a yellowback about cowboys and Indians. The hero was a man named Chesmore who, it seemed, changed disguises every few pages.

From his carpetbag on the floor next to the bed, Uncle Septemus took a pint bottle of rye, swigged some, then put his head down and closed his eyes. He left the bottle, corked, lying on his considerable belly.

"You trying to take a nap, Uncle Septemus?"

Uncle Septemus opened one brown eye and looked at James. "Guess I was till you asked me if I was."

"A man came."

"A man?"

"A lawman."

"A lawman?"

"The sheriff."

Uncle Septemus propped himself up uncomfortably, still giving James the benefit of only one eye. "He say what he wanted?"

"Said he wanted to talk to you."

"He say about what?"

James was careful not to say "No sir" and sound too deferential. "Nope."

Uncle Septemus closed his eye, lay back down flat, uncorked the rye bottle with his thick fingers, poured a considerable tote down his throat, corked up the bottle good, then gave the impression that he was deep asleep.

"Uncle Septemus?"

"Yes, son?"

"I know you're tryin' to sleep."

"If you know I'm tryin' to sleep, why are you bothering me then."

"Because, I guess."

"Because?"

"Aren't you worried?"

"About what?"

"About why a sheriff would come up to our room and ask to see you."

"Maybe he's somebody I know."

"Huh?"

"Maybe he's somebody who came to my store and bought things before. A lot of people do that, and from all over the area, because I've got such good merchandise. They remember me but I don't remember them. Whenever I visit other towns, there's always somebody who comes running up and asks me do I remember him."

"You really think that's why the sheriff came up here?"

"Your mother sure has turned you into a worrier, hasn't she, James?"

There he went again. Another jibe at James's mother. "Uncle Septemus."

Septemus sighed. His eyes had remained closed and he was obviously getting irritated. "What is it now, James?"

"I don't want you to insult my mother anymore."

"I haven't insulted your mother. I've just expressed my concern that a woman can't turn a boy into a man. Only another man can do that. Nothing against your mother at all. She's a fine woman, a fine woman."

"You really mean that?"

"I really mean that."

Now James lay down and closed his eyes. The black fly was back, walking on his red freckles.

Uncle Septemus said, "I want you to wear that fancy linen collar tonight."

"Where are we going?"

"Someplace special." He hesitated. Now he rolled

over and up onto one elbow. He looked at James with
both eyes. "Look at me, James."

James rolled over on the bed across from his uncle
and opened his eyes.

"Do you want to be treated like a man?"

"Sure."

"A man can give his word to keep a secret and then
keep that word. Do you think you can do that?"

"Does this have something to do with the sheriff?"

"Forget about the sheriff, James. This has nothing to
do with him at all. This has to do with you being a man.
Now can you give me your word that you can keep a
secret?"

"Yes."

"Then I'll tell you that tonight I'm going to take you
someplace very special."

"The opera house?"

"Nope."

"The racetrack?"

"Nope."

"The nickelodeon parlor?"

"Don't even try to guess. It's someplace so special
you wouldn't guess it in a hundred years. Now let's take
a nap."

So James lay back down. In the stillness of the dying
afternoon, the stillness and dust and heat of the dying
afternoon, he heard the clatter of horses and wagons and
the shouts of men and the fading laughter of children.
This town was very much like Council Bluffs and, thinking about home, James just naturally thought of Marietta.

But then he forgot Marietta because of his uncle's

promise of something "special" this evening.

James wondered what it could possibly be.

2

People made jokes about the way Dodds kept his office. Three times a week he had it dusted, twice a week he had the floor mopped and waxed, and once a week he had the front windows cleaned. When his fancy rolltop desk was open visitors could see that his fastidiousness continued into his personal belongings as well. Everything had its proper drawer or slot. Nothing was left loose inside the desk except a small stack of almost blindingly white writing paper on which Dodds wrote in a labored but beautiful hand, always in ink with an Easterbrook steel pen. He had a son in Tucson and one in New York, and he wrote to them frequently. His wife dead, the sons were the only family he had left and corresponding was the only way he could stay in contact with them.

Unfortunately, they weren't so good about writing back. One of the sons had gone and had a baby, Dodds's first grandson, but before Dodds knew anything about the birth let alone the pregnancy, the kid, named Clarence, was born and already walking around his home in New York, where his father worked as an accountant. Dodds lived in a sleeping room two short blocks from the sheriff's office. He'd moved here after the missus died, selling the white gabled house they'd lived in on the edge of town, and making himself available to whatever kind of trouble arose.

Many nights you could see Dodds running down the

middle of the street still pulling his suspenders up. The law—the jail, more exactly—was Dodds's life. He was sixty-one and would soon enough retire, and he meant to store up as many war stories as possible. He had some good ones. A drunken Indian, defiant beyond imagining because Dodds had arrested his brother, snuck into the office one night, jimmied up the rolltop desk and took a crap right in it. Then he'd locked the desk back up and waited for Dodds to come in and learn what had happened.

Another time Dodds had swum out against a hard current on a rainy day and rescued a two-month-old lamb that had fallen into the river. And then there was the Windsor woman, a genuine redheaded beauty with a touring opera company, a woman who also managed to steal a goodly number of diamonds and jewels and rubies from the local gentry who'd given her a fancy party. Oh, yes, he had some good tales, and he loved to tell them, too, over a bucket of beer on cool nights inside screened-in porches. It was too much trouble to find another woman and, anyway, he couldn't ever imagine loving anybody else the way he had Eva; so he said to hell with it and indulged himself in those pleasures that can only be enjoyed by solitary people. Such as being a fussbudget, which he most certainly was. It was said among the town's lawyers that you might not piss off Sheriff David Dodds by breaking into his room in the middle of the night but you'd piss him off for sure if you wore muddy boots while doing it.

Now Dodds sat at his desk, rolling his Easterbrook pen between his fingers the way he would a fine cigar, thinking about the former Pinkerton man he'd run in last fall for being drunk and disorderly. O'Malley, the man's name had been. For the first week O'Malley had been there, Dodds hadn't been able to figure out what the man was doing in Myles. The check he'd run indicated that O'Malley had been let go from the Pinkertons. When that happened, it usually meant that the man had been found morally corrupt in some way; Alan Pinkerton was a stickler. So what was O'Malley doing there? During the long and noisy night that O'Malley had spent in one of the cells in back, he'd given Dodds at least some notion of why he'd come to Myles. A man had hired him to find out who had killed his daughter. Dodds had thought immediately of the killing in Council Bluffs, so it was not difficult to intuit from that that O'Malley was looking for those bank robbers people had been seeking so long.

During O'Malley's last three days in Myles, Dodds had followed him everywhere. He never learned exactly who O'Malley had decided on but, given the places he stopped at, O'Malley seemed to be giving most of his attention to three men—Griff, Kittredge, and Carlyle. Then O'Malley was gone.

Since then, Dodds had kept close watch on the three men, noting that while Griff and Kittredge saw each other occasionally, they stayed clear of Carlyle. The three men used to be close friends. He wondered what had gone wrong between them.

Earlier this afternoon, when he saw Septemus Ryan and James ride into town, he knew immediately that he was looking at the man who had hired the Pinkerton. He remembered from pictures that this was the man whose little girl had been killed.

He liked trouble, Dodds did. He believed it kept him

young. He sensed that he was now going to have plenty of trouble, and very soon.

The black man and the Mexican in the next cell stared at the nineteen year old who was balled up on his straw cot like a sick colt.

"Couldn't you let me go till my pa gets here? You know he'll go my bail, Sheriff."

"I suppose he will. But that don't mean I can let you go. I didn't hand down that sentence. Judge Sullivan did. And there ain't a damn thing I can do about it, even if I wanted to."

"All I did was raise a little hell."

Dodds had been in the cell block with this kid for ten minutes now. It was enough. He didn't especially like seeing a boy like this thrown in with a bunch of hardcases, but then again, the kid should have thought about what he was doing when he got drunk the night before and shot up a tavern. He could have killed a few people in all that ruckus.

Dodds went to the cell door and called for his deputy to let him out. Dodds never took any chances. Only a fool brought keys into a cell with him.

Through the bars on the high windows, Dodds could see that it was getting dark. His stomach grumbled. He was looking forward to meat loaf and mashed potatoes and peas at Juanita's Diner down the street. It was Tuesday and that was the Tuesday menu.

Deputy Harrison, a twenty-five year old with lots of ambition and a certain cunning, but not much intelligence, came through the cell-block door and said, "The pretty boy here giving you any trouble, Sheriff? If he is, I'd be happy to take care of him for you."

"No, no trouble," Dodds said, weary of Harrison's bluff swaggering manner. Dodds had two deputies, Windom and Harrison. Windom possessed wisdom but no courage and Harrison possessed courage but no wisdom. Together they made Dodds one hell of a deputy.

"Had to come back and get you anyway, Sheriff," Harrison said.

"Oh?"

"Yep. You got a visitor."

"Visitor? Who?"

"Man named Ryan. Septemus Ryan."

"Hear you were looking for me, Sheriff."

Up close, Ryan gave the same impression he had riding into town this afternoon. A kind of arrogance crossed with a curious sadness. The mouth, for instance, was wide and confident, even petulant; but the brown eyes were aggrieved, and deeply so.

Ryan put out a hand. He had one damn fine grip.

"Coffee, Mr. Ryan?"

"Sounds good."

When they were seated on their respective sides of Dodds's desk, tin cups of coffee hot in their hands, Dodds said, "You look familiar to me, Mr. Ryan."

Ryan smiled. "You were probably a customer of mine at one time or another. Ryan's Male Attire in Council Bluffs. The finest fabrics and appointments outside Chicago." He smiled again. He had a nice, ingratiating smile. His brown eyes were as sad as ever. "If I do say so myself."

Dodds decided not to waste any time. "I saw your picture in the state newspaper not too long ago."

Ryan just stared at him with those handsome brown eyes.

"They was lowering a casket into a grave and you was standing topside of that grave. They was burying your daughter, Mr. Ryan. Or are you going to deny that that was you?"

Ryan shook his head.

Dodds leaned forward on his elbows. "Then not too long ago an ex-Pinkerton man came to Myles. He seemed to be looking for somebody special." A hard smile broke Dodds's face. "He probably didn't tell you this part, Mr. Ryan, but one night he got drunk and in a fight down the street, and I had to bring him back here to cool him off for the night, and during that night he told me all about this man who'd hired him. I got a good notion of who that man would be, Mr. Ryan."

Ryan continued to stare at him. There was no reading those eyes, no reading them at all.

"You were the one who hired him. And I know why, too. You had him backtrackin' the men who killed your girl. And that eventually led him here. Isn't that about right, Mr. Ryan?"

"I'd be a foolish man to interrupt a sheriff as well-spoken as you."

"So now you're here, Mr. Ryan, and there can only be one reason for that."

"And what would that be, Sheriff?"

"You plan to take the law into your own hands. You plan to kill those three men."

Ryan sat back in his chair. "Are you going to arrest me, Sheriff?"

"Wish I could. All I can do right now is warn you. I'm not a man who abides vengeance outside the law. I grew up near the border, Mr. Ryan, and I got enough lynch-law justice in my first fifteen years to last me a lifetime. I seen my own brother hanged by a pack of men, and I seen an uncle of mine, too. It's one thing I don't tolerate.''

Ryan kept his eyes level on Dodds's. ''Oh, I expect there's a lot you don't tolerate, Sheriff Dodds.''

''And why the hell'd you bring that boy along? If I ever seen a sweeter young kid, I don't know when or where it'd be.''

''Maybe that's his problem. Maybe he's too sweet for his own good.''

''So you invite him along so he can see you kill three men?''

''You're the one who keeps saying that, Sheriff, about me killing those three men. Not me.''

Dodds's chair squawked as he leaned back. ''I make a bad enemy, Mr. Ryan. I'm warning you now so you won't make no mistakes about it. When I took this job twenty years ago, it wasn't safe to walk the streets. My pride is that I made it safe and I mean to keep it safe.''

Ryan drained his coffee and set the cup down on the edge of the desk. ''That about the extent of what you've got to say?''

''That would be about it, Mr. Ryan.''

''Then I guess I'll get back to my nephew. Promised him a fancy dinner and a good time in your little town.''

Dodds pawed a big hand over his angular face. ''If you've got proof they're really the killers, Mr. Ryan, give me the proof and let me take them in. I'd be glad to help hang the men who murdered your daughter.''

Ryan stood up. ''I appreciate the offer, Sheriff. And I'll definitely think it over.''

With that, he tilted his derby at a smart-aleck angle, nodded goodbye to Dodds, and went out the front door.

Dodds listened to the front door close, the little bell above the frame tinkling. He sat there for a time thinking about Ryan and his brown eyes and what those brown eyes said. Sorrow, to be sure; and then Dodds realized what else—it could be heard in his laugh and seen in his smile, too—craziness, pure blessed craziness, the kind you'd feel if somebody killed your little girl and got away with it.

3

It was a place of Rochester lamps whose light was the color of burnished gold; of starchy white tablecloths; of waiters in walrus mustaches and ladies in low-cut organdy gowns. Several tables away from where James sat with his Uncle Septemus, a pair of men got up to resemble gypsies walked around the restaurant, dramatically playing their violins. Even though nobody paid much attention—and even though some of the men looked damned uncomfortable with such displays of passion and emotion—the would-be gypsies lent the place its final touch of sophistication.

"They kind of make me nervous," James confided.

"Who?"

"Those gypsies."

"Why should they make you nervous?"

"I don't know. Like they'd just sneak up behind you all of a sudden."

"And then what?"

"I don't know. Play some really corny song."

"And embarrass you?"

James nodded. "Yeah, sort of."

Uncle Septemus raised his wineglass. He was notorious, within the family, for being an easy drunk. He'd had three glasses of wine so far this evening, and he was showing the effects. His words slurred, and his handsome brown eyes seemed not quite focused.

"Wait till you're a little older," Septemus said.

"Then what?"

Septemus smiled. "Then you'll appreciate things more."

"Like gypsy violinists?"

Septemus laughed. "Like gypsy violinists." And then his smile died. "And memories."

The silver tears came clear and obvious in his brown eyes. "Do you ever think about her, James?"

"Who?"

"Why, Clarice, of course. My daughter."

James felt embarrassed. He should have known who his uncle was talking about. Much of the time, his uncle talked about little else. "Sure."

"Are you just saying that?"

"Huh-uh, Uncle Septemus, honest."

Septemus drank from his goblet and then rolled the wine around the fine glass that filled his hand. Septemus was a lover of fine foods, he was. "What's your favorite memory of her?"

"My favorite?" James was stalling for time. His favorite? He'd never thought of it that way. "Uh . . ."

"Don't worry," Septemus said. "I have the same problem. I have so many good memories, I don't know which one is my favorite."

"When we used to go sledding, is one of them. She

never got afraid like the other girls. She'd come lickety-split down those hills and sail right onto Hartson Creek. Not afraid at all.''

Septemus smiled again, looking beyond James now. James wondered what he was seeing.

Septemus said, ''Winter was her favorite time. You'd think it would've been spring or summer or even fall but no, it was winter. I remember how she used to get snow all over her face so it looked like she had these big bushy white eyebrows and how red her cheeks would get and how her eyes would sparkle. I think about her eyes a lot.''

James was afraid his uncle was going to start sobbing right in the middle of the restaurant. James was never prepared for such scenes. All he could do was kind of sit there and sort of scooch down in his seat and more or less hold his breath and hope for the best.

Septemus said, leaning across, ''If I tell you something, will you promise not to tell your mother?''

''Uh-huh.''

''You promise?''

''Honest, Uncle Septemus. Honest.''

''Because she worries about me. I'm sure she's told you I'm not quite right in the head since Clarice was killed.''

James felt his cheeks get hot. That's exactly what his mother had told him, and many times.

''No, Uncle Septemus, she never said anything like that.''

''She talks to me. All the time.'' Uncle Septemus was staring right at James now.

''My mother?''

''No, Clarice.''

"Clarice talks to you?"

"Clear as a bell. Usually at night, just when I'm going to sleep."

"Oh."

Septemus's eyes seemed to press James back in his chair. "You don't believe me, do you, James?"

"No, I believe you."

"Do you think I'm crazy?"

"No, Uncle Septemus, I don't." He hesitated before speaking again. "I just think you miss her an awful lot."

"More than you can imagine, James."

"It was like when Blackie died."

"Your dog?"

"Uh-huh. He was all I thought about all last summer. Sometimes I'd look up on the hill by the railroad tracks and I'd see him running there, black as all get out and going lickety-split, but when I'd tell Mom about it, she'd just kind of get sad looking and say, 'You'll get over it, dear.' But I saw Blackie; I'm sure I did. And I'm sure Clarice speaks to you, too. I'm sure of it, Uncle Septemus."

The tears were back. "You're a good boy, James, and I love you very much. I want you to know that."

"I do know that, truly."

"And those things I said about being brought up by a man—I only meant it for your own good."

"I know."

"The world's a harsh enough place but for men who can't deal with it—it's especially harsh for men like that, if you know what I'm talking about."

"I know. My friend Ronnie's got a cousin like that. People make fun of him all the time and about all he can do is run away and hide. It must be awful."

"You can bet it is awful, James." He sipped some more wine. "I'll say hello for you next time."

"To Clarice?"

"Umm-hmm. If you'd like me to."

"Tell her I'm thinking about her."

Septemus smiled again. "I'll be happy to tell her that, James. Happy to."

Septemus raised his wineglass. "But for now, let's toast our adventure for tonight."

"Our adventure? Is that the surprise you were telling me about?"

"Indeed it is, James. Indeed it is." Earlier Septemus had asked the waiter for two wineglasses. One had stood empty for the length of the dinner. Now Septemus filled it halfway up and handed it over to James.

"Maybe I hadn't ought to," James said. "You know how my mother is with us kids. She won't even let us sample the cider."

"You're with me now, James, not with your mother."

"You sure it's all right?"

"It's man to man tonight, James. It's what's expected of you."

Septemus raised his glass in toast again. "Now raise yours, James."

James raised his.

"Now we'll toast," Septemus said, and brought his glass against James's. "To our adventure tonight. Now you say it, James."

"To our adventure tonight."

"Perfect." They clinked glasses.

"Uncle Septemus," James said after he'd had a sip of wine and the stuff tasted sweet and hot at the same time in his throat.

"Yes?"

"What exactly is our adventure going to be, anyway?"

"You mean you haven't figured it out yet?"

"Huh-uh."

"You really haven't?"

"Honest, Uncle Septemus. I can't figure it out at all."

"Well, tonight's the night you become a man."

"I do?"

"You do." Septemus looked across the table with great patriarchal pride. He smiled. "Tonight I'm taking you to a whorehouse."

Chapter Four

1

"You going out?"

"Thought I might take a walk," Dennis Kittredge said.

"You be gone long?"

"Not too long."

"You thinking of stopping by the tavern?"

He was by the front door, the lace covering the glass smelling of dry summer dust. In the trees near the curb he could see the dying day, flame and dusk and a half moon. "I might have me a glass or two is all."

She was in the rocker, knitting, a magazine in her lap. He'd seen the magazine earlier. It had a painting of a very pretty Jesus on it. Jesus was touching his glowing heart with long fingers. "You forgetting what night it is?"

"I'm not forgetting."

"I don't often ask that you pray with me but I don't see how fifteen minutes one night a week is going to help."

"And just what is it we're praying for?"

She paused and looked down at her poor worn hands. She worked so hard and sometimes he felt terrible for resenting her prayerfulness. She looked up then. "I had the dream again last night."

"I see."

"Don't you want to know which one?"

"I know which one."

"The son we would've had. I saw him plain on a hill right at dawn. He was running right toward us. We were on a buckboard on a dusty road and we didn't hear him or see him. He kept running and running and shouting and shouting but we didn't see him or hear him. Finally, he fell down in the long grass and all the animals came to him at night and comforted him—because we wouldn't comfort him."

Kittredge sighed. "I won't be gone too long."

"Don't you know what the dream could mean?"

"No. I guess I don't."

"Why, it could mean that He's forgiven us, that the Lord has forgiven us for sinning before we were married, and that now He's ready to let us have children."

"I see."

"Don't you believe that, Dennis?"

"I'm not sure just what I do believe," he said, and pulled the door open. The sounds and smells of dusk—the robins and jays in the trees, a hard relentless chorus, the scent of flowers as they cooled in the dusk—he took all this in with great affection. He wanted to be out in the night, a part of all this.

"I won't be gone too long," he said again, and before she could respond he was out the door and moving fast toward the sidewalk.

He liked walking downtown at night. He liked the way the lamplight glowed and the way women in picture hats and bustles walked on the arms of their gentlemen to the opera house where shiny coaches and rigs stood outside waiting. He liked the sound of player pianos on the lonely Midwestern darkness and he liked the smell of brewer's yeast that you picked up as you passed tavern doors. He liked the sound of pinochle and poker hands being slapped down on the table, and the sweet high giggle of tavern maids. This was, by God, 1901 and this was, by God, civilized and he took a curious pride in this, as if he were personally responsible for it all.

It was not quite eight o'clock, so he walked down to the roundhouse tavern where the railroad men drank. It was his favorite place unless there were too many Mexicans in there from some road crew. He hated the way Mexicans resorted to their knives so quickly; he'd seen it too many times. A man stabbed was much worse than a man shot—at least to the man watching it all.

The place was nearly empty. At the far end of the plank bar two Mexes drank from a bucket of suds, and at the other a white man played blackjack with the bartender. In the corner a player piano rolled out the melody to "My Sweet Brown Eyes" while an old man, nodding off in his cups, lay facedown on the piano's keys, spittle running silver from his mouth to the floor. The bartender paid him no mind.

A maid appeared from the back and served Kittredge his beer. He stood there with his schooner, enjoying the player piano. It was playing Stephen Foster songs now, a medley, and his toe tapped and in just a few swallows he felt buzzy, not drunk, but buzzy and blessedly so. He forgot that in an hour he would meet Griff and Carlyle and that together they would have to decide what to do about Septemus Ryan. That was the funny thing about the whole event: he did not feel responsible. It had been an accident, though obviously most people had chosen not to believe that, an accident because Dennis Kittredge was a good and responsible man and had been all his life.

He felt that if he could open his heart and look inside he would find fine things—patience and courage and understanding. He was not the sort of man who cut up other men the way Mexes did and he was certainly not the sort of man who killed young girls. It all had a dreamy quality to it. He would always be, in his heart, the little kid making his first communion—why couldn't people understand that?

"Nice night for a walk."

Kittredge turned around and saw Sheriff Dodds standing there. The sheriff tossed a nickel on the bar plank. The maid brought him a schooner with a good foamy head on it.

"Sure is," Kittredge said.

The sheriff sipped his beer, studying Kittredge as he did so. "You still think about the days when the wagon works was up and runnin'?"

"Sure. Everybody does."

"Them was good times."

"Sure was."

"Hell," Dodds said, "I remember seein' you and Griff and Carlyle everywhere I went. You three was some friends."

"Some friends is right," Kittredge said, then swigged some of his own beer. For some reason, his stomach was knotting and he had started having some problems swallowing, the way he did sometimes when he got nervous. Dodds came in there often enough, had a schooner or two a night, nothing to scandalize even church ladies, and often as not he spoke to Dennis, too. But there was something about his tone tonight, as if he were saying one thing but meaning quite another. Kittredge wondered what the hell Dodds was driving at.

"You boys don't hang around each other much anymore, do you?"

"Guess we don't, Sheriff."

"Too bad. You bein' such good friends and all. At one time, I mean." He said this over the rim of his schooner. He was still watching Kittredge very closely.

Kittredge looked toward the door. "Well," he said.

Dodds followed his gaze to the front of the tavern. "Going on home now?"

Kittredge met his glance. "Thought I might finish my walk."

"I'd be careful if I were you."

"Careful?"

Dodds drained off his beer. "Hear there are some strangers in town."

"Why would strangers bother me?"

"Well, you know how it is with strangers. You can never be sure what they want."

Now Kittredge finished his own beer. He belched a little because he'd put it down too fast. "Well, guess I'll be saying goodnight, Sheriff."

But Dodds wasn't done. Not quite. "Too bad you don't have any children, Kittredge."

"Yep. I suppose it is." What the hell was Dodds getting at, anyway?

"Man who don't have no children of his own don't know what it means to lose one. Take this man a while back, this Ryan fella, over in Council Bluffs. His little girl got killed in the course of a bank robbery."

"I guess I heard about that. Don't remember it all, quite."

"Little girl's father went insane, some people said. Just couldn't get over it. Hired an investigator fella to start backtrackin' the robbers. Guess the investigator fella had some good luck."

Kittredge felt faint. Actually, literally faint, the way women got. He put a hand for steadiness on the plank bar. "Sure hope they catch those thieves."

And all the while, remorseless, Dodds staring at him. Staring. "If I was them boys, I'd be a lot more scared of Septemus Ryan than the law."

"Oh?"

"Law'll give them boys a fair hearing. If it was an accident that the little girl got killed, which some of the witnesses say it was, law'll take that into account."

"But not the little girl's father?"

"Oh, not the little girl's father at all. Put yourself in his place, Kittredge. Say you had a pretty little girl and one day she got killed like that. Wouldn't make no difference to you if it was an accident or not. Least it wouldn't to most fathers. All they'd want to do is kill

the men who killed their pretty little girl. You ever think
of it that way?''

"Ain't thought about it much one way or the other,
Sheriff," Kittredge said. His voice was so dry he could
barely speak, but he didn't want to order another schooner because then he'd have to stand there and drink it
with Dodds.

Dodds nodded. "Well, if you ever do sit down and
start thinking it over, Kittredge, that's just how I'd figure
it—that I'd have me a much better chance with the
lawn'n I would a grief-crazy father. You might pass that
along to Griff and Carlyle, too?''

"Now why would they care about that, Sheriff?''

Dodds made a face. "Carlyle, he's too dumb and too
shiftless to care. But Griff, well, he's smart. You tell
him what I told you and he's likely to agree with me.''

So he knew, Dodds did. There could be no mistaking.
Somehow he'd found out about the robbery and the little
girl and knew that it was the three of them who were
involved.

Dodds said, "You have yourself a nice walk, Kittredge.''

"I will.''

"And you say hello to Mae. She's a fine woman; but
I guess you know that.''

"She is a fine woman, Sheriff, and I appreciate you
sayin' that.''

Imagine what Mae would think of him if she ever
found out he was involved in the robbery of that bank
and the death of that little girl.

"So long, Kittredge," Dodds said, then swung back
so that he was facing the tavern maid. He ordered himself another schooner.

Kittredge left.

2

When James was younger, just after his father's funeral, his mother's sister, a shy and unmarried woman named Nella, stayed with the family for three months till, as she put it, Mrs. Hogan "saw that there were things still worth living for." It was Nella's habit to bathe in the downstairs bathroom, where the tub with the claws and the wall with the nymphs on it sat in the rear of the house. Nella always waited till everyone had gone to sleep before bathing. The family was too polite to ask why, of course, respecting their aunt as they did, even if she was "eccentric" as their mother had rather shamefully said of her one day.

One night, when he badly needed a drink, and had found his mother in the upstairs bathroom, James had gone downstairs, thinking he'd get water from the kitchen, which the colored maid had cleaned only that afternoon. He descended the stairs in darkness, liking the way winter moonlight played silver and frosty through the front window. Then he heard the sighing from the back of the house, from the bathroom.

At first the sound reminded him of pain. But why would Nella inflict pain on herself?

On tiptoe, sensing he should not do what he was about to do, James went down the hall to the bathroom. The closer he got the more pronounced the moaning and the signing became.

He was about to raise his hand and let it gently fall against the door when she said, "Oh, Donald; Donald."

And that stopped him. Was there a man in there with her?

He did not knock. Instead he did what so many co-medians in vaudeville did. He fell to one knee and peered through the keyhole.

Aunt Nella was nude. The body she had kept mod-estly hidden was beautiful and womanly and over-whelming to him. She leaned against the wall with the nymphs so that he could see her clearly, her eyes closed so tightly, her mouth open and gasping, her hand fallen and moving quicksilver fast at the part in her white legs. ''Oh, Donald; Donald.'' And he saw now that she was alone and only summoning the man as if he were a ghost who could pass through walls and visit her, touch her as she now touched herself.

He never forgot how Aunt Nella looked that night; she would forever be the woman with whom he com-pared all other women, and for many years after, in stern Midwestern February and in soft Midwestern October, he would see her there projected on his ceiling. Oh, Nella; Nella (just as she'd called out for Donald). Nella.

Just after his third drink, just after Uncle Septemus dis-appeared down the hall, just after the door closed and the girl came in and dropped her shabby dress to her wide hips, James thought of Nella, thinking the most forbidden thought of all, that he wished it were Nella he was with on this most important of nights, and not some chubby farm girl with bleached hair and the smell of too-sweet perfume.

The whorehouse shook with the relentless happiness of player pianos (one up, one down) and the even more relentless happiness of girls determined in their

somewhat sad way to show the men a good time. He
could smell whiskey and cigar smoke and sweat, and
could see the flickering shadows cast by the kerosene
lamp on the sentimental painting of the innocent but
somehow erotic young prairie girl above the brass bed.
James supposed that that was how all the girls saw themselves—idealized and vulnerable in that way, not crude
and harsh and defeated as they really were.

She came over and stood by him and said, "My
name's Liz."

"Hi, Liz."

She smiled. "It's all right if you look at them. That's
why I took my dress down. So you could see them."

He couldn't stop staring at her breasts. He'd raise his
eyes and look into her eyes or he'd glance up at the
painting above the bed but always his eyes would drop
back down to her breasts.

She reached out and took his hand. Touched it in such
a way that he could tell she was making some character
judgment about him. "You're not a farm boy, are you?"

"No, ma'm."

She giggled. "I ain't no 'ma'm,' I bet I'm younger
than you. I'm fourteen."

He didn't say anything. Stood straight and still, heart
hammering.

"You want to kiss first?"

"I guess so," he said.

"You don't know what to do, do you?"

"I guess not."

"You look mighty scared."

He said nothing.

"If you just relax, you'll enjoy yourself."

He said nothing.

"You kinda remind me of my brother and that's kinda sweet." She leaned forward and kissed him gently on the lips. "That feel good?"

"I guess so."

She laughed. "You sure 'guess' about a lot of things."

He said nothing.

She took his hand again. She led him over to the bed. They sat on the edge of it, the springs squeaking. She was prettier in profile than straight on. He wanted her to be pretty. On a night like this you wanted your girl to be pretty. He wondered if he'd be so scared now if he were sitting here with Marietta. Or Nella. That was a terrible thought and he tried not to think it, about sitting there with his own aunt, but he couldn't help it.

He said, "Do you go to school?"

She turned and looked at him. "Do I go to school?" She smiled and patted his hand. "Honey, they wouldn't let girls like me in school."

"You got folks?"

"In South Dakota."

"Do they—"

"Do they know what I do? Was that what you were gonna ask me?"

"I guess."

"No. They don't know. A year ago I run off. This was as far as I got. I wrote 'em and tole 'em I'm working for this nice woman." She laughed. "Miss Susan is nice; that part of it ain't a lie."

He sat on the edge of the bed and stared down at his hands. They were trembling. "We don't have to do anything. I wouldn't ask for my money back, I mean."

"You afraid you can't do it?"

He didn't say anything.

"A lot of men are like that. Even when they've been doin' it regular all their lives. They just get kinda scared and they get worried if they're gonna make fools of themselves but, heck, you'll be fine."

"You sure?"

"Sure. I mean, we'll take it real slow. We'll lay back on the bed and just kind of hold each other and take it real slow. I like it better that way anyway."

"You do?"

"Sure. More like we care about each other."

"You want to lie back now?"

"You talk good, don't you?"

"Good?"

"Proper-like."

"English is one of my best subjects."

She laughed. "Honey, none of 'em was my best subject. I'm thick as a log."

"You ready?"

"Any time you are."

"And I just lie back?"

"You just lie back."

"I don't take my clothes off yet?"

"Not yet. I'll do that for you later."

"And then we just . . . do it?"

"That's right. Then we just . . . do it. But maybe I should teach you a little trick."

"A trick?"

"I ain't a beautiful girl, honey. I know that. I got a nice set of milk jugs but that's about it. So Miss Sue tole me about this little trick to pass on to men."

"What sort of trick?"

She giggled. "You're getting scared again, honey. It's

nothing to be scared about at all.'' She leaned over and touched his chest. He liked the weight and warmth of her pressed against him. ''You got a sweetheart?''

James thought about it. Should he even mention Marietta's name to a girl like this? ''I guess.''

''Well, then, while we're doin' it, you close your eyes and pretend I'm her. It'll be a lot better for you that way.''

''But isn't that kind of—'' He shook his head.

''Kind of what?''

''Won't that kind of hurt your feelings?''

She looked up at him in the soft flicking lampglow. How hard she seemed, and yet there was a weariness in her young gaze that made him sad for her. She was fourteen and no fourteen year old he knew looked this weary. ''Nope,'' she said. ''It won't hurt my feelings at all.''

But for some reason he didn't think she was telling him the truth. For some reason he thought she might be happy to hear what he said next.

''I'm happy to be with you,'' he said.

''You are?''

''Sure.''

''Well, that's nice of you to say.'' She pointed to her mouth. ''Let me finish chewin' my gum so my breath gets good and sweet.''

She finished chewing her gum, then set it with surprising delicacy on the edge of the bureau and lay back down next to him.

''Would you like it better if I turned the lamp out?'' she said.

''Yeah, maybe that would be better.''

So she turned the lamp out.

He lay there in the darkness listening to both of them breathe.

After a time she kissed him and it was awkward and he felt nervous and afraid but then she kissed him a second and a third time and it felt very nice and he began stroking her bleached hair and she took one of his hands and set it to her breast and then everything was fine, just fine, and all the whorehouse noise faded and it was just them in the soft shared prairie shadows.

3

Tess was his littlest girl. She was four. Because of the heat she wore a pair of ribbed summer drawers. Her sister Eloise was asleep. Tess was at the doorway, giving Griff a hug he had to bend down to get. Her body was hot and damp and as always she felt almost frighteningly fragile in his arms. He kissed her blue eyes and her pink lips and then he hugged her, feeling the doll cradled in her arm press against him.

"Will you kiss Betty, too?"

"Kind of hot for a kiss, isn't it?" Griff said playfully.

"You kissed me, Daddy. Can't you kiss her?"

Griff looked over at his wife in the rattan rocker and winked. "Oh, I guess I could."

So he picked Betty up and kissed her on the forehead and handed her back.

" 'Night, punkin'," he said, bending down and holding Tess to his leg. She was so small, she scarcely touched his thigh.

"Will you bring me ice cream?"

"I'm afraid I can't tonight, hon."

"How come?"

"I have some business to take care of."

"What kind of business?"

He laughed. "Dora, don't you think it's time you put your little girl to bed?"

Dora got up from the rocker and came over. She leaned down and picked up Tess. Tess held tight to Betty.

Dora said, "How about a kiss for me, too?"

Griff obliged. He held her longer than he meant to and he closed his eyes as he kissed her. He knew that she knew something was wrong. He'd told her that Kittredge wanted to talk to him about some haying later on in the fall, that the hay man wanted an answer tomorrow morning. But she knew. All during dinner he'd felt her eyes on him. Gray, loving, gentle eyes. Now, holding their youngest, she touched him and the feel of her fingers on his forearm made him feel weak, as if he were caught up in some kind of reverie. He wanted to be younger, back before the holdup and the little girl getting killed. How stupid it all seemed now, being so concerned about not having a job, feeling so afraid that he'd been pushed to such extremes. Hell, he didn't have nearly as good a job even now but they were making it and making it fine.

"You don't have to go, you know," Dora said. A tall woman, not pretty but handsome in her clean purposeful way, she tugged on his shirtsleeve much as Tess had done earlier. "You could always tell Kittredge you just weren't interested."

"Could be some good money. You never can tell."

She said, "Is Carlyle going to be there?"

"Carlyle? Why would he be there? I haven't seen Carlyle in a long time."

"It just feels funny, tonight."

"What's 'feel funny,' Momma?" Tess said.

He leaned in and kissed them both again. "I won't be too long," he said, and then he was gone.

Long before there was a brick-and-steel bridge near the dam, Griff used to go there as a boy and throw his fishing line in and spend the day. He'd always bring an apple, a piece of jerky, and enough water to last the long hot day. Other boys would come but Griff always managed to stay alone, liking it better that way. But much as he liked it during the day, he liked it even better at night, when the water over the dam fell silver in the moonlight, and when fishermen in boats downriver could be seen standing up against the golden circle of the moon, casting out their lines and waiting, waiting for their smallmouth bass and catfish and sheepshead and northern pike. In the war, where he'd served in the Eleventh Infantry under General Ord during the siege of Corinth and the occupation of Bolivar, he'd lain awake nights thinking of his fishing spot, and the firefly darkness, and the rush and roar of the dam, and rain-clouds passing the moon.

He was hoping to be a little early tonight so he could appreciate all this before Kittredge and Carlyle got there, but as soon as he left the main path over by the swings he saw two figures outlined against the sky and he knew that tonight there wouldn't be even that much peace.

Kittredge said, "Good thing you got here now. Carlyle's gone crazy."

"Crazy, hell," Carlyle said. "I'm just sayin' we

should take care of him before he takes care of us.''

Griff sighed. Things hadn't changed any in the years the men had been apart. Kittredge and Carlyle had never gotten along; it had always been up to Griff to keep things smooth between them. Tonight was especially bad. Even from several feet away, Griff could see and smell that Carlyle was drunk.

''Plus we've got some complications,'' Kittredge said. ''And I don't mean just the little girl's father.''

''What're you talking about?''

So Kittredge explained how Sheriff Dodds had come into the roundhouse tavern and pretty much said that he knew the three men had stuck up the bank and killed the little girl—maybe not killed her on purpose but killed her nonetheless—and that if he, Dodds, had to choose fates, he'd take his chances with the law instead of with some crazy man with a Winchester.

''That's why I say we kill Ryan,'' Carlyle said, ''before he kills us.''

''Shut up,'' Griff said.

They stood downslope from the dam so they could talk over the roar. Griff rolled himself a cigarette, taking the smoke deep into his lungs, savoring the burning. He said, ''Maybe we should take it to a vote.''

''Take what to a vote?'' Carlyle said.

''What the sheriff said.''

''You mean turning ourselves in?'' Kittredge said.

''Yup,'' Griff said. ''Maybe that's the easiest way to do things.''

''That what you want to do, Griff?'' Carlyle said.

''I didn't say one way or the other; all I said was that maybe we should take it to a vote.''

''I been in Fort Madison,'' Carlyle said. ''I'd never

last in there again. I'm too god damn old for prison."

"So you're voting against it?" Griff said.

"God damn right I'm votin' against it."

"Kittredge? What do you think we should do?"

Kittredge ran a hand across his face, turned slightly to look out at the water over the grassy hump of the slope, then spat into the earth. He turned back to his partners. "You think he'd listen to our side of it?"

"Who?" Griff said.

"Ryan."

"Doubt it," Griff said. "Put yourself in his place. Your daughter gets killed by three men and they come and try and tell you their side. Would you listen to them?"

Kittredge thought a moment. Then, "Maybe there's a third way, instead of turnin' ourselves in or just waitin' for Ryan to shoot us."

"What would that be?" Griff said.

"What Carlyle said."

"Damn right," Carlyle said. "What I said."

"Shoot Ryan, you mean?" Griff said.

"Yes."

"Damn right," Carlyle said again. "Let's vote right now."

Griff paid him no attention. He turned to Kittredge. "That's the tempting way, I know. But think about it. You said the sheriff pretty much believes we're the men involved in the robbery. But maybe he doesn't have hard evidence."

"So what?" Carlyle said.

Griff kept talking straight to Kittredge, even though Kittredge wasn't responding. "So if Ryan gets killed, who do you think the sheriff's going to blame? Us." He paused. "There's at least some possibility that the sheriff will never be able to prove we had a part in that robbery. But if we go after Ryan ourselves—"

"I want a damn vote," Carlyle said.

"He's right, Carlyle," Kittredge said.

"What?" Carlyle said.

"He's right. Griff is. By goin' after Ryan, we'd just be admitting that we were guilty."

"You votin' with him, then?"

"Yes," Kittredge said. "I am."

Griff allowed himself a small sigh. "We wait."

"We what?"

"We wait, Carlyle. We see what Ryan's going to do next. That's the only way we stay out of trouble."

"What if he tries to kill us?" Carlyle said.

"Then we have the sheriff take care of him. You know how Dodds is. He won't allow anybody to start shooting people. He'll either run Ryan in or run him out of town. Either way, he takes care of our problem for us."

"You make it sound pretty god damn simple," Carlyle said.

"It's a lot simpler than shooting somebody," Griff said, anger in his voice now. "You seem to forget something, Carlyle. We're not killers. Hell, we're not even thieves. We didn't get any money at all from that robbery. We killed a little girl by accident and we're going to fry in hell for what we did. But that still don't make us killers. That still don't mean we could pick up a gun and kill a man in cold blood." He nodded to Kittredge. "At least Kittredge and I couldn't." He turned back to Carlyle. "And I don't think you could, either. Not when you came right down to it. You like your hootch and you like your whores but that's a long damn way from bein' a killer.''

''You didn't see his eyes this afternoon,'' Carlyle said.

''We killed his little girl. How do you think he'd look?'' Griff said.

''So we wait?'' Kittredge said.

''Yes,'' Griff said, ''we just wait and see what happens.''

''Shit,'' Carlyle said, and pulled away from the two men, wobbling drunkenly over to a huge elm tree. In the darkness they could hear him splashing piss against the tree.

''He gets crazier the older he gets,'' Kittredge said.

Griff nodded. ''The way I see it, we've got two problems.''

''Two?''

''Ryan and Carlyle. Either one of them could do something crazy. Damn crazy.''

Kittredge sighed. ''My stomach's in knots. I couldn't eat tonight.''

''We'll keep an eye on him,'' Griff said, ''and we'll be alright.''

But he couldn't muster much conviction in his voice. All he could do was just stand there and watch Carlyle come wobbling back, zipping up his pants as he moved through the grass.

Griff just wanted to be home in bed with his wife and have his daughters come laughing in just after dawn, ready for a new day. But he had the terrible feeling that that simple pleasure was beyond him now. Maybe forever.

"I still want a god damn vote on the subject," Carlyle said as he swerved up to the two men.

Which was when Griff slapped him hard across the mouth. Slapped him as hard as he could, hard enough to knock him to his knees.

"Maybe you shouldn't have done that," Kittredge said, sounding tense.

Griff nodded. "Maybe I shouldn't have."

"You sonofabitch, you sonofabitch," Carlyle said, furious but drunk enough that he could not get easily to his feet. "You sonofabitch."

Griff walked away from the other two men. He went over and stood by the dam, the silver foaming water falling in the mosquito-thick night air. Thirty years ago, the boy he'd been had stood here all filled with great unbounded hope. How could he have known that all these long years later he would be standing here, the killer of a little girl, and the little girl's father come to pay him back?

He shook his head and stared with great sorrow at the roaring, tumbling water.

Then he went back to tell Carlyle he was sorry for slapping him.

4

James did the most unlikely thing of all, fell asleep just after he finished making love to the girl. Several glasses of wine had made him drowsy. The girl had let him sleep. She'd felt sorry for him. Not only was this the first time for him, drinking had also led him to talking about his old man. James had gotten teary, telling her how much he'd loved his father; and then he'd fallen asleep. His uncle had paid for two full hours; she was going to let him take advantage of the time even if all it meant was lying next to him thinking about her own parents. Anyway, James was gentle and sweet compared to the coarse men she was used to. Earlier tonight, for instance, a miner hadn't even let her get lubricated. He'd just pushed in, hurting her. Now, like James, she closed her eyes and dozed.

The gunshot woke him. He sat straight up in bed, muttering through the mists of sleep and booze. ''What happened?'' James said.

Next to him in the darkness, coming awake, too, the girl said, ''I don't know. I never heard no gunshot in here before. Something terrible must have happened.''

Outside the door you could hear heavy boots clomping on the wooden floor; men cursing and pulling on their clothes; women saying over and over, ''What happened? What happened?'' as they came out of their rooms. It was like a fire drill.

James pulled on his own clothes. As he started to leave, the girl grabbed him by the wrist. ''You be careful out there.''

''I will.''

There in the moonlight, she smiled. She sure wasn't pretty but he sure did like her. ''I'm glad it was with me, the first time.''

''So am I,'' James said, and squeezed her hand.

The hallway and the staircase were packed with retreating men. Obviously, nobody who had to make any pretense of being respectable wanted to be caught in a whorehouse. The notion now was to get the hell out of there.

On the way down the stairs, jostled in among other men, James was gawked at, pointed at, and smirked at. Old men with white hair and old men with muttonchops and old men with gold teeth peered at him wondering what the hell a fresh kid like him was doing there.

All James was concerned about was Uncle Septemus. Where was he and was he all right?

But even being pushed and shoved down the stairs by the crowd, even worried about what was going on, even sort of hungover from the alcohol . . . James was still smilingly aware of tonight's significance. It wasn't that he felt like a man exactly, it was more that he felt as if he'd learned something, that women, even ones who had to earn their living pleasing men, were every bit as real and complicated as he himself was. He'd actually liked the girl upstairs and that to him was more amazing than making love, which was wonderful and something he sure wanted to do again, but was not quite the heady mystical experience he'd assumed it would be after years of building up fantasies about it. He knew he'd never forget the girl, and not just because of the physical experience, either, but because of her rough intelligence and kindness in the face of his fears and patience in the face of his inexperience.

At the bottom of the stairs, he found his uncle.

Septemus sat in a straight-backed chair, so drunk he couldn't hold up his head, his six-shooter lying on the floor. You could smell the gun smoke, acrid even above the whiskey and perfume. The player piano was just now being turned off. Men were piling out front, side, and back doors.

The madame, a wiry little woman in a fancy blue silk dress and a hat that looked like a squatting porcupine, glared down at Uncle Septemus and said, "Who knows this sonofabitch anyway?"

"I do."

She whirled around to James.

"What'd he do, ma'm?"

"What'd he do? Why, the sonofabitch started talking about some little girl gettin' killed or some god damn thing and he went crazy. Started tearin' up the room and callin' out her name and then he started firin' his gun!"

"He didn't hurt the lady, though?"

"The lady?"

"The girl he was with."

She smirked. "Ain't used to hearin' 'em called ladies." Several of the girls standing around laughed about this. "No, he didn't hurt the girl." She shook her head. Her anger went abruptly, and something like pity came into her voice. "Poor god damn bastard. Was it his daughter got killed?"

"Yes, ma'm?"

"She young?"

"Thirteen."

"Poor god damn bastard."

"Somebody shot her."

She shook her head and sighed. "Get him out of here, kid. The gunshots'll bring the sheriff and you don't want to answer a lot of questions to that sonofabitch."

James went over and got his arm under Uncle Septemus and helped him to his feet.

It was obvious Uncle Septemus had no idea where he was. Sometimes his head would roll back and he'd try to focus his brown eyes but he couldn't. Once he said

''Clarice,'' as if she were somewhere around him and he were waiting for her.

''C'mon, kid, I'll help you,'' the madame said.

She got them out the back door and into the night.

There was yellow lamplight angling out the back door and making the long dusty grass green. Then the madame closed the door and everything was a rich dark prairie blue, the moon clear and round, the banking clouds gray, the elms and oaks and poplars black silhouettes against the ebony sky.

By the time he reached the street—four blocks from the hotel—the madame had turned the player piano on again. On the night air it managed to sound festive and lonely at the same time.

James dragged Uncle Septemus back to the hotel. He got sort of underneath him so Septemus could lay across his back and then he just started walking, Septemus's feet dragging in the dust. James was sweaty and winded and sore in no time but he didn't stop.

Only once did Uncle Septemus say anything. He seemed to say ''Kill,'' and he seemed to say it two or three times. Then he was unconscious again, James taking him down alleys to avoid curious lawmen. What did Uncle Septemus mean by ''kill'' anyway?

Chapter Five

1

Septemus Ryan woke up at dawn. He didn't know where he was. He rolled over on the bed and looked in the gray morning light at his nephew asleep and snoring in the bed across from him. Close by roosters crowed and dogs barked. A milk wagon or a water wagon or a freight wagon jangled by in the street below. He was hot from the heat, which was already in the eighties, and also hot from his hangover. He even felt a little feverish. He'd had several hard years drinking, ever since the death of Clarice, and the drinking was taking its toll. Bloody stools, sometimes frighteningly bloody ones, from hemorrhoids that liquor only inflamed. Dry heaves in the morning sometimes, sticking his finger down his throat till the vomit came up in a hot orange gush that had a recoil like a hunting rifle. And disorientation. His employees had long ago started making jokes about his drinking, winking and smiling to each other and even shaking their heads in pity. Poor sonofabitch. Daughter's dead and he can't get over it. These days he wanted whores. He wanted them even though much of the time he was too drunk to do anything with them. He just got kind of crazy sometimes. He was always paying bills submitted to him by angry madames. Come back here and try that shit again and you god damn see what happens. He never hurt the girls. He just destroyed the rooms he was in and then usually broke down bawling. He had no idea what this was all about. He didn't care, either.

He got out of bed. James started to wake up.

"You go back to sleep now," Ryan said. "You hear me?"

But James didn't need convincing. Between the early hour and his hangover, James had barely been conscious when he'd glanced up. He fell back asleep, snoring wetly.

Ryan went down the hall to the bathroom. He filled

the basin with clean tepid water that he poured from the pitcher. He washed his face and then shaved with a straight razor, getting all lathered up, and then he washed his neck and his armpits and dropped his trousers and washed his balls and his butt. He took water and a comb and got his hair to lie a certain parted way and then he was satisfied. He was a handsome man and he knew it and that was his vanity, so even on a morning such as this he wanted to look his best.

Back in the room, he put on a clean white shirt and a nice light jacket. He looked over at James only once. He smiled to himself. James would always remember last night. His first girl and most likely his first drunk. He didn't want James to be a woman and a woman was exactly what his sister was turning her son into.

The last thing he did was pick up the Winchester. Then he was ready. He left the room.

The hotel he sought was down by the tracks. The back door was flanked by garbage cans. The garbage stank, gagging sweetly like a corpse left in a hot room too long.

People weren't up and around yet. It was scarcely five A.M. Another half hour and then they'd be about their tasks.

He went up three flights of stairs to the top floor and then he went in through the fire door and halfway down the hall to room 307.

He glanced left, glanced right. Seeing nobody, he rapped on the door with one knuckle.

"God damn fucking sonofabitch," a male voice said from the other side of the door. "Who the hell is it?"

A muzzy female voice muttered something Ryan didn't understand.

Ryan rapped again. One knuckle.

''You're gonna be one sorry pecker when I get there, let me tell you,'' Carlyle said.

Ryan could hear covers being thrown back. Even in weather like this, some people liked covering up. He could hear Carlyle pulling his pants on. Carlyle continued to swear. The woman said nothing. Hopefully she'd gone back to sleep.

Carlyle opened the door and Ryan put the muzzle of his Winchester right in Carlyle's face.

Ryan saw that behind Carlyle the woman was still sleeping.

He got Carlyle out into the hall. The man wore pants. No socks. No shirt. He had a lot of gray chest hair and little fleshy titties like a young girl.

Ryan said, ''Walk downstairs now, Carlyle. There's a buggy and you're going to get into it.''

''You got the wrong man, mister,'' Carlyle said. It was easy to see how scared he was. It was almost disgusting to see. You'd think a man who had played a part in the death of an innocent young girl wouldn't be scared of anything.

Ryan said, ''Move.''

''Hey, listen,'' Carlyle said. ''You got the wrong man. Honest.''

Ryan slammed the barrel across the back of Carlyle's head.

Carlyle, who appeared to be just as hungover as Ryan, started crying.

Ryan said, ''Move. You understand?''

Carlyle, looking confused and baffled and imploring, snuffled some snot up into his sinuses and starting walking down the rubber runner leading to the fire door, and down the stairs outside.

Ryan made Carlyle take the reins of the top buggy. He held the Winchester on Carlyle where passersby couldn't see.

As they left town they passed the morning's first citizens, a black man washing down horses, a Mexican throwing out fry grease, and a chubby priest in a dusty black cassock sweeping off the steps of his church.

As they reached the sheriff's office, Carlyle started looking around for any sight of Dodds or his deputies. But the squat adobe building with barred windows on three sides appeared to have no one awake inside.

Carlyle looked as sad as any man Ryan had ever seen.

They rode on out of town.

"You ever have children?"

"Huh-uh."

"How come?"

"Whaddya mean how come?"

"Most men have kids."

"Just never did is all."

"Ever married?"

"Nope."

"How come?"

"What the hell you askin' me all these questions for?"

"We got a ways to go. Just trying to make the time a little more tolerable."

"You plannin' to kill me?"

"I don't know yet."

"You should look at your god damn eyes sometime, mister."

"That's enough for now," Ryan said. "Just keep your eyes on the road."

The horse was a big bay. Every ten yards or so he dropped big splashing green shit on the road. It splattered all over his fetlocks. The smell made things worse for Ryan. He shouldn't have had so much to drink last night. This morning was important.

When they got to the timber land, Ryan had Carlyle pull the wagon over.

Ryan said, waving the Winchester, "Get down."

"Get down?"

"That's what I said, isn't it?"

"Why am I gettin' down?"

"Because you're going for a walk."

"You're gonna kill me, aren't you?"

"I don't know yet."

"You liar. You liar."

This time Ryan smashed the butt of the Winchester into the back of Carlyle's head. A bloody hairy hole showed on the back of Carlyle's head now.

"You sonofabitch," he said, but he got down. He held his head, trying to stop the blood, but red kept pouring between his fingers.

Ryan dug in his pocket and took out his handkerchief. "Here," he said.

Carlyle took the handkerchief and applied it to the back of his head. The white cloth turned red almost instantly. Ryan must have hit him harder than he'd thought.

"Move," Ryan said then.

"Where?"

"Into the woods. To the river."

"You sonofabitch."

But he started walking.

"You remember the dress she had on that day?" Ryan asked.

The trees were spruce and elm and maple. The shrubs were red bud and lilac and mock orange. In the underbrush were fox and rabbit and gray squirrel. You could smell the heat already. You could smell the dry dirt on the narrow winding trail through the woods. Ryan could smell the sweat and the piss on Carlyle. Ryan could smell the sleep still on himself.

After a time, them moving faster now, Ryan said, "Calico."

"Huh?"

"The dress she wore that day. Calico."

"Oh."

"She'd only worn it twice. It was her birthday dress."

"Mister, look, I—"

"You should've seen how the bullets tore up the dress. You should have seen the blood."

"God damn, mister, you got the wrong—"

"Stop. Right here."

"Mister, look—"

"I said stop."

He jammed the Winchester in Carlyle's back.

They were in a clearing. A doe stood on the edge of the long grass. Ryan could smell thistle and thyme. The deer looked so sweet he wanted to go up and hug her. Clarice at the zoo had always hugged the deer.

Ryan said, "Turn around."

"Mister—"

"Turn around."

Carlyle turned around.

"You know I'm going to kill you, don't you?"

"Mister—"

"I'm going to gut-shoot you. It's going to take a long, long time to die."

Carlyle started crying. You could smell how he'd shit his pants just then. Just standing there, just then, shit his pants.

"Mister, please—"

"There's no pleasure in this for me. I want you to know that. I'm only doing what needs to be done."

"Jesus, mister, if you'd just listen—"

Ryan put a big sopping red hole in Carlyle's stomach. There was the sound of the gunfire and the scent of gunsmoke. Carlyle's cry was a pitiful thing. He fell to the ground. He was twitching pretty bad. It was ugly to watch.

Ryan walked over and stood next to him. Ryan looked down and said, "You should've seen that calico dress, Carlyle. You should've seen it."

Carlyle was sobbing. Ryan could see every piece of beard stubble on Carlyle's chin and every whiskey and tobacco stain on his teeth. "Holy Mary, Mother of God," Carlyle was saying, praying out loud without any kind of shame at all.

Ryan watched him for a time. Stood there. Just watching.

After a time the convulsions started.

"Shit, mister, just shoot me. Please. Jesus, please. Please."

The blood soaked into his trousers now. You could see life fading in the blue eyes. Fading.

"Please," he said. "I can't take it no more. Please."

Ryan lifted the Winchester and pointed it directly at Carlyle's face. He didn't have the taste for torture after all. He put the weapon right on Carlyle's nose. "You sure you want it this way?"

Carlyle was in so much pain he couldn't even talk. All he could do was nod. His lips were already dry and white and chapped.

"You should've seen what that calico looked like," Ryan said.

Ryan shot him in the face. He blew his nose off. All that remained was a ragged hole with blood chugging out. Ryan stared until he couldn't stand to stare any longer.

A jay came and sat on Carlyle's forehead and pointed a delicate beak at the hole in the dead man's face and started tasting the blood. Already you could see plump black ants coming up.

Ryan took one more look at Carlyle then hefted his Winchester and left.

2

"Morning, Mrs. Griff."

"Morning, Sheriff."

"Wondered if your husband would be around?"

"'Fraid not. He went over town early."

Dodds smiled. "Darned early. It's hardly seven."

"He was needin' some kind of wrench he didn't have. Said he could borrow one from Charlie Smythe."

Dodds nodded to the barn in back. "He still works on his buggies, huh?"

"They're his pride and joy."

"Guess they would be," Dodds said. "He built some good ones when the wagon works was open." Seeing that he'd made Mrs. Griff melancholy—he was not what you'd call steeped in the social graces, particularly where women were concerned—he bent down to look more closely at the two little girls who stood on either side of their mother. "Now let me see. One of you is Eloise and one of you is Tess. Right?"

The older girl giggled and blushed. "Uh-huh, Sheriff, uh-huh."

"You'd be Eloise, wouldn't you? The oldest one?"

"Uh-huh."

"How old are you, sweetie?"

"I'm six and Tess is four."

"Four!" Dodds said, turning to the littlest girl. She had golden braids—her sister had dark hair—and wore a blue calico dress. "Why, I thought you were five for sure."

Tess blushed and buried her face in her mother's apron. Dodds looked up at Mrs. Griff and winked. "Last time I saw your mother, I said that, didn't I, Mrs. Griff? I said, why I thought that Tess was five years old for sure."

The girls giggled and flushed some more, thoroughly charmed.

Dodds straightened up, his bones cracking as he did so. The older one got, the more noises one's body made. "Do you suppose you could walk me down to the corner, Mrs. Griff? Maybe have Eloise and Tess stay here?"

He could see the instant alarm in the woman's eyes. He hadn't wanted to put it there but there was no other way.

"Why don't you girls go back and finish your breakfast," Mrs. Griff said. He could hear the tightness in her voice, the fear. Something was wrong and now she knew it. She was a plump woman, but pretty even though her hair had started turning gray. She had always struck Dodds as one of those women who can handle any crisis, much stronger than most men at such moments, himself included. But now, panic besetting her gaze and sweet pink mouth, he saw her vulnerability. He was almost disappointed.

They set out down the walk.

"Just tell me straight out," she said. He could feel her trying to remain calm.

"I think he's in some trouble, Mrs. Griff."

"What kind of trouble?"

"Old trouble, actually. A bank robbery a few years back."

"A bank robbery?" She smiled with a kind of pretty bitterness. "Believe me, Sheriff, you go take a look at the food on our table and then you tell me that we ever saw any money from a bank robbery."

"That was one of the problems, at least from the robbers' point of view. A young girl got killed and the robbers got all het up and took off without any money."

"A young girl?"

"Thirteen. Delivering something to the bank for her father."

"My Lord." She sounded shocked and almost angry. Obviously she was thinking of her own girls.

They walked a time in silence. Kids were invading the green dusty summer day, streaming clean from the small white respectable houses of Tencourt Street, eager to soil shirts and trousers and dresses and, most especially, faces.

"Why do you think my husband had anything to do with this?"

"An ex-Pinkerton man was in town a while back. He'd traced the robbers to here."

"And he said Mike was one of them?"

"That's what he said."

"Who else?"

"He said Kittredge and Carlyle."

At the last name her face turned sour with a frown. "Carlyle, I could understand. But not Mike or Kittredge. They're good men, Sheriff, and you know it." She was watching him now, expecting him to agree.

"That they are, Mike and Dennis," he said. "Good men. But think back to when the wagon works closed. Think how desperate men were around here." He didn't have the courage to look at her as he said this.

They reached the corner. A small band of kids stood ten feet away pointing at the sheriff, or more specifically at his badge. It always brought a lot of ooohs and aaahs of the sort kids muster for people in uniform.

Now they faced each other and Dodds said, "The girl's father came to town yesterday."

"My God. Does he think Mike is responsible?"

"I'm pretty sure that's what he thinks."

"Are you going to tell him otherwise?"

This was the hard part for Dodds. "Mrs. Griff, I'd like you to talk to Mike and have him turn himself in at my office."

"My God. You think he did it, don't you?"

"I'm afraid I do."

"My God."

"If he don't turn himself in, Mrs. Griff, he's at the mercy of this fellow Ryan. So far Ryan has done nothing

I can arrest him for. That means he'll have every opportunity to kill the three men." He hesitated a minute. "You'd rather have Mike alive, wouldn't you?"

"He couldn't have killed a girl. He just couldn't have."

"It was an accident. Even the bank employees agree on that. An accident. So in all likelihood he wouldn't be facing any murder charge. Least not a first-degree one." His jaw clamped. "You've got to see this Ryan fellow to know what I'm talking about, Mrs. Griff. He's insane. He's so grieved over his daughter that nothing else matters than killing the men responsible. If Mike don't turn himself in, Mrs. Griff, Ryan's gonna kill him for sure."

"My God," she said.

The kids watching them inched closer. One kid said, "Sheriff, did your badge really cost two hunnerd dollars?"

The sheriff winked at Mrs. Griff and said to the kid, "Oh, a lot more than that, Frankie. You just can't see the jewels I got on the other side."

"Jewels! Wow! See, I tole ya!" Frankie said to the other kid and then they took off running, tumbling into the morning.

"You tell Mike to turn himself in, Mrs. Griff," Dodds said after turning back to the woman. "That's the safest way for everybody." He touched her elbow. "Please do it, Mrs. Griff. I don't want anybody else to die because of all this. The girl was enough."

Mrs. Griff was crying now; soft silver tears in her soft gray eyes. "He just couldn't have killed any girl, Sheriff," she said. "Not on purpose; not on purpose." That's all she could think of, the girl.

"You tell him," Dodds said quietly. "Please, Mrs. Griff. All right?"

He went back to his office.

3

The hangover felt like a fever in James, but not so much a fever that he couldn't think about the girl last night. He was changed, and this morning the change felt even more important than it had last night. He wished he had a good male friend in Council Bluffs, somebody you could really talk to—partly to impress, of course (not many boys his age had ever actually slept with a girl), and partly just as a confidant. Obviously he couldn't tell his mother and he couldn't tell Marietta. And his uncle already knew about it and . . .

His uncle. James looked across at the empty bed. Apparently Septemus had gotten dressed and gone downstairs for breakfast. James thought about last night. It was pretty sad, really, Septemus getting so drunk and sort of shooting up the place and then starting to cry. James thought about what his mother had said of Septemus ever since Clarice had died. How his uncle wasn't quite right somehow . . .

For the twenty minutes James had been awake, shoes and boots and bare feet could be heard passing by on the other side of the door. Every time he'd think it was his uncle, the sound would move on down the hall. So, lying there now, he held out no hope that the sounds of leather squeaking would actually be his uncle. But the door opened abruptly and in came Septemus.

"Good morning, James!" Septemus said, striding in

and shutting the door behind him. "Are you ready for a big breakfast? I certainly am."

James rolled off the bed and started getting into his clothes. He kept looking at Septemus. Despite the good cheer of his booming voice, there was something wrong with Septemus. He couldn't look James in the face.

"Then we'll go for a ride," Septemus said, rummaging for something in his carpetbag.

James saw Septemus take his Navy Colt from the bag, open his coat, and put the weapon inside his belt. Then he closed the coat again.

"You ready, son?"

"Mind if I wash up?"

"Of course not, James."

Septemus slapped James on the back. He would still not let his eyes meet James's.

"Uncle Septemus?"

"Yes, James?"

"Is something wrong?"

"Wrong? Why would you say a thing like that? Look out the window. It's a fine morning. And listen to all the wagons in the street below. It's not only a fine morning, it's a busy morning. The sounds of commerce, that's what you hear in the street below. The sound of commerce." His voice was good-naturedly booming again. But then why were his eyes filled with tears?

Something was terribly wrong. James wondered what it could be.

"I'll be right back," James said, and went down the hall.

A man was coming out of the bathroom just as James was ready to go in. The smell the man had left behind was so sour James had to hold his breath while he poured fresh water into the basin and got himself all scrubbed up.

When he was all through, he stared at himself in the mirror with his hair combed and a clean collar on.

Yes, he definitely looked older. Seventeen, maybe; or even eighteen. He had to thank Uncle Septemus for taking him along last night.

But when he thought of Uncle Septemus, he thought of his strange mood this morning. Where had Septemus gone so early in the day? And why was he putting on this blustery act of being so happy? Septemus hadn't been a happy man even before the murder of his daughter; afterward, he'd been inconsolable.

When he got back to the room he saw Septemus sitting on the edge of the bed staring at the rotogravure of Clarice he carried everywhere with him.

"She was a fine girl," his uncle said.

"She sure was."

Septemus looked up at him. "You miss her a lot, don't you, James?"

"Yes, I do."

Septemus continued to stare at him. "It changed all our lives, didn't it, when she was killed, I mean?"

James thought a moment. He felt guilty that he could not answer honestly. Sure, he was sad when Clarice had died, and he did indeed think about her pretty often. But change his life? Not really; not in the way his uncle meant. "Yes; yes, it did."

"You're a good boy, James."

"Thank you."

"Or excuse me. After last night, you're a boy no longer. You're half a man."

"Half?"

Septemus's troubled brown eyes remained on his. "There's one more thing you need to learn. You know firsthand about carnality, and the pleasures only a woman can render a man, but now you need to learn about the opposite of pleasure."

"The opposite of pleasure?"

"Responsibility. You have to pay for the pleasures of being a man by taking on the responsibilities of a man."

James noticed how Septemus had gone back to staring at the picture.

"What responsibilities?"

Septemus put the picture back in his carpetbag then stood up, putting on the good mood again. "Come on now, young man, we're going down to the restaurant and have the finest breakfast they've ever served."

James couldn't quell his appetite, even while he was beginning to worry about what Septemus must have in mind for them today.

"Bacon and eggs and hash browns," Septemus said as they strolled down the hall. "How does that sound?"

"It sounds great."

"And with lots of strawberry marmalade spread all over hot bread."

James could barely keep himself from salivating. In the onslaught of such food, he gradually forgot about Septemus's ominous talk of responsibility.

4

She had sat at the kitchen table rehearsing what she would say to him. How easy it was when it was words spoken only to herself, only in her mind.

Be honest with me, Mike. Whatever you've done, tell me, and I'll stand by you. I know you couldn't have killed that young girl, so tell me your side of things, Mike. Let me hear the honest truth from you.

Then she saw him coming up the walk, the girls hurling themselves at him so he'd pick them up in his strong callused hands and strong muscular arms and carry them inside.

The three of them came bursting through the door, the girls laughing because he was tickling them. He set them down and Tess said, "He said I was five years old, Daddy."

"Who said?" Griff said, tickling her again.

"The sheriff."

"The sheriff?" Griff said, fluffing her blond hair. "Was he trying to arrest you?"

Tess nodded to her mother. "He came here to see Mommy."

Griff's face tightened. "Dodds came here?"

His wife said, "Yes."

"When?"

"Not long after you walked over town."

"What did he want?"

She scooched the girls outdoors.

"How come we have to go outside, Mommy?" Tess said.

"Because it's summer and that's where little girls are supposed to be. Outside."

She closed the door and turned around. Griff was pouring himself a cup of coffee from the pot on the stove. No matter how hot it got, Griff always liked steaming coffee.

He went over and sat at the kitchen table. "What did he say?"

She decided against any sort of coyness or hesitation. "He said you were in trouble."

"He say what kind?"

"There was a bank robbery. A young girl was killed."

He stared at her a long time. "You believe that?"

"I'm not sure. Not about the girl, I mean. I know you well enough to know you could never hurt a child."

"How about the bank?"

She came over and sat down across from him at the table. The oilcloth smelled pleasant. "He said it was right after the wagon works closed. I remember what you were like in those days. Desperate. You thought we might lose the house and everything."

"What if I told you that I did help rob that bank?"

"I'd do my best to understand."

"What if I told you that the girl dying was a pure accident?"

"I'd believe that, too."

"Dodds tell you that the girl's father is here?"

"Yes. He says the man means to kill you."

He met her gaze. He looked sad and tense. "Can't say I blame him, can you?"

"It was an accident."

"What if it was Eloise or Tess? Would you be so forgiving just because it was an accident?"

"I reckon not."

"Dodds going to come and arrest me?"

"He wants you to turn yourself in."

"How do you feel about that?"

"I wish you would."

"It'd mean prison."

"I've thought about that, Mike."

"Not all women want to wait for their men."

She touched his coarse strong hand. "I love you, Mike. You made a mistake but that doesn't take away any of my feelings for you."

"I don't think I could tolerate prison. I'm too old. Too used to my freedom."

"What's the alternative?"

"Let this man Ryan try something. Then Dodds will have to run him in."

"Won't Dodds turn on you then?"

"He doesn't have any evidence. He just has the word of this ex-Pinkerton man who was through here a while back."

She put her head down and said a quick prayer for guidance. Then she raised her head and smiled at him. "The girls and I'll come see you. Every week if they'll let us."

"It'd be a terrible life for you."

"We'd get by."

He stared out the back window at the barn where his buggies were. She could tell he was thinking about them. Next to the girls and herself, the buggies were his abiding pride. He picked up his steaming coffee and blew on the hot liquid and said, "Let me think about it a little while."

She touched his hand again. "I love you, Mike. And so do the girls. Just remember that."

His eyes left the window and turned back to her. "I don't know what the hell I ever did to deserve you, but I sure am a lucky man."

She laughed and there were tears in her laugh. "You expect me to disagree with that?"

Then he laughed, too, and went back to staring out the window at the buggies.

5

"Your father coming back?"

James smiled up at the waiter. "Oh, he's not my father."

"Well, I certainly noticed a resemblance, young man."

"I suppose it's because he's my uncle."

"Uncle, is it?" the waiter asked. He had a gray walrus mustache and a thick head of wavy gray hair. His short black jacket was spotless and the serving tray he bore was shiny stainless steel. He also had a heavy brogue. "Uncle would explain it."

"He left this," James said, and slid the bill and several greenbacks to the edge of the table.

The waiter fingered the money with the skill of a pickpocket. "I'll be bringin' you your change," he said, though given the slight hesitation in his voice, James knew that the man hoped there would be no change.

"He said it was all for you."

The waiter laughed hoarsely. "Well, now, isn't that a way to gladden a man's day?" He offered James a small bow. "And I hope your day is gladdened, too, young one."

"Thank you."

"And thank you," the waiter said, and left.

In half an hour a rented wagon was to pull up in front

of the restaurant and James was to go out and meet it. Septemus said he would be driving. He said that James should come out fast and jump up and ask no questions. His appetite sated, his hangover waning, he had started wondering again exactly what his uncle was doing.

Why the wagon? Why come out fast? Why ask no questions?

He put his chin in the palm of his hand and stared out the window at the dusty street filled with pedestrians walking from one side to the other. He started thinking again of last night, of what he'd done with the girl, and he decided that the first thing he was going to do when he got back to Council Bluffs was get himself a good friend so he'd have somebody to tell about his experiences.

Then he started thinking of Uncle Septemus's comment that James was only half a man, that only when he took ''responsibility'' would he be a full man.

James started wondering where Uncle Septemus was right then.

6

In the lobby, Dodds went over to the desk and asked if Septemus Ryan was in his room.

The clerk shook his head. ''Saw both him and his nephew go out a while ago.'' The clerk wore a drummer's striped shirt and a pitiful scruffy little mustache and had a lot of slick goop on his rust-colored hair. He was the Hames's eldest, nineteen years old or so, and this was his first job in town. As far as Dodds was concerned he took it far too seriously. The only law and order the kid respected was that of Mel Lutz who owned the hotel and two other businesses.

"I'm going up to their room." He put out his hand. "I'd appreciate the key."

"Sheriff, now you know what Judge Mason said. He said you shouldn't ought to do that unless you check with him first. 'Bout how people had rights and all. And anyway Mel says I shouldn't ought to do it unless I check with him first."

"He in his office?"

"Yup."

"Then go check an' I'll wait here."

"What about the judge?"

"The judge'll be my concern. Now you go talk to Mel."

"Who'll watch the desk?"

"I'll watch the desk."

"I ain't sure that'd be right."

"What the hell you think I'm gonna do, boy-kid, steal somethin'?"

"No offense, Sheriff, but you ain't one of Mel's employees. And Mel's rule is that only a bona fide employee can be behind the desk."

"Boy, I just happen to be sheriff of this here burg. Now if that don't qualify me to be behind that desk, what does?"

"Guess that's a fair point."

"Now you go tell Mel I want the key."

"Can I tell him why you want the key?"

Dodds sighed. "'Cause I want to go up there and look around."

"Can I tell him why you want to go up there and look around?"

"Kid, you're lucky I don't punch you right on the nose."

"I'm just askin' the questions Mel's gonna ask me."

"I think Ryan's up to somethin' and I want to see if I can get some kind of evidence on him."

The kid leaned forward on his elbow and said, "What's he up to?"

"Git, now. Go ask Mel. That's all I'm gonna say."

The kid stood up, frowning. Obviously disappointed. Like most desk clerks, the kid was a gold-plated gossip.

"Git," the sheriff said.

The kid got.

In all, Dodds leaned on the desk for ten minutes while the kid was away. He said hello to maybe twenty people, sent icy stares at a couple of others he suspected of being confidence men working the area, and helped three different ladies out the front door with their packages.

Dodds liked the hotel's lobby, the leather furnishings, the ferns, the hazy air of cigar and pipe smoke, the bright brass cuspidors, the seemingly endless pinochle game that went on over in the corner. This was where the town's men spent their retirement years. Didn't matter if they were married or not, they always came down there. It was almost like working a shift at a factory. The missus made breakfast and then one took a morning walk and ended up at the hotel. The first thing to do was sit in one of the plump leather chairs and read the paper and then discuss any pressing politics and any pressing town gossip and then help oneself to the pinochle game. Dodds was a piss-poor pinochle player. He would have to get one hell of a lot better before he retired.

"Here's the key, Sheriff," the kid said when he came back. "Mel said five minutes."

"So he's setting time limits now, is he?"

"I'm only tellin' you what he tole me, Sheriff."

Dodds took the key. "Thanks, kid."

The kid held up the five fingers of his left hand and pointed to them with the index finger of his right hand. "Remember, Mel said five minutes."

Dodds restrained himself from telling the kid what an aggravating bastard he could be.

Dodds had always liked hotels. He liked the idea of all the different kinds of people and different kinds of lives being led in them. After his wife died, he'd thought of giving up the small house they'd lived in and moving in to the hotel. He still thought about it, about taking three meals downstairs at a long table covered with a fresh white linen cloth every time, sitting up in his room with a cigar and a magazine and a rocker and watching the sunset and listening to people on their way into the festive night, just sitting there smelling of shaving soap and hair oil, clean as a whistle and without a care.

He thought of all these things as he moved along the corridor to Ryan's room. Taking no chances, he pulled out his revolver, put an ear to the door, and listened. That kid desk clerk could easily have missed Ryan coming back up to his room. Or hell, maybe for some reason Ryan snuck up the back way.

He tried the door knob. Locked. He took out the key, fit it into the lock, and turned it.

He'd been in these rooms many times. In the daylight they looked somewhat shabby. The paint had faded, some of the wallpaper had worked free, the brass beds were getting a little rusty, and the linoleum was pretty scuffed up.

The first carpetbag he tried belonged to the kid. Or at least he assumed it did, unless a grown man carried a slingshot and a Buffalo Bill novel.

In the second carpetbag he found the newspaper stories. There were ten in all, clipped carefully from the front pages of newspapers around the state, some with pictures, some not. It was the same terrible story again and again, the thirteen-year-old girl slain during the bank robbery, the huge rewards offered for the capture of the men, the grieving father and the outrage of the towns-people.

Dodds also found the letter.

The thing ran three pages on a fancy buff blue stock and it was written in a fine, clear longhand that managed to be both attractive and masculine. It said just about what one would expect such a letter to say. While reading it, Dodds kept thinking of Ryan's brown eyes, for-lorn and angry and mad all at the same time.

Dodds had to smile about who the letter was ad-dressed to—it was addressed to him. Ryan had thought of everything. He would come to Myles and do what he wanted and, when it was done, Dodds would have the letter for explanation as to who had done it and why it had been done and what was to be made of it in the common mind.

Shaking his head, Dodds tucked the letter back inside the unsealed envelope, put the letter back inside the car-petbag, and left the room. He moved very quickly for a man his age.

If he didn't find Ryan fast, things were going to get real bad in town. Real bad.

Chapter Six

1

There was something wrong with a man in his forties sitting in a small, crowded confessional telling the priest that not only had he taken the Lord's name in vain, not only had he missed mass several times in the past few months, but also that he'd defiled himself. That was the term Kittredge had been taught, "defiled." Kittredge had a prostate problem. The damn thing got boggy as a rotten apple. This was because of Mae, of course; ever since Mae had miscarried, she'd shown little interest in sex, and Kittredge never felt like forcing himself on her. He felt sorry enough for her as it was, what with the sheets a bloody mess that night and Mae not quite right about anything ever since. He'd tried whorehouses twice but afterward he felt disgusted with himself. There he was liquored up and laughing with some woman who had no morals at all and there was Mae at home in the shadows of their little house, her hands all rosary-wrapped and her gaze fixed far away on something Kittredge had never been able to see.

Earlier this morning, just after waking, the day in the open window smelling of impending rain, these were the thoughts Kittredge had.

Soon after, he went downstairs and scrubbed and shaved for the day. He took the clothes Mae had set out for him and tugged them on and then went into the kitchen where she had two eggs, two strips of bacon, and a big slice of toast waiting for him. She sat across from him, watching him as he ate. This always seemed to give her a peculiar satisfaction he could not understand but found endearing. She would have looked even more fondly at their child eating, he knew. Maybe that's what she pretended, watching him this way, that he was their child.

"You got any special plans today?" she said.

"Sloane says there's no work. Thought I might go down by the creek and do some fishing. Maybe I can catch us something for tonight."

She smiled, watched him stand up and go to the door. "Maybe I'll bake us a cake."

"Now I know I'm gonna have to catch us a fish."

"A chocolate cake with white frosting."

It was his favorite kind. He walked back to her and took her face tenderly in his hands and kissed her gently on the lips. "You're a good woman, Mae."

"You keep on tellin' me that often enough, Dennis, I'm likely to start believin' it."

This time he kissed her on the forehead.

Two hours in, he'd caught nothing. He sat on a piece of limestone. The day was hot but overcast. The water was cloudy. A wild dog came by and tried to steal the lunch he'd brought along but he shooed it away, though for a few moments there the damn animal had scared him some. The county had been infested with rabies just a year ago and doctors everywhere were warning folks to be careful.

His favorite time to fish was autumn, when the days were gold and red and brown with fall colors and the nights were silver with frost. Then he worked fyke nets and basket traps and moved downriver in his johnboat where he made driftwood fires to keep warm. The autumn embraced him and held him in a way furious summer did not. There was solace in autumn and in summer none.

Ryan pulled the buggy into a copse of poplars. The soil there was red and sandy, the bunch grass brown from heat. His hangover was still pretty bad. He had to stop every mile or so to pee, and he kept thinking he had to vomit. The food hadn't helped all that much.

He left the Winchester in the buggy and set off across the woods to Kittredge's house.

Almost immediately after he knocked, a small, worn-looking woman came to the door.

"Mrs. Kittredge?"

"Yes."

"I'm Special Deputy Forbes."

"Special deputy?"

He knew instantly she was alarmed. It was just what he wanted her to be.

"I need to speak with your husband."

"With Dennis?"

"Yes."

"Has he done something wrong?"

Ryan shook his head. "Not at all, ma'm. Not at all. He may have seen something the other day and we need to get his testimony."

"Seen something?" She still sounded suspicious, wary.

"An incident in town." Ryan smiled. Now he wanted her to ease up some, relax. "Something was taken from the jewelry store. We're told your husband was standing in the middle of the street at that time. He may have seen the thief.''

''Which jewelry store would that be? I didn't know we had no jewelry store.''

It was Ryan's intention to remain calm. He inhaled sharply, put the smile back on his face, and said, ''Forgive me, ma'm, I'm down from the state capital so I'm not all that familiar with the town here.''

But she wasn't trying to trap him. In fact, she helped him out of his dilemma. ''Ragan's sells jewelry. That's the general store. They keep some jewelry in the back. Maybe you mean Ragan's.''

''That's exactly what I mean. That's exactly the name the sheriff used.''

He saw her face slacken, the heavy worry lines fading some. She shook her head. He thought he even detected a small, oddly bitter smile. ''Wouldn't that be just Dennis's luck?''

''Ma'm?''

''Goes over town on a completely innocent errand and gets himself mixed up in some kind of robbery.''

''I see.''

''No offense, but you know how it is when you get tied up goin' to court and everything.''

''Yes, ma'm, that's one thing I'm very familiar with.''

''Poor Dennis. He won't be happy to hear that.''

''No, ma'm.''

''But I s'pose it's his civic duty.''

''Yes, ma'm.'' He paused and said, ''Where might I find him, ma'm?''

''He went fishing.''

''Do you happen to know where?''

"He's got a favorite spot just north of here. Up near the bluffs." She pointed in the direction of ragged clay hills. "He'll probably be back in a few hours."

"Oh, I'm sure I can find him, ma'm."

Wariness showed in her eyes again. "You seem to be in a pretty big hurry to talk to him."

"Just like to get this settled so I can head back on the evening train."

"And you say you're a special deputy?"

"That's right, ma'm."

"Working with the sheriff?"

"Yes, ma'm. Down from the capital to help on the jewelry investigation."

"Never heard of such a thing."

Ryan smiled again. "It's an election year, ma'm."

"Election year?"

Ryan nodded. "The governor makes his special deputies available to anybody who asks."

"I see."

"Good politics, ma'm."

The suspicion died in her voice again. "I suppose." She put her face up into the air the way a small dog might. "You can smell rain coming. Dennis'll probably get soaked." She nodded to Ryan. "You tell him I'm working on that cake I promised him."

"I'll tell him, ma'm."

She gave him a curious look, then. "And tell . . . tell him I'm thinking about him."

Ryan knew that she really wanted to say "Tell him I love him," but that she was too inhibited. Somehow she knew, Ryan saw; knew what was really going on, much as she tried denying it to herself.

Ryan tipped his hat. "Good luck with that cake, ma'am."

But she was still giving him that curious, wary gaze. She didn't say good-bye. She just nodded and wiped her hands on her apron again and went back inside the house, closing the door behind her.

By the time Ryan went over the hill to his buggy, the first drops of rain had begun to fall. Plump, clear drops that were hot against the skin. He wished he hadn't liked the Kittredge woman as much as he had. He felt sorry for her. What he was about to do would destroy her life forever. He wished she could have been mean or stupid or offensive in some way.

He got in the buggy and started up the dusty trail that wound into the red clay foothills.

He kept thinking of the Kittredge woman. Maybe because he saw some of his own sorrow in her. They were not unalike, the two of them. Maybe that was it.

2

Half an hour later, the rain was coming down hot and slow. Black clouds covered the already faint sun. It was dark as dusk and the temperature had dropped ten degrees. Coming up over the clay cliffs, Ryan smelled how the rain stirred up the dust and gave it a chalky odor.

He leaned against a poplar and looked down at the bank below. The creek was wide there, deep and fast enough to look treacherous for animals, and the water hitting the surface of it made wide, soft circles.

He hefted the Winchester, aimed, and shot the hat directly off the head of Dennis Kittredge.

Kittredge put on a little show. Knowing that there was nowhere to hide, that he was several precious yards from either boulders or trees, he pitched himself to the right and started rolling in the dust.

Ryan put another shot a few feet ahead of where Kittredge was about to light.

This time Kittredge let out a crazed animal yelp. A fella didn't like to think that circumstances were completely beyond his control, but obviously they now were.

"Just stand up, Mr. Kittredge," Ryan said, starting down the slope, keeping the Winchester right on Ryan's chest. "That way you're not likely to get shot."

Kittredge got to his feet. His fishing pole had rolled off the bank and dropped into the water.

"What the hell do you think you're doing?" Kittredge said. Unlike Carlyle, Kittredge didn't seem so much frightened as angry. He was casual enough to dust off his trousers.

Ryan didn't answer. He came down the clay to the bank and then put the Winchester in Kittredge's face.

"You know why I'm here, Mr. Kittredge."

"I know why you say you're here. I talked to Carlyle. He said you think we had something to do with a bank robbery."

Ryan smiled. "We're beyond pretenses, Mr. Kittredge. I'd say ask Carlyle, but I'm afraid you can't do that. Not anymore."

"What's that supposed to mean?"

"It means he's dead."

For the first time, some of Kittredge's anger waned and something resembling fear narrowed his eyes and pulled his face tight. "You kill him, Ryan?"

"I did."

Kittredge didn't say anything.

Ryan said, "You should've seen it. He was pleading with me to do it."

"I don't want to hear about it."

"He was on the ground and I put the rifle hard against his nose."

"He didn't have that coming."

Ryan considered him a long time. "It's my understanding you don't have any children, Mr. Kittredge. It's my understanding that your wife can't bear you any."

Kittredge glared at him.

"Then you can't appreciate what it is to lose a child. Oh, I know that you *think* you can, Mr. Kittredge. But believe me, until you see your child—"

He didn't finish the sentence.

Thunder rumbled across the sky; lightning trembled gold and silver beneath black clouds. The rain fell in steady monotonous drops.

Ryan said, "Anyway, Mr. Kittredge, it's not something you can imagine. It's something you have to experience." He smiled at Kittredge. "You know what my daughter's very last words were to me, Mr. Kittredge? I'll never forget. She came up to me from the back of the store and said, 'Daddy, I'd like to take the bank deposit over now. Then I'm going to stop and pick you a bouquet of flowers because I love you so much.' Those were her very last words, Mr. Kittredge."

Kittredge let his gaze fall to his feet.

Ryan said, "She never did get to pick me those flowers, Mr. Kittredge. I keep wondering what kind she would have gotten me." He looked at Kittredge and smiled again. "What kind do you think she would have gotten me, Mr. Kittredge?"

Kittredge said nothing. He would not look up.

"You think she would have brought me roses, Mr. Kittredge?"

Nothing.

"Or maybe daisies."

Nothing.

"You going to answer me, Mr. Kittredge?"

Kittredge shuffled his feet. Still he said nothing.

"Seems to me an intelligent man could make an intelligent guess about what kind of flowers she would pick for her father, Mr. Kittredge. Roses or daisies or zinnias." .

Kittredge's head came up slowly. He looked at Ryan for a long time.

Kittredge said, "I'm sorry your little girl died, Ryan."

"You didn't answer my question."

"I really am sorry."

"Do you think she would have picked roses for me, Mr. Kittredge?"

"This won't bring her back. Killin' Carlyle or killin' me. It won't bring her back, Ryan. It won't bring her back."

Ryan hit him so hard with the butt of the rifle that Kittredge easily went over backward, his arms flailing all the way down.

Ryan went over to him then and kicked him once, hard in the face. You could hear his nose shatter and splatter. Right away the bleeding was bad.

Ryan said, "If you think I'm going to get it over with fast, the way I did with Carlyle, you're wrong, Mr. Kittredge. Carlyle didn't have the brains of a rock. But you—you and Griff—you're smart men, responsible men. So you've got a special price to pay and you're going to pay it.''

Through a very bloody mouth, his eyes wild now the way Carlyle's had been, Kittredge said, ''I'm sorry about your little girl, Ryan. I really am.''

This time Ryan kicked him hard on the side of the face, along the jawline.

Kittredge rolled into the dirt, facedown. He made moaning and sobbing sounds.

The rain hit Kittredge's back so hard it sounded like bullets being absorbed by the flesh.

The creek rattled with rain now.

Ryan stood over Kittredge and then finally he took the rope from his pocket.

Ryan said, ''Here you go, Mr. Kittredge. Here you go.''

3

By this time James was beginning to think his uncle had forgotten him. James had been sitting in the restaurant for two hours now, looking and watching out the rain-streaked window, and he was beginning to feel like a little boy kept indoors by a spring downpour.

Every ten minutes or so the hostess would come around and ask if he wanted another spafizz but James would only shake his head and smile bleakly.

Then he would turn resolutely back to the window, expecting his uncle to be there suddenly, like a gift left on a doorstep.

It was while he was watching that he saw the girl across the street trip on the boardwalk and go falling to her knees in the mud. Her parasol went flying into the path of a wagon. The horses trampled right over it. The girl, not one to take such a slight politely, raised her tiny fist and shook it in the direction of the retreating wagon.

Several of the older male customers inside the restaurant had also watched this little nickelodeon adventure played out in the rain and mud. They rubbed their muttonchops and patted the plump bellies they'd covered with silk vests and pointed to the girl.

One man said, "It's that young whore, Liz."

Looking into the street again, James saw that it was indeed the girl he'd spent much of last night with.

Another stout man laughed. "A little mud never hurt a girl like that."

Liz obliged her oglers by starting to stand up, mud clinging to her hands and arms and the whole of her skirt, and promptly falling right back down to her knees.

The men in the restaurant began poking each other and pointing out of the window as if they were spectators at a particularly funny play.

"Too bad she doesn't put on a show when you go up to see her," one man laughed.

James, disliking the meanness and arrogance of the men, got up from his chair and started running down the aisle to the door. He tromped hard on one man's shoes as he fled out the door, stomping down directly on the instep. This was the man who'd referred to Liz as a "young whore." The man cursed James and shook a fat fist in the boy's direction.

The rain pelted him immediately. It was a cold rain and hard. It was also difficult to see through.

He waded out into the street that had become a vast mud puddle. He sank in halfway to his knees. The mud made faint sucking sounds as he raised and lowered his feet.

He noticed that several people stood on the boardwalk under the overhang pointing to Liz and smirking much as the men in the restaurant had. It was obvious they knew who she was and what she was and would make no move to help her. The women twirling their parasols and peering out from beneath their picture hats looked particularly mean.

The street was so swampy it took him two full minutes to reach her. By this time she had fallen over yet again, and now even her face was mud-spattered.

She didn't recognize him at first. She was obviously angry and hurt and ashamed and so instead of thanking this helpful stranger, she tried to slap him.

The people along the boardwalk started laughing again.

James took the hand she meant to slap him with and said, "Don't you remember me, Liz?"

There in the drenching rain, there in the echoes of the crowd's harsh laughter, she narrowed her eyes and looked more closely at him. "You're the kid from last night."

He noted how she said that. She had not called him by name. There had been no warmth or even surprise in her voice. She was simply identifying him.

He said, above the rain, "I had a nice time last night."

She shook her head. "Kid, just help me get out of here, will you?"

But he felt hurt. "Didn't you have a nice time?"

Now she shouted above the rain. "Maybe you didn't notice but they're starting to laugh at you, too."

"Let them," he said. "I just want to know if you had a good time last night."

"I had a great time."

"You don't sound as if you mean that, Liz."

There in the rain, them both shouting, both soaked and mud-mired, she leaned over and kissed him on the cheek and said, "You know something, kid? You really are a kid. A sweet one."

The crowd found this even more wonderful entertainment. A few of them even applauded.

"Will you help me get across the street to the boardwalk?" Liz said.

He slid his arm in hers. "I'd be proud to."

She smiled at him uncertainly. "You haven't been drinking again today, have you, kid?"

He smiled back. "Not so far."

They walked across the street, step by inching step. By now James was mud-soaked, too.

Once, she fell and he had to help her up. Once, he fell and she had to help him up. The crowd loved it.

"They really make me mad," James said as they drew near the boardwalk.

"Why?"

"Because of how they treat you."

She stopped and stared at him through the silver rain. "Kid, I'm a whore. How do you expect them to treat me?"

"You should have more pride in yourself than that."

She squeezed his arm and smiled again.

Now he smiled. "And stop calling me kid. I'm nearly two years older than you."

So they resumed their walk.

Now it was apparent they were going to make it without further incident, the crowd began to disperse. Their entertainment was over.

When they finally reached the protection of the overhang, she began to look herself over, shaking her head. "No wonder they was laughin'."

"Why?"

"I ain't real pretty on the best of days. Lookin' like this . . ." She shook her head again. Her hair was formed against her head like the sculpted hair of a statue.

"Who said you aren't pretty?"

She had been scraping mud from her skirts. She stopped and looked up at him. "Kid, I don't think I can take any more of your chivalry."

"But Liz, I'm just trying to be—"

"I know what you're trying to be!" she said. She glanced over at two townsmen standing there watching her. Smirking. "Kid, sometimes being nice hurts worse than anything else. Because I'm not used to people being nice to me."

And he saw then in her tears and heard in the stricken sound of her voice the pain and dread she tried not to acknowledge.

"Kid, just go be nice to somebody else, all right?"

And then she left, her footsteps sharp against the wood of the boardwalk, a muddy little farm girl aging too quickly in the harsh city.

"Don't worry, son," one of the onlookers said. "There's plenty more back at that house where she came from."

James felt as if he wanted to take a swing at the guy, but it was just then that a male voice shouted his name through the rain, and he turned to see, standing in front of the restaurant his uncle Septemus.

Septemus was waving for James to cross the muddy street again.

Huddling into his soaked clothes, ready to feel the cold steady rain on his head and back again, James set forth across the swampy street.

4

In the night the Mexican prisoner and the white boy had taken a keen dislike to each other. Dodds was in the cell with the Mex kid trying to get him to talk about what had happened.

"I rolled over, and I fell out of bed," the Mex kid said. He looked over at the white boy and grinned.

The white boy had a narrow, feral face. He wore jail denims. He badly needed a shave but wouldn't accept the razor Dodds had several times tried to give him. He had eyes that were a mirror of all the things that had been done to him by others before he could defend himself, and all the things he wanted to do to people now that he was big and strong and dangerous. Once in a while Dodds felt sorry for kids like this but then he always reminded himself what a luxury such pity was. It had cost more than one lawman his life.

Dodds wanted the Mex to talk, but there he was intruding on the most sacred pact you found behind bars— no matter how much prisoners might hate each other, they hated a lawman more.

"I'd like to get this sonofabitch," Dodds said. "First because he snuck himself a knife into my jail. And second because he committed a felony while in my custody. That's the kind of thing that can really piss a man off."

"I don't know nothing about it. Nothing."

"What happens tonight?"

"Tonight?"

"Sure. When he gets another crack at you. Maybe you won't be so lucky tonight."

The white boy sat in the corner of his own cell, glaring first at Dodds then at the Mex kid.

For the first time, the Mex looked as if he just might believe what Dodds was saying.

The Mex raised his head and stared over at the white boy. "You s'posed to protect me while I'm in here."

"What the hell you think I'm *trying* to do?"

The Mex looked at the white boy again. "Let me think it over, okay?"

"Okay. But I wouldn't think about it much past sundown." Dodds grinned over at the white boy. "Not if you want to keep that punk off your back. He managed to stab you through the bars. That means he's got a good chance of killing you next time whether you're in separate cells or not."

"Sheriff," the deputy said through the barred door leading to the front office. "You got a visitor."

"Thanks," Dodds said, standing up. "If I ain't here, you give your statement to Eulo out there, okay?"

The Mex nodded.

The white boy grinned. Obviously he figured he had the Mex scared away.

Dodds hoped the Mex would surprise everybody and turn the white boy in. Assault with intent to commit great bodily injury would land the white boy in prison, where he belonged. All the white boy was doing time for was drunk and disorderly, but you could see that if somebody didn't stop him, he was the kind of kid who'd kill somebody for sure.

He started to make an obscene gesture behind Dodds's back as the sheriff headed for the front door.

Dodds turned around just in time to see what was about to happen. He grinned at the kid. That was one thing about punks. Mentally they never got much beyond second grade.

Dodds had always like Mae Kittredge. To some she was too religious, to others too strange, but she bore her disappointment over her lost child with a gentle dignity that touched Dodds. He remembered how Mae had helped the victims of the factory layoff, going door-to-door every few days to make sure that everyone had sufficient supplies of food and medicine, and sufficient supplies of tenderness for each other. Dodds had always joked to her that she'd make a fine sheriff; she could settle down riled-up husbands faster than any lawman he'd ever seen.

Now Mae sat in his office, her clothes damp from the rain. Her hands were folded in her lap, her eyes shaded by the bill of her bonnet. The way her lips moved softly, it was easy to tell she was praying.

Dodds came in and sat across from the desk and said, "Nice to see you, Mae."

As he said this, he realized he was going to be seeing a lot of the woman in the coming weeks. Her husband was, after all, implicated in a killing and a bank robbery.

"Nice to see you, Sheriff," she replied.

"How can I help you?"

"I just wanted to check up on that special deputy. After he left, I got suspicious."

''What deputy you talkin' about, Mae?''

''The one who came out to the house. The one who works for the governor. The one who's helping you.''

''My deputy's in back, Mae. He didn't go out to see you.''

In her somber gray eyes came the realization that she'd been tricked.

''He asked about Dennis,'' she said.

''What about Dennis?''

''He wanted to know where he could find him.''

''He say why?''

''He said Dennis had witnessed a jewelry robbery and he thought Dennis could testify against the robber.''

''I see.''

''It was a trick, wasn't it?''

He wanted to keep her calm. No reason to excite her. She'd had enough grief in recent years.

''I'm sure everything is fine, Mae,'' Dodds said, taking his pipe from his drawer. He stuck it between his teeth and inhaled it. He could taste the sweet and satisfying vapors of tobacco burned days ago. ''He ask you where he could find Dennis?''

''He did.''

''You tell him?''

''I did.'' Pause. ''I shouldn't have, should I?''

He sucked a little more on his pipe. He tried to remain as composed as possible. The hell of it was he felt a little tic troubling the corner of his eye. He always got it when he got scared and he was scared now. Ryan was a crazy sonofabitch. Just in case he forgot how crazy, all he had to do was read the letter Ryan had written and left in his carpetbag. ''Where'd you tell him he'd find Dennis, Mae?''

"Out on Lambert Creek. Up near Grovers Pass."

"Fishing, huh?"

"Umm-hmm."

This was the part he had to make sound really relaxed and nonchalant. "Why don't you let me do you a little favor, Mae?"

"A little favor?"

"Why don't you let me ride on out there and just see if I can find this fella. Ask him if there hasn't been some kind of mix-up or something."

She sighed. "I'd sure appreciate that, Sheriff."

"By the way, Mae, you haven't told me what this fella looks like exactly."

"Oh, he's a nice-looking man. You can tell he's successful and you can tell he's educated. He doesn't look like a criminal or anything."

"Could you be a little more specific, Mae? How tall he is and what color his hair is and what kind of clothes he's wearing."

She shrugged her narrow shoulders. "Sure, Sheriff. If you want me to."

The man she then proceeded to describe was, of course, Septemus Ryan.

5

The rain came hard enough to bother the bay that pulled the buggy. The animal spooked every so often on the mud road winding up through the clay hills.

James huddled back against the seat, trying to avoid getting any wetter than he already was. His clothes were still damp from trying to help Liz there in the street, and he hoped they would soon start to dry.

His uncle hied the horse and stared straight ahead. He leaned outside the protection of the top. Rain smashed against his skull and face but, if this bothered him, he didn't let James know it.

After a quarter-mile, James said, "Where we going, Uncle Septemus?"

"You'll see." Septemus didn't turn around to address him.

"It's awful muddy."

"So it is."

"You're not worried about getting stuck?"

"The Lord is with us," Septemus said, speaking up so he could be heard over the downpour.

Then he hied the horse with the lash again and they sluiced through the gloom.

In forty-five minutes, Septemus and James came to the top of a draw. Through the rain James saw below, set between stands of white birch, a small cabin cut from hardwoods. The windows on either side of the door had been smashed and were stuffed with paper. There were no outbuildings except for a privy and no animals of any kind.

"We'll walk from here," Septemus said.

He jumped down, taking his Winchester with him, wrapping it inside his coat to protect it from the water.

"We're going down to the cabin?"

"Yes, we are."

They started walking.

"This the surprise you told me about?"

"Indeed it is, James. Indeed it is."

Septemus still wasn't looking at James. Instead he kept his gaze fixed on the cabin.

James knew he wasn't going to like the surprise. Something was wrong with Septemus and James knew that this meant the surprise would be something terrible. He kept thinking of what his uncle had said about responsibility. It had something to do with that.

When they reached the cabin, which smelled of wood and mildew in the rain, Septemus stood aside and waved James on to precede him.

James put his hand on the doorknob and said, "I'm not going to like this surprise, am I, Uncle Septemus?" Septemus shook his head. James had never seen him look this way before. So . . . strange. Rain dripped off the roof and fell onto James's head. "Am I?"

"You may not like it, James. But I know you'll fulfill your responsibility to Clarice anyway."

"To Clarice?"

"She was like your sister, wasn't she, James?"

James knew how it would hurt Septemus if he denied this. "Yes, she was."

"Then you won't have any trouble doing your duty."

And with that, Septemus leaned forward and kicked the door inward. He kicked it hard enough that it slammed against the opposite wall. Dust rose up in the doorway and through the dust James saw a meanly furnished cabin with a cot that rats had eaten the straw out of, and a cast-iron stove already rusting, and enough bent and dented cans of food to last a short winter.

But it was the man tied to the chair in the center of the one-room cabin that got James's attention.

You could see where the man had been badly beaten, his face discolored and his mouth raw with dried blood.

There was a cut across his forehead and his left eye was blackened.

At first the man didn't speak—James wasn't certain he *could* speak, he looked so beaten up—he just stared at the two of them as they entered.

This was obviously the surprise, the man here, though what it meant exactly James wasn't yet sure.

Septemus said, "Do you know who this man is, James?"

"No," James said. "I don't."

"Run," the man said. "Run and get the law, kid. Get Sheriff Dodds." He strained against the bonds of rope that held him.

"He's one of the men who killed Clarice," Septemus said. "Kittredge."

"He's crazy, kid. Look at 'im. You can see it, can't you? That he's crazy?"

Septemus seemed not to have heard. "This is what I meant by responsibility, James. You've got to do what's right for Clarice."

"Kid, if I die, my wife won't have nobody. Nobody." The man looked as crazed with fear as Septemus did with anger.

James felt embarrassed for the man and had to drop his eyes. This was all so terrible; there was something unreal about it. It might almost have struck him as a nightmare except for the stink of the cabin itself and the raw look of the man's face. People just didn't have dreams that well detailed.

"Run, kid," the man said again.

Septemus held out the Winchester to James and said, "You take this, James, and you do right by Clarice. You hear me?"

James looked at the man in the chair. "Did you kill Clarice?"

The man looked miserable. "Kid, nobody killed the girl on purpose. It was an accident. We was out of work and couldn't find no jobs—that's the only reason we stuck up the bank in the first place."

The man was whining; again, James felt sorry for him.

"Why don't I go get the sheriff?" James said to his uncle.

"For what?"

"This man confessed, Uncle Septemus. All you have to do is turn him over. The law'll take care of it from that."

Septemus said, "You know why I brought you along on this trip?"

James knew better than to say anything.

"To learn how to be a man."

James hung his head.

"I show you one of the men who killed your cousin— the cousin who loved you—and what do you do? You talk about going to get the sheriff." Septemus waved the Winchester in the direction of Kittredge. "You're getting two things confused here, James. You're mistaking law for justice."

He walked over to Kittredge and stood next to him. Kittredge watched nervously. It was easy to see that Septemus wanted to start hitting him again.

Septemus said, "Now, in a court of law, Kittredge here might well convince a jury that Clarice's death was accidental. But we'd know better, wouldn't we, James? We'd know that that little girl would never have been killed if those men hadn't been there in the first place. Isn't that right, James?"

James nodded and glanced at Kittredge. Kittredge's eyes were huge and white, following Septemus around as the man paced.

"But being mature men, James—you and I—we won't settle for law. We want justice. We want what's right." He raised the rifle. This time he didn't offer it to James, he merely held it out for James to see. "That's where personal responsibility enters into it, James. That's where you've got to act like a grown-up and do what's right."

This time he did hand James the Winchester.

Much as he didn't want to, James took the rifle in his hand and brought it close to his body.

"Kittredge is your turn. I've already killed Carlyle."

When Septemus said this, James felt a terrible chill come over him. "You killed a man, Uncle Septemus?"

"I most certainly did. One of the men who killed my Clarice. The same Clarice you yourself loved and cherished."

"Look at his face, kid," Kittredge said. "You can see he's crazy. Run and get the sheriff. Go on now before it's too late."

"You shouldn't have killed anybody," James said to his uncle, realizing abruptly what he'd been sensing ever since leaving Council Bluffs—that while this man might look like Septemus Ryan, he wasn't. No, there Kittredge was right. This was an insane man who bore only a passing resemblance to his uncle.

Septemus said, nodding to the Winchester, "Raise the rifle and sight it, James. Just like I showed you when you were a boy. Raise the rifle and sight it and do your duty."

"Go run and get the sheriff, kid. Hurry."

"You going to listen to the man who killed your Clarice, James? Now raise that rifle and sight it and make Clarice proud."

"Please, son. Please don't listen to him. He's insane. He already killed one man and he'll surely kill me."

"James, don't let me down. Now raise that rifle and sight it and do what's right."

"Please, son."

"Raise the rifle, James."

And James—looking at Septemus, loving Septemus and knowing his uncle's relentless grief and agony ever since the death of his daughter—James raised the rifle into a firing position.

"That's a good boy, James. Now sight it, just like I always showed you."

Squinting, James sighted along the barrel. All he could think of was that maybe Septemus was right. Maybe he wasn't being a man. Maybe he did owe it to Clarice. Maybe the only way he was ever really going to grow up and have the respect of others, let alone the respect of himself, was to pull the trigger on the man who'd helped kill Clarice. James thought of his little cousin, how sweet and gentle she'd been, and how both his aunt and uncle had been destroyed by her death.

"Kid, I ain't got this coming. I really ain't," Kittredge said. "Please, kid."

Kittredge started crying.

James sighted the rifle.

"Make me proud of you, James," Uncle Septemus said. "Make Clarice proud."

Kittredge had closed his eyes, waiting for death.

James said, "I can't do it."

"You can do it, son. Just relax. You can do it fine."

"You'll be a killer if you do it, kid. You'll be a killer and they'll put you in prison."

"You just relax, James. You can do it fine."

James said, "I can't do it, I really can't. It isn't right."

Septemus slapped James harder than James had ever been slapped before. A terrible hot feeling filled James's face, and his head spun with stars.

"Now you get up there, James," Septemus said. "You get up there and do your responsibility."

Kittredge said, "You know what's right, kid. Don't give in to him. If you do, you'll be just as crazy as he is. You know what we done was an accident, don't you, kid?"

Septemus took James by the shoulder and turned him around so he was again facing Kittredge. He took the rifle and moved it into a firing position in James's hands.

"Now don't waste any more time, James. Shoot."

"Kid, listen, please—"

"Shoot!"

Their voices filling his head, the dank stink of the cabin filling his nose, the pathetic and somehow irritating spectacle of a man pleading for his life filling his mind—James let the Winchester slip from his hands to the floor.

He turned and ran from the cabin.

He went outside, just out from under the overhang, so he could stand in the rain, and the sound of it would drown out the madness of his uncle and the mewling of Kittredge who had, after all, been at least partly responsible for Clarice's death.

The rain came down silver and seemed to cleanse him and he put his hands out and opened his mouth to re-

ceive it, letting the drops splat on his face and trickle
down his neck and soak into his coat.

Then, even through the snapping rain, he heard it, the
gunshot, and knew what had happened.

He didn't feel any regret for Kittredge; the regret was
for his uncle. There would be no way back now.

He turned and stood in the rain and after a few
minutes Septemus came out of the cabin.

Septemus came a few feet up the slope of the hill. He
didn't seem to notice the rain soaking him.

"You let me down, James."

"I know."

"I always considered you like a son. Loved you in
that same way."

"Just the way I loved you, Uncle Septemus."

"But when the time came to prove how much you
loved me and loved my Clarice—" He fell silent. Rain
pocked the summer-brown grass and drummed against
the cabin roof. Blue-gray gunsmoke wafted out the cabin
door. You could smell the blood of an animal kill on
the air. In this case the animal had been human.

"You should let me help you, Uncle Septemus."

"I don't want anything more to do with you, James.
Your mother has not raised you to be a man and it's too
late now for me to do anything about it."

"I don't want them to hurt you, Uncle Septemus.
That's why I wish you'd give me the rifle and let me
take you into town."

Septemus raised his head in the rain and looked directly at James. "I know what the dead men say."

"What?"

"I know what the dead men say. They whisper to me,
James. They tell me secrets. They reassure me. This"—

he waved his arms in a patriarchal way to indicate the land and the cliffs surrounding them—"none of this is what it seems, James. Even Clarice tells me that when she talks to me."

"There's one more, isn't there?"

Through the beating rain, Septemus studied him. "Are you thinking of redeeming yourself with Griff, with the last one?" He waggled the rifle in James's direction. "Are you saying that you want to take this Winchester and do what's right?"

"I'm saying that you should leave him be. Killing two men is enough."

For a time, only the rain made sound. It seemed to be saying something, its hissing and pounding and spattering a language James yearned to understand, a dialogue shared only by rock and soil and leaves and grass.

"He has two daughters."

"Who?"

"The last one," Septemus said.

"They didn't kill Clarice."

"I want him to know how it feels."

The rain continued to speak.

James said, "Please give me your rifle, Uncle Septemus. Please let me take you in. They won't blame you for what you did. They'll understand."

"I'm going now, James."

Septemus started up the hill. "Please let me help you, Uncle Septemus!"

James slipped and fell on the wet grass. Septemus walked on ahead, never once looking back.

Scrambling to his feet, James went up the hill again, trying to grab his uncle's sleeve.

"Please, Uncle Septemus, please—"

With no hesitation, Septemus turned around and doubled his fist and hit James square on the jaw.

James felt as if he'd been shot. He saw darkness and felt a rush of cold air go up his nose and sinuses. He felt himself fall back and slam against the soggy earth. And for a moment then there was nothing at all, just a horrible spinning that made him nauseous and an overwhelming pain in the lower part of his face. He wondered if his uncle had broken his jaw.

Then, on the hill, there was the clop of hooves and the creaking of the buggy. Septemus hied the horse.

Septemus was gone.

He wasn't sure how long he lay there.

The rain soaked him, running into his eyes, his mouth, his nose.

Sometime during the darkness, before he had quite recovered his senses, he heard a horse on the road above. Then he heard a man, breathing hard and cursing under his breath, move carefully down the hill that was by now a mudslide.

When he opened his eyes, he saw Dodds peering down at him. "You all right, boy?"

"He hit me."

"Who?"

"My uncle Septemus."

"Where is he now?"

"I don't know."

"What happened?"

"You'd better look in the cabin."

"What's in the cabin?"

"Just go look."

While Dodds was gone, James struggled to his feet. He felt as if he would never be dry again. He had heard stories of Indians leaving white men out in downpours and by so doing drove them insane. James could see how that would be possible.

He had taken two steps down the hill when Dodds came out of the cabin.

"He did that, didn't he, your uncle."

"Yes."

"The crazy sonofabitch."

"That's his problem, Sheriff. He's crazy. Crazy over his girl dying. He said that that was one of the men who did it." He hesitated. "He killed another one, too. At least that's what he said."

"He tell you the name?"

"Carlyle."

"God damn it." Dodds said. "I've got to stop him." He looked back at the cabin. The rain hit him steady on the back of his balding head. "He was a pretty decent man, Kittredge was." He turned back to James. "It's sure as hell none of those men killed that little girl on purpose. Not even Carlyle. He was a lout but not a killer. Not of little girls, leastwise."

"That's why he's going to Griff's," he said.

"Why?"

"Because Griff has two little girls of his own."

Dodds stared at him. "You may have to help me, son. You willing?"

"He's my uncle."

"I know that."

"And I love him. He's pretty much been my father since my real father died."

Dodds nodded to the cabin. "You should go back in there and take a look at Kittredge."

James gulped. "I don't want to."

"He shot him in the face. Dead on. You ever seen that before?"

"No."

"Well, believe me, son, it's nothing to see."

"You aren't going to shoot him, are you?"

"Not unless I have to."

"Let me talk to him, then."

"Long as he don't hurt nobody else, talking to him is fine. I can't tell you what I'm going to feel like if he hurts either of those little girls."

"I feel sorry for him."

"I feel sorry for him, too, son. But I feel a hell of a lot sorrier for those girls."

Dodds started up the hill. "We're gonna have to ride double, so we better get goin'. That poor old horse of mine ain't that fast anymore."

As he made his way carefully up the hill, James said again, "You promise me you won't shoot him, Sheriff?"

Dodds looked back at him and said, "It's a little late for promises of any kind, son. We're just gonna have to see what happens."

Chapter Seven

1

He stood beneath a dripping oak, feeling tired suddenly, older than he ever had.

An early dusk gave the rain an even colder feel now, and put lights on in the windows of the small white houses on the small respectable street where Griff and his family lived.

He could see Griff in the window now, bending to turn up the wick in a kerosene lamp. He wondered if Griff had any sense that his two companions were dead.

Septemus Ryan hefted the Winchester and started walking down the block to where the alley began. Getting into Griff's house would not be easy. Going in through the rear would probably be best.

He passed picket fences and flower beds, neatly trimmed shrubs and tidy green lawns.

Griff's barn dominated the alley. The other buildings were small white garages. He did not have to worry about being seen because it had been raining so long and so steadily that nobody would be looking out the window. Or so he told himself.

As he strode over the wet cinders of the alley, he heard the voices, faintly. There was Clarice, thanking him for his brave actions today. And then the chorus of dead men—relatives and friends who'd gone on before—telling him that they were waiting for him, that the other side was good and he would like it and there was nothing to fear.

An uncle spoke to him, and then a brother dead early of consumption, and then a schoolmate killed in the war, and then an old muttonchopped mentor who'd advised him in the ways of business . . .

All these people whispered to Septemus Ryan, and said that Clarice was with them, and that like them, she awaited sight of her father as he crossed over.

And as he walked, there in the rain, the unrelenting hissing rain a curtain that lent everything a spectral cast, he had the sense that he was already walking the land of the dead, all humanity fading, fading behind the curtain of rain, alone in a curious and endless realm of phantoms and whispered voices.

He reached the barn and went in through the back door. He stood in the center of the dark, dusty place smelling the hay and the lubricating oils Griff used on his buggies and the sweet tart tang of horseshit from the stall where they kept the gelding.

He felt tired again, exhausted.

He looked enviously at the gelding. He wanted to go over and lay down next to it in the straw and hay, share the colorful threadbare horse blanket, and sleep with his arm thrown across the fleshy warm side of the animal, the way he'd once slept with his wife.

He went to the front sliding door and stood watching the rain fall in big silver drops from the roof. He could see nightcrawlers and worms swimming in the clear puddles around his feet; he could smell rusted iron tangy from the rain; he could see mist rising like ghosts from the slanting roof of the Griff house, and hear faintly, the way he once heard Clarice, the clear pure laughter of a little girl.

I remember you sleeping between your mother and I remember your soft pink cheeks so warm when you kissed me your eyes so lovely and blue how you made little snoring sounds in the middle of the night and kept your doll pulled so tight to you.

He saw her in the window now, just her head, the little girl.

He hefted his Winchester and started across the soggy grass.

There was a screened-in back porch with chairs for sitting. He eased open the back door and went inside. He could smell dampness on the stone floor and dinner from the kitchen just behind the door. It smelled good and warm and he realized how hungry he was.

There were no voices. From his glimpse in the window a minute ago he'd been able to see that the little girl was probably alone in the kitchen. That would make it easier.

We used to swing till dark in the summertime on the rope swing in the backyard, your hair shining gold even in the dusk and the firefly darkness and your mother calling lemonade's ready, lemonade's ready and the way you'd giggle and writhe as I'd tickle you on the way inside and your mother and I reading to you in the lampglow of your room as you fell asleep.

The door was open.

He went up two steps and found himself in the kitchen. It was about what he'd expected, modest but quite orderly. A girl of six or seven stood at the sink, drying dishes and then stacking them neatly on the sideboard.

He went straight up to her.

Just as she heard him, just as she started to turn to see what the noise was, he brought his hand around to the front of her face and covered her mouth.

With the other hand, he put the Winchester to her head.

"I want you to call out for your papa, you understand?"

Against the palm of his hand, he could feel the girl's hot breath and her saliva and the tiny edges of her teeth.

The girl nodded.

"Go ahead now," he said.

Before she called out, the girl twisted her neck so she could get a quick glimpse of him.

She looked terrified.

She said, "Papa. It's Eloise. Could you come out here, please?"

"Couldn't I finish my pipe first, hon?" he said.

Ryan nudged the little girl.

"I need you to come here now, Papa."

This time when she talked her voice broke with tension.

This time her papa came right away.

He came to the doorway of the kitchen and saw them.

He surprised Ryan by not saying anything.

He just stood there gawking, as if he could not believe it.

Finally, Griff said, "She doesn't have any part in this."

By now, his wife, apparently curious, came to the kitchen doorway, too.

She immediately made a noise that resembled mewling. "Oh, Eloise," she said.

"She doesn't have any part in this," Griff said again.

"My little girl didn't have any part in your robbery, either."

"Please, mister, please let her go," Griff's wife said.

Her mother's tone was scaring the girl even more. She strained against Ryan's hard grasp.

"I'm taking her," Ryan said.

"Oh, no!" her mother said and tried to lunge through the door to take her daughter.

Her husband put out a strong arm and stopped her. He said, "Go in the other room and make sure Tess is all right. I'll take care of this."

"Why would he want Eloise?" the woman said. She was becoming so distraught she sounded crazed.

"Go take care of Tess," he said.

Then, his wife gone, Griff said, "Take me, Ryan. You let Eloise walk over to me and you can take me anywhere you want. And do whatever you want. Just don't take it out on my daughter, you understand?"

Helping you with your homework at the dining room table how you always had the tiny pink corner of your tongue sticking out of your mouth when you were stumped by a problem and how you always had ink stains on the index finger of your right hand and worried that boys wouldn't think you were pretty because of the stains.

Ryan said, "I wanted you to know that I'm taking her. I wanted you to see it, Griff. To fear for it."

Eloise started crying.

Griff said, "I'm sorry for what happened to your daughter, Ryan."

It was then that he dived across the small kitchen to try and snatch Eloise away from Ryan, and it was then that Ryan shot Griff—two quick explosions of the Winchester—directly in the arm and leg.

2

Half a mile from town, the horse James and Dodds rode began to give out. He not only slowed, his legs were unsteady in the mud.

Dodds reined him in at a tree and said, "We'd better go on foot from here."

In the rain the horse looked cold and sick, his hazel eyes glazed, ragged breath rocking his ribs every few seconds.

Dodds saw how James was watching the horse over his shoulder as the two set off walking fast for town.

"Don't worry, son," Dodds said. "He just has the same problem I do."

"What problem's that?"

"Same problem you'll have and your own son'll have. Age. He's just old and the rain's got him spooked a little. I'll come back for him in a while and put him up in the livery and hay him and rub him down and he'll be fine."

"He's a nice horse."

"You get real attached to things, don't you, son?"

James shrugged, wiping rain from his face. He had been out in the downpour so long that he knew it would feel odd when the rain stopped. Human beings seemed to get used to things, even things they basically didn't like. "I guess I do."

As they walked, Dodds looked over at him and said, "I want to tell you something."

"What?"

"That I'll do my best not to shoot him."

"I appreciate that, Sheriff."

"I just hope he doesn't back me into a corner."

"People do that to you?"

"All the time. They get distraught or they get drunk or they get heartbroke and then they do very foolish things and they don't leave me much leeway."

"I'll talk to Septemus. He'll listen to me."

"I hope so, son. I hope so."

3

Dora got bandages and worked on her husband's arm and leg. There was a lot of blood. The first thing the two girls had done was scream. The second thing they did was start crying. Now they were silent, just watching it, how their mother was on her knees patching up their father, how Ryan just stood there with his Winchester.

"You shouldn't have shot him, mister," the wife said.

"He shouldn't have shot my daughter."

She just shook her head, looked at her husband's wounds again. Griff had his eyes closed. He'd tried to stand up several times but his wife wouldn't let him. He lay on the kitchen floor now with his head propped on three dishtowels she'd rolled up for a pillow.

Tess, the youngest girl, said, "I don't like you."

Ryan said, "Well, I like you. I like all little girls. Every single one of them."

"You hurt my papa."

"Well, he hurt somebody I cared about very much."

"Who?"

"My own little girl."

"Tess get over here," her mother said.

"How come Eloise can't come over with us?"

Her mother said, "The man won't let her."

"How come?"

"Get over here, Tess."

"My papa didn't hurt nobody," Tess said, and then kind of ambled over to stand next to her mother.

Ryan gripped Eloise's shoulder tight again and said, "I'm going to walk out of here with her now, ma'm."

"No!"

The woman jumped to her feet.

Her husband's eyes opened and the man tried to struggle to his feet. This time his wife didn't stop him.

Tess, sensing all the alarm, started sobbing. "What's he going to do, Mama?"

"Be quiet." The woman glared at Ryan. "No matter what happened, mister, my daughter don't deserve to be treated like this."

"Neither did my daughter."

"You let her go, you bad man," Tess said.

Griff had now managed to get himself upright. He was white from loss of blood and pasty-looking. His eyes didn't quite focus. There was blood all over his clothes. "I told you, Ryan. Take me. I'm the one you want."

"No, Griff. This will be worse. Taking your daughter. Then you'll know what I've been going through."

And with that, he picked the girl up and tucked her under his arm. He was strong enough to hold her even when she wriggled. He backed out of the kitchen to the stairs.

To the woman he said, "I'm sorry about this, ma'm. But it's the only way."

Eloise started screaming.

Ryan got one step down the back stairs and then two steps and then he moved quickly out the door.

4

By the time James and Dodds reached the alley that ran behind the Griff house, they could hear shouts and screams even above the rain.

"He's there," Dodds said, pulling his Navy Colt from his holster.

"You said you weren't going to shoot him," James said, panic filling his chest.

"Son, I said I'd try not to shoot him. But I didn't say I'd be foolish. He'll be armed and so will I." He nodded to a small garage to their left. "You could always go in there and stay till it's over."

"I want to go with you. I want to talk to him."

"All right," Dodds said, "c'mon, then."

They went up the alley. Even the cinders were squishy underfoot.

A hundred feet away they saw Septemus come into the alley, Eloise Griff pulled close to him, the Winchester not far from her head.

Dodds shouted, "Stop right there, Ryan."

Dodds and James started running toward the man and the little girl.

Around the corner of the barn came Mrs. Griff and her husband. Griff was crudely bandaged; blood soaked through several places in his shirt and trousers. He looked as if he were about ready to collapse.

Mrs. Griff was slowly, painfully pleading with Ryan to let her little girl go.

When Dodds and James reached them, Dodds walked as close to Ryan as Septemus would let him.

Ryan put the muzzle of the Winchester directly against Eloise's head. "I'm going to kill her, Sheriff. Stand back."

James stared at the man who'd once been his uncle. This impostor bore no resemblance. "Uncle Septemus," he said.

As if recognizing his presence for the first time, Septemus glanced over at him and shook his head. For a brief moment there, he did resemble the old Septemus. Concern filled his eyes. "You shouldn't have come, James. I shouldn't have brought you along. It was a mistake. You shouldn't have anything to do with this."

"Uncle Septemus, you can't kill that little girl," James said, stepping up closer to Dodds.

All of them stood there in the rain, cold now and soaking but unable to take their eyes from the man and the girl.

"I know what I have to do, James. I have to make things right. I'm sorry, this is the only way I can do it." Septemus pulled the girl tighter to him. "Now stand back, James. Stand back."

"Please, Sheriff, talk to him," Mrs. Griff said. One could hear how hard she was working at keeping herself sane, fighting against the impulse to be hysterical.

"Ryan," Dodds said, advancing another step or two. "Hand me the Winchester and let the little girl go."

"Don't make me shoot you, Sheriff," Septemus said. "I've got nothing against you. This is between Griff and me."

Griff hobbled up closer himself. "Just take me, Ryan. Just take me and let Eloise walk away."

Dodds, seeing that Ryan was momentarily watching Griff talk, took another step.

Ryan lowered the Winchester and shot him in the shoulder.

Dodds flailed, pieces of his shirt and his shoulder exploding. He went over backward and lay in a puddle in the middle of the alley.

Mrs. Griff went to him much as she'd done with her husband. She had his head up against her forearm. Dodds's eyes were open and he was saying something to Mrs. Griff in a slow, small voice. James couldn't hear them. Now all he could hear was the rain; the rain.

As James turned back to Septemus, he noticed the Navy Colt that Dodds had dropped.

Impulsively, he bent and picked it up.

Septemus watched him.

When James turned back to his uncle, he held the Navy Colt.

"You go on, now, James," Septemus said. "You go to the depot and get a train back to Council Bluffs."

"I want you to let the little girl go," James said.

He stood ten feet from his uncle, the Colt in his hand.

"Put the gun down," Septemus said.

"Uncle Septemus, you can't see yourself. You can't know how you look and sound. I know how much you loved Clarice but this isn't right. Not with this little girl."

Septemus looked down at Eloise a moment. His grip seemed to loosen.

"Please, Uncle Septemus," James said. "Please, let her go."

To his right, James could see the Griff woman saying

a silent prayer that Septemus would just let the girl walk away.

Septemus's grip let up considerably now.

James could see Eloise start to slip away.

"No!" Septemus shouted.

It was as if some spell had come over him suddenly. He was no longer James's uncle but the crazed, ugly man he'd been a few minutes ago; the one that he'd been back at the cabin where he'd killed Dennis Kittredge.

He grabbed the girl and jerked her back to him and slammed the Winchester against her temple once again.

James started walking toward Septemus, the Colt level in his hand. He wasn't even sure he could fire it properly. At this point he didn't care. Now that he knew how insane Septemus had become, all James could think of was freeing the little girl. He loved the man who'd been his uncle too much to do anything else.

"Let her go, Uncle Septemus," James said, advancing.

"I'll shoot you, James," Septemus said. "Don't think I won't."

Two, three, four more steps.

"Let her go, Uncle Septemus."

"You heard me, James."

Five, six, seven more steps.

"Let her go, Uncle Septemus."

"Please, James; please don't come any closer."

Septemus pulled the Winchester from the little girl and leveled it directly at James.

James dived then, not knowing if his uncle would fire or not; dived directly for the little girl.

He slammed into them hard enough that Septemus's grip on the girl's shoulder was broken.

"Run!" James shouted to her.

Eloise ran, stumbling across the cinders and puddles. Her mother ran out to swoop her up.

By now, James was flat on the ground.

Septemus had run into the darkness of the barn. He stood in the shadows, holding the Winchester at his side.

James got to his feet, picking up the Colt again. He felt an idiotic happiness that Septemus was still alive.

Dodds saw what James was about to do. Still lying on the ground, Dodds raised a hand and said, "Don't you go in there, son. Wait till some deputies get here."

But James didn't listen.

He went through the barn door. Rain dripped and plopped off the door into the silver puddles.

Septemus stood in the shadows.

He said, "I'm glad I didn't kill that little girl."

He started crying then.

James had never heard sounds so terrible.

After he had sobbed for a time, Septemus raised his head and said, "Do you love me, James?"

"You know I do, Uncle Septemus."

"Then will you help me?"

"I'll do anything you want me to, Uncle Septemus."

"You know what they'll do to me. The trial and all. It won't be good for anybody. You know what something like that would do to your mother."

"She loves you, too, Uncle Septemus. She knows how Clarice's death affected you."

"Raise that Colt, James."

"What?"

"Raise that Colt and shoot me."

"Uncle Septemus—"

Septemus shook his head. "It'll be better for everybody, James. You can see what all this has done to me. I'm not a killer, James, yet I've killed two men and I almost killed a little girl. I don't want to live anymore, James, yet I'm not sure I can take my own life because I'm afraid I'd be damned to hell."

"Uncle Septemus, I couldn't do that. I couldn't."

"I can hear her, James. Clarice, I mean. I want to be with her again. I want to hold her in my arms and sing to her and tell her how much I love her." Then his eyes in the gloom took on the clarity of the insane; that terrible vivid truth that only they can see. "Take the Colt, James. And do it. You'll be helping everybody."

"I can't."

"Just raise it up to my chest, James."

"I don't want to, Uncle Septemus."

"It's your duty, James. I was wrong about you helping me kill the others. But this time I'm not wrong, James. You need to grow and take the responsibility for the whole family, James."

"He's right, son; it'll be better this way."

From the door, Dodds hobbled inside. The blood on his shoulder was faded from the rain. His scratchy, wavery voice told how weak the gunshot had left him.

When Ryan saw him, he said, "I'm sorry I shot you, Sheriff."

"I know, Mr. Ryan. I don't hold you accountable. Not really." Dodds looked at James. "I'm going to get some deputies, son, so we can take Mr. Ryan into custody and so I can get somebody to do something about my shoulder. But I want to tell you something."

James shook his head. "I don't want to do it, sir."

Dodds said, "He's right about it, son. It'll be better for everybody. He can't help the way he is now and about the only thing we can do for him is to get him out of his misery.'' Dodds nodded to the door. "I'm going to walk out of here and I won't have any idea what happens. If your uncle gets shot and you tell me it was self-defense, then I'm just going to have to take your word for it, won't I, son?''

Dodds looked at Septemus then. "I'm sorry about your little girl, Mr. Ryan.''

He left the barn.

They stood alone facing each other. In the stall in the back they could hear the horse get restless with nightfall.

Somewhere beyond the rain there would be stars and the vast darkness of night. James just wanted to be a boy and sit in his bedroom window and dream idly about all the mysteries of the universe.

He did not want to be standing in a barn smelling of hay and horseshit and oil and facing his uncle in this way.

"You've got to help me, James,'' Septemus said, and fell to crying once more.

But this time he let the Winchester fall from his hands and he came over to James and embraced him.

James had never heard or felt this kind of grief before. His uncle's sobbing was too painful for either of them to abide for long.

"Help me, James; help me,'' Uncle Septemus said, leaning back from the boy.

Septemus took the barrel of the Colt and raised it to his chest and said, "Please help me, James. Please help me.''

"Uncle Septemus—''

"Please, James.''

James shot twice, the first shot not seeming to do anything, Septemus just hovering there, his face that of a stranger again.

With the second shot, however, Septemus fell to the ground on his back.

He looked up at James. "Thank you, James. You did your duty."

Then it was James who began to cry, wild with grief and fear, filled with disbelief that he might have done such a thing.

"Uncle Septemus!" he cried.

But it was too late.

Septemus's eyes had closed. In death he was himself again, the lines of his face softer, gentleness joining the intelligence of his brow.

"Uncle Septemus!" James cried out again.

But only the horse in the back was there to hear.

James rose then and went to the barn door and looked out through the rain. In the distance he could hear the slapping footsteps of men running. In the gloom their shouts were ugly and harsh. The deputies.

He felt so many things, and yet he felt nothing. He thought of his mother and Marietta and Liz; he thought of his dead cousin Clarice and the sound of the gunshot back there at the cabin where Kittredge had died; and he thought finally of Septemus, of the terrible things that can happen to human beings and of the terrible things those very same human beings are then capable of visiting on others.

If this was being a man, perhaps he didn't want to be a man. Maybe it was better to be a dreamy boy, passing by Marietta's house on a night of fireflies and banjos, her idle flirtations making him happier than he'd ever been before.

But something had changed in him now; and no matter how much he yearned to be the boy he'd been, he knew he could never be that boy again. He possessed some terrible knowledge now, some insight that would stay with him forever like a curse.

Then the men were there, the deputies, and the air was filled with the harsh barking curses of men who tried to convince themselves and each other that they were in control of things.

5

"You sure you don't want to do anything? You already paid, you know."

"I just want to lie here."

"In the darkness?"

"Yes."

"Till it's time for your train?"

"Yes."

Liz said, "You seem very different from last night."

He said nothing.

"I'm sorry about your uncle."

"I know."

She paused. "I'd like to kiss you, James."

He said nothing.

"I'd like to kiss you like a friend, James. Like somebody who cares about you very much."

She kissed him. He held her there a long time. He liked the warmth of her body against his. In the room next door a man laughed and his whore giggled.

"You shouldn't stay here a lot longer," James said.

"I been thinking that myself lately."

"Do you s'pose you'll really do it? Get out of here, I mean?"

She said, "I sure like to think so, James. I sure like to think so."

6

The train was a Chicago, Milwaukee, and St. Paul. A Short Line with Pullman sleepers and a long dining car.

James got a seat and the train rumbled away and was then hurtling through the vast prairie night. The rain had stopped and there was a hazy moon out now, casting silver on the cornfields and wheatfields and the cows in silhouette on the distant hills.

And James sat there alone, no longer James, not the old James anyway, but somebody else now, somebody he was not even sure he liked at all.

PERMISSIONS